JASON ANSPACH NICK COLE PETER NEALEN

ORDER OF THE CENTURION

ALWAYS LEGION

GALAXY'S EDGE

ISBN: 979-8-88922-042-8

Edited by David Gatewood
Published by Galaxy's Edge Press

Cover Art by Jermiah Humphries
Cover Design: M.S. Corely

Website: www.GalaxysEdge.us
Facebook: facebook.com/atgalaxysedge

Newsletter (get a free short story): www.InTheLegion.com

The Order of the Centurion is the highest award that can be bestowed upon an individual serving in, or with, the Legion. When such an individual displays exceptional valor in action against an enemy force, and uncommon loyalty and devotion to the Legion and its legionnaires, refusing to abandon post, mission, or brothers, even unto death, the Legion dutifully recognizes such courage with this award.

98.4% of all citations are awarded posthumously.

1

Rain shrouded the towers of the spaceport in gray and completely obscured the low, rocky hills beyond. On the landing pad, while everything was damp, the rain itself was little more than a fine mist.

Dav Toron grimaced as he looked up at the gray curtain over the sky. *Long way from Fereston.*

"Sket." Len Aguilar stepped down the shuttle ramp to stand next to him. "Cold *and* wet." The lean, hawk-faced man shook his head. "Why couldn't it be the desert?"

"Closest Temugol has to a desert is the polar ice caps." Dav started toward the fence line at the edge of the landing pad. "Come on. Let's get the vehicles before Vin decides he needs to micromanage some more."

Aguilar grunted. "If I hear one more sergeant major catchphrase, I think I'm gonna snap." He shook his head. "I feel sorry for Sayavong and Sones, having to stay back with him."

"Sones can handle himself. And I think even Vin's scared of Sayavong."

"He should be." Aguilar chuckled. "That boy's big enough for two of Vin, and he don't take no sket."

Both men started across the wet duracrete, Aguilar hunching his shoulders under his jacket. Dav was somewhat surprised at the volume of traffic to the Temugol Spaceport, as another ship descended on its repulsors onto the nearby pad. He shook his head at himself.

Of course there are more ships coming and going. This half-frozen backwater turned important all of a sudden. Why else would we be here?

They soon reached the glowing red, ray-shielded security fence. It wasn't so much the weather that made them hurry as it was the desire to get away from the shuttle and their principal, at least for a little while. The trip aboard the corvette *Inspiration* from Utopion had been entirely too long. Dav was already looking forward to the end of this particular contract.

Got out of the Legion because of a point, just to babysit the same sort of pukes times ten. Real smart, Toron.

He looked at a holographic port map projected near the gate, peering past graffiti scrawled on the edges. He found the Republic Admin Campus—a few city blocks where administrative staff—mostly bots—and other Repub resources were kept. Like sleds.

Dav looked to a nearby rental facility loaded with repulsor sleds, their forward viewscreens collecting beads of misting rain. That would be the quickest way to do the job, but the job was to escort a special aide of House of Reason Delegate Sandar Mahat named Macha Yuso.

Republic escorts required Republic vehicles.

"How far?" Aguilar asked.

Dav turned around. "Two klicks. Looks like we've

got a walk." The distance was *just* short enough that hiring a taxi would be reason enough for Vin to make it an issue, and unfortunately, they could trust their client to back Vin up.

"Looks like it." Aguilar hunched his shoulders against the wet as he scowled, turned away from the map, and headed through the spaceport toward the city. "At least it's a little bit of time away from babysitting."

Yeah. Dav shoved his hands in his pockets, next to his concealed blaster, and walked alongside the other man as they headed out onto the street. *Seems like most of us feel the same way. Gone from being high-speed death machines to glorified chaperones. The credits are good, but most of us seem to wonder if they're really worth it.*

He didn't know Aguilar's background for sure. They'd talked about this and that, but personal histories among contractors were something that was rarely asked about. He was a hell of a shot with the Garmian E7 blaster they all carried, he knew his way around the job, both the boring administrative parts, and the more kinetic parts that they all simultaneously prayed for and dreaded, and that was about it.

Dav had his suspicions. He could smell another leej a mile away, and Aguilar hadn't given him that impression. He'd had training, but there was an edge to the other man that wasn't *quite* military.

Shaking his head at the world, the weather, and his own life, Dav shoved his hands into his jacket pockets and followed.

They hadn't gotten much more than a half a klick, passing through the spaceport security gate, before a new sound made them both look up, scanning the cloudy sky and the rest of the spaceport with an alertness born of training and experience. That was a distinctive sound, and one that was almost standard across the Republic.

That was an attack alarm.

A rook might have hung out there on the street, looking for the source of the threat. Neither contractor was a rook, though, and they both moved fast to the lee of a low duracrete bunker that formed part of the spaceport control terminal, getting to some semblance of cover first of all. Their Garmians wouldn't do much good against an air raid.

The scream of repulsors went by overhead, and Dav caught a glimpse of a trio of dark, chisel-nosed shapes, flying so low and fast that their shock waves blasted whorls in the misting rain. Their passage shook the ground, even as the distinctive whine of blaster fire started up somewhere nearby.

Both men had their blasters in their hands, and Dav was starting to regret leaving his comm behind. That choice had promised to give him some peace on the way to getting the vehicles, but now it could be a bit of a liability.

Shouldn't have figured that it was just another babysitting gig, after all. Not that the bare-bones briefing they'd gotten aboard the *Inspiration* had given them much to work with.

For a moment, he considered just going ahead and pushing to the Republic complex, getting the sleds, and racing back to the spaceport. Movement would be preferable to having Yuso stationary in a landed shuttle. It wasn't like they could expect much backup from the corvette in orbit. Captain Ustinov hadn't instilled the former legionnaire with a great deal of confidence in his combative nature or initiative.

The odds of getting shot if they came careening back to the landing pad with a pair of unidentified repulsor sleds and no comms, however, were probably high. Even if old man Sones was on watch, both Vin and Hesand were going to be pretty high-strung with all the blaster fire out there.

Dav didn't have to ask whether Aguilar trusted either of the former basics not to open fire on a friendly. He sure didn't.

That left running back the half-klick they'd traveled so far. But before either of them could do much more than look at the gunships in the sky and back at each other, a balloon-wheeled utility truck raced down the street. It stopped at the end of the block, dropped its panels and spilled out half a dozen blaster-wielding men in ragged working coveralls.

Dav abandoned his plan to run back to the shuttle and ducked back behind his cover, almost colliding with Aguilar in the process. A wild fusillade of blaster fire came their way, the bolts smacking into the duracrete and zipping overhead. The weapons fire looked brighter than usual in the dimness of the weather.

Aguilar was at Dav's elbow, blaster in his hands. "Looks like we didn't come all the way out here for nothing, after all."

"Sure seems that way." Dav watched the blaster bolts and the space between them and the gate. He considered the open ground between the gate and the landing pad. "We're gonna get dusted if we try to run for it."

Aguilar wasn't arguing. "You got your comm?"

Dav shook his head in frustration. "Left it back like an idiot."

"Sket. So did I."

So, we both got complacent. Wonderful. Now we're cut off and without comms.

That left two options. Fight or hide. Dav knew what he was more inclined to do.

"On me." He didn't know for sure which way Aguilar was inclined to jump, but initiative has a way of winning out.

He moved back to the corner of the bunker and eased one eye around, wishing that he'd geared up before heading out. His Krall Mk 2 armor was nothing like Legion armor—at least the good stuff, before the shinies started to show up after the Battle of Kublar—but it was still a lot better than being out there with nothing but his shirt and a jacket between him and the blaster bolts. *And* it had built-in comms, too.

Still, a leej is as good naked as he is with his gear. So, he'd have to adapt.

The group of blaster-wielding militia, or whatever they were, hadn't moved far from the truck. They were blazing away at anything that moved, while more blaster fire echoed through the streets, the alarm wailed, and the chisel-nosed attack craft came around again, the heavier howl of their blasters joining the cacophony reverberating over the spaceport.

"High, low?" Aguilar had definitely had training.

Dav nodded, dropping to a knee at the corner. Aguilar stepped close to him, and then they both popped the corner at almost the same moment, blasters leveled.

Dav shot the first one through the head as soon as his blaster cleared the corner. The man's skull snapped back and his blaster clattered to the street. By then Dav was already shifting to the next one, a younger, long-haired man in the same ragged coveralls, crouched behind one of the truck's big balloon tires. A bolt took that one through the throat, and then Dav was shifting aim again as that gunman fell out of sight.

He might not be a leej anymore, but he'd been one once, and real leejes don't miss.

The hair on the back of his neck had stood up in the discharge when Aguilar opened fire above his head. The other contractor had dropped the other three, leaving one with two smoking holes in his coverall as he sprawled in the wet street. The urban battlefield went quiet, the faint patter of rain restored as the bolts stopped flash-boiling it by their passage.

That peace lasted about two whole seconds before the gunships came around again and strafed the spaceport, their brilliant blue bolts slamming into impervisteel, duracrete, and composite. Something blew up under that onslaught to send a fireball roiling into the cloudy sky.

"There's our ride. Come on." Dav nodded toward

the truck. Since the bad guys had just provided them with transportation, he opted to take it. The truck was easily big enough to carry Yuso, his entourage of flacks and hangers-on, and the six-man detail. It might not be comfortable, but it was better than waiting around on the landing pad while those gunships strafed every ship on the ground. Even as he sprinted toward the truck, a passenger liner rose into the air from its landing pad, repulsors throbbing, only to take a dozen blaster cannon bolts to the flank. The blue-and-white hull exploded, raining debris and fire down onto the pad beneath it and the next one over, setting a squat cargo hauler ablaze.

Dav ducked as the shock wave rolled over the spaceport and the burning space liner sagged, too many of its repulsors blown out to keep it in the air. He sprinted to the truck, Aguilar falling in beside him and dropping to a knee by the tailgate, his blaster held ready while Dav yanked the door open.

Aguilar paused before getting inside to glance down at the ground, then hastily snatched up a fallen blaster rifle. "Let's take these and then get in."

The two contractors collected the short, snubby-looking things and tossed the weapons into the truck bed. Dav clambered inside and looked up to watch for another pass of the fighters through the front windshield.

Instead of running around to the other side to get in, Aguilar vaulted into the bed and beat a fist against the cab. Dav sent the truck surging toward the gate. Hopefully no one waiting with the shuttle would decide to open fire on the unfamiliar vehicle, but he'd deal with that when they got there. Vin had been Repub Army. He *should* be able to deconflict without losing his head, even without comms.

Should.

The gate was shut, but the ray shielding was powered by simple, non-reinforced pylons. Dav picked one and drove right into it, knocking out the shielding as he passed by the adjoining guard post. The stationed security guard didn't budge from where he'd taken shelter under the post desk, which was probably for the best. Dav had a feeling Aguilar would have shot him if he'd tried to stop them.

He probably would have done the same if he hadn't been so busy driving.

It didn't take long to reach the landing pad, though he had to take the long way around to avoid the slow-motion crash as the space liner's repulsors finally gave up the ghost and the bullet-shaped vessel sank to the ground with a tooth-rattling *boom*. More fire and smoke billowed into the sky, carrying more whickering fragments of hull as something else cooked off inside the wreck.

Approaching from the south side actually worked to their advantage, Dav realized. They were now on the opposite side of the shuttle from the ramp, which meant they were a lot less likely to get shot by friendly fire.

He resisted the urge to fishtail into a wild stop and instead slowed the vehicle to a non-threatening complete stop. Then he swung out of the cab, arms raised as he ducked under the shuttle's stubby wing and approached the ramp. "Friendly!"

"Who's there?"

He felt a surge of relief at hearing Alben Sones's voice. Sones, at least, he was pretty sure he could trust not to open fire indiscriminately at sounds or movement.

"It's Toron. I've got us transport. We need to get the hell away from this sitting target." He came around the end of the ramp, waving at Aguilar to join him. Sones, skinny as a rail and burned a deep mahogany by a lot of different suns, was wearing full kit and on a knee at the top, blaster held ready. Behind him clustered the rest of the team, Cade Hesand and Thomas Sayavong only recognizable by their difference in height and build, as both were in their otherwise identical Hestra combat suits with their helmets on. Martin Vin had his helmet off, probably so that Dav and Aguilar could see his scowl, as if the attack was somehow their fault.

There was no sign of Yuso or the rest of the entourage and the shuttle flight crew. They must be on the upper deck, cowering. They'd have done better to be down in the cargo hold with the contractors, since they'd have marginally more cover from the aerial blaster fire there.

"What is karking going on, Toron?" Vin demanded.

Dav pushed past the team leader, ignoring him as he moved for the back of the shuttle where his gear was. It wouldn't take that long to get loaded up, and there was no way he was going back out there without his armor and his rifle.

"I'm talking to you, Toron!" Vin had followed him aft.

Dav didn't even look at him but continued to don

his armor. "Well, stop talking at me and get Yuso and everybody else aboard down here and into that truck I parked outside. It's not stylish, but it'll get us to the governor's complex." When Vin didn't move, but stood there glaring at him, Dav paused and fixed the former basic sergeant major with the icy stare of a man who had just killed three people and wouldn't mind making it four. "*Now*, Martin. Unless you want to sit here while this tin can turns into a fireball."

As if just to punctuate his words, the gunships made another pass, and another spaceport explosion rocked the shuttle.

Looking like he'd just bitten into something sour, Vin turned reluctantly before taking two steps to the ladder leading up to the top deck. "Our ride's here! We've got to go, now!" Of course he pulled out his Senior NCO bellow, making it clear to their principals that *he* was in charge.

From the sounds of things, Sones and Sayavong hadn't exactly been waiting around for Vin's word on the matter, and were already herding Yuso's entourage onto the truck.

Dav ignored him, strapping the last bit of his armor in place and grabbing his bucket. It was as close as he'd been able to find to a leej bucket. It wasn't the same, but it was close. Fortunately, Sunil Kakar Security had allowed the contractors to bring their own gear and weapons. Not all the companies getting House of Reason contracts were that flexible.

Shoving his bucket on his head and starting the boot-up sequence, he ran down the ramp to find Sones already behind the wheel.

"You can't drive worth sket, Dav."

Just as well. Dav clambered into the back and stationed himself just behind the cab. *Means I can get in the juice that much more easily if we take contact on the way.*

When *we take contact.*

He hadn't felt this alive in years.

2

Getting Yuso himself into the truck took entirely too long. The delegate's senior staffer wasn't exactly athletic, and the expensive suit he wore wasn't intended for any sort of kinetic action. He and his entourage dithered about how to even begin to get into the truck bed—there wasn't a ramp or steps to speak of—while the gunships made yet another strafing run, fortunately on the city beyond the spaceport this time.

Blaster fire was raging through the city itself. Dav guessed that more trucks than the one he and Aguilar had taken made their deliveries of rebels, who were not engaged in a running gun battle.

Sones looked at the gray sky warily. "Does this kelhorned planet even have a kelhorned defense fleet?"

He made a good point. These rebel ships had completed multiple runs at the star port closest to the Repub infrastructure and not a single interceptor was around to do anything about it. All the more reason to move.

Dav pounded his fist on the side of the vehicle to punctuate each word he sent to Yuso's entourage. "Get. In. The. *Truck.*"

He wasn't technically in charge, but they were

sitting blants on the landing pad. The truck wasn't exactly armored, and even if it had been, it probably wouldn't have stood up to the enemy flyers' heavy blaster cannons, but if they were moving it would at least become a harder target.

As the trio of gunships banked once again to come around toward the spaceport, a strobing burst of heavy blaster bolts reached up from the outskirts of the city toward them, forcing two of the repulsor vehicles to veer aside before they could line up their next gun run. The Temugol Defense Force had woken up.

About karking time.

The intensity of blaster fire out in the city sounded like it was rising. The attackers were running into more resistance. That was good, but it was still going to make the run to the governor's compound that much spicier.

Not that Dav was complaining. Yes, on a purely professional level, it was making his mission of keeping Yuso alive that much harder, but on a personal, visceral level, he was back in armor, behind a blaster, about to KTF.

Finally, Sayavong had had enough of watching Yuso and his hangers-on trying to climb into the elevated truck bed. The former hullbuster grabbed Yuso and physically picked their principal up off the wet duracrete pad then *threw* him into the back of the truck. Sayavong was big enough and mean enough that no one objected, though the staffers all looked at him like he was a rampaging bullitar.

The sight of their boss getting tossed like a rag doll, followed by Sayavong's faceless bucket turning toward them, put a sudden end to any coquettish difficulty climbing into the truck. A few might have ripped their expensive clothes, but they got in with admirable quickness.

Dav beat an armored gauntlet on the roof of the cab, and Sones sent the truck lurching toward the disabled gate. They roared through the wreckage and past the bodies in the street, heading into the city as more blaster fire slammed into the spaceport behind them, sending up another series of fireballs to join the roiling orange flames and black smoke already blotting out the gray skies.

Unfortunately, the city beyond the star port, which sprawled over the hills before the gray cliffs to the north cut it off, had not been laid out in what might be considered a logical pattern. From what little Dav had been able to see from the air while coming in through the storm, it had looked like at least three or four different smaller cities that had simply grown together. The holomap had verified that, showing neighborhoods, one with a more circular layout, and the others with habs and buildings dropped wherever the terrain and the colonists' whimsy had decided.

That meant they didn't have a straight shot at the governor's complex. Especially since that compound, a late addition, stood on a hilltop on the edge of the city about six klicks away.

Sones took the first left after they'd gotten past the bodies, racing as fast as he could get the big truck to move between low, modular duracrete buildings clustered around the spaceport. More blaster fire flickered down two of the avenues as they passed them, but nobody shot at the truck, so Dav and the other contractors in the back held their fire, while Yuso and his entourage huddled flat in the bed, praying to Oba not to get dusted.

The immediate area around the spaceport was still laid out in a rough grid, most of the buildings warehouses and office habs, so the going was fairly quick. Sones only had to divert twice, once because of a dead end that hadn't been on the maps pre-loaded into their helmets, the second time because the street was blocked by the burning wreckage of a repulsor sled.

They weren't going to get out of the spaceport district that easily, though.

Sones took another right and stomped on the brakes.

Smoke drifted through the street, coming from another blazing wreck somewhere out of sight behind the blocky duracrete buildings. It dimmed the wan light of the rainy day, which only made the flicker of blaster fire that much brighter.

It didn't take Dav long to assess the situation, even though his helmet didn't come with the HUD of a Legion bucket. Bodies lay in the street, blood dribbling from still-steaming blaster wounds. The double doors leading inside a nearby building appeared to have been blasted open, leaving black scorch marks on the jamb and the frame.

Uniformed soldiers, probably the local militia if not the Defense Force, since this was a major spaceport and not the hinterlands, were hunkered down in the street and exchanging weapons fire with whoever was up in the building. The bodies of those who'd made an attempt to storm the building lay out in the open just a few feet away from the others.

"Push through!" Vin ordered. "Drive! Drive!"

Unfortunately, it looked like there wasn't a way past that firefight that didn't involve going right through. And while the truck *might* hold up to some blaster fire, it wasn't a tank.

Sones delivered the news. "They can shoot right down into our truck bed, Vin. They got no cover back there."

Dav's first instinct was to get off the truck and clear out that nest of raiders—or whoever was shooting the hell out of the city—but this wasn't a combat sled, this wasn't the Legion, and it wasn't the mission. Yuso was the mission, whether he liked it or not.

There was no question that they couldn't get past that intersection without getting shot to pieces without clearing that building.

Vin, predictably, was shouting orders, none of which were particularly smart or inspired. "Okay, let's get some covering fire on that building while we set up a blocking position!"

Dav gritted his teeth. That wasn't even by the Repub Army's book, and he'd been around enough basics to know that. It was like Vin was just pulling tactical words out of thin air.

Fortunately, while Vin might fancy that he was in charge, thanks to his former rank, none of the other contractors thought the same. Sones eased the truck back down the way they'd come, giving them some more cover, while Dav jumped out of the back, immediately joined by Aguilar and Sayavong.

"I'll cover. You guys get to that building."

Sayavong had a powerful CrimTech VS-3 blaster in his big, gloved hands. It wasn't quite an SAB, but that thing could put out a ferocious volume of fire. It fit what Dav had seen of Sayavong's personality. The man wasn't given to subtlety or precision.

He leaned into the corner, bracing that big, heavy blaster rifle, and opened up, spraying brilliant, eye-searing bolts across the front of the blocky duracrete building. The sporadic and murderous blaster fire from the windows slackened, and Dav and Aguilar broke into a dead sprint across the street, their armored boots splashing in blood-tinged puddles as they went.

Dav hit the door on the run, even as more blaster bolts smacked into the duracrete above and around him. Whoever was shooting at the raiders inside the building, their target discrimination wasn't great, or else they'd decided that the two armored figures rushing the building were raiders themselves.

The interior was dark, but while Dav's aftermarket helmet didn't have all of the Legion bucket's bells and whistles, at least it had light enhancement built into the visor. The hallway brightened as he passed inside, and he could clearly see the blackened pits blown in the wall and the small, crumpled body on the floor just at the base of the steps leading up to the next floor.

Aguilar stayed right at Dav's shoulder despite not

being a leej, so far as Dav knew. He paced toward the steps, his EH-7 leveled at the landing ahead, poised to dust anything that popped out from the dead space on the other side of the next flight of steps. He pivoted as he went up the steps, his boots essentially inaudible over the whine and crash of blaster fire, pieing off the opening as he moved up.

The hallway at the top of the steps was almost identical to the one below, though there was no corpse on the floor. Flashes of light spilled into the darkened corridor from an open door at the far end, matching the whine and snap of blaster fire. At least some of the shooters were in there.

Dav moved quickly along the wall, covering the doors on the other side, letting Aguilar trail him. When he was just short of the open door, he pointed to the portal across the hall, which was partially ajar. Red lights flashed through the gap. Aguilar picked it up immediately, stepping next to Dav so that he could see the other man's blaster pointed at the gap.

Then Dav went through the open door, hard and fast.

He was already shooting before he'd cleared the threshold. He put a blaster bolt through the back of the first man's head before his lead foot had touched the floor, and then he was tracking across the line of gunmen at the windows. Each got a single bolt. All six of them were down before the last one had turned halfway around to bring his weapon to bear on Dav.

Under different circumstances, he might have held

his position in the room, secured the weapons, and then moved on. He was in the building to clear the way for the truck, though, so he came right out, falling in behind Aguilar, who had started toward the next door. Dav didn't think that the other man had even entered the first room behind him.

Aguilar's tactics weren't quite as precise. He kicked the door open, quickly getting out of the doorway as he ventilated the room with what seemed like half a charge pack. Three more shooters went down fast, the last one with his clothes on fire.

The blaster fire from the building had stopped, though some of the shooters across the street were still taking potshots at the windows, despite that fact. Dav was tempted to end that, but somebody down there was yelling, and the sporadic blaster fire died down to nothing.

"Let's go." He kept his EH-7 at the ready as he led the way back down to the street, reaching the front with Aguilar just as the truck pulled up outside, joined a moment later by a Temugol Defense Force vehicle, spilling gray-uniformed men onto the street.

The planetary defense forces rushed inside the building, nodding thanks as they moved to verify the contractor's handiwork.

Vin was obviously fuming, his helmet off, as Sayavong reached down and hauled Dav and Aguilar up into the bed at the same time. Before he could say much of anything, though, Sones had them moving again, and he accelerated hard enough that they all had to grab for something to keep from getting spilled off the tailgate.

One of the rebel gunships took a hit from a heavy blaster bolt that flashed up from below only a few streets over. It wasn't fatal, but the craft dipped, smoking fragments blasted away from the impact, and began to smoke as the pilot dove and twisted to skim the rooftops and make his escape to the north, toward the cliffs.

The other two broke off, but they veered around for one more strafing run. One of them roared by just overhead as Sones took another turn, and the first bolts hit only a few meters away, blasting shattered duracrete and flash-heated, compressed soil over the truck as it rolled down the street as fast as Sones could get it to move. Dav thought he heard a faint wail from one of Yuso's entourage, but then they were past and driving toward the slightly more affluent district ahead. Only about three klicks to go.

The street had become slightly serpentine, necessitated by the rock formations that were apparently too much trouble to blast level. Some of the shops and buildings were perched in existing crevices, while a few others had been dug into the dark, wet rock. Some showed bright, colorful lights still; others were blacked out and pocked with blaster burns.

Ahead, through the smoke and the rain, Dav could just see the gate leading to the governor's compound, the tower that was the seat of Republic power on Temugol a dark shape through the haze, rising above the domes and blocky habs that stood between them. They had a pretty straight shot there, and Sones accelerated again, intent on getting them to the compound as quickly as possible.

They hadn't gone a half a klick before two repulsor sleds turned onto the street ahead of them, full of more shooters in ragged coveralls—Dav was starting to think they were supposed to be camouflage, rather than just worn-out mining or ranching gear—pouring more blaster fire down the connecting street before they lost their field of fire.

Both sleds were coming straight for the truck.

Even as their human cargo started screaming, Sones gunned the engine, driving the truck straight at the newcomers as hard as he could. Dav got low over the cab, leveled his EH-7, and opened fire.

His first shots weren't as dead-on as they had been earlier. Moving targets at that speed are a little more difficult. He punched smoking holes in the cab and winged one of the blaster-wielding raiders in the back before he got a little more on target.

Aguilar's burst burned through the windscreen and dusted the driver. The repulsor sled veered wildly, bounced off the second vehicle, and flipped over, spilling bodies out of the back to smash brutally into the building on the side of the road, tumbling limply and brokenly to lie in crumpled, motionless heaps on the pavement.

The driver of the second sled tried to correct for the collision, but he didn't have enough room. He plowed directly into the front of a store set into a low shelf of rock. The explosion rocked the truck as Sones drove by, the flash momentarily blasting the mist of rain clear for a dozen meters.

Then they were past and on the home stretch as

the gunships roared away over the ocean, leaving fire, smoke, and destruction behind them.

3

As the gate loomed ahead, Dav beat on the cab's roof again and said over comms, "Slow down. We don't want to get lit up by Repub security."

Sones didn't need the reminder. *Good man.* Dav looked over his shoulder at Vin. The team leader appeared to be doing his job for once. He was on a comm, his helmet still off, while holding on to the truck's sidewalls for dear life. From what Dav's bucket could pick up, their former sergeant major was coordinating with the governor's security detail.

So when they rolled up to the gate, they weren't faced with leveled N-50s. There were still two older UT-70 combat sleds pulled up in front of the gate as security, but while the men and women in gray fatigues and light body armor looked jumpy as all hell, they had their weapons slung, muzzles down, and they just stared at the truck as it rolled toward the gate. Dav couldn't see the front of the truck, but he could hear the rattle. They'd taken some hits during that short, sharp fight with the two raider sleds on the street, and there were probably a few blaster impacts on the hull.

The sleds powered up and moved in front and behind the truck, with a sled-sized gap in between as they escorted the truck through the gate. Yuso was now sitting up in the back, and some of the security personnel saluted, though the House of Reason staffer of course didn't return them. He probably didn't know how, even if he thought it was worth doing.

The inside of the compound looked markedly different from the rest of the city's drab, mostly duracrete and prefab construction. Five white domes rose above the outer wall, surrounding the twenty-story-high gleaming crysteel tower topped by comms arrays that disappeared into the deep gray cloud cover.

The truck came to a stop a half-klick shy of the tower.

"Guess we wait here," Sones said. They were at a checkpoint—an inner gate built from the same ray-shielded link-posts as the spaceport, only these looked *much* less susceptible to being ran over. You'd probably ruin your vehicle trying.

"That's right," Vin said, sounding proud to have knowledge of what was coming next, though he hadn't bothered to share it.

Two vehicles emerged from the tower's sunken parking garage. Anywhere else, Dav might have sneered at how soft the Repub politicos were, unable to even walk half a klick, but after what had just gone down, he had to admit that it was reasonably smart to avoid exposure in the open.

Even if he was still sorely tempted to indulge his contempt.

The vehicles themselves were wheeled instead of

repulsor craft, which surprised Dav a little, given the conspicuously slick and expensive appearance of the governor's compound.

Maybe all the budget got spent on the fancy buildings.

The hum of repulsors, higher powered than the older UT-70 sleds escorting them, drew Dav's attention behind him. Still at high alert, he swiveled his head, tracking toward the sound. It was familiar.

It should be. It hadn't been *that* long since he'd ridden on a Legion combat sled.

The LCS wasn't all that new; the hull was scarred and pitted in places, though it had been painted over. The twin medium-heavy blasters looked almost as beat up, though he could only tell by looking at the scarring on the finish. Functionally they were immaculate, without the carbon scoring that he could see on the gray-uniformed guards' weapons. At least somebody was making the basics do regular weapons maintenance.

That told Dav something, even if it probably didn't mean much to the rest of the detail. It meant that even though there couldn't be many legionnaires on Temugol— he hadn't heard about there being *any*—at least one of them was a real leej. That was good.

The feeling of comfort and confidence at this revelation surprised him a little, given the deep-seated bitterness he was still carrying around from his own Legion exit. He'd have thought he wouldn't give a damn about what happened in the Legion anymore. That he felt some gratification that the men wearing much the same armor he had weren't being led straight to hell meant something. He was pulling for the Legion to right the ship more than he'd realized.

The combat sled hissed to a stop just outside the gate. Dav turned his attention back toward the reception committee coming out in the wheeled groundcars. He'd have to make contact with the leejes later. If they had even a decent officer in charge, they would have a better picture of what was going on. The House of Reason intel packet had been sparse, at best, though that shouldn't have been a surprise to him after doing half a dozen of these contracts. It had boiled down to "gray-uniformed locals good, anyone else with weapons bad."

The House despised the men who protected their hides personally almost as much as they despised the Legion.

Even better, a Legion quick reaction force was something you could count on to come through. All the more reason to get cozy with a good, old-school Legion NCO.

So why are you a contractor with these meatheads instead of being a good, old-school Legion NCO yourself, then? It was an uncomfortable question that he didn't want to think about right at the moment.

The oncoming vehicles from the tower stopped just inside the gate. The cars were close enough that Dav could see the security personnel in the same gray fatigues driving.

The Legion sled had shifted to cover the gate leading from the compound walls to the street. Whatever else the Legion was doing here, they were set up to take the brunt of any follow-on attack on the governor's compound, leaving a secure area for the special aide to meet with the governor's staff.

Since, apparently, this meeting had to happen *outside*. Dav didn't have enough fingers and toes to count off all the problems with that. But, Repub politicians and worlds all had their own special customs and rules. Maybe it was rude on this planet to wait to greet a guest until after they had come into your house. Stuff like that existed.

It was still stupid, from a security standpoint. Even Vin, who eyed the clouds warily for more flyovers, seemed aware of that, though he'd never admit it.

The drivers stayed in the vehicles while three security personnel per vehicle disembarked, and spread out on either side, as if worried about the shot-up truck, despite the sheer firepower surrounding it and the so-obviously-Utopion-it-hurts aide clearly visible in the back. As they took up their positions, a man in a suit stuck his head out of the rear vehicle and peered around before stepping out of the shadow of the door. He waited, crossing his hands in front of him, trying to appear calm and dignified, even as heavy blaster fire echoed in the distance. The Temugol Defense Force must be fighting off the last of the raiders. The gunships had already vanished into the murk.

Dav stayed where he was. Yuso didn't need his help, and Dav was going to be a lot more comfortable keeping an eye on things from the elevated position, as long as there was still a fight going on.

Vin, however, was eager to help the special aide down from the back of the truck. Yuso was rumpled, flustered, and clearly out of sorts. The special aide waited for Vin, Hesand, and Sayavong to get down and surround him in a triangle of armed and armored contractors before moved to approach the two government vehicles.

The rain was still misting and little whips of wind caused it to swirl. Yuso hunched his shoulders against it. The man in the suit didn't seem bothered, at least not by the rain. He almost flinched as something *boomed* in the distance, though he was quite obviously trying very hard not to. "Special Aide Yuso? I am Rand Vosh, aide to Governor Shen Nisa. I'm afraid that your arrival has come right when Colonel Cel Tradat has decided to stage one of his raids." He was looking around at the misty sky, as if searching for the gunships, his shoulders slightly hunched as if expecting a blow. "The governor wishes to assure you that this is *not* normal, though we do have our problems here. But for now, let's get you to the cover of the tower. It's the most secure spot on the entire planet."

"Yes, please, let's go." Yuso might have tried to maintain a façade of unflappability, but another burst of heavy blaster fire, though it was so far in the distance that Dav figured it had to be nearly five klicks away, almost sent him diving to the duracrete. "Lead the way."

"Everybody, out of the vehicle." Vin was taking charge, as he loved to do when things were calm. "Sones, park this wreck out of the way, then come join the rest of us." He looked up at Dav. "That includes you, Toron."

Dav considered staying put until Sones had the

vehicle parked. Not because there was any immediate threat that would require him to stay on alert with the hijacked truck—they were in probably one of the more secure areas of the city, the Temugol Defense Force was chasing the raiders off, and there were leejes right here.

No, he was just tired of taking guff from this basic.

Still, his professionalism took precedence, and he turned and dropped off the bed of the truck, his armored boots splashing in a puddle on the pavement, as Yuso and Vosh ducked into the back of the rear-wheeled vehicle. Without waiting for the security contractors on the ground, the vehicle backed up and headed for the tower.

Dav knew that his helmet disguised his expression as he turned his gaze on Vin, but he was glaring at the man. Vin, for his part, looked disgusted, but carefully smoothed his expression. "Sones! Where are you going with that truck?"

Dav closed his eyes, just for a moment, and took a deep breath. When he opened them again, he saw Sayavong shaking his head slowly, his helmet turned toward Vin, disgust evident in every line of the big man's body.

This was going to be one of *those* jobs.

It took entirely too long to get things situated and into the tower. After pushing to catch up with Vosh's vehicle and haggling with the door guards for a place to park the truck, the contractors found themselves stationed outside the door where Yuso was meeting with the Republic governor.

There was a plush waiting room outside the governor's office, but they weren't placed there. Instead, they were shown to what looked to be a utility closet.

"What's this?" Sones had asked the admin bot who had led them there.

"This is the security escape room," the bot explained. "If there is an emergency, those inside the governor's office will exit through here and immediately link with security. If they need help inside the office, they will open the door. This allows maximum security without, ahem, potentially upsetting the peace and tranquility of any other guests who might be awaiting the governor's presence."

The bot left.

"This is some sket." Hesand sat on a box and punched his palm. "This is some black, *putrefied* sket. How are we supposed to do our job from in here?"

Sones inspected a panel on the wall. "There's an intercom. Only goes one-way, though."

Vin cleared his throat. "We're in the middle of a Repub government building." From the tone of his voice, he desperately wanted to add a rank to the end of that sentence, but none of them had ranks anymore. "There's nothing to do. The only reason we're all in here is because they haven't shown us our quarters yet."

Sones was leaning against the wall near the door, his arms crossed over his chest plate. "Still need *somebody* on the principal."

"We'll set up a rotation." Vin looked around the room. "Hesand, you're up first, as soon as we get someone to show us to our rooms."

Dav wasn't surprised. *Of course he'd pick the new guy instead of stepping up himself.*

For his part, Dav decided not to waste more time just getting more pissed at Vin. "I'm going to head out, take a look around."

Vin straightened up. "No, we need to stay here."

Dav thought about making it a fight, but it was going to be a long deployment as it was. "Look, you just said it yourself. We're in a Repub government facility. There's security on the gate and the wall, *and* there's a Legion contingent. Nobody's going to go after Yuso in here. We're just twiddling our thumbs. *But.* We're not going to be inside all the time. He's going to want to take the tour of the city, out to the hinterlands, and around to the other cities. That's his *job.* It's a 'fact-finding' tour, remember? And we just landed in the middle of a raid, which means Temugol is a hell of a lot more than a *potential* conflict zone, and the more we know about it, the better." He turned toward the door, slinging his EH-7.

Vin stepped forward, looking up at Dav as the younger contractor loomed over him. "I said we need to stay here."

"The client's not here to give you an audience and be impressed, Vin, so sit down." Sones's voice was a laconic drawl. "The man's right. This was supposed to be some unrest, that's all." He jerked a thumb over his shoulder to indicate everything outside the compound. "I don't know about you, but I wouldn't call that 'unrest.'" He got nods from Aguilar and Sayavong. "Dav's right. We need more information, and it makes no sense to sit here on our thumbs when one of us can go and maybe find some more out."

Vin looked around at the rest of the team, and got nothing but blank, faintly hostile stares from all but Hesand, who didn't make eye contact. He looked at Dav, but if he was going to say anything else, he thought better of it and sat down with a huff.

With a nod to the others, Dav headed out the door.

"Dav." He turned back as the door shut behind Sones. The lean, wiry man's leathery face was set in a look of grim, tired amusement. "Look, I know there's no love lost between you Legion boys and Repub Army, but if I've got to keep breaking the two of you up, this is gonna be one hell of a long trip."

Dav sighed. "I'm trying, brother. He just rubs me the wrong way."

Sones chuckled. "Legionnaire or not, that don't make you special. I had to keep Sayavong from choking him out just before you and Aguilar got back with the truck."

Dav's eyebrows went up. "Seriously?"

A tired nod. "Seriously. He was getting Yuso's people all spun up. You'd think he'd never heard a blaster bolt before." He clapped Dav on the shoulder. "Just saying. Don't let him get to you, because when you get too snappy around him, it just makes things worse."

With a nod and a returned shoulder squeeze, Dav

said, "I'll do what I can."

"All I can ask. I know he's a kelhorn, and there's only so much any of us can do about it, but we've got bigger problems." Sones turned back toward the security room, while Dav headed for the speedlift.

4

The misting rain hadn't lifted as he stepped out of the tower and into the compound, so he put his helmet back on just to stay dry. It was something he hadn't thought about that much when he'd been in the Legion, since they'd had their buckets on all the time. The bucket was one of the most vital parts of a legionnaire's kit, not only providing protection and climate control, but also a lot of information that could be extremely useful in combat. A lot of extraneous sket, too, but that could get filtered out with some fiddling with the settings.

Looking around the compound, he spotted a second Legion combat sled parked outside one of the domes and turned toward it, keeping his EH-7 slung. The Legion might have slipped a long way from what it had been back when he'd first earned his Legion crest, but walking up to a bunch of leejes just after a firefight with a weapon in your hands was a good way to get dead.

Especially if these guys weren't up to the old Legion standards. Actually, scratch that, the old guys could sometimes take KTF to an almost literal level.

That wasn't what suddenly made him hesitate, though, standing in the rain just outside the tower's main entrance.

You left the Legion. How likely are they really going to be to want to help out an ex-leej who's now a babysitter for a House of Reason lackey?

He gusted a heavy sigh as he started across the courtyard, hating his life and where it had led him.

No one popped out to shoot or yell at him as he crossed the quad toward the dome. The compound security all seemed to be out on the perimeter, except for the air defense up on top of the tower. The rest of the governor's staff seemed to want to stay out of the open. Dav didn't blame them. A few three-wheeled scooters zipped around between the tower and a couple of the domes, but there weren't really any people walking around.

It was somewhat gratifying to see that he hadn't gone unobserved. He got about twenty meters from the LCS before the door slid open and two legionnaires, albeit in that shiny, cheap armor, stepped out, their N-4s in their hands.

"You seem to be a little lost, sir." The voice was grating and threatening through the bucket's speakers. At least that hadn't changed.

"Not lost, Leej." He pointed toward where smoke was still rising from the spaceport. "I'm here escorting a special aide from Delegate Sandar Mahat of Corsica. Just shot our way through from the spaceport, right after we landed. I was hoping to have a word with your CO, get some idea of the lay of the land down here."

The two legionnaires traded a glance. He could almost read their thoughts, probably because he'd have the same ones. *Who the hell is this guy and why is he talking to us?*

One soldier glanced over his shoulder. Something about these two told him they were green as hell, probably not that long out of Legion training. There was a long silence, probably while they were on the L-comm with their squad leader or someone. Then he turned back to Dav. "The CO's not here." The flat rasp of the Legion bucket's speakers didn't transmit a lot of emotion, but there was some stiffness there that spoke of trouble in paradise.

Welcome to my world, kid.

"Can I talk to your senior NCO, then?" He knew that there had to be *some* good leadership here, just from the observations he'd made about the state of their gear.

Another pause, then a slightly shorter figure in Legion fatigues, his hair buzzed short and with a nasty scar alongside his neck, appeared in the doorway of the dome, which must be a sort of barracks or command center. "I'm Sergeant First Class Droma. Not going to find a more senior NCO here. What can I do for you, …?"

"Toron. Dav Toron." Dav took his helmet off. He still maintained the same short hair he always had. It made the Krall helmet fit better if he kept it short. He also hadn't lost much of that Legion fitness. "Used to be a leej myself. When I saw that there was a contingent here, I knew I had to swing by and touch base."

Droma looked him over appraisingly. Then he jerked his head to beckon him inside. "I'm not going to give you a guided tour, but let me grab my gear and then we'll go to the cantina. Should be a couple places where we can sit and talk."

Without being listened to went unsaid but implied.

Dav nodded as he stepped up to the dome's entryway. The place was painfully clean, the light strips above illuminating the white plastite brilliantly. Given the general dinginess he'd seen out in the city, at least when he hadn't been looking for targets, it told him that Droma was keeping his boys busy keeping their own space squared away. He'd mostly seen that in backwater posts where there wasn't much going on. Given the reactions they'd seen so far to the raid, he wasn't sure that applied here. There was a clue in front of him, but he wasn't entirely sure yet what it was.

Droma had gone into the back, exiting the entry room and letting the door slide shut behind him. There was an unmanned desk and a few chairs and tables, but Dav decided it was probably best to hang outside the doorway, his bucket tucked under his arm. Even when he'd still been in the Legion, walking into a unit's space when you didn't belong there was verboten.

It didn't take long for the Legion NCO to return, back in his armor. It was the shiny stuff, but something about the way he wore it was different from the rooks out front. Droma had been around.

"Because of the raid, we can't go anywhere without armor or weapons for a while," he explained. "SOP."

Dav raised an eyebrow. "And if there wasn't a raid?"

"Probably still wear my armor," Droma answered.

Dav laughed. "Ooah."

He pulled his own helmet back on and followed the platoon sergeant out into the rain again. He'd be keeping his own gear within arm's reach for a while too, at least so far as he could without running afoul of Yuso's ideas on propriety. He was pretty sure that, if they hadn't come under fire as soon as they'd made planetfall, they'd have been required to make the trip to the governor's compound in plainclothes.

Droma led the way, walking briskly across the compound to a slightly larger dome near the wall, his N-4 dangling from his hand. Dav took the opportunity to scan the area again, but the weapons had finally fallen silent. Two TDF Preyhunters went by overhead with a Doppler roar, but there was no blaster fire, no explosions.

Dav watched the starfighters with narrowed eyes behind his helmet's vision slit. *Where were they about two hours ago?*

All was definitely not well on Temugol, and it wasn't all because of Colonel Cel Tradat.

The cantina was almost deserted, despite the weather. It probably was a matter of time, since there didn't appear to be anything being served at the moment. Droma led the way to the kaff machine, drew a large cup, then found a table near the back. Dav got his own cup of kaff and joined him.

"So, where are you coming from, Dav Toron?" Droma set his bucket and his N-4 on the chair next to him and eyed Dav coolly.

"The 154th." Dav sampled his kaff. It wasn't bad,

but it wasn't great, either. "Tiger Company."

Droma's eyes narrowed as he placed the unit. "Off the *Reliance*?" When Dav nodded, he mirrored the gesture. "Heard your boys got in some trouble out on the edge. Something about a place called Keram."

Dav kept his face still. "That was it."

Taking a sip of his kaff, Droma watched him carefully. "I take it that had something to do with why you left?" There was a challenge, in his words, his voice, and the look in his eye.

"Keram itself? No." All the bitterness came flooding back. "The point who got six of us killed for nothing and faced no consequences? Yeah." He took a savage swig of his kaff, burning his tongue in the process. "That, and the fact that the Legion *promoted* the scum-sucker."

"Ah." Droma nodded. "That old song." He took a sip of his own drink. "To be fair, you're not the only leej who's demanded his walking papers after something like that." He sighed. "Just for your SA, though, I suggest you keep that story between you and me."

Dav's smile was thin and humorless. "I take it your CO..."

"Is a point, yes." The Legion NCO looked like he wanted to spit. "And he's firmly attached to the governor's fourth point of contact, so be aware."

"Great." Dav shook his head. "Bad enough I'm babysitting some House of Reason worm."

"You haven't answered my question." To his credit, Droma didn't visibly react to the news that there was a House of Reason staffer in his AO. From the sounds of it, it might not actually make things appreciably that much worse. "What is it you're looking for from me?"

"Information." Dav leaned forward on the table, his armored elbows clicking on the top. "I'm working close protection for a fact-finding mission from the House. I know, I know. I didn't exactly trade up in the career department. It's credits in the bank, though. Anyway. We didn't get much of a brief—you know how it is—and it became rather blindingly obvious as soon as we made planetfall that if we're going to keep this kelhorn from getting dusted, we need more intel. We dropped right into a hit on the capital city itself. What the *kark* did we fly into?"

Droma grimaced, looked around at the rest of the cantina, and leaned on the table, cradling his cup of kaff in his hands. "Okay. So, we're still sorting some of it out ourselves. Most of that is because Lieutenant Mastruk won't let us push out and do our own reconnaissance. First Platoon, Bullitar Company, 173rd Legion, is here on Temugol in an advise-and-assist capacity with the Temugol Defense Force, and that means we're entirely dependent on the Temus."

"Advise and assist?" Dav frowned. "Since when was *that* a Legion mission? That used to be the kind of thing Dark Ops did."

"Since the House of Reason and the points saw an opportunity to further spread out and dilute the Legion." Droma's voice was low as he said it. Dav could well understand why. He had no more need to temper his cynicism in public, but Droma was still a Legion NCO. He had to step carefully.

"At any rate, the TDF has been fighting Colonel Cel Tradat for the last two years, pretty much ever since Governor Nisa took over. The Repub is putting out every bit of propaganda they can about it. He's a would-be tyrant, a mass murderer, the usual. Some of the stories we hear from official channels, he may as well be a Savage, if they weren't adamant that the Savages are all gone."

"Isn't he?" Dav asked. "A tyrant? A murderer?"

Dav had been out on the edge awhile. Any warlord who would launch an indiscriminate attack on a city like this couldn't be any kind of good guy.

Droma shrugged. "I don't know. I'm sure he's a kelhorn, but like I said, we haven't been allowed to go out. We go from here at the compound to the main Temugol Defense Force base and back. That's it."

"That's no way for leejes to operate."

"Tell me about it." Droma peered down into his kaff cup, and studied it for a long time. There was an odd expression in his eyes when they met Dav's again. "What was it like? Getting out?"

Dav's answer came fast. "Like the best and the worst decision I'd ever made in my life."

They lapsed into silence again, both men absorbed in their thoughts. Dav might not be a leej anymore, but both of them had recognized the brotherhood, and while he'd only met Droma minutes before... they were still brothers.

That was a surprise. And, deep down, he wasn't sure if he deserved that regard.

An idea was forming in Dav's head. "Tell you what,

Sarge. I might not be in the Legion now, but some things you don't just turn off. I've still got my mission, and I think it dovetails with yours. I'll keep my eyes open and my ear to the ground while we're out and about 'fact-finding.' Any intel I pick up, I'll pass on to you. We're staying here in the compound, as far as I know. You do the same for me?"

Droma reached across the table, and the two men shook, gauntleted hand in gauntleted hand. "KTF."

"KTF."

The security group's quarters were a floor below Yuso's. The special aide and his entourage were still ensconced with the governor, but all the contractors had been sent to their living quarters, the reasoning being that since they were on a Repub compound, and the raid had finally been declared over, nothing could happen that would require their services.

Dav had a few thoughts on that theory, especially given what had just gone down, but nobody was asking him.

The security quarters were comfortable enough, though the rooms were small and stark, and everything a sterile white except for the furniture. There was a small common area, but not much in it. Perhaps they were expected to use the compound's cantina and entertainment facilities.

To Dav's great displeasure, Vin was waiting in the

common area when he came in. Dav saw that his duffel was sitting against the wall next to what he had to assume was his room.

Vin stood with his arms folded. "Where the hell have you been?"

Dav fixed him with a heavy-lidded stare, his helmet under his arm. "Talking to the Legion contingent. Getting some threat intel and making contacts that might give us some prior warning before something like that raid happens again." He didn't blink as he locked eyes with the smaller man. He sorely wanted to say something more, but Sones's warning echoed in his ears. If only out of respect for the older man, he was going to try to keep a tighter hold on his temper.

There was a warning in Dav's tone and demeanor, but Vin didn't pick up on it. From the looks of the other contractors who had stuck their heads out of their doors to see what was going on, several of them had.

Vin sneered. "Big, bad leej. Or should I say, 'ex-leej'?" He stabbed a finger at Dav's chest. "You're just another contractor like the rest of us, Toron. Don't you forget it."

Dav started to turn toward his room. "Oh, I'm not likely to."

He saw Vin's ugly grin out of the corner of his eye. "Yeah. How's it feel, *Leej*? Knowing you're getting paid the same as a Repub Army E4 like Hesand? What was it you leejes used to call us? Basics?"

"Hey, leave me out of this." Hesand might have a chip on his shoulder, but he'd always steered clear of Dav, and now he was very obviously uncomfortable, both with the confrontation and with having to talk back to a man he still thought of as a sergeant major.

Dav halted a few paces from his door. He considered just continuing on, ignoring the slights. But he couldn't quite do it.

He turned to face Vin again, and the shorter man's grin faltered. "You're right, Vin. I'm not in the Legion anymore." He stepped into Vin's space and dropped his voice. He stood almost half a head taller, and he was still in his Krall Mk 2 armor, while Vin was in shirtsleeves. "But you ain't a sergeant major anymore, either."

Vin took an involuntary step back. "What's that supposed to mean?"

Dav turned back to his door to pick up his duffel. "Just food for thought, Vin. Food for thought."

5

Nothing was said about the confrontation in the common area the next day as they got sleds together and prepared for the first tour around the city. This was shaping up to be a pretty standard fact-finding tour, and Dav was starting to come down from the combat high he'd hit on the previous day. On some level, he'd always known that there wasn't a House of Reason staffer alive who would willingly go looking for trouble, and thereby give his security detail a chance to get into a firefight.

There was also the factor that the governor probably wouldn't want to risk having a House staffer get into more trouble, and cast doubt on his own ability to govern.

Yesterday had been an anomaly. Today, they would cruise around the city, maybe visit a couple of the outer settlements—or more accurately, the wealthy Republic business magnates who'd decided to build their getaways on "exotic" Temugol—and then head back to Utopion with the governor's approved version of whatever it was that first got the House concerned.

For his part, Dav was still trying to find enough pieces to start putting the bigger picture together. The raid on the spaceport was a pretty good indicator that *somebody* here on Temugol had some serious firepower and was signaling that they might use it against the seat of Republic power. The next attack—if there would be one, could easily strike the domes or tower in the Governor's complex. Especially with how pitifully slow the defense forces had been in fighting back. Which was another piece Dav was still considering. Was that simple ineptitude or was the slow response as much a warning as the attack itself?

Temugol was relatively close in proximity to Craggock Three and its shipyards. If a planet so close Republic's primary carrier shipyards went rogue, there could be all sorts of long-term consequences.

Not that Dav necessarily cared. There were thousands of worlds across the edge, never mind the mid-core, that could cause problems if they broke away or just turned into war zones. Dav had seen enough in the Legion to not expect the House of Reason, of all things, to find a solution. More likely, they were making things worse.

He dismissed the thought as he stowed his armor and weapons behind his seat in one of the Repub luxury sleds given over to Yuso's purposes. Of course it wasn't one of the tactical models. It lacked any offensive weapons and its armor rating was sufficient for low-end blaster fire and little else. Anything more would have been asking a lot for an edge world.

The rain had lifted, though the clouds were still scattered across the sky. There was a damp chill in the air. They were about as close to Temugol's equator as they could get, and it never got comfortably warm.

Vin was, fortunately, in the lead vehicle and would ride with Hesand, the governor's aide, and Yuso. Once they actually came out of the tower. Dav, Sones, Sayavong, and Aguilar were all piled into the rear sled to follow along. At least the drive would be relatively quiet.

Sayavong sighed angrily, checking his chrono. "Of course we're running late. How long does it take one of those Utopion puffs to put on his makeup?"

"Hey, the special aide had an arduous evening yesterday." Sones was completely deadpan, his eyes fixed on the tower while the sleds hovered on thrumming repulsors outside.

If Dav hadn't been around Sones for a while, he might have taken his words seriously. As it was, he could hear the line of sarcasm, even if it wasn't entirely evident to anyone else.

They'd been relegated to their quarters, their presence deemed unnecessary while on the compound, for the entire night. Dav and Aguilar had considered going out in the sleds to familiarize themselves with the city, but Vin had raised sufficient hell—including calling the compound security to ensure they wouldn't get passage out—that they'd stayed put.

One of these days, they were going to have to deal with Vin. Dude was worse than a point.

Finally, the tower's side access doors slid open and four of the governor's security personnel, all in the same gray uniforms, though without much in the way of armor or weapons, came out and flanked the steps. Special Aide Yuso walked out a moment later, bundled up in a long coat and cold-weather hat, accompanied by a woman in much the same attire. The two of them completely ignored the security contractors as they went to the lead sled and got in.

"About time." Aguilar drummed his hands against the sled's steering wheel as the other three contractors adjusted their gear and weapons and got settled. It was probably going to be a long drive.

The sleds hummed out through the gate, passing the two old combat sleds that were now parked out on the street.

"What happened yesterday was... unexpected," the governor's aide announced in an all-comm broadcast to all the sleds. "Today will carry no such troubles."

Yuso answered on the open comm, apparently for his detail's benefit, "Yes, the governor told me the same."

The local government might be trying to act as if they had nothing to worry about, but the destruction on the streets from yesterday's action made the danger plain, and something in the tone of Yuso's voice told Dav that their principal wasn't necessarily buying the aide's reassurance. That was interesting.

The contractors stayed quiet as Aguilar drove behind the principal's sled. There wasn't much to talk about, and all of them had their eyes open and watching their surroundings.

It quickly became apparent that there were parts of the city where the governor's aide didn't want to go. Or at least that was Dav's guess based on the circuitous route they were taking. It seemed like they were steering around entire neighborhoods. Dav did what he could to scan those areas, but there wasn't much to see aside from the low duracrete structures and ancient pre-fabs that made up most of the city.

Sones noticed it, too. "What do you suppose they're hiding from us in those 'hoods?"

Nobody had an answer, so no one replied.

If there were any clues as to what was going on there, they couldn't see it from the sled.

So, drawing on lessons learned from years spent in various insurgency environments across galaxy's edge, Dav settled in to watch the people on the street.

Most of the inhabitants were human, though there were a couple of rough-looking male Tennar, some equally hard-knock Endurians, and what looked like a whole colony of Drusics working manual labor. For the most part, they all seemed to be ignoring the sleds and going about their business. If anything, some of them seemed to be going out of their way to avoid them.

Dav's eyes narrowed as he spotted movement near what looked like a sled garage. It wasn't much, but someone had just ducked into the shelter of the building as the lead vehicle had gotten close.

"Got something on the right. Somebody just took cover," Vin reported.

Dav clicked his comm to let the other man know that he'd heard and left it at that.

He kept his eye on the garage as they glided past. Nothing jumped out at him as a threat. Several mechanics were working on an old, broken-down repulsor truck, and there were a few dark glowers thrown their way, but nothing that looked to his practiced eye as anything but ordinary, everyday resentment of Repub luxury.

He'd been places where that resentment had flared into terrific violence, but he wasn't getting that feeling here. Not yet.

They kept moving, heading toward the higher ground above the bulk of the city, to the north. The route continued to meander back and forth around the city, pointedly avoiding the neighborhoods to the southeast, northwest, and just to the east of the center of the city.

Almost an hour of silent driving was broken up by Sayavong. "So, any bets on what the governor's trying to hide? Because this feels like a trip without a purpose. Just driving."

Aguilar snorted. "My guess is that he's got some under-the-table business arrangements he doesn't want getting out. All these connected types do."

Sones was still watching the city go by. "Over half the city? Seems a bit excessive, especially since he's only been here for two rotations."

Dav said acidly, "Don't underestimate these creeps." He didn't elaborate while he watched the street, his chin on his fist. He didn't need to. The grunts of agreement from the other three men in the sled were enough.

Leaving the city, the lead sled headed up the hill, toward a large dome set on top of a dark gray cliff overlooking the port. It stood by itself, towering over the low, squat shapes of the city's buildings, higher even than the governor's tower. The sled came to a stop near the entrance, on the far side from the city, and the aide got out, beckoning to Yuso to join her. As the two of them walked toward the dome, Dav noticed that there was a frown on Yuso's face, and though he couldn't hear what was being said, the special aide's impatience was getting ever more obvious in his body language.

Dav exited the sled as Aguilar halted a little behind the lead. The wet chill in the air was getting worse, as scraps of mist blew in off the highlands to the north. He scanned their surroundings, but there wasn't much to see. A few structures loomed dark in the mists in the distance, but the dome stood by itself.

"What in the Nine Hells is this place?" Sayavong looked around. "Another office?"

"It's a monument." Sones was looking at a plaque next to the door leading to the inside of the dome. "'To the resolve and intrepidity of the people of the Republic.'" He snorted, looking up at the plastite dome. "Why do I suspect this wasn't built by the original settlers?"

Dav agreed with Sones's suspicion, but that wasn't the thing that stuck out to him just then. He sighed. "So, I was right."

"Right about what?" Sayavong turned to look at him.

"This isn't a scouting expedition. It's a sightseeing tour." He spat on the wet rock underfoot. "Typical."

Despite his general suspicion of Yuso and every other Utopion creature he'd ever met, though, Dav was starting to suspect that the tactical tourism wasn't the special aide's idea. This was a diversion set up by the governor. Whatever was going on here, he suspected that Governor Nisa had a comfortable little existence going, despite the armed conflict that Droma had told him about, and letting Yuso think that the previous day's attack was anything but a fluke might get him more scrutiny.

Maybe. It fit some of the other edge worlds he'd been on. He couldn't be sure, but he was suspicious.

Sayavong shook his head. "After that dustup right after we landed, too. I thought this was gonna be a thing."

It would have been easy to relax, go back to the vehicles, and just wait for the bureaucrats to finish their tactical tourism, figuring that the locals wouldn't have let them go anywhere something was likely to happen. Something kept Dav outside, though, watching their surroundings, as empty and stark as they were as the mists rolled in off the glaciers to the north.

The sleds were still hovering on their repulsors, the thrum keeping the quiet at bay. That was why he saw the little triangular object—a bot?—before he could hear its own smaller repulsor drive.

He turned to follow it as it drifted overhead, moving down from the northeast, then started back toward the dome. Yeah, that was an observation bot, all right—a peeper. The little machine came to a hover above Yuso's sled and began to descend, rotating toward the entrance of the dome. Dav and Sones drew their weapons almost simultaneously and blasted it into glowing shards with twin, resounding *cracks*.

Vin was out of the sled like a shot. "What was that?"

"Peeper bot." Aguilar was already moving, heading toward the door in the dome, Dav only a couple steps behind him. "We need to go. Now."

Vin hesitated. "It might just have been a local's sightseeing bot."

"That doesn't make it any less of a threat. From some of the looks we were getting, that might actually make it *more.*" Dav was still scanning the sky as Aguilar yanked the door to the dome open.

"Mr. Yuso!" The hawk-faced man barked. "We need to go. Right now."

Yuso and the governor's aide were standing next to a black stone plinth buried in the ground surrounded by a duracrete dais. The plaque next to it declared that it had been set there by the first founders of the colony when they'd landed, claiming Temugol for the glory of the Republic. Dav thought that was unlikely, but that was the least of his concerns just then.

"Why? What's going on?" Yuso looked alert and worried, while his interlocutor's face was still and blank. Whatever was happening, it wasn't according to either man's plan. And these types rarely did well when their plans were thrown out of whack.

"We just got buzzed by a peeper. Might have been recon, might have been an assassin drone. We need to leave."

For a second, it looked like Yuso was going to argue. He looked at the governor's aide, then back at Dav and nodded. "Okay. Let's go."

Dav waited as the two VIPs got into their sled with

Vin. Sayavong and Sones were still on their feet, blasters in their hands, holding security. The mist had thickened over the last minute.

All was quiet. No new peepers. No speeders full of blaster-wielding terrorists. No gunships.

That didn't make Dav feel any better.

As Vin drove off, the three of them ducked back into the trail sled.

Aguilar throttled up fast, even as they shut the doors, but Vin had quite a head start. Now that his mind was thinking of threats, he was in a hurry, to the point of leaving his backup in the dust.

It fit everything Dav had observed about Vin so far, but that didn't make it any less infuriating.

Aguilar followed the principal's sled down the hill, heading back into the city as fast as they could maintain control.

Not quite fast enough.

They'd just come around a bend to find a pair of big utility trucks blocking the road. They were almost identical to the one Dav and Aguilar had commandeered to get to the governor's compound. Vin's sled barely came to a stop before slamming into one of them.

Realizing the trouble he was in, Vin began to back up as dark figures popped out of the buildings all around.

6

Aguilar brought the sled to an abrupt halt, swiveling the vehicle to one side and using the repulsors to arrest its momentum. The sled rocked, even as Dav threw himself out the door, his EH-7 already in his hands. Of course there was no time to armor up, but he was on the pavement and moving to cover fast.

Sones and Sayavong were right behind him. There wasn't much cover on the street, but they were barricaded on the sled and the nearest corners of low duracrete buildings in seconds.

It was immediately clear that they were massively outnumbered. Dav had seen that as soon as he'd dismounted. He couldn't see a lot of detail, as the attackers were mostly clustered in cover behind the balloon-tired trucks, but he could see enough to realize there were a lot of them. That didn't matter. They had to get Yuso out of there.

For a few seconds, nothing happened as Vin gunned his sled in reverse. You might have thought the ambushers were fine to let them go, the trucks forming more of a roadblock than a death trap. Then blaster fire snapped out from behind the stationary vehicles. Bolts tested the lightly armored sled and sent fractal impact patterns against the windshield.

Dav had to duck as bolts dug scorched holes in the duracrete just in front of him. He leaned out on a low knee and returned fire, tracking his own bolts down the side of the street, doing what he could to avoid hitting the lead sled. Vin had stopped and the doors were partially opened, but those inside looked frozen in place. That might have been because Vin was freaking out, but it was just as likely that Yuso and his host were doing the freaking out and Vin was trying to keep them from running out into the open. Dav had seen that sort of thing screw up a response before, even in the Legion.

"Up!" he roared, surging to his feet and running forward along the street, flaying the corner of the building ahead with rapid-fire blaster bolts. They had to get fire superiority, and fast, or this was going to go pear-shaped in a hurry.

Dashing to the next bit of cover, a sunken doorway in the duracrete wall of the long, low building, he pivoted and shot a bearded human in greasy coveralls through the head, his bolt streaking past the rear of the lead sled. Sayavong backed him up, scattering blaster fire across both sides of the street from his own cover in a storm of brilliant bolts that almost looked random, except that each one seemed to either drop a hostile, or else hammer into a window or other form of cover.

Aguilar reversed their sled with a deafening whine, until he suddenly stopped. More blaster fire snapped around the street behind him. Dav spared a look back and saw that things had just gotten worse. A long, flatbed utility sled had just pulled across the street behind them.

They were trapped.

There would be time to analyze how they'd been tracked and cornered later. That peeper must not have been the only one. The immediate concern was getting Yuso—and themselves—somewhere safer. Blaster bolts continued to punch into the lead sled. Vin and Hesand were returning fire from a cracked door. The attackers were still mostly staying behind cover, peppering the vehicles with blaster fire. If they'd intended to use the initial burst of fire to cover a dash to the vehicles, it had failed as soon as the contractors had dismounted and started fighting back.

The contractor turned back to the front door of the building at his side. A simple, two-story building without signage or ornamentation. It was locked, but a single bolt to the catch plate solved that problem. He didn't wait for Sones. There wasn't time. He forced the door open, and leading with his blaster's muzzle, he pushed inside.

The place was a residence from the looks of it, but if there was anyone home, they were wisely hiding. The entryway and the main living room were dark and still as Dav quickly stepped through the fatal funnel of the door and cleared the space around him. At least in the Legion, you had your armor to keep you alive in the event of a one-man clear. Oh well, necessity required the risk.

It took seconds to clear the rest of the residence. The building must have been partitioned into multiple dwelling spaces, and Dav had just picked one of several front doors. The whole block was probably tenements, then; the brutalist utilitarian style of the printed building made each one look like the next. The good news was that no one was home and the walls were thick duracrete intended to insulate against the damp chill that was Temugol City's climate even during the summer. Those would probably work to stop blaster bolts.

Quickly shifting back to the front, he got on comms. "This is Three. I've got cover in the building to the three o'clock. Bring it in."

Sayavong held his position. So did Sones, though he was now covering their six, peppering that big, flatbed utility sled with more blaster fire, keeping their unknown attackers at bay. Dav pushed out onto the street again, raking the corner with blaster bolts.

"Vin," he said into his comm. "Did you hear me? Get out of that sled and come to me while we can still provide covering fire."

The team leader didn't answer, but Hesand finally jumped out of the lead sled, dragged the rear door open, and, while the governor's staffer protested and shrieked, dragged the man out onto the pavement and propelled him, head down, toward the door.

Hesand might have been a green-as-grass basic, but he'd learned the close protection business well enough.

Vin did much the same with Yuso, though the House of Reason Special Aide was more dignified about it. Both of them crouched almost double as Vin scuttled to the rear, using his own open door as cover while he hauled their principal out onto the pavement and ran around the back of the trapped sled, which was now increasingly pitted with blackened blaster impacts. To his credit, Vin kept his own body between the blaster fire and the special aide.

With their two protectees inside, Dav bellowed over the comm. "Collapse on me!" He accompanied the call with another storm of blaster fire to cover Sayavong's movement. The big former hullbuster dashed across the street, chased by a few more stray blaster bolts, and dove through the door behind Dav. Aguilar had abandoned his sled and was right on Sayavong's heels.

Sones had backed up, and was now almost to the alcove where the door stood open. "On me!"

Dav sent one last burst down the street, then pivoted toward the door, clapping Sones on the shoulder as he went.

"Last man!" Sones announced.

Dav ducked through the door with Sones on his heels, turning to cover back the way they'd come. He was reasonably sure that no one had entered the house after he'd cleared it, and their immediate threat was right out front.

"Who's on the rear door?" Technically, it should be Vin asking that question, but Dav hadn't heard a word from him since they'd gotten hit.

"What back door?" Sayavong asked.

That answered that question.

"Hesand! Get to the back and cover that door before these kelhorns shiv us in the kidneys!" Dav gritted his teeth. He shouldn't have to do everything on this team, especially not when Yuso had consistently deferred to Vin as the detail lead.

"I'm on it, too." Aguilar ducked toward the rear, practically dragging Hesand with him. With Dav and Sones on the front door, it made sense to have two blasters on the rear.

The sounds of blaster fire on the street had died down, though it hadn't gone completely silent. As it got quiet, Dav eased his head out into the alcove, only to duck back as a blaster bolt smacked into the duracrete next to his cheek, spattering him with burning hot bits of frag. The attackers had learned some caution, but there were still at least several of them out there, keeping the front of the building covered. He'd seen two run to the corner of one of the halted repulsor trucks, trying to get a better angle, though they weren't trying to assault the contractors' position. Yet.

Sones returned fire, sending brilliant lines back toward the shooter, but there was enough mist and smoke out there by then that Dav couldn't tell if he'd hit anything.

He noticed then that he hadn't heard any comm traffic. He had his own comm set to monitor both their internal channel and the main TDF support channel, which was supposed to be their backup. "Vin! Have you called for the react force yet?"

"Sket!" The former sergeant major muttered some more imprecations before he calmed down. "Tango Delta Five Eight, this is Scribe One." Oba only knew who had come up with that call sign. "We are under attack and pinned down at..." He paused for a second. "Where are we?"

Dav took a deep breath, trying to suppress the sulfurous curse that sprang to his lips. Sones, however, had no such qualms.

"What the hell were you doing that entire drive?" He twisted his head to glare at their teammate. "We're at the corner of Ioren and Calk Streets. Get those kelhorns *moving.*"

For a moment Dav thought that Vin was going to snap back at Sones. He didn't do well with criticism, that had become abundantly clear. But team leader let it go and got on the comm again. "We are at the corner of Ioren and Calk Streets. Under heavy fire."

"Copy, Scribe One. Stand by."

The quiet stretched out.

"What are they waiting for?" Yuso sounded like he was trying very hard to sound calm, but the incipient panic in his voice was there for all to hear. "We're not that far from the compound or the Defense Force base."

"I don't know, sir." Vin sounded almost as scared as Yuso.

"Maybe they aren't that interested in saving a Repub rep." Sones's voice was pitched low enough that Dav was pretty sure he was the only one who could hear him.

For his part, Dav didn't comment, but kept his eyes and his blaster on the street outside. This wasn't the time or the place for that conversation.

He was really starting to think that they needed far more intel about what was happening on Temugol.

If they made it through the next hour, anyway.

Blaster fire snapped and whined in the distance. It was hard to say exactly where, given the acoustics of the alcove where he and Sones were covered down, but it was at least a block away. A moment later, a female voice came over the comm.

"Scribe One, this is Tregar Seven One."

Tregar. That was an interesting call sign. From the briefing materials they'd received on the planet, the tregar was a semi-amphibious, very dangerous animal that haunted the Temugol coasts.

"We are encountering heavy resistance and are under intense fire. We cannot reach you. You will have to —" The comm cut off.

Dav echoed Sones's curse, even as several others in the room uttered imprecations from half a dozen worlds. Either the TDF was sandbagging them, or things were a lot worse than they had looked on contact.

His money was on the former. He'd seen the TDF fight during the raid. The question then was, why?

Funny how the intel packet had more on local wildlife than it did on hostile activity.

"Scribe One, this is Bullitar One Five." Dav recognized Droma's voice over the comm. "Hold what you've got. We are en route. Five mikes."

Dav couldn't keep back a tight, feral grin. Let these kelhorns get a taste of what it meant to cross swords with the Legion.

In the meantime, they had to wait.

He shifted his position to get a slightly better view,

but the street remained empty. Their sleds, scarred and smoking, were still hovering about half a meter off the ground, providing the bad guys a certain degree of cover and concealment he wasn't happy with, but it wasn't as if he could very well run out there and move them.

Part of him wanted to try it anyway, if only to get his armor and the rest of his gear off the sled. He had one spare charge pack for his EH-7, but the rest was in the go bag next to his seat. Without a lot of cover fire, though, that would be a suicide run, provided the terrorists hadn't made themselves scarce. They certainly weren't making an effort to fight their way into the building.

The sounds of blaster fire in the distance had died down again. Had the TDF react force really run into stiff resistance, or had it just taken a couple of potshots for them to decide to retreat? Dav glanced at Sones then inclined his head toward the street.

It seemed like a good time to make a run for the sleds.

The older man glanced over his shoulder a little. Sones was as hard as they came, from what Dav had seen, but he was also getting a little long in the tooth, and not everyone took a job like this because they were looking for trouble. He'd been more than competent so far, but it was still asking a lot to get more aggressive than absolutely necessary in a situation like this. After all, the Legion was coming. They *could* just stay put and wait for those combat sleds. In fact, if they were being smart, they probably should.

That went against the grain for Dav, though, and it

seemed that it did for Sones, too. He nodded, and the two of them moved out into the alcove, cross-covering up and down the street as they did.

Another burst of blaster fire kicked grit into Dav's face, but he'd seen where it had come from—a window just up the street, above the utility sled which had blocked them in. He returned fire almost without flinching. His first bolt stabbed into the darkness where the incoming had originated, and the fire ceased.

Then the sound of a pair of twin N-50s crackled down the street, accompanied by the distant rumble of repulsors. Bright bolts of blaster fire ripped into the utility sled behind their halted vehicles. Glowing holes were blasted through the light metal skin and windows, and then the power cell blew up with a brilliant flash and a tooth-rattling *boom.*

The lead combat sled roared through the dissipating flames and smoke, its armored prow shouldering the wreckage aside. A shiny helmet was crouched behind the twins, their muzzles rotating from side to side like some predatory beast sniffing for prey.

Dav might have had his problems with the direction the Legion had gone in recent years, but it didn't make that sight any less beautiful.

Vin quickly made contact. "Bullitar One Five, this is Scribe One. We are in the second apartment of the one-story tenement block to your two o'clock. We'd appreciate it if you watched your fires."

"Good copy, Scribe One." The repulsors howled as the combat sleds—still spaced far enough apart to avoid getting caught in a single blast—pushed their way up to the initial roadblock, twins and N4 muzzles looking for targets. Everyone who'd still been standing seemed to have vanished into the tenement blocks, though.

The combat sled came to a halt just outside their door. "This is Scribe One, coming out."

Dav and Sones, already out of the alcove, carefully cleared the street outside the tenement, just to be on the safe side as the others began to make their way out of the tenement building.

Some habits die hard, and that's why Dav was still alive.

A man with sergeant's bars on his armor climbed down out of the combat sled. "You Toron?" He didn't take his helmet off, which was wise, since they weren't out of it yet.

"That's me." Dav didn't look to see the expression on Vin's face at the fact that the legionnaires were deferring to him as the point of contact. "You guys got here just in time."

The sergeant nodded, before turning his attention to the Repub sleds. "Can those still move, or are you going to need a ride? It's going to be a tight fit if you have to ride with us."

The blank faceplate of the helmet and the sandpapery, emotionless rasp of the external speakers didn't give away any expression or emotion, but Dav suspected there might be an ulterior motive in the legionnaire's caution. Nobody who wasn't a political animal looking for an advantage would want to share a sled—particularly an overloaded one—with a House of Reason creature.

"We'll have to see." Dav was already moving toward the sled he'd shared with Sones, Sayavong, and Aguilar. He wanted his armor and his gear. He wasn't the only one, either. The other contractors converged on the stricken vehicle, dragging go-bags out of the back as fast as they could.

There wasn't time to get armored up right there, though. Vin had moved quickly to the lead sled and climbed in. His voice came over the comm a moment later. "We're still running. Get everyone in and let's go."

Dav shook his head slightly and shrugged as the Legion NCO looked at him. He tossed his go-bag back into the sled's cab. "I guess you're leading out."

If he had a comment in mind, the legionnaire kept it to himself. "We'll slide over so you can get past. Follow the second sled." He jerked an armored thumb over his shoulder at the dim shape of another combat sled just barely visible through the thickening smoke that filled the street.

Dav nodded. "Thanks, Leej." Then he clambered into his own ride as the sergeant circled his fist above his head and climbed back into the rear of the combat sled. Aguilar spun their vehicle around on its repulsors and slid forward, bumping over the wreckage of the flatbed utility vehicle that had blocked them in before moving aside to let Vin's sled past.

Vin laid on the horn as he went by, as if to express his displeasure that they hadn't just gotten out of the way first.

Aguilar rolled his eyes. Dav shook his head and started shouldering into his chest armor.

They still had a ways to go to get back to the governor's compound, and he wasn't going to make the trip in shirtsleeves again.

7

It was an uneventful drive back to the compound. That was both welcome and unsurprising, what with Legion combat sleds in front and behind, the twins rotating around to cover every opening, every vehicle that might be out of place, as they went. With legionnaires on the street, it seemed as if no one wanted to stick their necks out. That was fine with Dav.

At least, it was mostly fine. He hadn't really had a chance to KTF in a long time, and while this job was definitely shaping up to be a very... kinetic one, he found that it was making him wish, more than ever, that he'd never left his armor.

One bad officer and you took off.

It was more complicated than that, and he knew it, but the call of the Legion was strong. Along with second-guessing his own life choices.

That one bad officer is becoming the norm, not the exception. It's only a matter of time before guys like Droma get forced out, and it's all points. Why else would that kelhorn have gotten away with what he did? Connections matter more than competence now.

Competence, courage, brotherhood. Those were things that the House of Reason hated and feared, and so they were busily taking their knives to the Legion so that they didn't have to worry about them anymore.

Yet here you are escorting a House of Reason toady. How does that put you in a better position? And you still had to call the Legion for help.

Dav kept his thoughts to himself, but the turmoil he felt as he watched the combat sled up ahead was weighing on his mind. He watched the combat sled's twins move back and forth, a hard-charging leej behind them, waiting for any chance to KTF. Never mind the cheap, shiny armor that had been foisted on him by the House of Reason. Dav watched that man, and he knew what he was thinking—just begging a kelhorn to try it.

They reached the gates of the governor's compound faster than Dav anticipated. The Legion escort had no problems about moving through neighborhoods that Yuso's guide had avoided.

And you didn't even think to notice or look, Dav admonished himself. *Too busy thinking about the past. Second-guessing. Keep your head clear.*

The security at the outer wall's gate was in sight, but the defense troopers on those old UT-70s sleds outside made the Legion combat sleds stop well before them. It looked like there were some hoops that needed to be jumped through. Sergeant Droma got down out of his sled and had a short—but presumably sharp—talk with one of their NCOs. The UT-70 dutifully slid out of the way to make the passage clear while Droma went back to his own vehicle.

Dav had seen things like this before. He'd been to

plenty of places where the Legion routinely got stonewalled at the gate through sheer weight of bureaucracy. Counterintuitively, it often got *worse* after an incident like the raid the day before. As far as delays went, this one wasn't so bad. The Legion sleds hovered away as soon as they were inside the wall, and the rear sled passed with a gauntleted hand raised from the turret. Dav returned the wave, wondering if the leej behind the twins would have waved if he hadn't talked to Droma the day before.

A skimmer came hauling out of the garage next to the tower and headed off the lead sled. Parking right in front of it, a man in a blue suit jumped out of the back of the skimmer and waved frantically at Vin, pointing the sled toward the garage.

"Get that heap off the grounds," the man shouted to Vin. "Last thing everybody needs to see is a sled shot to hell by rebels."

Vin drove as instructed, but Dav could see him shaking his head as he drove.

Aguilar drummed his fingers on the steering wheel. "Oba forbid they have a med-bot here to greet us instead of grounds and maintenance."

It seemed that the local bureaucrats didn't want a shot-up sled disturbing their delicate sensibilities. Typical.

There wasn't much any of them could do about it, and the more he thought about it, the less Dav thought it likely that protesting would do much more than make matters worse. The kind of kelhorns who treated ambushed personnel like this weren't going to have sudden changes of heart from a direct confrontation. They'd probably just double down and make life twice as miserable for the contractors.

"I can't quite put my finger on it," Sones deadpanned, "but something ain't right on Temugol."

Dav gave a half-laugh, half-grunt. "Step lightly. We'll figure it out."

Technically it would be *Yuso* who would have to figure out what was wrong. And from what little he'd been able to see over the last couple of hours, Dav thought that their principal might be ready to start digging, hard. All the contractors had to do was keep him safe.

Aguilar followed Vin into the garage and parked where the illuminated guide lights directed them. It was deep in the bowels of the underground bay. They *really* wanted the evidence of the ambush out of sight.

The contractors all got out as the drivers shut down the repulsors and settled the sleds to the ground. The governor's staffer scuttled away without even a word or a glance at the contractors. Yuso got out somewhat more sedately, though the man was pale and obviously rattled.

"Thank you, gentle sirs." He looked around at each of them, making eye contact, which Dav couldn't remember the man ever doing before. "I am going to have a meeting with the governor shortly. I would like all of you to come with me."

"Of course," Vin said and then glared at Dav, as if he was going to object. Dav returned his stare with an unblinking, almost bored gaze. Vin looked back at the special aide. "We'll be there every step of the way."

It was possible that the close call had given Yuso a renewed appreciation for his protectors. He might also be thinking of using them as leverage and intimidation in the meeting to come. Dav suspected that he was mostly just scared, but that could translate into appreciation. But it was the sort that could vanish as soon as Yuso felt safe again. Time would tell.

Slinging their gear and weapons, the contractors fell into a loose diamond formation around Yuso and accompanied him out of the garage and toward the tower.

The governor's audience hall was on the uppermost floor of the tower, with high, arching columns cast in ornate designs and set with brilliant, gold-shaded lamps. Vast floor-to-ceiling windows afforded sweeping views of the coast and the Temugol spaceport. Anyone who'd been in the hall could have watched the raid in perfect clarity from here, including the attack and the crash of the space liner that was still a twisted, blackened hulk at the center of the grim scar it had cut in the spaceport facilities.

Most of the hall was wide open and empty, with a raised dais in the center holding the governor's desk and a high-backed chair from which he could swivel to view any part of the room or the windows around the outside. It had been carefully designed to impress upon any visitor the power and grandeur of the Republic, while at the same time it had just enough businesslike starkness that the governor—or any other Repub functionary—could claim that they were just representing the grandeur of the *people* of the Republic, rather than the vast bureaucracy that they really worked for.

Dav imagined that was the reason for a desk, rather than a throne.

Governor Shen Nisa sat at the desk, his fingers steepled in front of his face. He was trying to look grave, but he was a sallow man with a scrawny, soft build that even his expensive clothes couldn't disguise. Beside him stood a tall, shapely woman in a uniform half covered in medals, a silvene braid hanging from her shoulder. It looked to have been tailored to accentuate her every curve. She was almost a decade younger than the governor, who had clearly had some rejuv treatments. Even so, she had to be far too young for the general's rank insignia on her shoulder boards.

Dav left the possibilities behind that situation in a deep, dark corner of his mind.

Yuso stood on the dais, towering over Nisa who remained seated in his oversized desk chair, arms folded. Special Aide Macha Yuso was not what Dav would ever consider an imposing man, but compared to Nisa, he seemed impressive.

The contractors stood at the base of the steps, finally armored up the way they wished they'd been during the ambush. Somehow they'd been permitted to carry their Garmians openly.

Yuso had been serious about keeping his detail

close since the ambush. He'd had words with the governor's security about it before entering. The memory made Dav smile inwardly.

They were waiting in an awkward silence for someone. That was about all Dav knew. Neither Yuso nor the governor had bothered with introductions. It didn't matter if the contractors shook the governor's hand or knew the name of the young general standing at his side or that of anyone else for that matter.

The last arrivals came through the door a moment later as the awkward silence stretched out. A pair of legionnaires, officer and NCO, the lieutenant with his helmet tucked smartly under his arm.

The officer walked with purpose and precision to Yuso and then shook the special aide's hand. "Lieutenant Ioin Mastruk, First Platoon, Bullitar Company, 173rd Legion."

The lieutenant was a lantern-jawed, handsome young man, his hair just short enough to fit under a Legion bucket. Droma was the other legionnaire, and Dav couldn't help but contrast him with the grizzled, weary look he'd seen on the man's face last, though now the NCO had his helmet on.

The lieutenant turned to face the governor. "You wanted to see us, Governor?"

Though Mastruk stood tall, and his voice was deep and projected well, there was something about his manner that rubbed Dav the wrong way. Like it was all a façade, an act.

Of course it was an act. He was a point.

The woman standing by the governor's chair stepped forward and leaned on the desk. "Yes, *Lieutenant.* The Legion's role here is very clear, and always has been. Your force's intervention this afternoon was a blatant violation of Republic laws on Temugol, and vastly exceeded your authority. You are here to *advise* and *assist.* Nowhere in that remit are you authorized to conduct unilateral combat operations in the center of Temugol City, of all places." She straightened, adjusting her uniform jacket with a huff. She was trying to look angry, but Dav figured it was owing to how the overly tight garment had ridden up. "We have no choice but to terminate this partnership and have you recalled."

Dav glanced at the lieutenant. The young man had gone pale. Dav was disappointed, but not surprised. The point clearly saw his political aspirations dying in front of his eyes. An appointed officer in any branch could get away with a lot, but if he was recalled from a command billet, the odds of getting much of anywhere in the Republic's maze of politics and government got a lot longer. Because if this point had a powerful enough patron to undo that sort of disgrace, the general wouldn't have dared recall him.

Which was why Dav could see his next move coming a mile away.

The Legion platoon leader glanced over his shoulder, at where Droma stood at parade rest. The sket was about to roll downhill. Dav had no doubt in his mind that the point was about to throw his platoon sergeant under the bus. The credit never stopped with a point. The point might have okayed the mission; he might not have. But he was going to do everything he could to make Droma pay for it.

You can't let this happen again. Dav looked up at Yuso, who was watching the little play with a faint furrow between his brows. *Screw it. Worst thing that can happen is you get sent back to the* Inspiration *and have to go looking for another job.*

"Just what kind of resistance did your people run into, General, that they couldn't come deal with three sleds' worth of Cel Tradat's terrorists?" Dav's voice echoed through the chamber.

Vin's head snapped around to glare at Dav.

Everyone was shocked into silence.

Except Dav.

"They put down yesterday's raid handily enough. It seems a little strange to me that we were sitting there under fire for almost ten minutes, until a single Legion *squad* broke through what your entire—what? Battalion? Regiment?—couldn't get through."

"*Stand down, Toron!*" Vin hissed, but it was too late, and he knew it.

The general had recoiled from the words almost as if Dav had marched up and slapped her in the face. She was pale around the eyes as she stared at him, pure venom in her gaze. "You are out of line! You are only here as a courtesy to Special Aide Yuso, nothing more. Your advice is not required or requested. You will do well to remember your job and be silent while your betters discuss these matters!"

The governor looked from Dav, to the general, and finally to Yuso. "An apology to General Huno is in order, I believe."

Yuso glanced back to Dav with a troubled look in his eyes. For a moment, Dav thought that his gamble had failed, but then Yuso turned to the governor with a frown.

"Special Agent Toron is correct, however." His voice was soft, but the impact of the words that followed were not in line with his tone. The governor almost flinched, and the general looked even more peeved. "Military matters might not be my area of expertise, but the timing and the degree of resistance do not seem to match. He correctly assesses that we saw a considerably faster and more effective response upon our arrival. So, General, I would ask you to answer the special agent's question on my—on the *Republic's*—behalf."

General Huno looked at Governor Nisa, looking unsure how to answer. She stammered and then replied, "Ongoing operations had much of our resources committed... elsewhere."

Yuso, while he might be a political animal, apparently wasn't a fool. "Ongoing operations? Interesting. I did not receive any briefings on these ongoing operations. In fact, based on what briefings I did get, it was my understanding that Colonel Cel Tradat's separatist forces were always moving between hidden bases on the northern tundra, and that repeated attempts to dig them out have been unsuccessful, with enough loss of personnel and equipment due to weather and terrain such that there hasn't been an expedition in over two cycles." He tilted his head with a frown. "I would think that any change in that situation might be worth mentioning."

Drawing himself up, he stared at General Huno until she could no longer meet his eyes. "Need I remind you, General, that I am a direct representative of the House of Reason, here on a *fact-finding* mission? I do have the authority to demand that I be briefed on *anything* of planetary importance. The fact that I apparently have to make that demand is already a problem."

Dav was tempted to let his regard for Yuso go up a ways after that, but he tempered the thought. Yuso wasn't doing any of this for Dav's sake or the sake of the Legion appointee. The special aide had his own reasons not to get walked over by a bunch of provincial bureaucrats on a half-frozen edge world. These people had disrespected his position... and apparently were willing to leave him to die.

And he was still mixed up with the House of Reason. As nice as the support was, it didn't mean he wouldn't throw the leejes and the contractors under the bus as soon as it became advantageous.

Dav had too much experience not to know better.

"The sensitive nature of the operation currently underway made it impossible to brief it outside of the operational units and the governor. There wasn't time to brief you either, especially not before you left on the morning tour. The operation was time-sensitive." Huno had regained some of her equilibrium, but she still seemed rattled.

Dav was pretty sure she was either lying outright or dissembling as hard and as fast as she could. She had to know there would be consequences if Yuso got off-planet—or even reported back to Delegate Mahat via hypercomm—and suggested that the Temus had tried to have him killed. Or even *let* him get killed.

Yuso raised his eyebrows. "In that case, you won't mind if I speak to the mission commander. I'd be very interested in finding out what progress has been made against this little insurgency."

Huno and Nisa traded a glance. It was so quick that it almost wasn't noticeable, but Dav picked up on it. From the way Aguilar shifted his weight, he had too.

Huno was attempting to sound cooperative while not at all delivering what the special aide requested. "I'm afraid that's not possible as yet. The situation is still fluid, and follow-on missions might be necessary. They will not be back to base for some time yet. We'll be sure to notify you when they return, though."

Meaning they'll stay in the field until we leave. I'd be willing to bet that they're rolling out right now, just to make sure there's no one on base to answer Yuso's questions if we drive out there.

Things were getting deeper and deeper.

For a moment, Yuso studied the two of them. Judging by the way his gaze lingered on Nisa, Dav suspected that it was not lost on him that the governor really hadn't said a word so far.

"I would appreciate it. In the meantime, I will go back to my quarters. I expect a full brief this evening, but for now, I'm afraid it's been a rather taxing day. If you'll excuse me." Without waiting for an acknowledgment from either the governor or the Temugol Defense Forces commander, Yuso turned and headed for the door, and the contractors followed.

Lieutenant Mastruk didn't look at them while they passed, but Dav got the impression that Droma had his eyes on him. He touched two fingers to his eyebrow in a mock salute as they passed. It wasn't Legion discipline, but then, he wasn't a leej anymore, was he?

8

Yuso might have decided that he needed his security detail closer now, but that didn't mean he was going to confide in them. While he'd had them move up into his apartments, once they got back to the entire floor of the governor's tower that had been set aside for him, he disappeared into his suite of rooms and left them out in the main room and the staterooms to either side.

Vin might have thrown a tantrum about Dav's interjection during the meeting with the governor, but fortunately, Yuso's intervention and agreement reduced the tirade to a hate-filled glare shot at the former legionnaire prior to stalking into his own stateroom.

Dav shook his head and turned to see Hesand, who hovered near his own door. He looked as if he were unsure whether he should hang out or follow Vin's example and go into his own quarters. There was definitely some disapproval in the way he looked at Dav.

For his part, Dav wasn't going to wait around for the team leader to return. There were things that needed discussing. "Okay, unless I miss my guess, that little byplay in there just made our entire situation way riskier."

"Definitely." Aguilar sat down on the couch and kicked his armored boots up onto the low table in the sunken center of the common room. He cocked his head to one side critically. "I wonder just what the backlash from your little extemporaneous speech might have been, but it might not really have moved the needle that much. Whatever's going on, they're covering something up. Maybe it's corruption, maybe it's just negligence. They don't want our guy around, though, that's for sure."

"But letting him get kidnapped or dusted?" Sayavong wasn't convinced. "That's a bit far for a Republic governor, isn't it?"

Dav and Sones both laughed, without much humor. "You must not have been around the edge that much."

Sayavong wasn't amused. "I'm not Hesand. Or Vin." He turned to the younger man. "No offense."

Hesand didn't seem to know what to say.

Dav held his hands up. "Sorry, man. Didn't mean it that way." He dropped his helmet onto the table. "We need more intel. I couldn't care less what kind of weird political games are going on here, but we're in harm's way, and I'd rather have a better idea of what to expect. I don't like just sitting around, waiting to get hit." He'd had to do that a couple of times in the Legion, both times under the point who had finally broken his last bit of determination to gut it out.

"Yeah well," Hesand said, "that doesn't really matter, does it? Whether we're in harm's way. It's about Yuso."

Dav looked at the guy. "Yeah... And if Yuso's a target, then we're in trouble, too. I'm going out to do some snooping. If Yuso wants to go anywhere, cover for me and give me a ping."

"Vin won't like it," Hesand warned.

Aguilar stood up and stretched. "If he wants to be in charge, he should probably get to know the job a bit better, not to mention actually be around when things are happening." He turned to Dav. "I'll come with you."

Dav nodded his thanks and slung his EH-7 over his shoulder, grabbed a long coat from the rack near the door and draped it over his armor and weapons. He'd have to leave the helmet. "We'll see you guys when we get back. Hopefully with some answers."

The two of them didn't head straight for the gate. Dav wanted to swing by the Legion dome first. The two leejes on security stopped him at the door.

"I'm—" Dav began, but the legionnaire stopped him by holding up a hand.

"Wait one." After a brief moment, probably while he spoke over the L-comm, the legionnaire said, "Sarge will be out to see you in a second, sir."

Dav nodded silently. He still felt a bit like an interloper, despite how well his first meeting with the Legion NCO had gone.

Droma was still in his armor, though he had his bucket off. He looked tired. "What can I do for you, Mr. Toron?"

"Aguilar and I are heading out to do a little snooping and listening. Need any ideas you might have of places to avoid, places we might hear things." He held up his hands. "I know. You haven't been able to get out much. You have to have heard *some* things from the locals, though."

Droma chuckled dryly. "We might have seen or heard a few things, but not much that's going to help. Your best bet will probably be the spaceport and the bars around there. Lots of RUMINT to be had. Just take it with a grain of salt. I doubt I have to tell you that, though."

Dav shrugged. "Hey. Why don't you come with us? Call it liberty call or something. Met up with an old leej who wants to buy you a shot of Kortan brandy?"

"I'd say make it Jorgan whiskey and we have a deal, but I've got orders." Droma kept his expression still, a testament to years of discipline. "The lieutenant doesn't want to piss off the governor any more than he already is, so we're not leaving the compound for the moment."

While the thought of that point effectively taking his platoon out of the fight to appease a politico enraged him on some level, Dav was able to just shrug. "Well, probably for the best, anyway. I can only imagine how bad the knockoff Kortan is around here." He waved as he turned toward the gate. "See you around, Sarge."

"Watch your back, Leej."

It had taken some talking, finally backed up by a credit chit, to get out of the gate. Dav and Aguilar would need to bring back a case of Collyridian ale, whatever that was, when they returned. The rain started again almost as soon as he made it out into the streets.

Dav hunched his shoulders against the drizzle, wishing he had his helmet even while he knew that it would only make him stand out that much more. Their armor already made both men look bigger than they were, but fortunately their coats covered most of it. The rain might keep people from taking much notice of them, too.

The streets bore the scars of the recent raid, though as he made his way toward the spaceport, he couldn't help but notice older marks, too. It was patched or painted over, but blaster fire had marred this city before. He wondered just how long this little bush war with Cel Tradat had been going on for. Droma had said two years, which still seemed like it might have been a low estimate, judging by some of what he was seeing.

Ostensibly, that was why Yuso was on Temugol in the first place. There was just a lot that hadn't been included in the briefing materials for the security detail, probably either because some intel scumsack hadn't thought they'd needed to know or because the House's intel prep had been sloppy. Either one was likely.

Judging by some of that exchange with the governor, it seemed a bit like Yuso was starting to take the situation far more seriously than some House of Reason flacks he'd encountered.

He found that he hoped so. It was a bit of a surprising thought, given his all-consuming cynicism.

The farther the pair of contractors went, the more Dav was glad that he'd brought his EH-7 as well as his Garmian. There was a tension on the streets, and some of it seemed to be simply because they were strangers. Those who were out in the rain—a common thing given the regularity of poor weather—took long looks at Dav and Aguilar as they passed. Strangers in a city of a quarter million people is no surprise, but even cities of that size have regional neighborhoods and networks, and they didn't belong to any of them.

"Locals seem a bit jumpy." Aguilar kept his voice low, still looking around as they walked down the side of the street, side by side.

"Can you blame 'em?" Dav nodded toward the spaceport, and the rubble where the star liner had crashed, which was just visible down the street. "Cel Tradat just shot the sket out of this place, and from the looks of things, definitely not for the first time."

"Not really." Aguilar sighed. "It's making *me* jumpy, though."

"Yeah." Dav frowned as he turned a corner, drawing Aguilar after him, and checking something out of the corner of his eye.

In the Legion, you sent in bots or relied on the Republic's various intelligence branches to find out what you were dealing with. Maybe there would be a specialized team of leejes who were feeding advance reconnaissance —Dav had heard of such things. It hadn't been a thing he was ever asked to do. But moving to the private security side of things, Dav had needed to get a lot more used to the shadier aspects of operations. He'd needed to spy, to learn how to operate alone and in plain sight in a way that the Legion didn't usually practice. That was paying off now.

For the last block, he'd gotten the feeling that they were being followed. He couldn't pin it down, and there'd been a time when he wouldn't have given any credence to the heebie-jeebies as a threat indicator, but time and experience had taught him to trust his gut.

As he turned the corner, he took the opportunity to check behind them without being obvious about it.

Aguilar had picked up on his movement. "Got something?"

"Maybe. Human in a dark jacket just got taken by surprise as we turned the corner. He cut his steps, then changed course to go into that alley." He nodded across the street.

"Sket." Aguilar faded back against the damp duracrete wall behind him, his eyes narrowed and his expression taut as he scanned their surroundings. "What do you want to do? Should we try to lose him?"

"Best bet, unless you want to try to grab him and interrogate him." Even though both of them were in pretty good shape, that didn't seem like a good idea. They didn't know this maze of streets, and their shadow presumably did.

"Lead on." Aguilar shoved his hands deeper into

his coat pockets. He'd slit one of them so that he could get to his Garmian faster.

With their shadow currently out of line of sight, Dav ducked back onto the street. He moved quickly to the next corner, then went around it, resisting the urge to break into a run. They still had to be careful. If Cel Tradat's forces had spotters in the city—and he had no reason to think they didn't, especially not after the ambush—then making it clear that they were doing more than just going for a walk would probably only get more bad guys after them.

Two more rapid turns, and he didn't see their tail again when he paused to look in a shop window. Maybe they really had lost them. Maybe not. He kept going.

The spaceport itself was locked down, with more of the TDF UT-70 sleds parked across the gateway that he'd smashed with the balloon-tired truck a couple days before. Fortunately, from what he'd seen on the way out, most of the bars and cantinas were outside the spaceport proper, so they didn't really need to go in there.

He'd been to his share of dive bars, usually around military bases and spaceports, and had developed a bit of a feel for them. The ones frequented by the spacers were never the same ones the locals patronized, for good reason.

The spacer bars weren't going to help them unless they wanted news from off-world. The local bars were their target, and they'd have to step carefully there. Both contractors were too obviously outsiders, their dress and mannerisms just different enough that they'd stand out. Just judging by the looks they'd gotten already, not to mention the tail on the street, winning the locals' trust enough to learn anything was going to be tough.

It took a little while to find the right establishment. There were a number of taverns and cantinas near the spaceport, and the pair walked by them slowly, trying to get a sense of when to pick one and head inside. There was a subtly different feel to each one, but Dav thought he'd identified the local watering hole, a few blocks back from the spaceport security gate, past the first ring of spacer dives.

"This one." He glanced at Aguilar to see if the other man agreed. It wasn't as if the place had "Here is Where the Locals Drink" on the front door.

Aguilar squinted at it, then checked up and down the street. "It has the right look. Most spaceport dives are a bit more busted up."

Slipping inside, the two of them got out of the doorway while their eyes adjusted to the gloom. It wasn't exactly the peak of the day, so there were only a handful of people inside, mostly humans, except for a couple of large, ape-like Drusics and an alien he didn't recognize, humanoid but with bluish-green skin and an extra set of tendrils extending from its wrists. Large, blank, golden eyes turned toward them when they first entered, but looked away as Dav met the alien's gaze.

Dav and Aguilar made their way to a table near the wall, Dav being careful to keep his coat closed over his armor and weapons. It was warm inside the bar, warm enough that he realized just how cold it was on the street.

The bartender watched them with a gimlet-eyed

stare that wasn't what anyone would call friendly. Their assessment from the street seemed to be dead-on. This was a local bar, with a local clientele that all knew each other. Not a spacer bar.

That meant the information they were looking for was probably here. He just had to find a way to get it and then leave before trouble could find them.

The humans and the Drusics were still watching them, even though they were now in a deeply shadowed part of the bar, partially obscured by the dimness. No one had made a move to speak to him or see if he wanted to order anything.

"There's no order pad." Aguilar had checked the seats, which felt slightly tacky to the touch. "Pretty bare-bones sort of place."

Movement drew Dav's eye. "Heads up." A Drusic and two humans were up and closing in on his table. Both men wore gray coveralls, and one had clearly had his nose broken more than once. Given the rejuv treatments available, he either couldn't afford them, or he'd kept the crooked nose to look more intimidating.

And he might be intimidating. But not to a legionnaire. Or whatever Aguilar had been before he'd gone contract.

"Can I help you?" Dav felt a deadly calm come over him. This was nothing compared to the ambush in the street, or the fight to get clear of the spaceport, but it could still turn nasty in a heartbeat.

And he loved it.

"This isn't your kind of place." The man with the

crooked nose loomed over the table, the Drusic blotting out the light behind him.

Aguilar shrugged. "I don't know. It looks like just my kind of place."

That seemed to irritate the man. "You don't get it, outworlder."

Dav might have played it out, but he glanced at Aguilar. The hawk-faced veteran was sitting with his hands on the table, having gone perfectly still.

No, his hands weren't *on* the table. They were resting on the edge, where it looked like they were on top, but could easily vanish beneath to draw a blaster. With a hulking Drusic involved, this could really get bad.

He traded a quick glance with Aguilar, and the other man gave him a nod. Then they both surged out of their chairs, sending the seats tumbling backward with a clatter and forcing the man with the broken nose a step back.

Everyone froze. The three who'd come to his table had been expecting to pick a fight, but not like this.

"Why don't you help us 'get it,' then?" Dav growled.

The man glanced at the other human, which was a misstep. Aguilar took a step to close the distance, though Dav put out a hand to forestall him before he over-penetrated. They had a good angle on the three of them from where they stood now, and from the look on one of the humans' face, their would-be bullies realized it.

That was when the Drusic decided to intervene.

"This is a place for Temus. Not outworlders." The huge alien pointed to the door with a hairy finger. "Nothing for you here, outworlder."

"We just want a quiet drink. Away from the noise of drunken spacers. Not bothering anyone." This was getting delicate, but Dav was committed now. "So why don't you step off and leave us alone?"

The Drusic blinked at him. A human wasn't supposed to call out a Drusic like that, not unless they were feeling suicidal. The risk was too high...

And that risk came home a heartbeat later, when the Drusic's nostrils flared and it threw a punch.

Fortunately, Dav had some professional training and as well as a few harrowing experiences when it came to fighting Drusics. Enough to keep from becoming an immediate red smear on the floor, anyway.

With a lunge, he ducked under the massive swing, and took a long step to close on the man with the crooked nose. He grabbed the man behind the neck before he could react and smashed an armored elbow to re-break the nose before he swung around the man, putting him between himself and the increasingly enraged Drusic.

The man staggered to the point that it was only Dav's strength that kept him from crumpling to the floor. Blood streamed from his smashed nose. Dav let go and kicked him right into the Drusic's path as the massive alien started to rage. The two of them got tangled up, giving Dav just enough time to back up and snatch his EH-7 out from under his coat.

Aguilar already had his own blaster out and the other human was suddenly staring at the black pit of its muzzle with his eyes almost crossed, his hands out by his side while he tried to avoid getting pulped by his enraged Drusic buddy behind him.

The Drusic still had the sense enough to fling its fellow out of the way; Dav had seen a few of those maim or even kill its friends once their aggression was fully fired up. The alien roared. Dav started to wonder if this was going to work. He didn't want to shoot one of the locals, but if the Drusic was in full rage, he might not have the choice.

"I said back off!" Dav jerked his head toward the back of the bar without letting his muzzle move a millimeter from where he could put a bolt through the Drusic's eye.

Fortunately, while the Drusics were famous for their speed, strength, and aggressiveness more than their smarts, this one wasn't quite so far gone as not to recognize the threat of a blaster rifle pointed at its skull from three meters away. It snarled, baring fangs the size of Dav's fingers, but it froze nevertheless.

The second human glanced at his fallen friend, then back at Aguilar. For a moment, the contractor just stared at him over his blaster, then he nodded. The human then ducked around the Drusic, which was still staring at Dav, its nostrils flared, chest heaving with the urge to lunge forward and smash this upstart outworlder to paste. The man picked up his semi-conscious companion and started to drag him away, watching Dav and Aguilar with obvious consternation. They really had expected to bully the spacers into leaving.

Holding his ground, Dav kept his blaster on the Drusic. The humans might have backed off, but that massive alien was still a threat, and was still watching him, breathing hard, a hair trigger of hormones away from turning into a weapon of mass destruction in that enclosed space.

The door opened then, and he had to force himself to keep his eyes and muzzle on the Drusic, trusting Aguilar to cover any newcomers.

This has not gone according to plan.

Two young humans had come through, both in long coats not unlike his own, showing just enough bulk underneath that he suspected they were wearing body armor and carrying blasters or short surge shotguns underneath. Behind them, a short, stocky man stood in the doorway, dressed similarly but with his coat swept back and his hands on his hips as he surveyed the tableau of the dim bar and the aborted fight. With a wave of his hand, he led the way over toward the table.

"This disagreement is over, Neka," the man said to the Drusic. There was a significant weight of authority in his voice.

The Drusic hesitated. One of the bodyguards standing inside the door shifted his weight and squared off with the Drusic. *Surge shotgun. No way any regular dude in his right mind is going to try to quickdraw on a Drusic with a hand blaster.* Dav might do it, but he was much more confident in his own speed and accuracy than any backcountry gunslinger should be.

The Drusic snarled again, then turned and shambled after its two human companions, though not without a glare at Dav that promised this wasn't over.

The stocky man pulled up a third chair to their table and sat down. He looked from Dav to Aguilar and back. "Have a seat, gentlemen. We need to talk."

9

Dav eyed the two bodyguards. They had shifted to cover both him and Aguilar, though they'd lowered the surge shotguns to point at the floor.

Sitting down was safe enough... for now. He glanced over at Aguilar, they traded a nod, and lowered their own blasters.

He slid into the chair, letting his EH-7 hang on its sling across his lap, while Aguilar did the same across the table. Probably best not to unclip the blaster and put it on the table. Those boys with the surge shotguns might get the wrong idea.

"You have us at a disadvantage," Aguilar told the stranger across from him.

"I'm Samuel Triste." The stocky man put his elbows on the table and waved at the bartender without looking away from the two of them. He had a peculiar accent that Dav had only heard from a few locals since arriving. "That probably means nothing to outworlders like you. Some history. My family was one of the first to settle on Temugol. We still have one of the largest turesk ranching operations on the planet." He folded his hands on the table. "As for you, I might not know *who* you are, but I know *what* you are. You're here with the Republic special aide."

Dav thought he was starting to understand. "You had us followed."

Triste didn't deny it. "With everything going on, my friends and I have good reason to watch the governor's compound."

He eyed Dav and Aguilar appraisingly, then seemed to decide that he could trust the men in armor carrying semi-concealed blaster carbines. Probably because he didn't have any choice.

"The reason I'm talking to you is because I have no other way to get a message to your boss. Nobody's getting in or out of that compound without some serious vetting by Nisa's people, and they sure as frakk don't want me talking to him. I'm a local, after all."

Frakk. That was a new one Dav hadn't heard before. Part of the fun of visiting far-off worlds. They had their own dialect of curses. Dav leaned back in his chair, his hand naturally coming to rest on the EH-7. "Are you saying that the local Republic government isn't interested in its constituents' concerns?" He was only half sincere in the question. But the inherent cynicism that he'd come by honestly over the last few cycles lent an edge of sarcasm to his words.

Triste snorted. "That's putting it mildly. There hasn't been a Temu governor on this planet in most of my lifetime. Which is where the root of most of our problems lies. Ours isn't a particularly wealthy world, but given our proximity to Craggock Three, the Republic wants a firm grasp. That doesn't bother me or my friends on any serious level. We are Republic citizens. Yet having an outworlder governing us doesn't follow the Republic charter."

Aguilar seemed to find that curious. "You didn't vote him in?"

Triste leveled a distasteful sneer at the question. "Certain... 'emergencies' allow for an appointment in place of elections."

Dav still didn't clearly see the connection, but knew he was close. "Even so, what would be the point of bringing in an outsider?"

Triste shrugged. "We don't know for certain. The decision was made arbitrarily, off-world, about ten cycles ago. Whatever the case is, we *do* know that Nisa has become obscenely wealthy during his tenure here. How, I couldn't tell you. But some of it is because of Cel Tradat."

There was that name again. A name that *should* have been all over their mission briefs but had been completely absent.

"Who is Cel Tradat, and what does he want?" Dav realized that they were getting at least some of the intel they'd come into town for. They'd have to take it with a grain of salt, but at least they'd have something to report. Whether or not Yuso took it seriously was another question.

Triste took a deep breath as he leaned back in his seat, seemingly settling in for a long story. "Exactly who he is, I don't know. The name he uses means 'The Betrayed' in our old language. I have my guesses, but they're only that. Guesses. He's been very careful.

"What he wants is total independence from the Republic—with himself in charge of the *new* Temugol. His actions are what gives the Republic the authority to appoint the governor we have now. These types never realize how much worse they make things. While I can sympathize with his discontent concerning our outworlder governor, and the Legion being brought in to train the TDF to fight a 'counterinsurgency' against our own people, like I said, most of us still want to be part of the Republic. We'd just prefer to be equal partners, not a protectorate."

Equal partners meant full membership into the Republic and sending a pair of senators to Utopion. As a protectorate, their governor was a planetary and Republic official and they could vote on their House of Reason Delegate who represented the vast expanse of space that the planet found itself in.

"How long has this insurgency been going on?" Aguilar asked.

"Since we became a Republic protectorate." At Dav's raised eyebrow, Triste nodded. "Oh yes. It's dragged on far too long. Which is all on Nisa." His expression hardened. "He's been treating this war like a game almost the entire time. Cel Tradat raids one of the cities, Nisa sends the Temugol Defense Force out after him, and then they conveniently 'lose' their quarry in the weather and the wilderness."

"That seems a little suspect. The Repub destroyer that dropped off the legionnaires—not to mention the leejes themselves—ought to have been able to wipe out what I've seen in a matter of days."

"Except Nisa refuses to let them give it a go; his right as governor. It's *extremely* suspect. So the Republic sends more resources—and those resources get turned into that big tower and complex you came from... but if you ask me, there ought to be a lot more credits to spare. If you'd seen the rest of this colony, you'd understand that they're not seeing the same upgrades."

"You think the governor is keeping the change." It wasn't a question.

"I know it. Worse, though I haven't been able to identify the source, or confirm it for certain, I and several of my associates suspect that *Cel Tradat* is also paying him off."

Dav shook his head, putting the pieces together. "He's buying time."

"Indeed. Nisa is a greedy fool. The other side, though, they're true believers. They're taking advantage of Nisa's greed and corruption now, but it won't last forever. Now I might not know who Cel Tradat is, but I know some of those who have gravitated to him. They haven't told me anything outright, but they've certainly implied that as long as Cel Tradat can exploit the governor's greed, and therefore keep the Defense Force off his trail, he will. But he's building up to something. And I think it's coming soon."

Triste leaned across the table again, his voice dipping. They were in a local bar, not a spacer watering hole, but it was clear that the man was concerned with snooping ears. "There have been ships coming in, not even bothering with the star ports, and they're not here to do business with us or with the governor. I think that Cel Tradat has made contacts and allies off-world, and that he's positioning people to make his final move." Triste laughed. "The irony of it. Our governor makes himself rich by making Cel Tradat powerful, and he can't see what that power is going to be used for."

"What do you want us to do about it?" Dav was already thinking through the implications. Yuso might be a creature of the House of Reason, but he'd demonstrated already that he wasn't going to get snowballed by the governor. This conflict might still be small enough that it could be squashed prior to becoming a regional flare-up that would require a full Legion campaign.

If nothing else, getting this story to Yuso might be enough to be allowed to do more digging along with some of the other contractors. Go looking for trouble. From the look on Aguilar's face, he was thinking much the same thing.

Assuming Yuso was willing to let his security thin out a bit to let it happen. No guarantee.

Dav would do what he could to make sure it happened. Not because he felt any kinship with the Temus, or even the Republic bureaucrats who had sent them out here. He just needed a mission, needed the action, and he smelled something a lot better than babysitting a special aide.

Triste brought Dav's thoughts back to the present. The man seemed about ready to be done. "If you can, speak to the man you are protecting. Let him know that the attempt on his life was a sign that things are about to start moving very fast."

"Was that the governor?" Aguilar asked. Dav wasn't sure if this man would or could know that, but it was worth the question.

Triste shook his head. "No. Governor Nisa has no reason to want to keep someone from the House of Reason close to his affairs. His part was only in letting them go."

"Cel Tradat, then."

Triste shrugged, but his expression made it clear that he guessed the same. He stood. "You have very little time left, if I am any judge of such things. I have delivered my message. If your employer wishes to speak to me, my home is to the west, in the hills above Barsota."

On his way out, Triste paused at the door. "It would be best not to leave this establishment together. Cel Tradat has eyes everywhere." With that, he stepped outside and disappeared.

Dav scanned the bar. The bartender was watching him, as was the Drusic, who was now sitting in a booth near the back. That was a concern. If they left and that mountain of muscle, fur, and fangs decided to follow them...

Well, that was why they'd brought blasters.

Communicating wordlessly with Aguilar, a tilt of his head indicating the Drusic, Dav settled in to finish his drink. The massive alien wasn't their only concern.

Ten minutes passed before he paid with his credit

chit—his main one, rather than one of the throwaways he was carrying for emergency use—then the two of them got up and headed for the door.

Slipping out onto the street, Dav squinted against the glare. The weather had cleared up some, though there were still plenty of clouds in the sky, and the brightness of the sunlight was painful after the gloom inside the bar. He scanned his surroundings quickly but carefully as he stepped out of the doorway and moved to where he could quickly turn to engage the Drusic if the big alien followed them out. Without a word, Aguilar had gone the other way, putting the pair of them into a good position to ambush anyone following too aggressively.

No one came after them though, and while several sleds and more than a few pedestrians were out on the damp streets, Dav saw nothing that appeared hostile. Not yet anyway.

Hunching his shoulders under his coat and making sure that both his Garmian and his EH-7 were hidden in its folds, he started down the street, heading in the same direction as before. Aguilar caught up quickly, though he was staying offset just enough that neither of them would block the other if they needed to suddenly draw and get down to the violence business. Other than their spacing, though, both men walked as casually as possible. No need to give additional suspicions to anyone watching.

The heavy-duty whine of repulsors caught his ear. That didn't sound like a normal vehicle, not even one of the heavy utility haulers. That sounded like a combat sled.

Sure enough, as he turned the next corner, he

slowed, though he didn't stop. Aguilar quickly crossed the street, just in case. An even older V-712 Kabrikkian combat sled, a relic of the Savage Wars, sat across the road. Men and women in TDF combat uniforms, with full gear and old Y19 blasters slung, were deploying to set up a roadblock.

While Dav might not have entirely believed everything that Triste had said, that didn't mean he was going to take chances with getting rolled up. It had already been pretty obvious that the governor had wanted Yuso only to see the tourist attractions while he was on Temugol. Let two of the special aide's security detail get picked up walking around the streets on his own, concealing battle armor and military-grade blasters, and some very uncomfortable questions might be asked.

Provided they didn't just kill the two of them, dump their bodies, and claim to have no idea what happened to them. Vin sure wouldn't try to dig very hard. Yuso probably wouldn't either.

With Aguilar covering their six, Dav ducked down a side alley and started to look for another route.

<h1 style="text-align:center">10</h1>

They got a couple of blocks before the next checkpoint popped up. It looked increasingly like every major intersection was getting locked down.

Dav told himself he shouldn't be *too* concerned about it.

If Triste had been telling the truth, then it was entirely possible that the governor was panicking after the ambush. And certainly, Yuso's displeasure would have only added to that panic. That might mean that he was just trying to keep things calm until Yuso left, and the lockdown was his way of making sure that Cel Tradat's agents didn't try the same trick twice. Maybe if he could keep things quiet long enough, then Yuso would think about his close call, remember the easy life on Utopion, and decide it was best to leave the planet to become someone else's problem. Then the governor could get back to business as usual.

Dav moved down another narrow alley, every sense alert, wishing more than ever that he had a Legion bucket to provide him some more early warning. His natural eyes and ears could only pick up so much. Even his aftermarket helmet would've been nice just then.

But you didn't bring it, so stop wasting time and

energy thinking about it.

Dav and Aguilar weren't the only ones on the street trying to avoid the checkpoints. So far, the few locals he saw ignored them, and he did his best not to eyeball them too closely, either. He didn't expect any of them to be friendly. Especially not if they were Cel Tradat's people.

He caught up with a group hustling off the street just ahead of him. The two nearest him were young humans, maybe in their early twenties, dressed in similar black jackets, the rest of their clothes looking intentionally ragged in that way wealthy core-world people dress to look cool. Only, on an edge world, things were hard enough that no one could tell the difference. They had their hands in their jacket pockets, and unless he missed his guess, Dav suspected they were clutching weapons. The look of the whole group just screamed "street ganger" to him, and that was without the tall, skinny guy with the long, greasy hair twitching like he was high on H8.

Things were about to get interesting.

He stopped in the shadow of one of the printed duracrete colony buildings, wishing there were some vehicles to hide behind. He didn't need to get tangled up with this bunch.

Unfortunately, they didn't just keep moving. Apparently satisfied that they were far enough away from the TDF forces, they glanced over their shoulders toward the street, then started to relax and spread out across the alley. One of the shorter ones dug into a pocket and came out with an H8 ball.

Sket.

Dav glanced over his shoulder, judging time and angles. The last thing they needed was to get into a fight with street gangers, especially within two blocks of a checkpoint. Blaster fire would inevitably bring the local defense forces or militia, and then they'd be in the middle of the very situation they'd been trying to avoid.

He couldn't see much in the way of escape routes, though. Those gangers had stopped before any branch alleys, so unless they were going to go through one of the nearby tenements, they'd have to go back to the street, and if any of those checkpoint troops were alert enough, they couldn't help but notice the two men who'd just gone into the alley suddenly come out.

That brief hesitation was almost their undoing. The H8 addict was so wound up that he looked up at the first sign of movement, and locked onto Dav. "Hey, chachek!" Twitching, the kid started toward him, one hand coming out of a pocket with a knife.

Dav braced himself. Going to blasters wasn't going to work, and he knew enough about H8 addicts to know that this probably wasn't going to be defused by just trying to walk away. With a sigh, he got ready to fight, hoping that his armor would keep that blade out of any of his softer parts.

Aguilar moved first. Stepping out into the street, he startled the H8 addict and his buddies, who must have sort of zeroed in on Dav. Aguilar had momentarily faded into the shadows of a recessed doorway before he moved out, letting his coat fall open and exposing his blaster and the combat armor underneath.

"Nothing here to take, sket-breath. Just a short trip to a dirt nap. Turn around and step off."

Dav held his ground, hoping that his companion knew what he was doing. Aguilar was locked in on the H8 addict, aggression written on every line of his stance. It was a gamble that might or might not pay off. H8 made people irrational, and so you couldn't expect a rational reaction.

Fortunately, the other gangers were still together enough to recognize the threat. Most of them immediately turned to find somewhere else to be, while a couple moved up to try to draw their stoned-out companion away. For a moment, it looked like the H8 user was about to go nuts, but maybe the drug was wearing off just enough. He finally allowed his companions to draw him back, and the gangers vanished into the rain.

As Dav let out a long breath, he saw Aguilar do the same. They traded a look and a shake of the head.

Sket, that was close.

The checkpoints got thicker the closer they got to the compound, augmented by patrols in police speeders. It was if every intersection was on lockdown. Governor Nisa really wasn't taking chances.

Chances on what, though, was the question. The more Dav watched the planetary defense forces, the more the tingling sense of danger that he'd shaped while with the Legion on a dozen worlds wracked by civil strife told him to stay away from them.

There wasn't anything preternatural about that sixth sense. It was just his brain putting together clues that he hadn't consciously connected yet. Something about the way these troopers carried themselves told him that their orders weren't just to keep the peace.

The two contractors found shelter in another inset doorway, and Dav peered out at the checkpoint about a block away. The gate to the governor's compound was just beyond it, about a hundred meters. It might as well have been halfway around the planet. He pulled out his comm and took a chance.

The ping was answered almost immediately. "Droma."

"It's Toron." Dav had gotten the legionnaire's personal comm and was relieved that the man answered it. "How much do you know about what's going on out here on the street right now?"

"Not enough." The expected frustration wasn't in the Legion NCO's voice, though. Dav recognized the tone. Droma was in problem-solving mode. "I've got a peeper up—no, the LT doesn't know about it—so I can see some of it, but we've had no contact with the TDF for the last several hours. They sure didn't tell us this was happening."

"I didn't think they would after what happened earlier." Dav took a breath. "We're probably not going to be able to walk back in the way we walked out. Call it a hunch. If they're not talking to you..."

"Then they probably won't have much interest in

talking to anybody who's not loyal to the governor. Especially not close in." Droma got the problem. "Tell you what. Not everybody in the TDF is necessarily one of Nisa's creatures. Let me make a couple of calls. Can you lie low somewhere for a bit?"

"Maybe. The thing is, the patrols and the checkpoints are forcing some of the less desirable elements into the same places we're having to go to avoid them. Already had one close call with some H8 junkies."

"Yeah, that'll happen. I don't know. Find a shop or something where you can get off the street. I'll be in touch." Droma cut the connection.

"Great." Dav looked around. There were actually quite a few shops in close proximity to the governor's compound, which made sense. The Repub government was going to have money to burn, so it was always good business to cater to those with the credits.

"We need to find a place to hole up."

Aguilar leaned out into the street. "Looks like a café of some kind right over there. Good place to get out of the rain, at least."

They waited until after the next patrol had passed by, then stepped out onto the street and casually walked the ten meters to the next door.

Dav forced himself to relax and they didn't get so much as a second glance from the proprietor after ordering a kaff and sitting down near the door. In fact, no one did. The locals were all more worried about the military presence on the street than random pedestrians. All eyes and conversation were fixed on what was happening *outside* the café. That was good.

Dav was halfway finished with his first cup of kaff when his comm buzzed. "Go."

"It's Droma. I've got a ride coming your way. A TDF officer who actually has a head on his shoulders. He's scraped up an excuse to come to the governor's compound. Go to the corner of Vagha and Unity. He'll be in a TDF staff sled. He's your way in."

"Good copy. And thanks."

Droma chuckled. "I'm not just doing this out of Oba's kindness. I expect a full intel dump in return. See you in a few."

11

The pickup went about as smoothly as Dav could have hoped. The staff sled, painted the same gray-green as all the other TDF vehicles he'd seen, but with a small crest of the Temugol Defense Force on the doors, slid to a halt on the corner as he walked up, and he got in as if he were stepping into a taxi.

"You don't look like legionnaires to me." The man behind the wheel was skinnier than Dav would have expected of a soldier, but still in uniform.

"It's complicated." Droma might trust this guy to make the pickup and get them back inside the compound, but that didn't mean Dav was going to get careless. His time in the Legion had already wired him not to trust much of anyone outside the Legion itself, and even a few inside it. His time outside the Legion had only reinforced that mindset.

The Temu soldier, for his part, just shrugged and headed for the governor's compound.

They neared the checkpoint that Dav had been watching when he'd called Droma. Two UT-70 sleds were set up on the street, slightly offset so that a vehicle could pass between them once the portable barrier was pulled aside. That barrier stood in front of two TDF troopers, while the medium-heavy blasters in the sleds' turrets covered the street.

His driver frowned as they got closer. Staff car or not, the barrier's micro-repulsors weren't being activated, let alone the blockage being pulled aside. The turret-mounted blasters remained leveled. One of the guards stepped up to the barrier and held up a hand to signal the TDF officer to stop.

"What is going on?" Dav's driver opened the window as two additional troopers came out from behind one of the UT-70s and approached, both in full battle rattle.

"We need to see your ID, sir." The trooper in front kept his voice emotionless, the half visor of his helmet disguising his expression.

The officer produced his identi-chit, prompting a slight stiffening of the trooper's posture and a salute. "What is going on here, trooper?"

"I have orders to check all vehicles and personnel at this point, and to detain anyone not authorized to come within the control area around the governor's compound, sir." The trooper sounded sullen, as if he didn't appreciate being questioned. He turned toward the back, where Dav sat. "I will need to see your passenger's identification, as well, sir."

"Stand down, trooper." The officer was getting irritated. "I'm authorized, and that means my passenger is as well."

Dav wasn't sure that was going to work. It wouldn't have with any professional military he'd worked with. It definitely wouldn't have flown with the Legion. He could almost feel Aguilar beside him, getting wound up for sudden, violent action.

The Temugol Defense Force, however, was not on the Legion's level. The trooper wavered, looking back over his shoulder, clearly unsure whether he should gainsay an officer.

"What's your name, rank, and unit, trooper?" the officer pressed.

That did it. The kid didn't want the scrutiny that an officer's inquiry might bring. For all he knew, this officer could make his life a living hell for the next year, making sure he got every sket detail there was. He stepped back and waved the sled through with a stiff salute.

The officer returned it vaguely as the barrier was drawn back. They slid between the two UT-70 combat sleds, under the muzzles of the medium-heavy blasters. Neither weapon pivoted to follow them, and Dav got a look at the gunners as they went by. They weren't watching the staff car, having apparently dismissed its very existence as soon as it had been cleared through.

Sloppy, but a good thing as far as Dav and Aguilar were concerned.

As they neared the compound gate, however, it was starting to look like the whole scene was going to play itself out all over again. And he couldn't be sure that the governor's personal guard weren't going to be a lot more conscientious than the regular slobs out on a street checkpoint.

His driver, however, was thinking along the same lines, and had apparently decided to get a jump on it.

"Here's my identification. I'm carrying an important message for General Huno, and I've already been delayed enough by those kelhorns at the checkpoint back there."

Whatever the man's justification for this trip to the governor's compound, it took some stones to just make up a message for the commanding general. Dav was impressed. Droma wasn't kidding about this guy having a head on his shoulders.

The troopers at the gate were off-balance from the officer's revelation. "Uh, sir... We have orders to..."

"You have to clear me through before I have you put on report, trooper," the officer snapped.

That was apparently enough. The troopers stepped out of the way and waved the sled through.

The officer drove toward the garage, letting out a long breath as he did so. "I'm glad that worked."

"I appreciate it," Dav said.

"Being an officer has its perks." The younger man winked as his passengers. He guided the sled into the garage and brought it to a halt, only then turning fully around in his seat. The look in his eyes was one that Dav could only describe as trepidation. It seemed to come all at once and out of nowhere. "I don't know why Sergeant Droma asked me for this favor. I don't want to know. Just... please don't make me regret it."

"You won't." Dav wasn't sure if he was telling the kid the truth, exactly, but he hoped so. He pushed open the door and dropped to the pavement. "Thanks for the ride."

Careful to make sure his weapons were still hidden, he looked around the compound for a moment as he stepped out of the massive vehicle garage. Yuso needed to know what he'd just found out, but so did Droma.

But who should he talk to first?

Droma had earned his loyalty. Yuso had only bought it.

"I'm going to go talk to the leejes. You want to come with me, or go brief the rest of the team?"

Aguilar cast an eye toward the Legion domes. "You've got an in with those guys that I don't. Probably best to get this to the client sooner, rather than later, anyway. Divide and conquer."

Dav nodded, traded a fist bump with his fellow contractor, and started across the quadrangle toward the Legion headquarters.

The leejes at the door were waiting for him. "Sarge is expecting you." Their gleaming buckets betrayed nothing. Dav nodded with a two-finger salute and headed in the open door.

Droma had come out to meet him, armored up, his bucket under his arm and his N-4 in his other hand. He tilted his head toward the inside of the platoon's housing. "Come on. The LT's up in 'consultation' with the governor and General Huno, so we shouldn't be disturbed."

Dav followed him farther into the dome, noticing that nobody seemed to care that he was packing blasters under the long coat. Apparently Droma trusted him, so that was good enough for the rest of the legionnaires.

He had to fight down that feeling that somehow, he still didn't belong there.

The Legion platoon sergeant led him to a briefing room in the center of the dome and fired up an information console. "Okay. Tell me everything."

Dav outlined their meeting with the man who'd called himself Samuel Triste. He left out the altercations with the Drusic and its pals beforehand and the H8 addicts on the way back. Those weren't really that relevant to the information he had to pass on.

Droma took it all in, hardly looking up as he took notes. "And you think he was sincere?" Meaning Triste.

"From what I could tell, yeah. And frankly, the sudden flood of troops on the street kinda backs up his story, doesn't it?"

"Maybe. Maybe it just took this long for a response to that ambush to get spun up." Droma looked up at him wryly. "You haven't been working with these people for the last half a cycle."

"You've got a point. Still."

"Still." Droma nodded. "It makes a certain sense. Especially given the fact that we've been effectively shut out over the last few days. It's not like we haven't bent over backwards to try to turn these yokels into a professional fighting force."

"Maybe that's *why* you've been shut out." Dav smiled grimly. "Don't get me wrong. I do think Triste's story is most likely true. But if the TDF resents you guys for trying to shape them up, that might only work to a corrupt governor's advantage."

"True enough." Droma frowned at the display. "This part about off-planet actors coming in to link up with Cel

Tradat worries me, though. *If* it's true."

"You're thinking MCR?" The Mid-Core Rebellion had been a thorn in the Republic's side for years now. Spouting ideals of independence and freedom, more often than not they used those ideals as justification for mass murder and grand theft. Dav had killed a few MCR types in his day, too.

"They would seem to be the most likely culprits." Droma ran a hand over his jaw as he stared at his notes. "Did he give you anything else? Numbers, times, maybe marshalling areas?"

Dav shook his head. "Nah. Sorry, Sarge."

"Well, if it's accurate, it's better than what we had before." The NCO, who had probably been a corporal when Dav had been in the Legion, thought for a moment. "You said you were on Keram?"

"I was." Dav wondered where this was going. Was that old debacle going to come back to haunt him again?

"I only ever read about it, but it sounded like a situation not dissimilar to this one."

Dav nodded. "I suppose. No MCR, though. There was a pirate network in that cluster that was getting delusions of grandeur, and they were doing much the same thing that Triste thinks Cel Tradat's been doing with Governor Nisa here. Buying him off until they were in position to kill him. They managed it, too. Would have had their own little fiefdom if the *Reliance* hadn't been nearby. Even then, it was a nasty fight to root them all out."

A fight that had turned out to be more costly than it should have been.

Droma searched his eyes. "And you think that's what's going on here?"

There was a lot behind that question, Dav realized. Droma was relying on Dav now as a fellow leej, one with experience. That meant a lot to legionnaires. Hotshots though they might be, they were professionals—the good ones. If someone had something to teach, they were willing, eager even, to learn.

Droma wasn't the sort to be totally lost, even when starved for information. He likely had his own idea of what was happening and, as he'd mentioned before, he'd been on the planet long enough to piece a few things together. Dav sensed that the man was looking for confirmation of a pre-existing gut feeling about the situation.

"Yeah, I do," Dav said, admitting it to himself and Droma at the same time. "I can't say exactly *why* I do, but Triste's story adds up a little too much for my liking." He mulled it over. "Aguilar's letting Yuso know. Even if he doesn't want to hear it, I think the ambush opened his eyes a bit. This is more than just occasional raids from the hinterlands. That ambush was aimed at *him*."

"And more might come, from a different quarter, if Nisa panics."

If Lieutenant Mastruk had been in the room, Dav doubted Droma would have said that part, but it was also shaping up to be true. Throwing checkpoints and patrols all over the city and keeping the Legion in the dark suggested that Nisa had something to hide. If he had decided that he couldn't put the genie back in the bottle, he just might do something desperate.

"Well, I know of at least one quarter that's safe." Dav inclined his head to indicate the Legion HQ.

"You think you could convince the LT?" Droma smiled wanly as he said it, almost as if he were joking.

Chuckling, Dav shrugged. "If we can convince Yuso, I might be able to convince your point CO. Maybe. It'll be good for *both* their careers. I dunno. I don't have the best record with points."

"Well, I'll do what I can." The NCO sighed. "That's my job, after all, not yours." He rubbed his eyes, then looked at his chrono. "Speaking of which, where is that kelhorn?"

Dav got up and turned toward the door. "That's your problem, Sarge. I've got my own to worry about."

"Look who decided to grace us with his presence again." Vin was standing in the middle of the common room, his hands on his hips. "This must be the vaunted 'Legion professionalism' I keep hearing about. Did all legionnaires slink off without permission in your unit, or was that just you, Toron?"

Dav didn't have the patience for the former sergeant major's power games. "Doing my job."

He barely looked at Vin as he brushed past him, heading for Yuso's rooms. The weight of his armor and weapons knocked Vin aside, but it didn't have the desired effect. The shoulder check had been Dav's counter to Vin's attempted intimidation tactics, but instead of getting the message, the smaller man just got angrier.

"I didn't give you permission to leave the first time! You're not gonna walk out of this room again! You were AWOL! The contract you signed says that you don't get to just decide when and where you work, Toron! You were a legionnaire. Fine. But get this through your kelhorned head: that does not mean—"

Dav pivoted to face him, his hands down at his sides, his coat hanging open to give Vin a good eyeful of his armor and weapons. After what had just gone down out in those streets, he'd had it with this pompous basic puke, who couldn't be bothered to do any of the hard work but would snipe at the guys who did just to pump his ego up a little bigger. "Mean what, Vin?"

The smaller man faltered at the look in Dav's eye. He took another step closer, forcing Vin to back up.

"Dav..." There was a warning in Sones's voice, but Dav waved him off and took another step close to Vin.

"You want to be team leader, want to tell everybody what to do, like your rank in Repub Army means sket here. You're just another contractor like the rest of us, but the difference is that you sit back here, resting on that same nonexistent rank, while we do the work. Even Hesand knows more about this sket than you do. Aguilar and I went out into the streets, by ourselves, so that we *don't* get blindsided again, and all you can do is bitch." He took another step, looming over Vin and forcing the smaller man back still more. "Now get out of my way."

For a second, Dav thought it was going to be a

fight. Vin turned white around the eyes, and his hands flexed at his sides, but the man wasn't stupid. Nor did he especially have the guts to go hand to hand with a legionnaire, former or not, especially when said leej was wearing combat armor. Even more so when he looked around at Sones, Sayavong, and Hesand, and saw nothing but stony stares, except from Hesand, who was frowning, looking between Dav and Vin as if he wasn't quite sure which side to take.

Turning contemptuously away from the man who'd essentially appointed himself detail lead, Dav headed for Yuso's rooms.

12

Two old Krestin-class bulk haulers dropped out of hyperspace well out from the planet's orbit. Aboard the Republic corvette *Inspiration*, the sudden appearance of two freighters in an edge-world system didn't raise any eyebrows.

Not that the bridge crew was on high alert in the first place. There was a small insurgency on the planet, certainly, but that was a local affair not likely to require the Republic's military might to resolve. In fact, as best Captain Ustinov understood it, the planetary forces were more than capable of handling the trouble on their own. Ustinov himself was getting along in age enough that he was happy for the simplicity of the mission. Retirement wasn't that far off, and a nice, relaxing vacation of a cruise was welcome, even if it was to a backwater like Temugol.

He lounged in his command chair on the bridge, sipping his kaff. The *Inspiration* was an old ship. She'd seen action well before the end of the Savage Wars, for Oba's sake. Still, she'd been kept up reasonably well, and she was comfortable. *Inspiration* was a good ship for his final few years before the deep chill of space gave way to the white sand beaches, cerulean waters, Lotonian cocktails, and all the scantily clad humanoid girls he could ogle in retirement.

Perhaps he might even behold the fabled beauty of a Cassari on that imaginary beach!

"Another cup, Captain?"

Ustinov looked up at the very *un*-Navy serving boy dressed in cascading white robes. Special Aide Yuso had come aboard with his own culinary staff, and they'd stayed aboard after Delegate Mahat's representative went planetside—presumably because the governor would set an even better table—so Ustinov got to reap the rewards, including some of the most exquisite kaff he'd ever drunk.

"Thank you," Ustoniv said happily.

"Captain?" The young ensign's voice interrupted his visions of blue water and green skin.

"What is it, Corbek?" Ustinov had a reputation for being less than formal. There wasn't much need for it. The Republic was at peace, except for the occasional MCR raid, but the Mids had no reason to be interested in this half-frozen lump of a world. And even if there were brush wars out on the edge—and Temugol *was* awfully close to the edge—this was effectively a diplomatic/governmental yacht now.

"Those two old bulk haulers." Ensign Corbek was watching the tracking display and the twin blips, barely a kilometer apart, closing in on the planet and had assumed the captain was aware of their arrival.

"What about them?" The captain quickly swept his eyes over his station holodisplays to catch up on recent events. Reluctantly, he put down his kaff and heaved himself to his feet. It probably wouldn't be a bad thing to stretch his legs a little, even if it was only to walk to the tracking station and lean over the young woman's shoulder.

After all, she's going to have a career in the Navy after I'm long retired and spending my nights in the arms of Cassari call girls. I should do her the favor of helping her learn the ropes.

When he leaned over to look at the tracking display, though, he blinked, then looked closer, a frown beginning to furrow his brow. "What in Tarkedes..."

The two freighters flying together wasn't odd in and of itself. Haulers did that all the time. It was their course that was odd. They weren't flying toward the natural orbital insert point, several hundred kilometers ahead of the *Inspiration*.

They were flying directly toward the corvette itself.

"Comms, open a hailing channel to those ships." The captain straightened. Well, so much for daydreaming. It would be good for the crew, though. It was probably nothing, but it was odd enough that it was worth checking up on.

The comms officer spoke loudly for the captain to hear. "Freighters *Starlight Carrier* and *Far From Home*, this is the Republic corvette *Inspiration*. You are on a course that will take you within our exclusion zone. Please announce your intentions and adjust your course."

Ustinov stood in the center of the bridge, watching the tracks on the holodisplay as they bore down on the corvette's position. He wasn't worried, but it did warrant caution. They were bulk haulers, and old ones at that. Nor were they moving especially fast. They were just on a strange course.

"No reply, Captain."

His frown deepened. "Send it again."

The comms officer did as he was told, but shook his head. "Still nothing."

"No change in course, Captain." Corbek was still watching the tracking display.

Ustinov stroked his chin. "Is there any risk of collision?" He didn't want to alter their orbit if it wasn't necessary. That would just make him look scared to the rest of the crew, and unless the haulers really were a collision risk, there was no need.

"Not at present, sir." Corbek sounded a little hesitant. She was worried, that much was obvious. This was a strange situation, there was no denying that.

"Shall I fire warning shots?" the weapons officer asked.

Corbek looked up at the captain expectantly.

He put his hand on her shoulder. "There's nothing to worry about. Just some rookie pilots who don't know what they're doing. You'll see that a lot out here on the edge. Light-freighter pilots who save their way into buying a large, bulk freighter and have to learn on the job just how different the big boats handle."

The impromptu lecture elicited chuckles from the bridge crew.

A moment later, he found out just how wrong he was.As the two freighters closed in, hatches along their spines opened, and concealed blaster cannons rose, their basic sensor packages taking scant seconds to get a lock on the *Inspiration*. With the corvette still not on alert, though, those seconds were all the time the ships needed.

Even as weapons lock alarms began to shriek aboard the *Inspiration* and red lights flashed above the main viewport, Ustinov looked up at the bulk haulers, confusion and surprise on his face. Before he could even open his mouth to order the ship to general quarters, the first salvo of blaster fire slammed into the *Inspiration*'s hull.

It wasn't all that accurate. Many of bolts missed, since the disguised attack craft had opened fire a little farther out than their weapons systems' capabilities allowed for. Those that impacted, however, punched through durasteel and synthplas along the corvette's spine. Brilliant explosions rocked the ship, spewing white-hot metal out into space and throwing the *Inspiration* into a spin.

Ustinov was thrown to the deck at the impact, his body battering against Corbek's chair as he fell. He levered himself painfully up to the console, blood streaming down his head from a cut just above his scalp. "Damage report!"

"Hull breaches on levels three, five, and six! We've lost maneuvering and power along the entire starboard side!" The damage control officer sounded borderline hysterical.

This was *not* supposed to be happening.

Hauling himself to his feet, Ustinov lurched toward his command chair. "Full alert. Get the engines to full power and arrest this drift." The ship shuddered again as another salvo of blaster fire slammed into it. "Where are my shields?"

"Shield generators took a hit, Captain."

"Sket." He strapped himself in. "Get me some weapons. Shoot back."

"Dorsal batteries are still functioning."

"Then get a lock and fire!"

Before they could even get the *Inspiration*'s own blasters up and running, another salvo lashed the ship from stem to stern. One engine exploded in a white-hot flash, making the ship's tumble worse, though the safety mechanisms kept the chain reaction from detonating the rest of the power plants. One entire blaster turret was sheared off with a massive explosion, sending sparks of molten metal showering out into space.

The third salvo punched through the bridge as the *Inspiration*'s spin accelerated with the explosion of the number two engine. The last thing Captain Ustinov ever saw was a brilliant flash as the viewport exploded into a million glowing shards and what was left of the bridge crew was sucked out into space.

Blaster fire flickered across the blackness of space from the two bulk haulers to the stricken corvette as more explosions rippled along her length. She was completely out of control now, twisting as super-heated debris spiraled off her hull to flash-freeze the vacuum. The two freighters maneuvered to either side of the hulk, pounding it with heavy blaster cannon fire. Neither had enough firepower to destroy the corvette outright, but it seemed like their gunners were hell-bent on breaching enough hull to kill every crew member onboard.

Meanwhile, the hauler's massive cargo bays opened and a small flock of assault shuttles fell away, igniting their engines and diving toward the cloud-shrouded surface of Temugol.

In the chaos of that attack, the *Inspiration* hadn't gotten a single message off. If any other ships in the vicinity had seen the attack—there was one within line of sight, an ancient Tulahel light freighter, currently just over the planet's horizon—they weren't going to get a message off anytime soon either, at least not within the system. Both the *Starlight Carrier* and the *Far From Home* had started blanket-jamming most common comms frequencies as soon as they'd opened fire. Anything short of military grade comms wouldn't get through.

The bulk haulers stayed in orbit as their cargo descended through the atmosphere on tongues of flame. The *Starlight Carrier* continued to take potshots at the wreck of the *Inspiration*, while the *Far From Home* maneuvered away, jockeying for position aside from the flight path of the assault shuttles that were already halfway to the surface.

Far From Home kept its cargo bay open to let loose one final surprise. The old XTN high-yield torpedo had been obsolete for the better part of five decades. Where this one had come from was a mystery, along with how well it was going to work. Small thruster packs floated it out of the cargo bay, then redirected its nose toward the planet below. Coordinates were synced via comm net, and the thrusters drifted the huge torpedo farther away from the bulk hauler. Finally, as the shuttles neared the surface, now lost in the haze of cloud above the ocean, the torpedo ignited its main engine and arrowed toward the surface and the spit of land sticking out into the sea that was Temugol City.

Dav was halfway to Yuso's door when the whole compound shook and a blinding flash stabbed through the windows. In the central room, they were spared the bulk of the brilliance, but the shock wave was brutal, the sound of shattering plastite drowned out by the end-of-the-world *boom* that almost knocked them all to their knees.

Vin was the first one to find his voice. "What in the Nine Hells just happened?"

Dav had a pretty good idea. "We need to get Yuso to the most secure area we can find. Best case would be the Legion HQ." He was at Yuso's door and fumbling with the controls. It was locked, and he didn't have the passcode. "What's the code?"

"I'm not telling you sket." Vin wasn't letting go of his little power trip. "I still don't know where you were or what you were doing for the last couple of hours. You're compromised, Toron."

Sones was at the door and entering the code.

When Vin turned his glare on him, the old merc just sneered. "Pull your head out, Vin. We've got bigger problems, and we need to get Yuso to safety. Dav's a lot of things, but he ain't no terrorist. And besides, Aguilar's already in there, and he was outside with Dav. You dumb kelhorn."

The door swished open and Dav stepped inside. "Mr. Yuso!"

He couldn't see their principal at first. The outer windows of the expansive suite were all shattered, glittering fragments scattered across the rich carpet and the even richer furniture. But his eyes were involuntarily drawn to the scene of devastation outside before he could search for the special aide. A cloud was rising above the main Temugol Defense Force base, just outside Temugol City. Whatever had done it was big. Capital-ship-missile big.

Dav returned his attention to finding Yuso.

The special aide wasn't hard to locate. The man was curled up in the fetal position behind a chair that had been partially shredded by flying bits of debris from the windows exploding inward. Aguilar was picking himself up off the floor on the other side of the desk, already moving to grab their principal. "It's not safe here, sir. We have to get to better shelter."

Dav stepped aside, turning toward the handful of staffers, their expensive clothing rumpled and some of them bleeding from flying bits of the window, huddled on the floor or against the walls. "Time to go, folks." None of them moved, several not even looking up, others staring at him with wide eyes.

Aguilar helped Yuso back to the other contractors where they would be sheltered from the suite and its windows. Aguilar started to check the special aide over. Yuso seemed to be in shock; he didn't fight the hasty and brusque search. He wasn't bleeding, at least not seriously. Then he looked up. "My staff. We need to get them out, too."

When Aguilar nodded that the primary was okay, Dav turned to Sayavong. "Thomas? If you don't mind."

The hulking former hullbuster, armored up and with that massive CrimTech blaster in his hands, strode into the wreckage of the office, picked the biggest, fattest staffer up, bodily, and *flung* him toward the door. "Time to go!" His bellow was amplified by his helmet, thundering through the entire room.

It did the trick. The staffers were up and moving fast, scuttling toward the door, while Sones and Hesand ushered them through and toward the stairs.

Dav stepped over to Sones. "We need to get to the Legion contingent. Somebody just detonated something big over at the TDF base. Nothing to gain by assuming that's a singular attack."

"That's a hell of a coup as it is." Sayavong sounded impressed. "Not easy to get your hands on that kind of weaponry."

"Yeah, that might be all they were going for." Hesand had taken up security on the main door, under Sones's watchful and baleful eye, but he was still looking around hopefully. "Hit the TDF base, then make demands."

"Aguilar and I got some intel out there that makes me doubt it," Dav said. A moment later, the distant sound of heavy blaster fire filtered through all the other noise of sirens, alarms, shouts, and screams. "Our source in town said there were off-world personnel coming in and joining up with Cel Tradat."

The tower shook again at another explosion, though this one was so much less than the hit on the TDF base. It felt almost gentle.

"Sounds like Triste was right," Aguilar said. He had Yuso down on the floor, standing over him, just in case.

Dav nodded. "Cel Tradat's making his big push, and he's got either pirates or the MCR to help him out."

"If we're going to move, we'd better do it now," Aguilar said. "We've got salties incoming."

"Salties?" Vin asked.

"Assault shuttles."

Salties. Dav had heard that somewhere before... where? It didn't matter now. The mystery of just what Aguilar did before going into private military contracting would have to wait.

Dav hurried to his stateroom, scooped up his bucket, and pulled it on. He immediately felt better inside its enclosed confines. "We've got two minutes. If you're not already armored up and geared up, get there." He fixed Vin with a stare, rendered inhuman by the blank visor of his helmet, as if daring the smaller man to try to assert some nonexistent authority. The former sergeant major turned and headed for his own room, where his weapons and armor were stowed.

He was the last one. The others had geared up fast while Dav had been going in to check on Yuso and Aguilar. In the meantime, while Dav and Sones held security, Aguilar turned to Yuso, who looked to be coming around somewhat, albeit slowly. "We're going to get you out of here and to somewhere safe, sir. But I need to finish what I was saying before things blew up. You need to understand what's going on." He waited until Yuso looked up at him with recognition in his eyes, then gave him a quick rundown of the intel he'd gotten from Triste. "Governor Nisa's dirty, and he's essentially handed this planet over to the separatists. We can't trust him, and he's entirely likely to move to try to eliminate you if he thinks that he's going to go down."

Almost as if those words had activated something, a new tone sounded through the room. Sones tilted his helmeted head a fraction, then moved to activate the door.

Nothing happened.

"Sket. We've been locked down."

13

Under any other circumstances, a lockdown might have just been a security measure. Dav was pretty sure that it was now, too, but not one with *their* security in mind.

"We need to get out before they send shooters in to make sure we become victims of the attack." He glanced at the open door to Yuso's suite just as the assault shuttles hammered the tower with blaster fire. Rappelling out might be an option, if they had the synth cord and if Yuso wasn't in the state he was in, never mind some of his staffers. "Who has any experience slicing locks?"

There was a few seconds' hesitation, as if none of them were eager to reveal such a skill set—and its accompanying past—in the hearing of a Repub special aide. But this wasn't the time for such scruples. With a faint sigh, Dav turned toward the access panel.

"Sket. Step aside." The weariness in Aguilar's voice was more than just tiredness at the stress of the last couple of days. He had just told them all something, though right at the moment, Dav was pretty sure that the only one who might have cared was Vin, and he was still putting his gear on.

Dav stepped aside and waved his teammate toward the lock. He was no slicer. Maybe if he'd gotten the call to join Dark Ops, he might have gotten that sort of training, but he had been a line legionnaire, a simple life taker and heartbreaker, hard as nails and able to smash anything in front of him. The subtler sorts of skill sets had been for other echelons.

Ripping the access panel off, Aguilar examined the circuitry. Dav had been to the Legion's basic breacher course, so he knew a few of the fundamentals. There was a difference between slicing and hot-wiring a door; a good slicer could get through without leaving a trace. What Aguilar did was more like hot-wiring, sidestepping the controls altogether and fusing the circuits. Tearing into the circuitry, he bridged a couple of connections, working faster than Dav would have trusted himself to do. There was a spark, a loud *crack*, and the doors fell limp into their housing.

"Help me lift this," Dav said.

Sayavong hurried to hold the door open, and Sones went through the breach first. This was a door made for style and not hardened security. They had been lucky.

Fortunately, Sones was on point instead of Vin or the green Hesand. Two men in gray fatigues and light body armor were already on their way toward the door, coming down from the upper floors. The pair of them started as the door was suddenly pushed upward in its housing and out swung Sones. Then they brought their weapons up to bear on the contractor.

Wrong move. Even if they'd only been surprised and thought that maybe there was an unexpected threat on the compound already, pointing blasters at a man in battle armor and with his own weapon already at the low ready was a bad call. Especially when that man was an old veteran who was charged with protecting a Republic official.

Sones gunned both of them down in a second, putting a single bolt into the first man's chest before transitioning to the second, double-tapping him and sending him crashing to the steps with his coat on fire and a blackened crater where one eye had been.

The others poured out in turn, Aguilar escorting Yuso, Dav took a cue from Sayavong and hurried out into the hallway.

"Oh, sket," Vin muttered, looking at the two corpses. "Sket, we're in it now."

"They weren't here to help us out," Sones said. "I could see it in their eyes."

"Well, that answers that question." Sayavong was at Dav's elbow. "With you."

Dav held his position, still covering the short hallway outside, and triggered his comm. "Droma, this is Toron." He'd prefer call signs, but he didn't know Droma's, and Droma wouldn't have known his either. Come to think of it, he would have preferred L-comm, too. There was no telling whether their personal comm channels were being listened in on.

There was no response from the Legion NCO at first. Probably because things were getting busy out there. He could hear more blaster fire outside, punctuated by explosions. A hell of a fight was brewing out in the city.

Either that, or Cel Tradat and his allies were going to every length possible to destroy as much of Temugol City's infrastructure as they could, rendering it unusable as the planetary capital.

"This is Droma. We're a little busy down here, Toron."

"I figured. We just had to shoot two of the governor's security goons. We're coming down to the quad and coming to you. We might be fighting our way out, so watch your targets."

Another pause. Droma probably had a lot on his hands at the moment. "Copy. Make it fast. Things are unraveling with a quickness."

There were several questions Dav wanted to ask, but this wasn't the time nor the place. With a nod at Sones, Dav took point and led the team down the hall toward the emergency stairwells.

One of the dead men's comms was squawking. Dav couldn't make out the words, even with his helmet's audio enhancement, and he didn't bother. The reinforcements were probably going to come any second, provided that Governor Nisa thought he could spare them. The man had to be panicking. If Triste had been right, his illicit house of cards was coming down around his ears, and if he was going to have any chance of salvaging his fortune and his life, he would have to keep Yuso quiet and make it look to the galaxy at large like he'd died in the attack, an unfortunate casualty of war.

While Sones covered the steps leading up to the next level, Dav and Sayavong led the way down the stairs toward the lobby, leaving Yuso's escort to Aguilar, while Vin and Hesand shepherded the gaggle of near-panicked staffers. Time was of the essence, and with only six blasters, speed was going to have to be their security.

They moved down the steps quickly, muzzles pivoting to cover doorways as they passed, eyes searching for threats. The lower levels of the tower seemed to be in pandemonium, and no one took much notice of them. The governor's security must have been withdrawn to his staterooms in the upper levels, which meant that the bulk of the threat might be behind them.

Blaster fire from above seemed to confirm Dav's suspicions. He almost turned back to support Sones and the others, but he had to worry about forward security and linking up with the legionnaires. Droma didn't know Sayavong, and he probably wouldn't accept the big hullbuster's assertion unless Dav coordinated. He might be able to run that coordination via comm, but it was going to be faster and smoother to make contact himself, and the quicker they got down there, the sooner they'd have a platoon of leejes to back them up. Nisa's goon squad would have second thoughts about facing Legion blasters.

Unless Nisa was so far gone, which he might be, that eliminating *every* Republic interest on this world would be the only way for him to keep his power... assuming he could hold off Cel Tradat afterwards.

With separatists—and possibly Mids—wreaking havoc outside, and a corrupt governor's bodyguard trying to tie up loose ends on the inside, this could get very interesting, very quickly.

They reached the ground floor. The blaster fire behind them had died down, and Dav hadn't heard either of the men on rear security call for support, so they were probably clear for now. "Droma, Toron. Coming out." He scanned the lobby as he and Sayavong quickly hit the base of the steps and swept the open space with their blasters, looking for targets.

All he saw at first glance were government functionaries huddled behind desks and any other semblance of cover they could find. For some of them, it was a good thing that the lobby wasn't currently under fire; they hadn't made particularly good judgments about the difference between cover and concealment.

Checking over his shoulder, he saw Aguilar with one hand on Yuso's shoulder, keeping their charge's head down, Vin trailing behind, leaving most of the work of keeping the staffers together and under cover to Hesand. The former sergeant major seemed completely out of his depth, hardly keeping his blaster at the ready or even pointed in a safe direction. He was lagging, not even holding security.

If they survived the next few hours, there were going to be words.

Sones came down the steps behind them, backing down step by step, an awkward and somewhat dangerous way to descend, but necessitated by the need to maintain coverage on the stairs, while too many of the rest of the team were bound up with their charges. The older man didn't complain or miss a step, though, and his blaster's muzzle didn't seem to move a millimeter as he worked his way down to the bottom floor.

Bright light flickered outside. The clouds were closing in again as the weather worsened, joining the smoke coming off the stricken TDF base and the fires springing up in the city, set by blaster fire or explosives. N-50 blaster fire streaked brilliantly across the gray of the day. Looking out through the few still intact windows at the quadrangle, Dav could see four Legion combat sleds drawn up in a semicircular formation outside the Legion's headquarters dome. One of the legionnaires on the twins sent another stream of bolts skyward, and something exploded, a small flyer tumbling in flaming wreckage to slam into the city beyond the wall with a catastrophic *boom*.

"On me." Dav stepped out of the front doors, making sure he had visual contact with one of the legionnaires standing behind the nearest sled before he started moving toward them. The last thing he needed was to trigger a blue-on-blue.

The legionnaire stayed still for a second, probably confirming over L-comm that he needed to let the blaster-carrying men in combat armor into the perimeter. Then he waved at Dav to come ahead, and the legionnaire-turned-contractor broke into a sprint.

He pounded across the quad as the rain fell in earnest. Skidding to a halt next to the legionnaire who had beckoned him in, he dropped to a knee and held security while the rest came after him. The leej next to him didn't say a word, just held his sector, his N-4 at the ready.

Dav counted the group in as they came after him,

not wanting to leave any behind. Aguilar still kept his hand on Yuso's shoulder, though the special aide wasn't moving nearly as fast as they needed him to. Neither was Vin, for that matter. He was now back in the rear with Hesand and Sones, though he wasn't keeping his head up and holding security the way those two were.

Sones came through the perimeter, clapping Dav on the pauldron with a gauntleted hand. "Last man!"

Dav glanced at the legionnaire beside him, but the man kept his focus on the yard and the tower. It occurred to Dav that the legionnaires must have seen the blaster fire on the stairs, since they were exposed to the outer windows in several places. Even the new guys had to know that something was very wrong inside the compound as well as out in the city.

The N-50s above his head thumped again, sending blinding red bolts skyward once more as Dav turned to look for Droma. He half expected the Legion NCO to be stuck with his CO, which would complicate things, but he found him at the rear of the central sled, his N-4 in his hands, looking like he was just watching the show, though he was probably fully engaged on the L-comm, analyzing the unfolding situation in his bucket's HUD.

Once again, Dav really wished he had his old Legion helmet back.

He walked up to Droma but let his blaster hang on its sling. He stood by the platoon sergeant's side to wait. When Droma was ready to talk to him, he'd let him know. Dav knew better than to interrupt whatever the NCO had going on. They weren't the main effort anymore; they were now the Legion's straphangers.

Vin, however, hadn't gotten the message. Now that they were somewhat out of harm's way, he came swaggering up to the two of them while Yuso caught his breath, leaning against the nearest combat sled.

"Hey, Leej. I'm in charge of Special Aide Yuso's detail. We need to get him to a secure area ASAP."

Droma ignored him. Either because he didn't believe that the shorter man who was slightly out of breath really was the detail lead or simply because, as far as he was concerned, the only individual in Yuso's entourage he was going to deal with would be the former legionnaire.

Or simply because he had bigger problems to deal with.

After a few seconds Droma moved, though he still didn't look at Vin, even as the latter was about to speak again. "Sket." The curse word was a harsh rasp through his bucket's speakers. He nodded to Dav and then up toward the top of the tower. "The LT's up there, in the governor's chambers. And the governor isn't letting anyone open the doors. The LT's convinced that there was a miscommunication or a misunderstanding."

"Blaster fire is one hell of a misunderstanding."

"No clint. He's more likely to figure that you got trigger-happy. Trust me on that one."

If the CO was a point, Dav could well believe it. Points had their own hierarchy of loyalties, and they tended toward politicians and high government officials before anything as mundane as brotherhood and common sense. The points he'd dealt with had all treated their legionnaires as suspicious at best, enemies to be punished at the slightest hint of opposition at worst. It wasn't a way to lead troops, but that wasn't the goal of the appointed officer program anyway.

They *might* be able to strongpoint the Legion dome for a while. Dav was about to suggest it when a fusillade of blaster fire sounded just outside the gate, the flickering lights of the blizzard of particle and directed energy fire lighting up the top of the wall. A tooth-rattling *boom* smacked earth and sky a moment later, and a fireball roiled skyward despite the rain, orange fire rapidly expanding beneath black smoke.

Given the proximity of those old UT-70s, one of them had just blown up, unless Dav missed his guess. Which meant that the assault on the compound had begun.

Another medium-heavy blaster opened up from a low-profile guard tower on the other side of the gates. What sounded an awful lot like an AP missile smacked into the tower an instant later, and the blaster went silent. Then something hit the gates, hard. Probably another missile.

"This isn't looking like the governor's in cahoots with the separatists, brother. Not gonna clint you." There was some doubt in Droma's voice. He was trying to figure out just what was going on, and which way to jump. "I'm getting orders from Lieutenant Mastruk to hold what we've got and defend the governor."

Of course, that wasn't *exactly* what Dav or his contact had communicated. Only that the governor and the rebel were playing a mutually beneficial game, one that they both intended to win for themselves at the end. Droma was drawing conclusions from Dav's own time as a legionnaire and misapplying them. But there was no time to argue that distinction.

The assault on the gates doubled in intensity, and something high-energy went to work on the heavy impervisteel. The center junction started to heat up. They might have brought up a mining laser or something like it.

"Not sure how viable a defensive position we have here," Dav said, looking at more than just the situation with the separatists burning through the gates. Those assault shuttles outside were laying waste wherever they flew, the anti-air batteries were as impotent as they had been during the last fight, and he didn't trust the governor or his security.

"Listen to me! Both of you!" Vin tried to shoulder his way in front of Dav to confront Droma, but Dav shoved him aside, turning to stare at the shorter man. His visor didn't convey the full force of his glare, but it was enough. Vin subsided, for the moment.

Then all hell broke loose.

An assault shuttle pilot, apparently deciding that the attempt to breach the gates with the mining laser was taking too long, dove down and strafed the front of the compound with heavy blaster fire. Brilliant bolts smacked into pavement, duracrete walls, and impervisteel gates. The gates sagged under the onslaught, and one bolt blew through the already weakened center section, scattering molten metal across the pavement just inside, before the gunship howled overhead, chased by a storm of N-50 fire.

More bolts smashed into its repulsors and something exploded, sending the wedge-shaped craft spinning away to crash onto the open ground behind the compound.

During that furious exchange of blaster bolts, one had, inexplicably, stabbed down from the direction of the tower. It took Special Aide Macha Yuso in the junction between neck and shoulder, practically decapitating him in an instant. He slumped to the ground, spattering scorched blood across the side of the combat sled where he'd been taking shelter.

Dav, Droma, and the nearest Legion twins gunner pivoted toward where the bolt had come from at the top of the tower. Hesand had been standing right next to the man, as Aguilar had moved to a better security position on the gates, and looked dumbstruck, his face reddened from the proximity of the blast.

"Sniper!" one of the legionnaires called out, evidently using his bucket's externals for the benefit of the contractors as well.

An onslaught of return fire from the sniper's position caused plastite and duracrete to shatter and blow apart in a haze of dust. The sniper, if he was still alive up there, must have decided that discretion was the better part of valor, for no more blaster bolts came from that direction.

Droma looked down at the special aide's corpse. "Looks like you were right. Sket."

Dav felt a curious stillness in his guts. He'd failed, in a way he never had before. He'd effectively taken charge of the protection detail when he'd led the way out of the apartments, and now the man they were supposed to protect was dead. It didn't matter that Hesand had been handling him and was now staring in shock at the scorched and bloodied meat that had been a House of Reason bureaucrat only a moment before. Dav was responsible.

He didn't doubt that Vin would quickly shed his assumption of detail lead now. Hell, Vin had been the one jawing to get Yuso to better cover.

Sket, how did this go so wrong?

"Hey. Toron. You with me?" Droma shook him. "It sucks, but there's nothing to do about it now, except stay alive to get word back to the Republic that Governor Nisa had your boss dusted. No doubt about that." He looked up at the tower, pausing just long enough that Dav was pretty sure he was back on the L-comm. "Kark. I think they just dusted the LT, too."

Blaster bolts stabbed from the lobby, even as the attackers burst through the last, weakened remnant of the gate. Not all of them were aimed at the assault force, either. Someone in the tower was hoping to eliminate all outside Republic forces, lest word of Governor Nisa's corruption and failure get off planet.

They should have known better than to shoot at legionnaires. You shoot at legionnaires, you die.

The gunners on the twins on the two nearest combat sleds pivoted and poured fire into the lobby, laying waste in a storm of super-bright, super-hot bolts that exploded plastite and flesh alike. In seconds, the entire lobby was an abattoir of blood, wreckage, and scorched flesh.

In the meantime, the full brunt of the rest of the Legion platoon's firepower poured into the breach in the gates. Two AP missiles slammed into the utility sled with an old repeating blaster mounted in the bed, blowing it back through the gate in a storm of fire and twisted, flying metal.

"Mount up!" Droma's amplified voice boomed over the compound. "KTF anything with a weapon!"

Dav moved back to Hesand, who was still staring at Yuso's body. "I was... I kept telling him to get down..."

Biting back the sudden feeling of relief that it hadn't been his fault, or even his teammate's, that Yuso had gotten himself killed through curiosity, Dav focused on the task at hand. He hauled Hesand to his feet and propelled him toward the nearest combat sled. "Get aboard. I've got him."

He might not have liked Yuso very much, but he wasn't going to leave the body for Nisa or Cel Tradat to take advantage of. If anyone was going to use the murdered body of a Republic special aide to make a point, it was going to be him.

Always make 'em pay. And there's more than one way to do that.

Heaving Yuso's corpse into a fireman's carry, he ran toward Droma's sled. The rest of the legionnaires were already in their vehicles, even while the gunners on the twins laid the hate as fast and as hot as they could. Sones, Sayavong, and Aguilar had taken charge of the staffers, quickly splitting them up and dragging them into one or another of the sleds.

Droma was the last man aboard, following Dav into the now extremely cramped troop compartment. There was nowhere to set the body except on the feet of legionnaires and staffers sitting on the benches, whose boots grew red from the man's blood.

"Should have left the meat for the tanzes."

Dav didn't know which legionnaire said it, but he faced the expressionless bucket with his own. "That meat is my ticket to signing Nisa's death warrant."

The contractor didn't have a spot to sit in, so he braced himself on the overhead with one hand and ducked his head to avoid scraping it off. "I'm not leaving it for Nisa to turn it against us or the Legion."

Droma crowded in behind him, bracing himself as the ramp closed and the sled surged toward the gate. The gunner up on the twins kept up a continuous stream of blaster fire as he rotated from side to side. These legionnaires might be green, but Droma had instilled in them the requisite aggression that was part and parcel of being leej.

Grabbing his shoulder, Droma leaned in. It was too crowded to talk bucket to bucket, so he had to speak in the open. "Where are we going?"

Dav realized that the NCO was relying on his intel, so the next step was at least partially on him. He thought back to his conversation with Triste. "Head for Barsota."

14

Shut up in a combat sled and without a Legion bucket to give him a HUD, Dav had to infer most of what happened next.

The Legion onslaught, led by those two aero-precision missiles, had driven the attackers back from the gate. The sheer volume of medium-heavy blaster fire that the gunners were putting out sent those rebels who hadn't already been dusted scrambling for cover while the five combat sleds roared out of the flaming wreckage of the gate, their repulsors sending the black smoke, flames, and sparks flying in hellish whorls. The attacking force that was still gathered at the front of the compound was wholly unprepared to withstand the sudden offensive. Legion blaster fire raked the buildings and every vehicle within line of sight, blowing glowing holes in metal and blasting flesh and bone apart.

The combat sleds turned hard left as soon as they could, the twin N-50 fire lessening as they cleared the initial cordon and targets grew light, but it never stopped altogether. Dav suspected that these guys were being a little less discriminating with their fire than legionnaires in his day might have. Still, they were looking to KTF, and they'd just gone through one hell of a fight just to get clear of the compound.

Roaring down the street, they headed toward the main highway out of the city, even as some of the attackers started to catch their breath and give chase.

A brief firefight between convoys flared up as the pursuing rebels sent blaster bolts sizzling past the Legion combat sleds. The legionnaires quickly coordinated fire on the lone pursuing vehicle and held down the butterfly triggers on the twins, flaying the street and puncturing the rebel technical with lurid bolts of pure destruction. The boxy wheeled vehicle with an ancient twinned G101 pulse cannon mounted above the cab slewed to one side as heavy fire cored out the cab and decapitated the driver. The truck hopped the curb and slammed to a stop into the corner of a duracrete building.

The legionnaires continued to fire until N-50 bolts penetrated the sled's power train and the power cell blew up with a satisfyingly thunderous detonation.

All the while, Dav could see the legs of the Legion gunner standing in the central turret as he did his work on the turret above. They weren't pulling any punches. Dav was almost surprised by their ferocity. Had he been out of the Legion so long?

Taking the next turn, the convoy accelerated, heading out of the city and toward the agricultural fields before speeding out into the seemingly endless moors and tundra that stretched along the Temugol coastline. The planet was cold enough, and the temperate areas limited enough, that aside from the taiga and mountains farther to the north and south, closer to the ice caps, there wasn't a whole lot of ecodiversity. Farmers overcame this by enclosing their fields beneath sprawling bio-habs tended to by low, rolling bots.

Several more sleds emerged from other city exits, but they were closing in from a distance. Anyone who had seen the wreckage left by the Legion gunners in the city were understandably reluctant to get too close to any of the combat sleds' twins. The real threat—if it chose to fixate on them—was going to come from the assault shuttles in the sky above.

Word was starting to spread about the breakout, though with some of the surviving Temugol Defense Force units on the street putting up more of a fight than expected, the response was slow. It was also disjointed, which would suggest to trained observers later that there was more than one command net in use.

Two of the wedge-shaped shuttles, heavy blasters slung beneath their chisel noses, banked and came around from the north, snarling toward the fleeing combat sleds.

The lead gunner spotted the dark specks against the lowering gray clouds as the legionnaires arrowed out along the packed vitrified earth road running between the ag fields to the south of the still-burning ruin of the TDF base, his HUD quickly identifying the target. The gunner pivoted his turret while his bucket pushed the alert, direction, and range, as well as algorithmically appointed firing assignments. The legionnaires almost opened fire in unison, it happened so fast.

A rippling curtain of blaster fire converged on the

oncoming skimmers, and the lead shuttle flew right into it. Torn apart by the blizzard of high-energy bolts, the flyer exploded spectacularly, the shock wave rocking its wingman, who hastily banked and dove for the deck, trying to get out of the line of fire. The rear two combat sled gunners shifted fire to follow it, dashed lines of red glowing annihilation spitting across the landscape almost too fast to see.

The ship's evasive maneuvers *almost* saved it. Instead of taking a fusillade of direct hits and exploding, it was only clipped by half a dozen bolts. That was enough to blow out one of its primary repulsors and detonate an air-to-ground rocket under one of its stubby wings. The explosion flipped the ship over and it plowed, inverted, into the ground beyond one of the farming habs, the impact throwing up a fountain of dirt, pulverized rock, and shredded, whickering metal.

Unlike most assignments Dav had ever been on, legionnaires were driving these combat sleds as opposed to Repub Army or Marines specially tasked with the job. The Legion was a fighting unit, and putting a leej behind the wheel meant he wasn't able to use his rifle. Perhaps those non-Legion personnel had been left, but that didn't seem like a thing Droma would do. Maybe they'd just made do, preferring to lose a man to the driver's seat than go without combat sleds at all.

The legionnaire drivers were pushing their sleds for all they were worth, as both wheeled and repulsor technicals came roaring out of the city from the north. Some desultory blaster fire reached out for the Legion vehicles, but it was way off, and the violent destruction of the two shuttles had been easily visible to anyone on the western edge of the city, lending even greater caution to those who hadn't known exactly what they were getting into when they got the word to pursue the fleeing sleds.

The incoming fire was ineffective enough that all but the rear vehicle's gunners ceased fire. There was no sense in trading ineffective bolts and soon even the rebels realized the pointlessness of the exchange.

Dav was hanging on for dear life, unable to see what was happening outside but letting his imagination fill in some of the blanks as he listened to the blaster fire and the distant explosions. He had enough experience that it didn't require a *lot* of imagination.

"We're going to need to halt and sort things out once we've broken contact." Droma was already thinking ahead. "You don't have comms for this Triste guy, do you?"

Dav frowned. "Unfortunately, no. He kinda interrupted a bar fight, then walked out after telling me where his ranch is."

Saying it out loud made Dav's confidence in the man, and the plan, dip slightly. It sounded a bit convenient. But so far... it had also been correct.

Droma didn't seem to think the lack of comms was an insurmountable obstacle. "Okay, so we're definitely going to need to halt, set security, and run some recon before we go charging into Barsota. We're going to need to get these scumsacks off our tail first."

The Legion NCO was already pulling up his battle

board and peering at the display, which looked like it was showing a three-dimensional map of the surrounding terrain. Dav didn't know if it was an old map downloaded before they'd come to Temugol, or one real-time mapped by the *Inspiration*. Who, come to think of it, really should be doing something about locking down airspace right about now.

Dav couldn't hear what instructions Droma sent out next, since they were all over the L-comm. He thought about asking for a spare, but he wouldn't expect the Legion NCO to give him one. He'd heard of points giving L-comms to sketchier characters, but Droma was a real leej, not a point. Former legionnaire or not, Dav wasn't under his command.

And Dav's reason for being on the planet at all was now rapidly cooling meat on the floor of the combat sled, so that probably didn't give Droma a whole lot of confidence in him.

He knew that he was thinking too hard about it, especially since they were still in active contact, but he couldn't help himself. A part of him had always wondered if he'd run away when he'd left the Legion, whether he simply hadn't had what it took to stay and push back against the points as well as the Mids, the zhee, and everyone else the Legion found itself fighting. Now those doubts were all coming back again.

He pushed them away. He wouldn't prove himself, redeem himself, if he descended into a death spiral of self-reproach. Yuso was dead. If Hesand was to be believed— and the kid was too shell-shocked to have made it up, Dav was sure of that—then Yuso had disregarded his security and gotten himself killed.

It didn't matter. The mission was a failure and whosever's fault it was, there was no going back and fixing it. He *could*, however, redeem himself. Perform to standard again.

Stay alive and KTF the kelhorns who'd kicked all this off.

As he was thinking this, Droma had apparently finished his platoon briefing over the L-comm, and held out the battle board to show Dav. "There's a good chokepoint about twenty klicks west, northwest. The road goes through a cut, with a knife-edge ridge on either side. If we move fast enough—and if they don't already have forces set in up ahead to cut us off—then we should be able to get through that cut and set up one hell of a kill box in the middle of it."

The T-shape of his visor was regarding Dav, not moving a millimeter. "Can I count on you and the rest of your contractor buddies to act as another fire team?"

"Ooah, Sarge." That was all he needed to say. He might have to put boot to fourth point of contact— especially if Vin got over his own shell shock and started to push back—but he'd get through to the others that this was a matter of self-preservation. Their survival was inextricably tied to the Legion platoon.

He wouldn't have it any other way.

The next twenty klicks went by fast. Almost too fast.

Dav couldn't get a reliable comms connection with the others though the armor of the combat sleds, at least not good enough with the equipment they had. He wanted to pass on what was happening and figured that at least a hullbuster like Sayavong would be able to wheedle the details out of their Legion counterparts. Sones could handle himself and Aguilar was capable if a mystery, but he wondered if Vin and Hesand were still in the dark—or if they'd even bothered to try to ask what was happening. Both were former basics, and his opinion of Vin aside, Hesand probably hadn't been trained to push for the word.

The sleds veered off the road just past the cut, and the ramps dropped. "Everybody out but gunners and drivers." Droma used his external speakers, probably primarily as a courtesy to Dav. He appreciated it, even as he left Yuso's body on the deck and pushed out behind Droma, clearing the way for the rest of the legionnaires to exit the sled.

The legionnaires pushed out fast, fanning out from the ramp with their blasters up, scanning for threats. Dav did the same, though he had other responsibilities. Like getting his team together, whether Vin liked it or not.

There wasn't a whole lot of vegetation, but there was cover. The knife-edge ridge that Droma had described wasn't quite so knifelike now that Dav got a look at it, but it was still a formidable obstacle to a sled or wheeled vehicle. Climbing over it on foot wouldn't be easy, but it would be doable. In fact, Droma had apparently issued full orders to his legionnaires over the L-comm while they'd been en route, because two squads were already clambering up the wet, rocky slope on the south side of the cut, their boots gripping the low, gray-green fungus-like vegetation easily enough. The third squad had pushed to a flanking position farther down the ridge, while the fourth squad set in security around the sleds. With a faint whine, three TT-16 observation bots rose into the air and winged through the drizzling, misting rain toward the city and their pursuers.

The Legion combat sleds were set into a modified herringbone formation, with two able to direct their twins down the cut, while the remaining three spread out to cover the flanks and their direction of travel.

Dav circled his arm over his head. "Team Yuso, bring it in." He didn't have another term for the contractors.

Sayavong, Aguilar, and Sones closed in on his position next to the sled closest to the cut. Hesand and Vin lingered, but when they looked around and saw that the legionnaires were paying them little to no mind, they came to join the small knot of men in combat armor that looked decidedly out of place amid the uniform silver of the legionnaire armor.

While he waited, Dav noticed that most of the legionnaires were throwing short, drab ponchos over their shoulders. He nodded faintly as he figured out the idea.

Droma couldn't do anything about the shiny armor, but he could cover it up. And without their point CO to insist on current SOPs, he could take some steps to correct a few of the more asinine decisions that had been handed down by the House of Reason.

It was encouraging.

"Okay, sounds like we're still dragging some pursuers, so Sergeant Droma's decided to put an end to it. We're setting in an ambush here, to break contact definitively before we continue on to Barsota."

Droma came over to join them as the legionnaires did their best to disappear into the rocks and undergrowth up on the ridge. "If you guys are game, we could use a few more blasters up on the north ridge with Second Squad." It was a request, but Dav recognized the test there. He might be somewhat trusted, thanks to the work he'd already put in, but Droma wasn't sure about the other contractors, and with the sudden loss of their principal, he wasn't sure if Dav was going to be able to keep them together and effective.

He was also wondering if he hadn't just hauled a bunch of dead weight along on a serious fight.

"We're on it." Dav watched Vin as he spoke, knowing he could trust Sayavong, Sones, and Aguilar to have his back. They might not have been legionnaires, but they were life takers and heartbreakers in their own right. Even old Sones, who almost looked bored behind his only slightly tinted faceplate. It was just another day at the office for him.

While Hesand was looking around at the

legionnaires, the sleds, and the ridge above them like a kid who was wondering just how he'd gotten there, Vin was staring at the ground. That prompted a frown from Dav, though his helmet hid the expression.

But right before a firefight wasn't the time to have that little dispute over authority hashed out. "I'll take the inside, where I can coordinate with Sergeant Droma. Aguilar, you've got the far side, linking up with that leej squad on the end."

Dav had noticed that Droma had told that squad to push out farther, giving Dav and his team the closer spot. Droma was no fool; he didn't want the contractors turning into a wild card out on the flank. He wanted them close, where he had some more control.

Legionnaires were professionals, some of the most professional killers the galaxy had ever seen, so they didn't need a lot of control. At least, the legionnaires Dav had served with hadn't. Things might be changing, as the House of Reason hollowed out the Legion, but from what he'd seen so far, Droma had taught his boys well.

"We're taking our cues from the legionnaires," Dav continued. "Nobody opens fire until they do. If any of you gets trigger-happy, I'll deal with him." His helmet might not have had the Legion's external speakers that changed a voice to a harsh, inhuman rasp, but right then, Dav didn't need it. He kept watching Vin, waiting for the man to decide that he didn't want to accept what was happening.

For once, though, Vin held his peace.

Dav nodded to Droma, to assure him—as well as Dav himself—that they were good, and he was about to head for the ridge when Droma put out a hand to stop him. "What's your comm channel? I can't spare an L-comm for you."

Dav hadn't expected him to, so that was no surprise. He rattled off the channel, and in a few seconds he heard Droma's voice inside his helmet. "Comms check." It wasn't quite as clear as an L-comm would be, and certainly not as secure, but it would be serviceable.

"Good copy." Dav was about to head up to the ridge when Droma stiffened, then pulled out his battle board again.

"Get moving." Droma turned and started to jog toward the other sled. "Gomers are maybe five minutes out from the kill zone."

Dav led the way toward the ridge, breaking into a run as he started up, but quickly slowing down. He'd maintained his fitness since he'd gotten out, but the slope was steep and the rocks were slick.

Sayavong and Aguilar kept up, but Sones and Hesand had to slow down even more. Vin trailed at the back. Dav wondered if he was sandbagging until he paused, just short of the crest, and looked back. Vin was visibly struggling, his chest heaving under his armor.

Never send a basic to do a legionnaire's job.

Then he was at the crest, getting down in the prone behind a boulder, his EH-7 in his shoulder, and the enemy was moving in.

15

The technicals came on through the rain in a column, sticking to the road, none of them willing to brave off-road driving. Whether that was because of the wet, the bumpy terrain, or just a lack of tactical imagination, Dav couldn't say. It put them in a nice, canalized kill zone, though, and he was fine with that.

Glancing across the gap, he caught a glimpse of a legionnaire, the hood of his poncho up over his bucket, prepping an AP rocket. The rebels were going to get one hell of a greeting.

He considered calling Droma and suggesting they stick to blasters for now. They didn't know what all Cel Tradat's forces had, and they might find that they needed those missiles later. He doubted Triste had any reloads for such a proprietary weapons system squirreled away in the hills. The man had seemed too law-abiding, and not nearly wealthy enough for that.

Ultimately it was Droma's show. Dav knew that he was just a supernumerary there to add a few extra blasters. If they were going to work together, he had to maintain that trust, and with Vin barely managing to drag himself up into position, that meant keeping his mouth shut and KTFing until that trust was solid enough that he *could* speak up on tactical decisions and be listened to.

So he settled in behind his blaster rifle and got ready to get stuck in.

The lead technical was an old Yarran S320 sports utility sled, scarred and rust-spotted, with more sheet durasteel welded to the back and a figure crouched behind a BAK89 repeating blaster.

Dav zoomed in on the gunner. His Krall bucket at least had that capability, though it was limited, relying on an extra lens in front of his right eye.

He frowned. That wasn't a human behind that blaster. Even from this distance, and with the helmet's admittedly limited magnification, he could tell that the yellow-skinned humanoid was Kimbrin. He hadn't seen a Kimbrin on Temugol since they'd landed, but knew of an outfit that was often ripe with them.

"Mids." Droma's voice was cold. He could see the same thing. "Looks like we've got confirmation of your boy's intel on off-world allies working with Cel Tradat, Toron."

"Looks like." That was something he would have been glad enough to have been wrong about. Adding the MCR to this already twisted equation was just going to make matters worse.

Still, it wasn't as if he was surprised. The MCR was backing yet another separatist movement. Shocker. So close to the carrier shipyards at Craggock Three, it was no wonder the Mids wanted a foothold here.

That was a concern for another time. Executing a successful ambush needed to be the focus here and now.

He laid his sights on the tiny yellow blotch that was the Kimbrin's head, even as the oncoming column of vehicles slowed. Somebody down there had enough tactical acumen to be cautious when approaching a chokepoint like the cut.

They had still let themselves get far too close though.

The first AP missile crossed the misty gap between the ridge and the lead vehicle with a *bang*. The old sporting sled died in a flash and a puff of smoke, the yellow face of the Kimbrin disappearing in a billowing cloud of black smoke and whickering shrapnel. The other vehicles tried to swerve off the road and out of the kill zone, but it was too late.

Even as Dav set his sights on one of the gunmen who had bailed out and was running for cover, he realized just how beautifully Droma had timed it. While the terrain out there wasn't nearly as rough as the ridge the legionnaires were set up on, it was just difficult enough to prevent the vehicles from getting far off the road without heavier-duty repulsors than what they had. And when a second AP missile slammed out and blew apart the big utility truck at the rear, the rest of the column was trapped.

Dav caught his target center mass with a single bolt, and the man in rough coveralls and makeshift armor went sprawling onto the rocks. The trooper didn't move, so he searched for another target.

The SABs were going to town from the ends of the ridgeline. The Legion squad leaders had set their squad automatic blasters as far out as they could, getting angles to maximize their field of fire on the road. The gunners raked the stalled vehicles with fire from both sides, bolts punching through thin sheet metal and even the makeshift armor of bolted on durasteel panels after enough hits.

Dav and the contractors were being just a bit more circumspect in their shots, since they were even more limited on charge packs than the legionnaires were. He did notice, peripherally, as he gunned down a human in ancient flak armor and helmet who had sprinted deftly away from the stalled column and set up behind another of the sleds, that no more AP missiles were flying. Those legionnaires equipped with them had gone back to their N-4s. Droma was all too aware of how limited their munitions were.

The return fire from below grew a bit more intense as the handful of rebels who had survived the initial onslaught—and had stood their ground to fight instead of fleeing into the moors and the tundra—got to cover and started to get organized. Someone down there had the brains and the guts to know that they had to fight or die.

Aguilar dropped one with a single bolt from his T8 blaster rifle.

"Toron, Droma." The platoon sergeant's voice echoed tinnily inside his helmet. "My boys can keep them pinned down. Bring your team down here."

Unsure whether the NCO had something in mind or just wasn't satisfied with the contractors' performance, Dav acknowledged and passed the word. Sones, Aguilar, and Sayavong moved immediately. Vin, down behind his blaster, didn't seem to have heard; he dumped random shots down at the kill zone. Those trigger pulls weren't hitting much, but he *was* providing some suppressing fire.

"Vin!" Dav wished, not for the first time or the last, that his helmet had the amplification of a Legion bucket. He had to use every bit of volume he could summon out of his lungs to bellow over the snap of blaster fire. "Get up and move! Now!"

Hesand, for his part, started, then hesitated when Vin didn't do the same. After a glance at the former sergeant major, though still a little hesitant, he scrambled back from his covered position and followed the other three contractors down the hillside.

Vin very deliberately took one more shot before he got up and followed suit, not looking at Dav as he moved. Dav watched him for a moment, his eyes narrowed. This was going to be a problem.

A problem to be solved when they *weren't* in a firefight. The fire coming from the rebel position was still ragged and sporadic, but it was enough that he kept his head low as he started down toward Droma's sled.

He arrived just behind Vin. Droma had ducked back behind the rear of the vehicle, by the ramp. The steam coming off the legionnaire's N-4 when the rain hit it broadcast that he hadn't kept himself out of the fight to coordinate.

Two three-man fire teams had fallen back from the ridge, and now they stood with Droma, their ponchos lank with moisture over their armor. Droma waited just long enough for Dav to get in hearing range. "Okay. We've got them pinned down, and we *could* break contact from here and put some decent territory between us and them before they can get rescued. But they *might* be able to get a couple of those vehicles running again and then we'd have to do this all over again." He turned briefly to Dav. "We've lost all contact with the *Inspiration*. Best guess is the Mids hit them. Don't know how, but it is what it is."

That attitude was refreshing after having been around points and politicians for so long. There was no pondering what couldn't be known. No freaking out. Just an acceptance of their limitations and lack of support before moving on to how to tackle the problem without wishing for things that couldn't be.

"Let's make damn good and sure that these kelhorns can't follow us. The squads up on the ridge will maintain covering fire." He pointed to the contractors. "Toron, since you and your boys just have blaster rifles, you're going to be more useful on a maneuver element than a base of fire, so you're coming with us."

Vin cocked his head. "Is that so?"

Dav gritted his teeth. Of all the times. "You don't want to be a team player, Vin, you can stay here with the Mids. We're taking your charge packs if that's the case, though." The tone of his voice, and the hand on the grip of his EH-7, made it abundantly clear that he was *not* karking around. Sayavong and Aguilar were also staring at Vin, pure murder in their stances.

Vin subsided with a reluctant nod. Dav turned back to Droma. "What's the plan, Sarge?"

"Mount up. We'll envelop around the south side,

sweep across the kill zone, then collapse back here, consolidate, and move out."

Short, simple, and to the point. The legionnaires and the contractors started to scramble aboard the sleds.

Dav caught Vin before he could climb aboard the maneuver sled. Touching his helmet to the squad leader's to keep his voice low.

"That was your one freebie, *Sergeant Major*. You kark around like that again and I'll dust you myself. If your ego's more important to you than our survival, I'll remove the obstacle." Without waiting for a response, he let go of the other man's arm with a push toward the sled.

"Don't talk to me about egos," Vin spat over his shoulder, but went into the sled willingly.

For a second Dav considered getting into the second sled, but he forced himself to follow Vin into that one. He wasn't going to give the other man the satisfaction of thinking that he was going to avoid the hard feelings that were metastasizing between the two of them. He also wasn't going to give him the opportunity to get any further into Hesand's head.

No one could spend much time in any military without running into someone who was a cancer, a malignancy eating away at the inside of a unit. Most of his time in the Legion, Dav had mostly seen that coming from points, but that was because the Legion was otherwise very strict in its vetting process. The Repub Army wasn't, and apparently neither was S-K Security, either.

Not that he should have been surprised. He'd seen it more than once on the contracts he'd drifted between over the last few years since he'd left the Legion. Most of the companies were more concerned with numbers than quality.

What's that say about you?

The ramp closed behind them, and the sled swiveled around on its repulsors, surging toward the south side of the ridge.

It was a short, fast trip. It felt like mere seconds had passed, Vin staring at the deck near the gunner's feet beneath the twins, Dav watching him balefully. They came to a stop and the ramp dropped. Dav was the first one out, beating the young legionnaire next to the ramp by a half a step.

The sleds had halted in a slight depression where the ridge had begun to curve toward the east. The legionnaires, led by Droma, were already spreading out on-line, taking cover along the rocky, mossy ground. Most of the fight was all but invisible through the rain and the mist, only the actinic flashes of blaster fire showing where the enemy and the friendly base of fire element were.

Dav quickly got his own team lined up on the inside flank, making sure Vin was right next to him. It felt like babysitting a problem-child private, something that he really hadn't had to do in the Legion, but, like Droma had said, it was what it was.

The line started moving, advancing at a patrolling pace, still moving mostly upright given the range. Dav watched his teammates, gratified to see that Sones, Aguilar, Sayavong, and even Hesand weren't having any difficulty falling in and keeping formation as they moved.

Vin, on the other hand, was dragging all too quickly.

Dav stayed even with the shorter man, who seemed to stumble every few steps as his boot slipped on a slick spot or a rock rolled under his foot. This was not the first time that Vin was having a hard time with the terrain. He'd let himself get out of shape, banking on a soft life as a House of Reason contractor, and now they were all going to pay the price.

While Dav saw his element start to lag behind the legionnaires, he didn't dare leave Vin behind him unobserved. Maybe that was paranoid, but he wouldn't put it past the man to get revenge for Dav's harsh words in the middle of a firefight.

Finally, necessity took over. Crossing to Vin, he grabbed the man by the drag handle on the back of his armor and started to propel him across the terrain. Vin stumbled and cursed, but after a moment he got his feet under him and got moving again, though not without a look at Dav that was no doubt a venomous glare on the other side of his visor.

They closed in on the embattled Mids, blasters up and looking for targets.

The terrain was rising as they advanced, and from where Dav was, he couldn't see the enemy shooters. They were in low ground on the other side of that rocky slope. Which meant this was going to be just about as close quarters a fight as he could imagine outside of a raid on a building. The legionnaires were starting to crouch down, keeping in cover as much as possible as they got closer, while the base of fire kept hammering the depression ahead with blaster fire. Every once in a while, a hotter, louder shot from one of the N18s up on the ridge cracked across the open ground, and the outgoing blaster fire got a little bit less.

Things were getting hot as Droma and the lead fire team of Legion assaulters took a knee just below the crest of the rise. Dav could hear not only the blaster fire on the other side, but could almost swear he heard raised voices as well. They were that close.

And the base of fire was still pouring blaster bolts into that defile, right in front of the attacking elements' faces, but no one seemed fazed except for Hesand, Sayavong, and Vin.

Sayavong was a little nervous, but he wasn't nearly as shaky as the two basics. Sones had seen it all before. And Aguilar... Dav wondered just what that guy had done prior to becoming a contractor. SOAR Marine, perhaps?

Droma looked left and right, saw that the assault force was on line, and then got up and moved, leading the way as he went over the crest.

Dav almost reached over to haul Vin to his feet, but for once the man didn't need any encouragement. Maybe the reality of their situation had finally come home to him. Maybe he was taking Dav's threat to end him seriously. Either way, he got up and followed the rest up to the higher ground.

The base of fire ceased just as they came up over the rise and got eyes on the enemy. The half-dozen or so Mids left were still huddled in the dubious cover of one of the wheeled trucks, which had gotten halfway off the road before it had been shot to scrap. Only one of the rebels looked up as the grim, cloaked shapes of the legionnaires appeared above them.

Droma's first shot was quickly drowned in a fusillade of blaster fire. Every shot was aimed and targeted. Not a single bolt missed.

It was over quick.

16

The terrain got steadily higher and more rugged as they made their way toward Barsota. After a high-altitude flyover by a craft they couldn't identify, Droma ordered the sleds off the road, and they struck out for the wilderness, heading up into the hills leading toward the snow-topped mountains that stood between the coastal settlements and the wide, empty taiga and tundra before the polar ice caps.

Those mountains weren't even all that high, but Temugol didn't have much of what Dav might call a temperate zone.

While getting into the hinterlands away from the road and therefore harder to spot, their advance was slowed down. The sleds could get over small obstacles and cracks in the ground without too much trouble, but they were ground effect vehicles, not flyers. Their repulsors weren't built to get them over some of the nastier bits of that rocky nightmare, so their progress slowed to a crawl in several places. They even had to get the winches out several times to negotiate some of the rougher areas.

The good news, Dav mused as he helped stow the winch cable of their sled after getting over a particularly steep rise, was that any pursuers were going to be slowed down by that much and worse. The Legion sleds had a head start that wouldn't be negated by anything but aircraft.

"We need to halt." Droma came over to join him as he straightened from ensuring the cable went back onto the winch without much trouble. "My boys are real leejes, but they're about to drop."

Dav nodded. His eyes felt gritty, and his every limb ached. It had been a while since he'd been on the move this long, with two firefights in the mix. The adrenaline dump alone had almost made him fall asleep in the sled several times since they'd consolidated after sweeping the kill zone of Mids, and that had been hours before.

With a glance over his shoulder, he lowered his voice. "Mine are in even worse shape, if we're being honest."

Droma didn't react. He probably wasn't surprised. In fact, while Dav had fought off sleep on the drive, he knew that Vin hadn't. The comments about the "contractor" snoring in his bucket had reached his ears a couple of halts ago.

"We'll push to that next rise over there, circle up, and set security for the rest of the night," Droma said.

Dav was grateful for that, and not just because he and the rest of his team were exhausted.

Droma was apparently reading his mind. "We're going to have to mostly operate in daylight, or have you guys on the twins, aren't we?"

With a shrug, Dav dusted his gauntleted hands off.

"I'm pretty sure we've all got some low-light capability, though it's nothing like a Legion bucket. I can see enough to fight, but I may as well be blind compared to you guys."

Droma nodded. "Either way, we do need to halt and get some rest. We've got another two hundred klicks to go to get to Barsota, and we have to pass Curwasta on the way." He turned back toward the command sled. "Meet up with me when we get set in. We need to go over the next step."

The sleds were circled up in a tight three-sixty on top of a bare-rock tableland overlooking a long river valley with a churning stream at the base, lined with the dark, feathery Temu equivalents to trees. Dav had just left his contractors, who had stuffed Yuso into a Legion body bag, thus ensuring the rot of death wouldn't permeate the sled carrying him, and now moved over to the command sled where Droma and his squad leaders had gathered just inside the ramp. Most of the legionnaires who weren't on security had stretched out on the rock, wrapped in their ponchos and with their N-4s within arm's reach, and gone almost immediately to sleep.

Every sled's twins were manned, and the sleds' observation bots were all up and sniffing around for the enemy.

"Okay, everybody's here." Droma had his helmet off, and he looked and sounded every bit as tired as Dav felt. "So, here's the deal. We've got to get around Curwasta, but that's going to be more easily said than done, even in country as sparsely populated as this. The reason is the terrain."

He swiveled his battle board so that the assembled platoon leadership—Dav included—could see it. "Curwasta's a major mining hub, which means while it's down here in the valley, there's continual traffic from the mines higher up, just below the snow line. We don't know what the disposition of forces around Curwasta is, though there is a TDF base there, primarily focused on security for the mining operation. It would be kind of out of place if not for Cel Tradat's raids. The mines are one hell of a target, and he's tried to take them at least once."

"We've been out there a couple times." The squad leader known as Meathook was chewing on a ration bar.

"We have," Droma acknowledged. "It's actually better than it was at the main base." He chuckled, though it wasn't much of a humorous sound. "Always stay as far from the flagpole as you can. These guys are luckier than they know."

"Provided the Mids didn't have another torp with their name on it." That was the fourth squad leader, Tiny.

"Provided," Droma replied. "Anyway, we don't know where we stand with them either. If the governor decided to flip on the Republic, they might have gotten orders to stop us. While one leej is worth a few hundred TDF squaddies, that's not odds I necessarily want to try."

He traced a pair of lines on the battle board. "We've got two options. We can head downhill, toward the coast, and try to cross the Kurga River before it hits the delta. That's going to suck, no doubt about it. The Kurga runs through a pretty deep canyon from the mountains all the way down to about two klicks from the delta itself. The delta might be an option, but there are some pretty nasty parts to try to get through if we go all the way down there. The other problem is how much of the mining product is shipped elsewhere on the planet by sea, which means that it goes down the Kurga. There isn't infrastructure all the way down the river, but there's enough, and there's the added chance that we might run into a barge on its way up or down. They won't necessarily be hostile, but they can't be trusted not to let word out that we're crossing there, either."

"What's the other option?" asked the dark, scarred NCO in charge of Second Squad known as Beauty.

Droma smiled, looking downright sinister in the low light inside the sled. "We go up." He pointed to the mountains above Carwasta. "It's going to be one hell of an overland, but while we might encounter enemy forces on the Kurga, there's very little chance they'll have anyone up there. There might be jrasks." He glanced at Dav. "One of the local animals. Big and hairy, with tusks that can put a hole in a sled. Also mean as hell." Turning back to the rest, he continued. "But there are unlikely to be any TDF forces up that high."

"Temus don't want to freeze up there for nothing, and most of them will think it's nothing." Tiny spat in disgust off the ramp. "Lazy kelhorns."

"Sounds like the smart move to me, Sarge." Beauty

leaned back against the inside of the sled.

"What do you think, Toron?" Droma was looking at him. All eyes turned to where he stood on the ramp, his EH-7 dangling from its sling, his helmet under his arm.

He shrugged. "I'm a straphanger, Sarge. You tell me where you want us, and I'll get us there."

For a handful of heartbeats, the legionnaires all watched him carefully. He'd had little to do with the other squad leaders, having mostly just communicated with Droma. They were sizing him up, trying to judge just what it was that had their platoon sergeant consulting this obvious civilian on tactics.

Droma got to the chase. "Doesn't matter. You were a leej, and we're one unit now, whether everybody likes it or not. You're a team leader and I'm trusting you to get your team to perform and pull their weight, so you get a hearing. Only thing is, once we've slapped the table, that's the plan."

Dav nodded. "I think Sergeant Beauty's got the right of it. It might be harder driving, but the mountains are probably a better bet. They'll put us closer to Barsota once we come down, too."

Beauty didn't seem to be impressed or gratified at Dav's agreement with him. He just leaned against the wall of the inside of the sled, chewing his ration bar. Meathook and Tiny glanced at Droma, and the final squad leader, a fireplug of a man known as Stump, nodded.

"You were a leej?" Tiny—who outweighed every other man in the sled by at least ten kilos—eyed him skeptically. "What are you doing as a contractor?"

"All because of a point."

Tiny spat out past him, off the ramp, again. Stump grimaced and shook his head, and Meathook and Beauty both muttered under their breaths. These guys knew what it was like to have a point for a CO, and none of them needed much more than that to explain Dav's status.

"What about those other dudes?" Beauty wasn't quite giving up. "If they were leejes, they've slipped a bit."

"Sayavong was a hullbuster. Two were basics. Sones has merc'ed it up across about half the galaxy. Aguilar... I'm not sure."

"Well, I'm glad they're your responsibility and not mine." Stump stretched. "You got anything else, Sergeant Droma?"

Droma shook his head. "Get some rest while you can. It's gonna be a hell of a day."

Tiny, Meathook, and Stump made their way down the ramp and toward their sleds. Beauty, though, stayed where he was, still studying Dav. "Who were you with?" He apparently wanted more information about his new teammate.

"Tiger Company, 154th."

Beauty raised an eyebrow, making one of the scars on his face pull at the skin. "Keram?"

"That was the last one for me."

"Sket." Beauty seemed to be impressed. "Heard about that sket-show. Among a few other little brushfires the 154th got into."

"No different from any other Legion on the edge. I was aboard the *Reliance* for a while."

"Well, if you were on Keram, that puts you higher in the experience bracket than anyone in this platoon except for Sergeant Droma." Beauty shrugged. "I'm fine with that." He levered himself off the bench and scooped up his bucket and his N-4. "See you boys at stand-to."

Dav looked at Droma. "You got anything else for me?"

Droma didn't answer right away. "How far can you trust your boys?"

It was an important question, and one that Dav had been asking himself for the entire day. He sank onto the bench at the side of the sled and leaned his elbows on his knees.

"From what I've seen so far, I'm pretty sure that Sones, Sayavong, and Aguilar will hang. They're solid dudes. Sones is the only one I'd worked with before this contract, but there's been zero drama, and they've maintained their professionalism every step of the way." He looked down at his gauntleted hands. "Hesand and Vin, I'm worried about. Hesand because of Vin. They were both basics, but Vin was a sergeant major, which carries weight for Hesand. He's just a kid; did one hitch and went for the big money."

"Joke's on him." Droma smiled faintly, though it was a tired expression.

"No clint." Dav sighed. "Vin's been resting on his rank for too long. I can hope that he'll wake the kark up, but I've already had to threaten his life once. He's fat, slow, and arrogant." A part of him wondered at speaking so harshly about a teammate with a man he'd only met days before, but it seemed that he hadn't let go of that Legion identity as much as he thought. He trusted Droma with his life, far more than he did any of the other contractors. "And if it's not me who puts him down, it'll be Sayavong or Aguilar."

"Well, we don't necessarily get to pick our teammates all the time, do we?" Droma was leaning back against the wall, looking up at the overhead. "We're outnumbered and outgunned and we can't spare the blaster right now." He huffed a deep breath, blowing it out past his nose. "So we're going to have to keep an eye on him and utilize his strengths while trying to offset his weaknesses."

Dav shook his head wearily. "More easily said than done."

"So step up, Leej." There was a hard edge in Droma's voice that made Dav's eyes snap to the younger man's face. "We don't have a choice. We've got the people and the blasters we've got. You're the contractor team leader. Most of your team seems to have accepted it. I've got to work with it. Or did you get soft when you got out?"

Dav knew what the NCO was doing, but he couldn't disagree. And he didn't have a rank to pull anymore, not that it had been his style. He and the rest of the team owed the legionnaires their lives. "Good copy, Sarge. I'll make it happen."

Even if I have to put Vin in the ground to do it.

Droma searched his face, then nodded. "Ooah." He turned toward the turret, where a legionnaire's legs were visible. "Hey, Dorf! You didn't hear sket, you hear me?"

"Roger that, Sarge." The leej's voice was muffled,

but clear enough. There wasn't any of the sort of wink-and-nod tone he might have expected from some privates, either. It was clear that Droma had formed this platoon, as green as many of them were, and they respected him.

He'd probably have them all beside the sleds, doing flutter kicks until the sun came up, if they sassed him. It was what Dav would have done.

Once upon a time.

Droma got up and stepped out onto the ramp, stretching as he got out of the sled's troop compartment. "Get some rest, Toron. We've got a hell of a movement in the morning."

Dav followed him out, pulling on his helmet as he got out from the shelter of the sled and into the misting rain. There was a biting chill to it that heralded considerably worse cold the higher they got. "See you in the morning, Sarge."

Droma just nodded before he stepped back into the sled, pulling his battle board out as he did so. He'd probably be up for a while yet, going over routes and contingencies.

For a moment, Dav considered offering to help out, but then he turned and started toward the sled he'd been riding in, where Vin should be sacked out. He needed to check on his team, and Droma would have said something if he wanted help.

It was tough, accepting his odd position here. He had more combat experience than most of the platoon put together. If he understood things right, and gauged their difference in age properly, he probably had more experience than Droma. But it wasn't his platoon. He wasn't even a legionnaire. He had to accept that and work with it, or he'd turn into Vin.

Kark that.

17

The weather was getting worse. The rain had intensified as they'd moved out in the predawn darkness, and by the time they started to get into the high timber several hours later, it had turned to sleet. The sleds didn't have trouble with it, but the guys on the twins had to be grateful for their armor's climate control.

Dav had ended up in a sled with Tiny's squad and Sayavong. Vin had been avoiding him since they'd ambushed their pursuers, and while Dav had to admit that it was somewhat refreshing, it was also a little concerning. The former sergeant major was keeping Hesand close, and that didn't bode well.

There was only so much he could worry about it, though. They'd have plenty of work ahead of them as it was. Also, the team had stayed close together while Dav had talked with Droma the night before. He was sure that Sones or Aguilar would give him a heads up if they saw anything too concerning.

That still worried him a little bit. They weren't passengers, like the staffers who had barely budged from the sleds since they'd left the compound, but they weren't leejes, either. He had to find a way to integrate them more with the legionnaires, even though they were acting as a separate fire team, or this could get uncomfortable, and therefore dangerous, as fatigue and combat stress took greater hold.

The hills were getting steeper and the dark, strange trees thicker. It was taking longer and longer to find routes through. The column had slowed to a crawl, the lead sled threading its way up one ridge and partway down another, weaving between the trees while the rain and sleet came down thick and gray, obscuring visual range ever more as they got higher. If the weather had been clear, they could have looked down the mountainside and seen Carwasta on the sides of the ravine several dozen klicks to their west, but as it was, they could barely see the rear vehicle from the front.

That was a blessing more than it was a curse, though. If they couldn't see the enemy, the enemy couldn't see them.

They had to halt more than once to negotiate an obstacle, and each time the legionnaires got out and set security while the observation bots flew up and scanned the area, ranging pretty far afield to make up for the limited visibility. Now, facing a ravine that hadn't been on the map, they were halted again.

Dav made his rounds, checking on the contractors where they were scattered between the multiple combat sleds. The Legion squads weren't going to break up to accommodate the contractor team, so they were spread out. Nature of the beast.

Sones and Aguilar were riding with Stump's squad, and they were right there with the legionnaires, on a knee behind cover, blasters ready, scanning their fields of fire. Both men nodded that they were fine when Dav checked on them. Sones was even more stoic and tight-lipped than usual, but that might just be because he had his game face on. Aguilar had never been especially forthcoming about his past or his experience. Most of what Dav knew or suspected about him had been inferred from his performance. But the legionnaires seemed to like the man, which went a long way in Dav's mind.

He fist-bumped Aguilar, which was about as much as he could expect in terms of a status report from the man who was almost as taciturn as Sones, then headed for Meathook's sled, where Vin and Hesand had been riding.

Somewhat to his surprise, he found the two of them out of the sled, both armed up and geared up, on a knee behind cover, holding security and as alert as any of the legionnaires. They were both cool but professional when he spoke to them, asking if they needed anything and how they were holding up. It was a far better interaction than he could have hoped for.

It didn't make him relax at all, though. If anything, it put him more on edge. Vin being conciliatory and disciplined was a warning sign. It was too abruptly uncharacteristic.

He moved over to Stump. "How have my guys been doing?" He kept his voice pitched low, so low that it shouldn't travel far, certainly not to the other side of the sled where Vin and Hesand were holding down their sectors. Stump's bucket should be able to amplify his words enough.

"Been keeping to themselves." Stump didn't look at him, but watched the perimeter and the curtains of rain, his bucket's enhancements letting him see farther into the rain and sleet than Dav could with his Krall helmet. "Neither one's talked much, but that's probably for the best. Basics wouldn't do so hot in this bunch."

Dav just nodded, glancing toward the other side of the sled. *What are you cooking up, Vin? And why do you have to be such a kelhorn?*

He didn't have an answer. He was going to have to do what Droma had said, and watch, wait, and hope that the smaller man wised up and realized just how dependent his survival was on being a part of the team.

Otherwise, things were going to get real ugly.

With a fist bump to Stump, who'd apparently decided that Dav was all right, being a former legionnaire, he headed back to his own sled.

Getting across the ravine required some scouting on foot, with the sleds finally backtracking downhill about a klick before they came to a broken bit of hillside that was shallow enough that they could get across, the repulsors setting the gurgling stream at the bottom boiling into a fine mist. They then headed upcountry again in order to avoid the nearest mining facility, which was so close that they could hear the noise of the machinery even over the hum of their repulsors.

The next halt was a little more complicated.

"There wasn't supposed to be anybody up this high."

It was the first thing Sones had said in over a day, and it kind of surprised Dav that he had been the one who'd said it. After a moment though, he had to shake his head. He'd almost missed the deadpan sarcasm.

Droma, however, must have been tired enough that he missed it completely. "Intel's never perfect."

Sones, his helmet off, eyed the Legion platoon sergeant for a moment, as if he was considering whether or not to answer. "I know that, Sar'nt. I probably should have kept my mouth shut."

It took Droma a second for it to register. Then he waved the comment off and brought his field mags back to his eyes.

Dav didn't have the optics to see it, but he could hear well enough to just make out some of the movement up on the ridge, less than half a klick from where they'd halted. There was at least one sled up there, and from the sounds of it, two or more repulsor craft flyers above, in the clouds. What kind of sensor suites they might have he didn't know, though what he'd seen of the TDF didn't suggest that they'd have anything more sophisticated than the sleds' observation bots. That didn't mean they were in a good spot. The MCR might have gotten their dirty hands on something more capable.

The trees provided them some overhead cover, but they were close to the snow line, and the sleds would show up on thermals, overhead cover or no. The thermal bloom had to be huge.

"What's the plan, Sarge?" Beauty was watching the distant sled through his own field mags. The squad leaders had consolidated on Droma's sled and then moved up to the point vehicle.

They were all using open comms instead of the L-comm, so Dav could hear and add his two credits. He wasn't sure if that was a sign of trust or just a way to placate the contractors.

"We need to scout it out." Droma lowered his field mags and pulled out his battle board, linked to the TT-16 observation bot that was hovering overhead. "If there's a way we can get around them without a fight, we'll have to take it." He sounded slightly frustrated at that, and Dav could see why. Legionnaires were life takers and heartbreakers. They lived to fight. This sneaking around stuff was more up a Recon leej's alley than a line leej's.

It was what it was, though.

Droma watched the screen on his battle board in silence. When he recalled the bot and put the board away, Dav could see the frustration had only increased. "They're scouts, all right. Looks like a TDF fire team with an unarmed sporting sled."

"We'll handle it, Sarge." Beauty put his field mags away. "Won't take long."

Droma nodded his approval, and Beauty faded, reappearing a couple minutes later with one of his fire teams, their ponchos draped over their armor and their hoods up, swathing their buckets except for their visors. There was still a lot of shiny armor under those coverings, but if they moved right, they might get close without being spotted, especially in the misty gloom of the day. The sleet had given way to snow, though even that had thinned out now.

With a gesture, Beauty led the way into the thicker woods just downhill from the gathered combat sleds, disappearing into the foliage in seconds.

Dav had to admit he was impressed. Disappearing like that would have taken some serious skill in the old gray armor. That Beauty could still stalk like a ghost in the new stuff said some good things about him, and about how well Droma had trained his platoon, probably in spite of their point CO.

Or maybe spite hadn't actually had anything to do with it. If Lieutenant Mastruk had spent as much time away from the platoon as it had seemed, Droma might have had a freer hand than Dav had seen with points during his time.

He couldn't see that well to catch what happened next with any detail. He saw movement, heard what might have been a muffled cry. Then the sound of the sled's repulsors out there shut down. A few minutes later, Beauty and his squad mates came back through the trees to the perimeter. Dav hadn't heard any deconfliction, so he had to assume they'd called ahead via L-comm.

"Way's clear." Beauty pulled back his hood as he joined the other squad leaders and Droma.

Not a shot had been fired. Maybe the younger generation of leejes would be all right. Points or no points.

Droma circled his hand in the air. "Mount up!"

18

Getting around Carwasta had taken a full day and a half, and it was in the dying light of the second day that they got up on the plateau to the northwest and got some smoother ground to traverse. It wasn't a road, but it wasn't as rough and broken, and it had fewer trees, which made for faster going for the sleds. The weather was clearing up, too.

The clouds lifted and began to break up, visibility improved. The enemy would have a better chance to spot them. It was awfully open country.

"Gunners, keep your eyes up. Remember, the bad guys may have more assault shuttles." Droma's call went out over L-comm and open freqs both. The gunner in Droma's sled, just ahead of where Dav was sitting with his blaster rifle between his knees, shifted his position, dropping slightly in the turret as he rotated the twins skyward, looking for targets.

Droma was up near the front, watching his battle board. There wasn't a lot of visibility from inside a combat sled, and none of these sleds were the command variant that provided a full war room partitioned off with the driver. Droma made do by having the sled's observation bot keeping pace with them. It would need to dock and recharge soon, but for the moment it was giving the legionnaires better visibility on their surroundings.

The platoon sergeant suddenly sat up a little straighter and peered down at the board, making a couple of adjustments. Then he handed it across to Dav. "Check this out."

Dav took the board. He was technically a team leader, even if he was a supernumerary, so he was getting the intel dump.

The battle board was a little different from the one he'd used in the Legion. It felt lighter, a little flimsier. Typical.

He also didn't have full use of all its features, without a Legion helmet. Droma had set it to show him what he needed to see, though. It gave a clear image from the observation bot. And it wasn't a pretty one.

A column of vehicles was making its way down the main coastal road, about twenty klicks south of the legionnaires' route. Most of them were technicals, civilian sleds, and wheeled trucks with hastily mounted and crude armor, weapons strapped on or welded in the beds. Not all of them were cobbled-together fighting vehicles, though.

There were at least two UT-70 combat sleds in the mix, as well as a light tank the battle board identified as a Goorithian Systems Atavist. He'd seen those before, on Keram. They weren't necessarily MCR, but they were common enough among various planetary militaries along galaxy's edge. They were vulnerable to AP missiles, and even the N-50s would put a dent in one, but they had a rapid-fire repeating blaster in the turret that could make for a very bad day for anyone downrange of them.

As he watched the screen, the column seemed to grow. More technicals. More UT-70s and a few XR-234 mortar carriers. More Atavists. That was close to a battalion on the road.

And it was going in the same direction they were. Toward Barsota.

That was quite a force, one Dav assumed belong to Cel Tradat. Perhaps Triste was a bigger fish than Dav realized and the rebel leader now wanted to see the man taken off the board.

Dav handed the datapad back over. "If they can spare forces like this for Barsota, I suspect Temugol City has been secured."

Ordinarily, Dav would have doubted that any force could pacify a spaceport city that fast, but from what he'd seen of the governor, and the destruction of the main TDF headquarters, he shouldn't be that surprised. Again, he was going off what Triste had told him, but it sounded like the locals *all* had resented Nisa, so anyone would have been an improvement.

The damage done by the raids could be justified, especially when the alternative was getting lined up against a wall and shot.

"That or the MCR just dropped a bunch more resources onto this planet," Droma replied.

"Looks like we might be headed for one hell of a fight."

"No clint." The platoon sergeant looked down at the screen. "I just hope your buddy back in the hills has more than political pull and the moral high ground to fight with."

"You and me both, Sarge. You and me both."

Even though they were moving across rougher ground, the legionnaires had the advantage in speed, mostly because they had a smaller unit and their sleds were all repulsor vehicles. The column down below, even though it was moving on the road, was larger, more spread out, and had to adjust its speed for the wheeled and tracked vehicles as well as the repulsor sleds. Within an hour, the Legion platoon was pulling ahead. Two hours after that, Barsota started to come into view.

Barsota was built around a central tower that might have been a marketplace, an early warning station, a seat of local government, or maybe all three. Calling it a "tower" was almost inaccurate, since it was almost as wide as it was tall, but the stubby cylinder still stood tall above the rest of the city of mostly one-story duracrete blocks or domes that looked to have been printed a long time ago.

Like every other settlement on Temugol, it was built for the extreme weather that came with the planet's winter, still several months away.

Droma had the platoon pull up into a security halt on a rise just to the east of the city. The coastal mountains had fallen away to the north, and Barsota sat in the middle of a vast bowl, framed by the snow-topped peaks that vanished into the gray haze in the distance. Somewhere north of there was Triste's ranch, though Dav couldn't see it with just his eyeballs and the limited optics in his helmet.

Droma passed him the field mags. The other squad leaders all had their own, so once again, Dav was the odd man out, having to rely on Droma to stay up to speed. It chafed a little, but he had to accept it.

There was movement down by the city, several sleds zipping around the outskirts like they were patrolling and more than a few VTOLs rising into the sky. They had to have gotten word about the column coming their way.

"Making contact without getting lit up is going to be interesting." Droma accepted the field mags from Dav as he handed them back. "We don't know what's going on down in the city, either."

Dav thought about it as he looked toward the settlement. "Might be best if my team tries to make contact."

When Droma turned to look at him with a faint tilt of his bucket, Dav shrugged. "If the city has fallen, some contractors with non-standard armor and weapons might be taken as either Mids or mercs working for Cel Tradat. Not so with legionnaires. Especially if they've put out an alert on the platoon, which they probably did after we shot our way out of the spaceport."

The platoon sergeant thought it over. "I knew I brought you boys along for a reason." He glanced back at one of the other sleds, and Dav knew what he was thinking. "You sure you want to take your *whole* team?"

It was a good question, and not just for the obvious

reason. Vin had continued with his quiet professional act, but the longer it went on, the more Dav expected a vibro-blade in the kidneys at any moment. The man just wasn't the type to have that abrupt a turnaround. At least he had Sones, Sayavong, and Aguilar watching his back. Though Vin probably resented those three almost as much.

The other factor, though, was footprint. Dav didn't know what they'd be getting into down in the city. Too many strangers all at once might attract the wrong sort of attention, especially if the rebel/MCR column hadn't gotten there yet. If he was going to get in, snoop around, and get out, walking in with a six-man fire team might not work.

He wouldn't turn down the firepower if things dropped in the pot, but it would be better to get in, get out, and report back to the legionnaires *without* things going sideways.

"I'll take a man with me." Dav knew that would be either Sones or Aguilar. Aguilar had demonstrated some considerable skill in moving through an urban area unnoticed, but he'd worked with Sones longer.

"We'll give you a ride down to an insert point once you're ready. You'll have twenty-four hours to be back at extract."

Dav and Sones were still in their armor, wearing borrowed Legion ponchos to cover it since they were without the long coats provided them back at the tower. They left their helmets back with the combat sleds. Dav still had his regular comm, though, and he'd synced it with Droma before they'd been dropped off.

They'd debated bringing their blaster rifles. Dav's EH-7 was compact enough that he could conceal it under his coat, but Sones's R-6 was a little long. In the end, Dav brought his, while Sones would fall back on his Garmian.

He and Droma had sweated out their insert point for a while. They couldn't just drive into town, but if they just walked in out of the hinterlands, that would look suspicious, too. They had to make it look right.

The obs bots had pinpointed the oncoming enemy column, still twenty klicks away on the coastal road. That gave them a bit of a window, so the sled that had inserted them dropped them a klick away from the city. They'd walk in from there.

Barsota's elevation was considerably higher than Temugol City, and the weather was accordingly colder. The wind came down off the snowy peaks of the mountains, but fortunately it wasn't snowing, sleeting, or raining.

Yet.

Clouds were building to the south, over the sea.

"So, how's Vin doing?" Sones asked as they walked. "I haven't been down by his sled in a day or two."

"Lucky you." Dav snorted at Sones's chuckle. "You know damned well."

"I guess the better question is how's Hesand doing?"

"Pulling his weight." Dav scanned the hills as he spoke. "It's funny. Being around the legionnaires seems to have changed something. He's not looking at Vin for guidance that much anymore."

"Professionalism will do that." Sones nodded, stepping over a rock, though not before looking down at where he was about to place his boot. The old man was careful. It was the only reason he'd lived as long as he had in this profession. "As will the realization that his idol is out of his depth." He glanced over at Dav. "What about you?"

"What do you mean?"

Sones snorted. "Boy, I've fought in over a dozen wars across twice that many worlds. You think I haven't seen how you act around the legionnaires? You're regretting leaving, and thinking that somehow that don't make you worthy. So, you're pushing to try to prove it to them, and to yourself. Tell me I'm lying."

Dav was somewhat grateful for his helmet, just to hide his wince. "I can't."

Sones stopped, though he didn't do it in the open, stepping into an overhang and almost disappearing into the shadows, his visor tracking across the visible hillside below them before he spoke. Dav moved in to join him, shifting to cover the security that the old man couldn't.

"Look, I get it. I've seen it. I've *been* that guy. And I'm not even saying it's a bad thing. Just don't get so wrapped up in trying to prove yourself again that you get somebody killed."

Dav nodded, keeping his eyes on his sector, if only to avoid meeting Sones's gaze. "I hear you."

For a moment, he could feel the older man watching him appraisingly. "Just needed to be said. Let's go."

There were eyes in the outskirts of the city. The sled came racing out to of a blind intersection to intercept Dav and Sones halfway to the edge of the first line of buildings, almost as soon as they cleared the curve around a low hill that had obscured them from any observers that weren't overhead.

Neither man spoke as the sled bore down on them. Dav felt a rush of adrenaline. All the sled's driver would have to do would be to run them over. Armor or no armor, it wouldn't make much difference. He doubted whether he could get his EH-7 out fast enough to dust the driver if it looked like they were just going to be targeted, no questions asked.

But the driver brought his vehicle to a smooth, practiced stop, and a man with a surge shotgun stood up in the passenger seat. "Hold there." He spoke Standard, but with a decided accent that Dav now recognized from the way Triste spoke. "This isn't a good time to be wandering around, strangers."

"We heard there was some security work around here." Dav took the lead, since Sones was hanging back and just watching with gimlet eyes from beneath his hood.

"That depends." The man with the surge shotgun

was being just as cautious. "If you're looking to sign up with Cel Tradat, you're in the wrong place."

"People don't like Cel Tradat much around here?" Dav decided to feel things out a bit. That surge shotgun wasn't pointed at them yet. He was fairly sure he could draw and put a blaster bolt in the man before he could bring the weapon to bear. This could be the intel they needed.

The man spat. Dav might have seen the sled's driver move, rather like he was rolling his eyes. "This isn't the Boraga family's territory, friend. We don't hold with letting them run the whole planet, much less their outworld friends."

Dav decided to take a chance. If Triste owned the bulk of the land around Barsota, then it wasn't too much of a chance. "I spoke to Samuel Triste back in Temugol City before things went sideways there. Figured we'd see if he was hiring."

The local squinted at him suspiciously, and Dav felt his every nerve going still as he began his draw in his mind, not moving a muscle even as he prepared to sweep his coat aside and pull his blaster.

Finally, though, the man motioned toward the back of the sled. "Get in and you can talk to him. But we'll be watching you, outlanders. If you try anything, or turn out to be Cel Tradat's spies, well. There are some high beams we can hang you from, if we don't just shoot you first."

Dav glanced at Sones and got a nod. They stepped to the back, but before they could get in, the driver said something and the guy with the surge shotgun rethought things. "Hold up." He brought his weapon a little closer to pointed at the two of them and motioned with the muzzle. "Let's see under the ponchos."

So, they weren't going to get in unsearched. Dav forced himself to relax. This was expected. It could turn out to be disastrous, but it was what he'd do in the man's place.

"We're armed," Dav said.

They both complied. The threat of the surge shotgun—which could cut one or both of them in half at that range—was one thing, but they were also going to play along, in case these guys really did work for Triste. Trust was going to be necessary.

The man's eyes widened a little at the sight of the armor, the Garmians, and Dav's stubby EH-7. "You brought a lot of hardware, outlander."

"I said we were looking for security work, didn't I?" Dav kept his tone reasonable. "Wouldn't have much to offer as a hired gun without a blaster."

That seemed to make sense to the shotgunner, but he wasn't fool enough to let two strangers with that kind of firepower into the sled behind him. "Set the weapons on the ground and step back."

Sones had stood, still as a statue, during the exchange. Now, slowly and carefully, he drew his blaster with two fingers, slowly and carefully setting it on the damp pavement of the road while Dav unclipped his EH-7's sling and did the same, followed by his own Garmian. They stepped back as the man with the surge shotgun climbed down from the sled and retrieved the weapons.

"We'll be expecting those back." Dav could only hold his peace on that for so long.

The driver answered. He was older, weathered and balding. He squinted at the two of them. "If you turn out to be what you say you are, you'll get them back. Mr. Triste could use all the guns he can get right now."

"You ain't lying." Sones spoke for the first time. "There's close to a battalion or more coming this way right now."

That stopped the man in his tracks, and his eyes widened. "That so?"

Dav nodded. "Saw them on the way in."

The shotgunner motioned toward the back seats in the sled. "Get in."

Dav and Sones did as they were told, and the driver spun the sled like a top before speeding back into town. He didn't stop, though, racing up the main drag between low slope-walled buildings with holographic signs in alcoves on their fronts, mostly advertising drinks or hardware. Barsota wasn't a large city, and they were through it in about ten minutes, heading up into the ag fields and the hills above.

Over the driver's shoulder, Dav could see what looked like a fortified compound up on the shoulder of one of the taller of the coastal mountains, even though that peak probably wasn't more than about two thousand meters above sea level. The snow level was still just above the compound itself, which was surrounded by more of the dark, feathery trees.

Once they were out of the city, the driver laid on the

throttle and they sped up, zipping between the field-habs toward the compound. Dav studied it as best he could without his helmet or Droma's field mags. There didn't appear to be turrets or weapons in evidence, but whoever had built it had clearly had defense in mind.

Maybe some of that defense was against the weather. The wind was already getting stiffer, and Dav could feel it rocking the sled as they went. He filed that away for later. Maybe they could use it against the oncoming Mids and rebels.

If they survived this part.

The sled slowed, and the man on the surge shotgun got on his comm and called ahead. He had to wait for his ping to be answered, and when he started talking, it wasn't in Standard. Dav didn't recognize the language, but that was no great surprise. Standard might be called that for a reason, but the Republic was full of local dialects, and not just for aliens.

After a long conversation, the driver slowed to a halt just short of the massive gates leading into the compound. The comm call ended and the gates started to grind open.

The sled hummed inside the compound as soon as the gates were open wide enough. Several armed men were waiting on the steps leading up to the big house at the top of the shelf, and a familiar figure stood behind them.

"You come talk to Mr. Triste now." The doors opened and their escort got out, carrying their blasters. "Weapons'll be here waiting for you."

Triste started down the steps as Dav and Sones got out. "It seems my warning came none too soon." He extended a hand and Dav shook it.

"Looks that way."

Triste glanced over his shoulder. "Did you bring your boss?"

"Yuso's dead." Dav kept his face still. "You were right. The governor wasn't going to let him get off-planet with any reports that things weren't going swimmingly here. He was shot by one of the governor's security before we could break out."

"I'm sorry to hear that." Triste's shoulders slumped. "He was the last hope I had of heading this off."

"There's no heading anything off now." Dav gestured over his shoulder. "But there *is* a platoon of legionnaires in the hills, waiting for me to report back. We linked up with them on the way out, just before one of Nisa's sharpshooters killed Yuso. Figured we'd come here, since you're about the only one I think we can trust at the moment."

Triste tilted his head in some surprise at the announcement, but he didn't take long to come to a decision. "The Legion's help will be welcome. Especially if Cel Tradat is now turning his attention here, which your escort says you told him."

Dav nodded to confirm.

Trist gave a wan smile. "I am his biggest rival on the face of the planet, though I haven't pushed the matter before now."

"Now he's pushing." Dav described the column of

technicals, APCs, and tanks that was on its way. Triste's face turned slightly slack and gray as he listened to the full extent of the firepower that was currently bearing down on his city.

"How far are the legionnaires?" Triste clearly believed that they were his best hope, even considering how few of them there were.

"Maybe twenty minutes out," Dav said. Probably faster, if the younger leejes were really cut loose. They'd gained a lot of confidence handling their sleds on rough ground over the last few days. It had somewhat surprised Dav, until he'd thought about the fact that Droma had told him that they'd been essentially held to their own quarters and the TDF base outside the city for the majority of their deployment.

"Call them in. Tell them that we'll follow their lead and lend any support we can, if they'll assist us." He pulled a small datapad out. "I can show you a good route to come here fastest, though we will have to move down to the city if we are going to hold it."

"Thank you." Dav was already digging his comm out.

Droma answered the comm almost immediately. "Talk to me."

"I'm dropping a data link with a route here in a second. Triste's on board."

"Good, because we just shot down another peeper. They know we're in the vicinity. Things are about to get heated."

19

There wasn't time to secure the city, even if a platoon of legionnaires with six contractors as supernumeraries could have done it in the first place.

Triste had been on the comms with Barsota's mayor, who seemed to be a distant cousin, since right after Dav called the legionnaires in. Things got a little heated, as the mayor was presumably reluctant to fall back and abandon the city to the Cel Tradat and the Mid-Core Rebellion, but Triste either had the weight of the reality of the situation or else his personality and seniority in the area to fall back on. He got his way.

Droma pinged Dav while the contractor was retrieving his weapons from the man with the surge shotgun, one of Triste's workers named Shota. He holstered his Garmian and answered with one hand as he took his EH-7 back with the other.

"We're not going straight to the compound." Droma's voice was raised over the rumble of the repulsors in the background. "That column's getting too close. We're going to the hill just outside the city, where we'll set up an ambush. You should be able to join up with us before they hit the kill zone."

Droma might not have said as much, but Dav could read between the lines. The platoon sergeant wanted his straphanger team leader there, just in case one of the two basics got froggy.

"Roger. We'll be on our way in a heartbeat." He looked up at where Triste was still on his comm. "Hey, Shota, we need a ride again."

"Mr. Triste…" The man looked up at his boss.

"Mr. Triste will understand. We need to go link up with those legionnaires to put some hurt on that armored column that's on its way. Maybe keep them from blowing up your place." Dav had no idea whether Shota lived down in town or up there in Triste's compound, but it was worth a shot.

The balding man glanced down toward the city, then back up at Triste. For a second, Dav was afraid that it wasn't going to work, that he was going to be stuck and wouldn't make it down to join up with the leejes in time, but Triste had apparently heard, and he waved his assent at Shota, who nodded. "Let's go."

If Shota's buddy, Korgov, had been driving fast on the way up to Triste's compound, it was nothing compared to the hair-raising drive down to the outskirts of Barsota. To say that the pugnacious but silent man was heavy on the throttle would be putting it mildly.

Dav noticed the old PK-9 blaster rifle next to the man's leg. He was loaded for bear, and probably itching to get into the fight too. It *was* his town, after all.

"You lookin' to join us?" Dav asked the man.

"Yep."

Well, Dav wasn't going to turn down another blaster. He was pretty sure Droma wouldn't, either, though he had a bit of a sinking feeling that he was going to get put in charge of any local augments. May as well put the irregulars with the irregulars.

Shouldn't have gotten out.

He was about to direct Korgov toward the hill that Droma had pinpointed when the Legion combat sleds came down out of the hills, moving fast and slithering between the terrain and the sparse vegetation while the twins tracked to cover every angle around them. "Hold up here." Dav keyed his comm. "Droma, Toron. We're in the sled directly to your two o'clock."

"Got eyes on you. No time, so fall in behind the rear sled." Droma wasn't asking questions or even wondering about who else might be in the vehicle with them. It was KTF time, and from the sound of his voice, the platoon sergeant was ready for it.

Somewhat to his surprise, Dav didn't even have to pass the word. Korgov had heard it, and he nodded. "Rear vehicle. We don't have twins, though."

Korgov's accent was considerably less pronounced than Shota's. In fact, he sounded like more than a few leejes Dav had met over the years.

"Were you ever..."

"Thirteenth, Invicta Company, off the *Resolute*." Korgov didn't turn around, but Dav could see part of the faint smile that creased his squarish face. "Been a while, but I remember a few things."

Dav just nodded. Right at the moment, though, it was time to focus on the upcoming fight.

They reached the hill a minute later, Droma already out of his vehicle and directing the sleds to positions where their twins could cover the road. Dav stepped out of his own ride while it was still moving, and jogged over to join the Legion NCO.

"We might have another shooter." He jerked his thumb over his shoulder. "Says he was a leej, back in the day."

Droma had his bucket on, and turned his head to see Korgov getting out of the sled, his PK-9 in his hands. "Every blaster helps." He clapped Dav on the shoulder. "Guess what, though?"

"He's my responsibility, I know."

He could almost hear the platoon sergeant's grin. "Got it in one, Leej. You're the expert with a multi-service team."

Dav grimaced as he headed for the sled to grab his helmet before he started rounding up the team to get them into position. "Roger that, Sarge."

"KTF, Leej."

They had only minutes to get set in before the first of the technicals appeared around the curve in the road.

Dav crouched behind a boulder with his EH-7, Korgov on one side of him and Vin on the other. The latter hadn't talked back, hadn't given any real indication that he resented the rapid-fire orders Dav had snapped at him and the other contractors, but he'd been just slow enough getting into position that Dav knew their feud wasn't over.

The lead technical was a relatively new sporting sled. It almost didn't look like it could be called a "technical," since the armor appeared to be some sort of purpose-manufactured package, instead of the bolted-on durasteel that was more common on planets from Etaros to Kublar.

It wouldn't to be enough to fend off what was coming, though, and the Mid on the mounted rocket launcher in the back was facing the wrong way, looking toward the city instead of the hill where the legionnaires were waiting.

Still, the sled passed by unmolested, turning toward the low, gray skyline of Barsota and moving by the hill.

Droma was waiting for the right moment.

Just for a second, Dav wondered if he was really going to try to hit the entire column so hard that it would stop them cold. He wasn't sure if that was possible with the numbers and the firepower they had. Even with the one mortar bot they'd gotten out of Temugol City, it was shading the edge of impossible.

Fortunately, Sergeant Droma wasn't feeling delusions of grandeur. Not that day.

Two aero-precision missiles slammed out of the shadows of the hill and turned the lead technical and one of the Atavist tanks into fireballs, the vehicles throwing blackened, twisted sections of metal flying and flipping through the air as they tumbled from the impact and the explosion.

Most of the other vehicles between the lead

technical and the light tank were thin-skinned sleds or lightly armored trucks, which was why Droma had targeted two of his sharply limited supply of AP missiles that way. Now that the vehicles in between and behind halted abruptly, their gunners and passengers desperately looking for where the catastrophic fire had come from, he unleashed the rest of his firepower.

Dav leaned into his EH-7 and stitched bolts across what looked like it had once been a luxury sled, just behind a balloon-wheeled flatbed with something strapped down under a tarp in the back. The plastite and sheet durasteel weren't rated for blaster fire, and he quickly punched half a dozen smoking holes through the door and the bodies behind it.

The mortar bot coughed four times, and a blizzard of energized explosives tore through the vehicles in the kill zone and any Mids or Temu rebels who tried to dismount and run to cover on the wrong side. Explosions sounded beyond the Atavist, which was now burning fiercely, the mortar rounds slamming down into the vehicles bunched up behind it.

Three men in flak vests piled out of the far side of the luxury sled, one of them firing wildly over the roof as they scrambled for cover in the rocks just off the road. Vin ducked, almost burying his face and his visor in the mud, but Dav and Korgov both shot back coolly, even as blaster bolts went overhead with harsh snaps. Targeting was a little difficult through the smoke pouring down the road from the burning wreckage of the lead technical and its mounted rockets, but Dav winged one and Korgov blasted another through the throat.

The sleds were moving up now, the twins pouring heavy blaster fire into the column. Three more sleds were immolated as brilliant spears of energy punched all the way through their bodies, one striking a power cell and turning the sled into a fireball.

Dav lost track of the men he'd been shooting at as the explosion knocked everyone down by the road off their feet, and fire and smoke billowed through the low ground.

"Mount up!" Two more of the Atavists were maneuvering out of the column behind the kill zone, and Droma clearly didn't want to stick around for those heavy repeating blasters to come to bear.

Dav was up on his feet in a heartbeat. Korgov was a little slower, and Vin was still down on the ground.

Grabbing the shorter man by the carry handle, Dav dragged him to his feet and propelled him toward a sled. "Move if you want to live!"

He all but threw Vin into the back of the sled, and the man was engulfed a moment later as Droma's legionnaires poured in after him. Then Dav ran for his own sled. "Korgov, get in your vic and get out of here!"

A glance over his shoulder showed him Korgov running as fast as his stubby legs would carry him down the hill toward the civilian sled they'd ridden out there. The man was no dummy.

Dav threw himself into the sled right in front of Droma. Not because he was that desperate to save his own hide, but because he knew Droma wasn't going to budge until everyone was loaded up.

With the twins letting out a steady stream of white-hot hate, the sled swiveled around and headed down the hill, faster than Dav probably would have driven if he'd been in the cockpit. The legionnaire on the twins kept up the fire as long as he could, until the terrain cut off his field of fire and the platoon raced away, heading around Barsota and toward Triste's compound.

Droma was in the seat right at the inside of the ramp, his head bowed, probably getting ACE reports over the L-comm. Dav reached for his own comm, though it wasn't going to penetrate the skin of the combat sled as well as the L-comm would. He didn't know what kind of sorcery went into the L-comm, but he'd *never* seen it go down. He hadn't realized just how unusual that was until he'd gotten out and had to use civilian comms.

Before he could get the call out, Droma looked up. "Got the word from your man Aguilar. Everyone's up. No casualties."

Dav nodded his appreciation. That had been for his benefit. Any of the others would have heard the check-ins in their own buckets.

"Now things get sketchy."

20

"We bought some time," Droma said, studying the feed from his sled's observation bot, which was currently circling above the city. "They haven't advanced past the kill zone, though they've spread out to set security and those tanks are up on the high ground. Anybody trying to come at them from the city is going to get dusted with a quickness."

They were now inside Triste's ranch compound and going over their options inside Triste's dining room, a massive, cathedral-ceilinged room that could probably hold the entire platoon as well as most of Triste's household. Dav was looking over Droma's shoulder, along with Meathook, Beauty, Stump, and Tiny. Triste and his head of security—a small, wiry man with enough of a resemblance to Triste that Dav suspected he was a cousin or something—stood nearby, with an old holomap brought up on the table.

Yuso's body was still in its Legion body bag, but now in Triste's basement. It would stay there until this was over. The rest of his staff were in a similar state, though several of the locals were making sure they were fed and had a place to sleep. They'd stay there until this little war got sorted out.

What their ultimate fate would be depended on what that meant.

"How many AP missiles do we have left?" Dav asked.

"Enough for those tanks, but not much past that. And we'd have to get close enough." Droma pointed to the hill where they'd set in their ambush. "It looks like they already have sharpshooters and heavy repeating blasters set up overlooking the road. We'd have to get all the way behind them to get a shot at them, and this bunch has suddenly gotten a whole lot more security-conscious for some reason."

Tiny snorted.

"What about air?" Dav hadn't heard any more assault ships, but that didn't mean they weren't out there.

"Nothing so far, but the fact that they're holding their position, and have been for the last couple of hours, makes me nervous." That a legionnaire would admit to being nervous in front of anyone who wasn't also a leej lent some considerable weight to the seriousness of their situation. Droma looked over at Triste. "Any word from the city?"

As far as they'd seen from the rancher's compound, there hadn't been much movement down there.

"Mayor Yalorak is rallying the constabulary and those TDF forces we can trust. There have never been many stationed here, and most of those in recent years have been largely tasked by the Republic governor to keep an eye on me." Triste's lip curled with disgust. "The majority of the unit that was here has been taken into custody by the constabulary."

"Are the constabulary loyal to the mayor, then?" Beauty had chosen his words carefully, omitting *Or to you?* Dav figured that most everyone in the room heard the unspoken part.

Triste likely picked up on the subtext, but only nodded. "They are all local boys. Well, there have been a few immigrants from some of the outer settlements, and even some transplants from Carwasta and Temugol City. Mostly it's miners who would prefer a more country life."

Droma pursed his lips and said, "And those boys are probably even more likely to be dedicated to their new home."

Dav had seen it before. So, it seemed, had Droma.

The contractor watched the interplay with a carefully neutral expression, taking it all in. Droma was no one's fool. He had to suspect that there was more going on here than Triste was saying. Dav had dealt with the man only a little more than Droma had at this point, and he figured that they could trust him, but not blindly. Every leej had to learn whenever he got mixed up in one of these perpetual brush wars out on the edge that you could only fully trust the man next to you.

Several years of contracting after Keram had only reinforced that lesson in Dav's mind. Triste had talked a good game so far, and he'd backed it up with action, but they couldn't ever forget that Triste's loyalty would ultimately be to Triste and his family's position on Temugol.

This was an alliance of necessity. Such alliances were subject to change at the drop of a charge pack.

Droma no doubt understood that the fight to come was ultimately going to come down to the legionnaires KTFing the Mids and rebels, and watching each other's backs.

And here I am with a squad of straphangers that Droma—rightly—isn't so sure he can trust.

"What kind of hardware do they have?" Droma was vague as to who "they" was, but Triste gathered that he was talking about the constabulary.

"Mostly blasters and a few surge shotguns." The rancher shrugged. "This is the edge. We don't get a lot of fancy tech out here unless the first colonists brought it with them, let alone fancy weapons."

Dav could dispute that, from a few nasty encounters out on the edge, Keram not even the least.

Droma spoke quiet and patiently. "What about the TDF? If the constabulary has taken them into custody, they couldn't have had much."

"Oh." Triste hesitated, and Dav watched him carefully. "They have never amounted to much more than military police, so, much the same."

"It seems to me that, even before the MCR arrived, TDF and your forces were outgunned?" Droma was searching for more intel, if only to make sure they didn't get a vibro-blade in the kidneys as soon as they turned to engage the Mids.

"Truly spoken," said Triste.

Tiny and Beauty shared a look. The legionnaires in

Droma's platoon might have been relatively untested when they'd come to Temugol, but they weren't dumb.

Well, hell. I'm the outsider here, so I may as well draw some fire.

"If Cel Tradat has it out for you the way you described it to me, and he's had you outgunned, then he's got to have one hell of a reason to have stayed out of Barsota until now."

Triste looked at Dav coolly. "There's a column of soldiers massed outside the city that would challenge your assertion, Mr. Toron."

"*Now* there is," Dav said. "But what was keeping him out before? I don't think that a man who'd launch military raids on the capital city and the spaceport would just stay away out of respect."

Triste's expression froze, even as Droma turned a languid eye toward him, one eyebrow climbing toward the platoon sergeant's shorn scalp. The Legion NCO didn't say anything, just waited.

For his part, Triste didn't bluster like Dav had half expected him to. So far, the man had come across as the voice of reason, a man who just wanted the best for his planet, but this little inconsistency made Dav wonder. Not that it surprised him. He was long past that.

The rancher sighed. "No, it wasn't out of respect, exactly. He knew what I am capable of, and that was warning enough."

Droma drummed his fingers on the table. "If you've got something up your sleeve that we can use against them, I need to know."

Or else what? Dav asked himself. What would Droma do if Triste held out. Leave? Where would they go?

Of course, Dav figured that Droma had a few ideas. So did he. So would any leej in this situation. Dav's mostly involving a cross-country E&E before sneaking back into the spaceport and hijacking a freighter, if one could be found.

Triste's shoulders slumped. Maybe he thought that Droma was going to do just that, and he didn't want to cross the legionnaires right in his dining room. Or maybe he really believed that he needed to cooperate fully if he had a chance of survival.

"We have a cache of old weapons," Triste admitted, albeit reluctantly. If this was true, he was revealing some serious cards. Cards he might not want the Republic to know about.

Of course, he wasn't telling the Republic. Yuso was dead. He was telling the Legion.

How that worked out for him would depend on a number of factors, not least of which was Droma's opinion of the man.

"You won't be pleased with what I'm about to say, Sergeant, but the truth is, we can't say exactly what all is in the cache. It was here when my family pushed out from Temugol City, about fifty years ago. To the best of my knowledge, no one knows for certain who left it. It's human. The markings are in an old dialect of Standard... and it was buried in this hill when my grandfather came here."

Tiny rubbed a hand against his jaw as he watched

Triste. "If you don't know what's in it, then how do you or anyone else know that it's going to be effective against Cel Tradat, let alone the Mids? And why would an unknown keep Cel Tradat away?"

Triste gave a sly smile. "Just because I've shared the truth about what we have with you, does not mean I did the same with *him*. Cel Tradat believes that we possess enough weapons to equip a small army with a level of firepower that hasn't been seen since the Savage Wars."

Dav nodded, understanding. "And that's been enough. And the TDF forces? Had the governor heard the same rumors?"

"A distinct possibility."

"And a moot point if I am to understand that you haven't actually been into this cache," Droma said. He rubbed the bridge of his nose, no longer able to simply handle the whole situation with complete equanimity.

"The seal in place at its discovery has remained." Triste shrugged. "We may be a backwater edge world, but we are aware of some of the horrors of the Savage Wars. My family knew better than to meddle with such things."

"But evidently didn't feel the need to contact the Republic about it," Dav said.

"We knew better than to do that, as well. Though I mean no offense to those in this room."

"Sket." Droma shook his head. "You've maintained your position through a bluff that has now been called. Great." He sighed. "Let's see what you've got. If it really does have firepower that we can use, we'll need it. If they bring up more assault shuttles and tanks, right now the most my legionnaires and I can offer is a blaze of glory to go out in."

Triste looked almost like he was going to argue. Dav watched the byplay in silence, his eyes moving between Droma and Triste. The Legion squad leaders were watching Triste as well, with that coiled-spring readiness that characterized men who'd already been in a fight for their lives and weren't all that picky about fighting some more.

Their current ally, however, wasn't interested in that fight. At least not one against the Legion. He sighed. "Come on. I'll show you the way. It might not be as simple as you hope it to be, though."

21

Triste hadn't been kidding about the cache being *buried* in the hill. The passageway opened in the back of the house's subbasement, leading down to a steel door with an old-fashioned dogging wheel in the center of it. Dav had only seen doors like that in holos.

"This is what was initially found, though this isn't the entrance to the vault itself." Triste twisted the dogging wheel and pulled the door open with a creak. Beyond the doorway was a landing made of steel grating, with steps leading down into the darkness.

Triste hit a switch, and a string of work lights flickered to life, illuminating the steps in a shaft that looked like it went almost a hundred meters down into the bedrock. Whoever had built this, they hadn't been fooling around.

Droma nodded to one of his squad leaders. "Tiny, you've got point."

Dav had figured that Droma would put his team of contractors on point. They had to be more expendable to the NCO than his own legionnaires. There was probably only so much that Droma was willing to let his legionnaires defer to the contractors, if that was the way he was thinking about it. The other three squads were out on security outside the compound.

Tiny, easily identifiable by his size as he stacked up behind one of his legionnaires, pointed toward the door. The two of them went through fast, N-4s leveled, the leej in front dipping his muzzle to cover down the steps.

Boots clanged on steel grating as the legionnaires streamed down the steps. Dav could only wait, his EH-7 in his hands, listening for the inevitable burst of blaster fire.

"LS-201, LS-678. We're at a sealed hatch. You'd better get down here."

"On me." Droma started down, not without a glance at Dav, which he responded to with a nod. He fell in behind the Legion NCO as he headed down the steps.

The stairwell turned out to be a lot deeper than he'd thought. They went down easily two hundred meters before they reached the bell-shaped chamber at the bottom where Tiny and the rest of his squad were spread out, at least four N-4s pointed at the massive doors that formed one entire wall.

"Holy strokes." Droma couldn't hold back. He looked at Triste. "This was here when you got here?"

Triste, who had accompanied him and Dav down the steps, nodded. "The entrance was camouflaged. My grandfather might not have found it if he hadn't decided that this hill was where he wanted his home."

"This is some major construction." Tiny was looking over the doors and the control panel next to them carefully. "Whatever's down here, somebody really didn't want just anybody getting into it."

Dav looked over the markings. They were in

Standard, but mostly alphanumerics that he didn't recognize.

They were also strangely crude. Like they'd been painted on by hand.

Droma asked Triste, "I don't suppose you ever figured out what the entry codes are, since you say nobody's ever been inside?"

Triste shook his head. "The console still has power —no idea from where—but nothing we've ever tried has opened it. My father was convinced that it was better to leave it sealed and leave the contents a matter of guesswork for our enemies, than to risk opening it."

Dav suppressed a disgusted shake of his own head, but Droma didn't seem bothered.

A glance at Aguilar drew a slightly reluctant nod. Dav waved subtly toward the Legion platoon sergeant, and the other contractor stepped forward. "I'm a decent breacher, Sergeant."

Droma simply waved an inviting hand toward the control panel.

Slinging his blaster, Aguilar knelt in front of the panel.

It was clearly old tech, and Dav hoped that, wherever Aguilar had gotten his slicer/breacher training, it had touched on some of the older stuff. He stepped back a little, while the rest of the contractors and legionnaires held their positions. The legionnaires maintained security, as did Sones and Sayavong, though Vin seemed to just be hanging out, and Hesand wasn't sure where to stand, especially since every angle seemed to be covered, and

Vin wasn't visibly concerned.

Dav considered addressing that little problem, but with Tiny's legionnaires watching and listening, he didn't figure it was the time or the place. Vin was a team problem.

Aguilar carefully removed the housing, pausing for a second before taking the faceplate all the way off. Pulling an ultrabeam from his gear, he shone it inside, grunted, and reached inside, holding the housing at the same distance.

Dav tried not to fidget as Aguilar carefully tried several connections in the ancient circuitry, feeling his nerves get stretched a little tighter with every failed connection. He could only imagine what sort of traps might be set for a slicer trying to get through that door, traps that may or may not be something that a later slicer would even know about.

Finally, Aguilar paused and turned to look at them. "Everybody might want to stand back a little. This is the last connection I can make, and if it goes wrong, well... either the doors are going to fuse shut, or something very unpleasant might happen."

The legionnaires backed off without a word, and his contractors followed their lead. Not that they needed to move that far. None of them were hanging out in the fatal funnel of the doors as it was.

Aguilar made the final connection, and something clunked deep in the rock wall beyond. There was a hiss, and then the heavy doors started to come apart. Aguilar, as stoic as he usually was, let out a long sigh of relief.

The doors had barely opened a meter when a storm of blaster fire ripped through the opening, tearing into the stairs and the frame and blowing glowing pits in the stone on the far side. Tiny tossed a banger through the opening, but the blaster fire didn't slacken.

Dav started to ease out as the doors continued to open, looking for a target.

The continual stream of blaster fire didn't change its angle, which gave him reason to think they weren't dealing with war bots. Sure enough, as the doors continued to slowly roll back, he got a glimpse of a sentry gun set up just inside, spraying bolts through the opening and against the far wall. It was traversing from side to side, but it didn't seem to be tracking in on anything. A second turret was firing from the opposite side.

He put two bolts into the first sentry gun, and it stopped firing.

Tiny did the same to the other sentry, and the blaster fire from inside the vault abruptly ceased. The entryway went quiet, and Dav could smell the ozone and superheated metal even inside his helmet.

"Moving." Tiny stepped forward and swept through the door, his N-4 leveled. Dav did the same from his side, since he was closest, the rest of the legionnaires flowing in behind them, followed by the contractors.

They found themselves in a massive impervisteel half-cylinder. The two wrecked sentry guns stood in front of a simple, manual door. The floor was made of more metal grating, showing Dav that the whole construct was a massive cylinder about the size of a ship.

Someone had gone to a lot of trouble to build and conceal this facility.

Tiny was moving carefully, scanning the entire room slowly, his visor just above his N-4's sights. He was probably checking for lidar traps, which Dav's Krall helmet wasn't equipped for.

They closed on the door, the legionnaires once again stacking up on either side of it.

Aguilar moved up to continue in his role as breacher, but was waved away.

"Step back." Tiny reached for the handle. "We'll take this one."

Dav assembled with his team and half expected the door to be locked, but the outer blast doors seemed to have been the facility's primary line of defense. It swung open with a protesting creak, the hinges having seized a little in the damp underground.

The legionnaires flooded through the door, blasters up. It was dark as pitch on the other side, and even with his helmet's light amplification, Dav could barely see anything when he and Droma swept through behind Tiny's squad, Sayavong and Sones right on his heels, the rest of the team taking up the rear. He could see enough, though, to tell that they were in a tunnel that extended deep into the mountainside.

"Who built this?" Sayavong asked no one in particular. The tunnel was silent as the grave, except for the faint click of armored boots.

"Markings are all in Standard, so it had to be humans," Droma answered, keeping his volume down.

"Maybe some pre-Savage Wars colony?"

Sones spoke up. "Not with those defenses. Those turrets shot blaster bolts—those didn't exist prior to the Savage Wars."

That seemed to be news to both Dav and Droma.

Sayavong chimed in his own expertise. "Those sentries are old, but they weren't ancient."

The Legion NCO offered another guess. "Pirates, then. Maybe. But more successful pirates than I've heard of lately."

"Still feels pretty old," Dav insisted. "Maybe some group we've never heard of, who got wiped out by either the Savages or the Legion." He scanned the walls as they continued to move inward, the legionnaires splitting up to either side, cross-covering for each other as they paced their way down the tunnel while the contractors worked security.

The tunnel didn't curve left or right, but continued straight back into the mountain. *If there are more of those sentry bots at the end, this could get ugly.*

Dav checked behind him. He'd been absorbed enough in what was in front of them that he'd lost track of his own team. Vin was behind Droma, but instead of Hesand, Sones was right behind him. The older hullbuster was keeping a close, gimlet eye on their resident problem child. Dav would have to remember to thank him for that.

Tiny's point man stopped, holding up a gauntleted fist that glinted in the faint glow coming from the doors behind them. Everyone halted and dropped to a knee, getting as close to the walls as possible.

Dav just hoped that whatever second line of defense on this vault there might be, the people who'd set it up hadn't anticipated that and set their next sentry guns to shoot right along the walls.

It was what he'd do.

Tiny was peering through the darkness ahead with his bucket.

"Looks like another set of blast doors with two more sentry guns in front of them. Old stuff, still. Their sensors can't have picked us up yet, since they haven't started shooting." Tiny looked over his shoulder at Droma. "What do you want to do, Sarge?"

"Wish we had some bot-poppers," Droma muttered.

"Not sure those would work," Sayavong put in. "These sentry guns tend to be dumb as bricks and about as delicate. We ran into some in a raid on Yubosh Station, back in the day. We *had* bot-poppers, and they didn't do sket."

"Can you make the shot, Tiny?"

Tiny's reply was a rapid pair of blaster bolts. Somewhere down the tunnel, something died in a flash in a shower of sparks. Then another.

"Way's clear, Sarge."

"Move out."

They continued, not rushing, but not moving slowly, either. Dav fell into that combat glide as if he'd been doing it all his life—which was pretty close to the truth. When he checked over his shoulder, he saw that Aguilar, Sones, and Sayavong had done the same. Hesand was trying to follow suit, but Vin was basically walking.

He was seriously starting to wonder about whoever it was that vetted Vin's qualifications when he'd first signed up for a high-risk protection job. Maybe they'd just seen his rank and assumed he knew what he was doing.

They closed the last two hundred meters to the smoking remains of the sentry guns and the next set of doors.

"Big doors." Tiny looked back at where Triste was still trailing the contractors, half hidden behind Sayavong's bulk. "This is one hell of an installation. Seems like more than just a small arms cache."

"I don't care how big it is if it leads us to a few more AP missiles. Maybe a heavy repeater." Droma spoke through his robotic external speakers, probably for Triste and the contractor's benefit. They weren't exactly in the greatest position to be exploring, though it occurred to Dav that if they really needed to, they could defend this vault indefinitely. Cel Tradat and his MCR allies would have a terrifically tough job prying them out.

That wouldn't get them off the planet, though, or even get word to the Republic that the MCR had taken over.

Aguilar moved up to find the control panel. It was almost the same as the first one, and he got it open quickly enough, but after checking a couple circuits, he abruptly stopped.

Dav thought he understood the other man's hesitation. They'd had sentry guns in front of this door, too.

Would they be all that confident?

Aguilar retraced the circuits, then grimaced. "Clever little kelhorns." He leaned back and shone his ultrabeam at what he'd found, Dav and Tiny peering in over his shoulder. The explosive built into the casing had been hard to spot, but if he'd made the same connection that had opened the outer blast doors, the entire panel would have blown up in his face.

"There." He made the right connection, which would have been the first on the original panel, and the blast doors rumbled open.

No blaster fire came at them this time. The vault beyond was dark and silent.

Once again, the legionnaires led the way, spreading out as they flowed through the still-opening blast doors. Dav went in behind the squad's SAB gunner, who was still packing his repeating blaster. Not what Dav would have picked for a close-quarters weapon, but he'd seen worse.

The other legionnaires had stopped. As his vision adjusted to the dimness of the cavern he'd just stepped into, Dav could see why.

This wasn't a weapons cache. This was a base. And not some pirate hideout, either. At least, not compared to the sketched-out asteroid mining facilities Dav had cleared out during his deployments aboard the *Reliance*. This had taken major effort and resources.

A thin layer of dust coated everything in the massive room. Faint lights glowed on old machinery that was somehow still functional, but the main lights were off, bathing the entire chamber in gloom.

Hulks of old KSR-74 mechs stood lined up in the center of the space. Ancient machines, technologically speaking. They wouldn't stand a chance against an HK-PP. But they were a sight more formidable than anything else the legionnaires had.

Stacks of equipment lined the walls, and another steel staircase led up to a higher level, with more grating forming a ceiling just above the KSR-74s' hatches. The legionnaires started to move toward the stairs, clearly intending to make sure they really were alone in this old, mysterious installation.

"Toron, you and your boys start checking this room. I want to know if those mechs are serviceable, and if so, if we have munitions for them." Droma was already moving to follow Tiny toward the stairs. "Those could come in handy."

Dav turned to see Sones eyeing the mechs speculatively. "You heard the man."

They spread out around the room, examining the equipment cases and the machinery. Much of it looked like it was support gear for the mechs—including reloads for their rocket launchers. Those would be handy, as well... if they still worked.

Sones stood in front of one of the KSR-74s, looking up at the bulbous cockpit. He seemed to sense Dav watching him. "Been a while since I've seen one of these." He reached up and touched the handholds in the front, intended to give the pilot some assistance in mounting the machine.

Something about the way he said that gave Dav a clue. "Seen one? Or run one?" While he knew that Sones had been around, working as a mercenary in, as he'd said, a dozen wars along galaxy's edge, there was still a lot Dav didn't know about him, even after more than one contract alongside him. But if he knew how to run a KSR-74 mech, that could be invaluable. Especially if they went up against those Atavist tanks. Dav was pretty sure he could figure out the mech's controls, but someone with real experience would be way ahead of him.

Sones's helmet hid his expression. He was ordinarily so taciturn and emotionless that Dav couldn't even guess what he was thinking. "There was a time."

He didn't elaborate, but Dav thought he could read between the lines. The KSR-74s hadn't been front-line combat vehicles on any Republic-aligned world that he knew about for a long time. Which meant that if they'd been in use, it had probably been by pirates or some splinter group of separatists or even the MCR, somewhere out on the edge. Or a mercenary company, which the House of Reason often considered worse than pirates or the MCR. A company that had probably fought on both sides in some of those edge wars.

That last one made the most sense to Dav. Sones's history might have just become a little clearer.

Right then, though, Dav really didn't care. If the man had the experience and the expertise they needed, Dav wasn't going to worry too much where he'd gotten it. Besides, he knew he could trust the old man. They'd been through too much already. Somebody like Yuso might have thrown a fit if he knew that Sones might have fought against the Republic at some point. Vin almost certainly would, if only to advance himself. As far as Dav was concerned—and he suspected that if he asked, Sayavong and Aguilar would agree—Sones was on their side for this one, and that was all that mattered.

"Well, see if you can get it fired up. And then, if they're running, we're going to need some quick and dirty training." Dav looked up at the mech. It was perhaps four meters tall and almost as wide, heavily armored and sporting a small, reinforced cockpit window on its chest. It had no head to speak of, just a broad set of shoulders studded with weapons pods, sensors, and a what to Dav's eyes looked like a comically oversized comms relay. "I've never driven a mech in my life."

Sones sounded like he was smiling. "Well, you'll get to start with a classic, then."

22

Sones had fired up three mechs by the time Droma and Triste had returned from telling those topside of the discovery. Dav met the pair on their arrival. "Everything looks like it still works, and there are charge packs and missile reloads along that wall."

He pointed to where Sayavong was already manhandling one of the missile cases toward his chosen mech. The KSR-74's missiles weren't nearly as capable as even a modern AP missile, but they could still pack a punch, at least according to Sones.

"Good." Droma pointed to the ceiling overhead. "This place goes up another three stories. Most of it's living quarters and storage, including some ration packs that look like they expired about a century ago. But there are weapons. Unfortunately, no charge packs that will fit N-4s or SABs, but enough old TK-17s and charge packs to go around as backups. No AP missiles, either, but there are about two dozen single-shot Slammer rocket packs."

Dav nodded as all eyes turned to one of the mechs. Sones was in the cockpit, the canopy still raised, and was putting it through its paces, running diagnostics to make sure nothing had seized up over the unknown amount of time it had been sitting underground. With a growl of drive engines, the machine took its first step, the *boom* of its metal claw echoing through the chamber. The KSR-74s weighed a lot less than an HK-PP, so Dav heard it more than felt it, but in a few moments, Sones was demonstrating just how agile the smaller mechs could be. He took the machine on a quick circuit of the floor before bringing it to a halt right in front of Dav and Droma.

From the open hatch, Sones looked down at the two of them. "Runs fine. Everything appears to be working."

"What are they doing here?" Despite the urgency of their situation, Dav couldn't help but ask the question. Droma looked up, apparently curious himself.

Sones's lips were drawn tight, as though he were considering just how much he wanted to say. "I don't know for sure; I can give you a guess. There used to be a pirate gang out this way called the Sons of Vren. Intel said they were originally a merc company back in the Savage Wars. Their last commander, Kostet, tried to set up his own little empire.

"The Legion killed him about thirty-five years ago. My encounters involved cleaning up the last lingering elements trying to keep the Sons of Vren name alive. Pretenders, but in this same sector of space. My guess is that this was one of Kostet's bases. He was spreading things out, setting up to carve about a dozen worlds off the Republic to be his own fiefdom." He looked around the inside of the cavern. "This fits him."

Tiny had been tapping his feet somewhat impatiently and then blurted out, "Kinda curious how a

Repub contractor knows what fits some pirate who got dusted thirty-five years ago." The legionnaire wasn't being particularly subtle, but from what Dav had seen, subtlety wasn't exactly Tiny's strong suit.

"I know because I was with Rackham's Raiders thirty years ago."

Dav felt his eyebrows go up. He'd never heard of the Sons of Vren, but there wasn't a legionnaire in the 154th that didn't know about Rackham's Raiders. They'd fought both for and against the Republic on half a hundred worlds over the last century. Colonel Mateusz Rackham himself had become a legend, to the point that no one knew for sure who he'd really been or where he'd come from. He was nowhere near General Rex in stature, but in his little corner of the galaxy, he'd been larger than life.

"I'm surprised you got this job if you fought with Rackham's Raiders," Dav admitted.

Sones snorted. "Son, I didn't tell S-K Security *everything* I've done."

Droma was starting to get a little impatient. "The history lesson is interesting, but we've still got a battalion minus outside, ready to get KTF'd. Triste has his men getting some bots assembled to help get this equipment topside where we can use it. Toron, if you haven't already, let's see about getting the freight lift working so we can bring these mechs out into what passes for sunshine on this rock."

Sones powered down his mech and then slid out of the hatch, skipping the final rungs of the ladder that ran up its leg to the driver's compartment and dropping on the deck. "It's going to take a few more minutes to get the rest up to speed, but we should be able to walk them out shortly."

"Ooah. I'll get the lifter bots down here for the rest of the cargo." Droma looked over at Triste, who was examining one of the mechs on the opposite side of the garage. "Toron, keep an eye on our host, will you? We're on the same side for now, but you never know what opening another man's treasure vault might do to him."

Dav glanced over his shoulder at the man.

He's got to know that we're the best chance he's got. Hell, he *sought* me *out.*

Reality, though, is always different from the plan. The plan might have seemed good to Triste in the orderly shelter of his own home, but it had to be different now, with strange legionnaires running roughshod over his property and breaking into the vault his family had safeguarded for half a century.

Yes, Triste would definitely bear watching.

The lift was easy to get working and free of any traps or complications. Dav didn't have to do much beyond make sure a power supply was in place and then press a few buttons. Sones had those designated to pilot the machines, Dav included, learn the ropes by walking the mechs into the freight lift and then outside via a tunnel leading out of the compound that sloped steadily upward.

Dav was starting to wonder whether it came out at the top of the ridge. Finally, though, it terminated at another set of blast doors about half a klick from the silo, nearly a klick to the east of Triste's compound. He had no idea if any of the generations of ranchers that had preceded Triste had discovered these doors.

With Dav in one mech, Sones in another, and two of Tiny's legionnaires, Travis Nichols and William Westphal, driving the other two, the rest of their little force trotted along behind the mechs and Triste's lift bot, an old, rattling monstrosity that had to have been built when General Rex was a corporal. Triste and his head of security had not accompanied them, electing to stay back and organize the rest of the cache with an impromptu militia raised from Triste's family, staff, and select Barsota citizens.

Droma probably wouldn't be crazy about Dav no longer keeping tabs on the man, but he couldn't be two places at once. They'd just have to keep their heads on a swivel and be ready to KTF.

Dav was about to get down from his mech to hot-wire the door when Tiny jogged forward and slapped a switch on the duracrete wall. The blast doors started to grind open, and Dav shook his head at himself.

Of course they'd open easily from the inside. It was outsiders that the builders had been concerned about.

Driving forward behind Sones's mech, he stumped out into the cavern that formed the concealed exit.

It was low-ceilinged and dark. For a moment, Dav wondered if they weren't going to have to get out through yet another set of blast doors, but as he strode forward, he saw that the cavern turned sharply, opening out onto the hillside through a relatively narrow crack that would be difficult to see from anywhere but right on top of it.

This Kostet that Sones had talked about—if it had been him who'd built the vault—had known what he was doing.

Sones led the way out, trudging into gently falling snow. Dav followed, pivoting his mech to sweep the low shelf where the cavern had opened up, grateful that the vehicle's scanners and targeting systems all seemed to be in good working order. The machine was clunky, old, and stiff, and likely something would break before too long, but the KSR-74s had been built for hard duty in places where maintenance would be difficult.

The hillside was still and empty, except for a bit of thermal signature and movement up higher. Dav pivoted the repeating blaster mounted on the mech's shoulder, but quickly realized that it was just an animal, one of the prowling, six-legged pseudo felines that harried the locals in the north. The creature disappeared into the snow.

He kept pushing out toward the tree-studded slope below them, stretching the mech's sensors as much as he could while Sones delivered the occasional tip to all the drivers to help them handle the weather and terrain. The markings were archaic and the controls were sluggish, but he could make it work. Soon he was sure that they were alone and undetected. The storm wasn't bad, but it would help disguise their movement as they headed out to link up with the platoon and defend Barsota from the Mids.

Dav and the other mechs spread out behind Sones as he started down the slope toward the settlement and Triste's compound.

The mech's sensors sounded the alarm before he could hear anything. Alert graphics were projected on a recessed display screen dug into the center console, and lights began to flash. Dav looked confusedly at the unfamiliar symbols and displays.

"Artillery!" Sones shouted, deciphering the icons for Dav and the other drivers.

Dav's blood ran cold.

The Mids were bombarding the town from farther down the road.

23

Shells and rockets came howling down out of the clouds and slammed into the rocky ground with heavy crumps, vibrating the snowy terrain on the southern edge of Barsota. Black fountains of dirt, frag, and smoke cascaded from the impacts.

"Well, that changes things." Droma was on the comms with all squads. "They can continue to advance ahead of a rolling barrage, if they know what they're doing, and there ain't sket we can do about it. Unless we take out that arty."

Dav checked his instruments as he sat in the cockpit, somewhat grateful that the anemic heater inside the machine was still, somehow, working. The mech's computer traced the arcs of the artillery fire back to some point beyond that ridge. The blaster cannon on his mech's shoulder might be able to reach that far, *if* he had line of sight, but the curved lines disappeared behind the rocks and the trees. He wasn't eager to try to take a mech over the ridgeline that lay between them and the presumable point of origin for the artillery, but that might be the surest way to neutralize the artillery.

"We can use the KSR-74s," he said.

"Negative. The mechs will be too slow on this

terrain." Droma was firm. "Toron, I hate to jerk you around and make you do gofer work all the time, but you're the closest we've got to a liaison with Triste now, and I've got to get back to the platoon and coordinate in case the Mids have the sense to advance while they roll this barrage forward. I need you to park your mech by the compound and go back in. See if Triste's got any flyers we can use for a nap-of-the-earth insert."

Dav acknowledged and started his mech stumping back the way they'd come. He wasn't in charge. Droma might be about the same age as the brand-new rooks out of Academy before he'd punched out of the Legion, but Droma was the platoon sergeant. *He* was in charge. Dav was just a former action guy turned contractor. He had to swallow his pride and accept that.

He parked the mech at the gate, turning it around so that its weapons were pointed back down the hill, across the fields and toward the town, which was still getting pounded by artillery fire. He wondered, as he swung down to the ground from the open cockpit, just where the enemy had gotten all that firepower. Had the Mids brought it all with them? Or had Cel Tradat been preparing a lot more for a lot longer than Triste had told them?

Either way, they had to take those guns and rocket batteries out. They could worry about where the bad guys had gotten the weapons after the killing was done and the dust had settled.

With a wave at the rancher's security and one hand still on his EH-7 just in case, Dav went looking for Triste.

It turned out that their host did indeed own a flyer, a surprisingly new Mykova MYK-77 utility speeder. It wasn't designed to carry troops, but it would do the job well enough. They would just have to offset enough that the speeder didn't come under fire, since it was pretty thin-skinned and they had only their blasters to return fire with. And even that was small comfort, since they were flying with the side doors closed.

The pilot wasn't military-trained, so she was probably flying a little too high. Dav had been on Legion inserts via speeder that had been so low, the repulsors had brushed the treetops. This young lady was far too nervous about a collision to try that. So Stump was right beside her in the cockpit, directing her course up over the ridge and around toward the enemy's rear, all the while scanning the jagged rocks and snow with his Legion bucket to make sure they weren't about to fly right over a Mid flanking maneuver.

The ride wasn't smooth, even as the pilot did her best to keep them moving level. The storm might have been light for Temugol, but it was still heavy enough—especially over the mountains—to rock and buffet the flyer. Dav wanted to lean up front and tell her not to worry so much about it, that the leejes and his contractors—well, the majority of his contractors—had plenty of experience with rougher rides than this. But she was white-knuckling the flight yoke. Probably best to let her focus.

She banked around a peak and the speeder rocked alarmingly as a gust blew off the top of the mountain, bringing a feathery blast of snow with it. She held it together and turned south.

"Thirty seconds!" she yelped, the comms amplifying her voice quite well. "I know it's still putting you guys a few klicks out, but if this thing takes a hit, we're done for. I've got to keep us all safe."

Not the first concern in combat, lady, but I guess you've got to make allowances for lack of experience.

The speeder dipped toward the ground below, the snow turning to sleet and rain as they passed below the snowline. The taller trees rose toward them as the pilot flared the aircraft and slowed, closing in on a clearing about five klicks ahead.

In the distance, Dav thought he could just see where the batteries were situated. It looked like the Mids had set up a firebase on a hill that they'd passed in the combat sleds on the way out from Temugol City. Tube artillery flashed and occasionally rockets streaked brightly toward Barsota. There wasn't much of a pattern to it. It looked like they were just firing as they got reloaded; the barrage was pretty ragged.

That lack of professionalism was welcome, but even poorly disciplined artillery could do a lot of damage.

The pilot brought the speeder to a hover about a meter above the ground. The trees were behind them. In front was only rolling moorland and rocky hills, covered in the mosslike growth that made up most of the coastal vegetation. The doors slid open.

"This is our stop." Stump was already dropping to the ground, his poncho wrapped around his shoulders and his hood up. "Move out. Time's wasting."

Dav got out right behind him and moved up to put a hand on the young sergeant's pauldron. "Hold up just a second, Sergeant."

Stump looked over at him, and while his bucket hid any emotion, Dav was pretty sure he was glaring at the old man in the civilian armor. Stump was the squad leader, and therefore the mission commander. Why was this has-been countering his orders?

Dav pointed to some of the rough terrain they still had to get across, including some of the higher points where a sniper or scout team could be watching their landing zone. "Let's find some cover and make sure we're alone and unobserved before we run right into a fire sack, shall we?"

He thought Stump was going to argue with him, but then the younger man looked around and took in their surroundings more thoroughly. "You're right." Despite the robotic tone of the Legion helmet's external speakers, he sounded a little abashed. "Got ahead of myself." He lifted a hand and circled it above his head even as he put out the call over the L-comm.

Dav just faded back to his team. It was a lesson he'd had to learn the hard way as a young, hard-charging Legion NCO, too. There's a fine balance between speed and security, but if their insert had been observed, they wouldn't do the rest of the platoon back at Barsota any good by running into concentrated blaster fire.

Legionnaires are hard kelhorns, but it's easy to be hard. Sometimes it's a lot harder to be smart.

The squad and their contractor support spread out to covered positions, getting low behind rocks and into folds in the ground. Stump found his own spot and dug his TT-16 observation bot out of his gear, tossing it into the air before he got even lower behind a boulder, pulling up his battle board to watch the bot's feed.

The bot made checking for enemy presence a lot faster than it might have been back in the old days. After Stump had swept a half-kick radius around their position, he recalled the bot. "*Now* time's a-wasting." He hung back as his point man, a tall, almost skinny kid named Brad Stumpp who was called "Sheldor" to avoid confusion, started toward the high ground across from the mid firebase.

Leaning in to catch Dav's attention, Stump kept his voice low. "Thanks for that, Leej. Can't forget nothin'."

"KTF." No more needed to be said.

The legionnaires spread out into a wedge as they moved across the wet ground, the rain passing over them in sheets of gray. Their ponchos did a decent job of covering their armor, but every now and again Dav saw a glint, even through the wan gray light of the wet, stormy day. Curse the House of Reason pukes who, safe and warm on Utopion, had forced that garbage on the Legion. It might get these boys killed. So far, they'd survived— thanks to the sheer ferocity of Legion combat tactics, a testament to Droma's leadership and insistence on training his boys while his point CO had been off doing other things. How long could that last, he wondered.

Meanwhile, Dav had worries of his own. He checked on his team. As expected, Sayavong and Aguilar were keeping up, their heads on a swivel and their blasters ready to engage, executing a truncated V formation at the rear of the Legion wedge. Hesand wasn't as squared away, but he was doing his best. Sones was back with the mechs.

And Vin... Vin was all the way at the rear, and he was struggling.

Again.

But you had to bring him, didn't you, Toron? Dav thought that an unsupervised Vin would be even more a liability than a gassed out, dragging Vin. Maybe not.

Dav slowed for a moment, watching the man. The former sergeant major was genuinely fighting to keep up, losing his footing several times and falling. He was out of shape, having never expected to be conducting a cross-country movement on foot to engage in straight-up infantry combat. He was retired. If he'd even been infantry in the Repub Army—which Dav wasn't even sure about—then he probably hadn't had to do a forced march or combat patrol for years, even before he retired.

You don't belong here, in this business. But that hardly mattered now. He had the squad mates he had. They needed to adapt.

Stump had looked back, too, and had seen the same thing. He paused, watching Vin, but then he looked at Dav, turned, and kept going. Dav understood. Vin was his responsibility. Stump's responsibility was taking out that artillery, and the longer it took to do that, the more people were going to die.

Dav considered leaving Vin to catch up. It would serve the man right. But if he was going to lead this team, he had to lead it.

Cursing silently inside his helmet, he signaled Sayavong and Aguilar to slow down. They'd have to catch up with the legionnaires at the attack position.

24

Stump hadn't launched the attack by the time Dav and the contractors joined the squad in the rocks that formed their attack position. The Legion squad leader found the last covered and concealed point before hitting the enemy. Vin had sucked it up and made it the rest of the way, though he was almost falling down by the time they got into position. He was going to need a second to get his wind back.

There was no guaranteeing the legionnaires would let him have it before commencing their attack.

Dav joined Stump, crouched behind a boulder. "Looks like we might have to be the support by fire position."

He didn't have to point Vin out. Behind them, the man was flopped on the ground—but still making some attempt to hold security.

Progress.

"Thing is, I'm not sure we can spare the blasters for a support by fire position." Stump turned back toward the Mid firebase and handed over his field mags. "Check it out."

Dav took the optics and zoomed in on the enemy artillery. "Holy strokes."

He counted about half a dozen heavy cannons and

at least two mobile rocket launchers. Furthermore, there were three heavy lift speeders full of troops staged and waiting. They looked like they were getting ready to hop over the hills to do much the same thing as the legionnaires were doing.

Stump nodded in agreement. "We didn't bring any of those AT rockets, just det packs. So, we can call a warning back—and I have—but we need to do something about those Mids." He stuffed his field mags back into his gear under his poncho. "Trouble is, with one SAB and an N-18, we can put a dent in them, but we can't get all of them."

Dav peered across the misty valley between their position and the enemy firebase as another ragged volley of artillery fire arced skyward, shock waves blasting away from the gun muzzles. He couldn't count all of the Mids with blasters huddled around those speeders, but there was at least a platoon.

But there was also no sign that they had any idea there were nine legionnaires and five contractors right within blaster range, either. Surprise could count for a lot.

"I'll leave three of mine here to provide *some* support by fire and hold an escape route." Dav was thinking tactically, but he was also thinking about the fact that Vin was going to need some time to recover before he tried to move anywhere. Dragging him into a firefight was only going to get somebody killed.

Probably wouldn't be Vin, either.

Stump glanced over his shoulder again, as if he was reading Dav's mind. "Ooah." He pointed. "We can move up that little draw there, and get behind those two guns. From there, we'll have some cover and we can get right up on those Mids and their speeders."

Dav nodded. Legion combat doctrine was aggressive, and in that situation, getting to a position where they could mow down as many Mids in the first burst of blaster fire as possible was the best option. They'd come to knock out an artillery battery, so they had to get up close.

"You coming or staying?" Stump didn't look at him as he asked the question, but Dav got the impression the legionnaire was watching him anyway. The leejes were still feeling him out.

Unless he put the armor back on, it was going to stay that way, too.

"I'm coming."

Dav wasn't going to sit back here, out of the fight, just to babysit Vin. As far as he was concerned, the legionnaires' esteem was more important. He could sort things out with Sunil Kakar Security when they got off Temugol. If they got off.

"We're moving in thirty seconds. Get sorted." Stump was in charge, and while Dav might have bristled at the man's tone, he didn't object. He waved a two-finger salute off the corner of his visor and moved back to the rest of the contractors.

"Vin, Aguilar, and Sayavong. You're base of fire. Hesand, you're with me." Dav didn't want Vin left with Hesand to keep poisoning the kid's attitude. The fact that Hesand looked at Vin first, as if seeking his approval to follow Dav's orders, might have pissed Dav off if he hadn't already been in combat mode, calm and detached. Plus, he'd seen it so many times by now, it was hard to get worked up over it.

Fortunately, Vin nodded to Hesand. If he hadn't, it probably would have been a fight. So far, so good.

Sayavong didn't even look at Vin, but was already getting settled in behind that big CrimTech blaster of his. He might have done most of his career in the Repub Marines aboard ship, but the big man was a born SAB gunner, and Dav didn't doubt that he'd reap his share of souls with that thing.

Aguilar looked back over his shoulder at Vin. He might have sighed, but then he just nodded. He got what Dav was doing, and while he might prefer to be down in the fight, he also recognized that he was getting left back because Dav trusted him, above all, to keep an eye on their problem child.

Gathering Hesand, Dav moved back to rejoin Stump, who was already heading down through the rocks into the narrow valley below.

The legionnaires moved fast, hunched under their ponchos to hide the shine. Dav wished that he'd taken point. That armor was going to backfire.

And he was right.

Stump and Sheldor had almost gotten to the cleft in the ground that they were going to use to get up onto the high ground next to one of the big howitzers when there was a yell. A blaster bolt slammed across the valley, lighting up the gloom. Someone had seen something.

Vin, Sayavong, and Aguilar responded with a withering hail of blaster fire. Bolts flickered across the gap between the hills, and even from where he crouched, as low to the ground as he could get and scanning the horizon for targets over his EH-7, Dav could tell that his men were doing more than just spraying fire to get the Mids' heads down. They were killing as many as they could, as fast as they could.

He would have expected no less from Sayavong and Aguilar.

Stump didn't freeze. He surged up the hill, the rest of his squad right with him, except for Sheldor, who was down on the ground with a smoking hole through his shiny bucket. Things had started off badly.

Dav and Hesand moved with Stump. Hesand was young enough that he could keep up, though he was still sucking wind. It's a rare man outside the Legion who can get within a *pimble*-hair of matching their conditioning.

More blaster fire erupted from atop the hill as Stump and a leej named Scott Sloan reached the crest and began gunning down Mids as fast as their trigger fingers could keep up the fire. More of the legionnaires poured over the top behind them. Dav and Hesand were the last ones to arrive.

The firebase was complete pandemonium.

Blaster fire from the hill where the legionnaires had set up slammed across the gap. The Mids, despite sending down the shot that had killed Sheldor, were caught off guard. Now most of the enemy shooters were hunkered down, even as more corpses dropped when Sayavong or

Aguilar found a target.

Dav was pretty sure he could pick out Vin's fire. That was the wild bolts that were mostly flying overhead and disappearing into the storm. How had someone like this been cleared to even carry a rifle, let alone lead a security team?

Unfortunately, while the support by fire team was doing a good job of keeping the Mids' heads down, the legionnaires remained stuck in a hell of a fight. Blaster fire flickered and snapped between positions less than thirty meters apart as the legionnaires who crested the hill had to seek cover from the sheer number of MCR shooters. These enemy fighters had gotten themselves sufficient cover from the support by fire position and couldn't shoot back at Vin, Sayavong, and Aguilar, but they had a shot at the men in shiny armor coming out of the draw.

Two more legionnaires were down by the time Dav came up and threw himself behind one of the big howitzers. The automated cannon boomed again a second later, battering him with the muzzle blast, and a dozen blaster bolts glanced off the weapon's armor plating as Mids tried to gun the contractor down. Dav threw himself flat in the mud, shooting wildly underneath the mobile gun, and was rewarded with a scream as a man in gray fatigues collapsed, his knee having exploded under the impact of one of Dav's bolts. Dav finished him off with a bolt to the head, then rolled to his side, shoving his head, shoulders, and blaster just far enough past the mobile cannon's treads—and praying hard that the operating crew didn't just put the howitzer into reverse and crush him—to start shooting back at the Mids clustered near the closest speeder.

Stump was positioned in a slight depression in the ground on the other side of the draw they'd used as an approach, along with Steven "Star Fox" Smead, the SAB gunner, who was laying the hate as fast as he could. Hesand was still down in the draw, his blaster up but unable to get a shot. He wasn't moving, and even with the kid's visor covering his face, Dav could tell he was petrified.

Basics.

Two more legionnaires reached Dav's blaster cannon and took cover beside him.

As Dav slid out into the open, he started picking targets and shooting. He and Stump shot the same Mid twice in the same instant, four blaster bolts practically obliterating the Kimbrin's head.

He kept moving out into the open between the mobile cannon and the speeder, scraping his shoulder through the mud, blasting at any vaguely humanoid shape that blossomed before his sights. The legionnaires in the hollow at the edge of the hilltop with Stump were picking up their own volume of fire, and soon it looked like a Folkan thunderstorm on that hilltop.

The legionnaires had taken good cover, and between them and the contractors on the other hill, they had the Mids in a hell of a crossfire. A human MCR trooper rose up from behind a pile of bodies with a grenade launcher, only to lose his head to another pair of blaster bolts from the hill.

Dav shot straight down the side of the cannon's hull, and heard the engine rev. *Sket.* If he stayed put, he was karked. "Stump! Throw me a det pack!"

The Legion NCO chucked the brick of explosive to him. Dav slapped it against the hull, twisted the detonator to thirty seconds, and threw himself back into the cleft in the hill, landing in the muddy rocks next to Hesand.

"Get your head down, but then you'd better be ready to get some, kid," he growled, hoping he got the message across.

The det pack went off with a catastrophic *crack*, tearing through the cannon's hull with a brilliant flash, followed by an even more deafening and tooth-rattling *wham* as the gun's magazine exploded. Shrapnel whickered across the hilltop, and a piece of impervisteel screamed over Dav's head with a sound like a meteor tearing through the air. The shock wave flattened everyone on the hilltop, and the blaster fire stilled.

That was their chance. Dav surged to his feet, hauling Hesand up by the drag handle on the back of his plain tan armor. "Let's go, kid. Ain't nobody gonna live forever."

Surging up onto the hilltop, he joined Stump and the surviving legionnaires as they pushed out into the gap between the fiercely burning remains of the destroyed howitzer and the thoroughly wrecked speeder. A chunk of the howitzer's hull had punched right through the speeder's cockpit. No one was lifting that flyer again.

Dav got to the front of the destroyed mobile gun and almost got his head taken off by a storm of blaster bolts. It took him a second to realize that they were going the wrong way. They were coming from the other hill.

"This is Toron. Shift fire, shift fire."

For a moment, he wondered if Vin was going to ignore him and keep pouring fire into the conflagration on the hilltop. That was why he'd left Aguilar and Sayavong back there, though. Then the blaster fire ceased.

With Hesand beside him, and Stump and the other legionnaires on the other side, next to the wrecked speeder, Dav started to move up, cross-covering across the speeder's nose while Stump did the same for him. Stump fired twice, his bolts going past Dav's head, even as he spotted a small clump of Endurians, humans, and Kimbrin rallying near the second speeder.

Leveling his blaster, he dumped what felt like half the charge pack into the clump of them.

Blaster bolts punched through fatigues, flak armor, and flesh. A few desultory bolts came back toward him, but they were wild. In seconds, the entire group was down, dying or dead, and Dav ducked back to change charge packs.

Then Hesand chose that moment to play the hero.

Getting up as Dav ducked back into cover, Hesand rushed toward the next mobile gun battery. Unfortunately, Dav hadn't quite killed all of the Mids.

A blaster bolt took the young contractor in the head as he moved past the hulk of the burning howitzer. He stiffened for a second, then dropped limply to the mud.

Dav didn't have time to even think or feel much about the kid's death. He slapped the charge pack into his

EH-7 and laid down covering fire past the nose of the speeder, while Stump readjusted and started his legionnaires back toward the vehicle's rear. They moved quick, and in seconds another storm of blaster fire flashed and crackled behind the wrecked speeder.

The fire fell silent a moment later, as Dav continued to shift his position out past the burning howitzer, which was starting to get dangerously hot even through his armor, backed up by two of Stump's legionnaires. More bodies lay in the mud, while the legionnaires stalked forward, blasters up and looking for targets.

A legionnaire near Dav fired, the bolt stabbing toward one of the other mobile guns. A blackened, cratered helmet fell back into the hatch.

The outgoing artillery fire had ceased for the moment, and the hilltop was weirdly quiet.

"Let's finish this before they get a react force over here." Stump was already moving toward the nearest howitzer, pulling another det pack out of the bag at his side.

The det pack went against the side of the howitzer's hull. Hatches opened, and the crew started to get out, but they made the mistake of leading with blasters. They were smoking corpses a second later, and the cannon blew as the legionnaires ran to the next one.

Dav and his companions moved on their next target, one leej slapping another det pack against the hull of the next mobile gun. Those crewmen had bailed and were running down the hill, away from the firebase, but they didn't get far. More blaster fire from the support by fire position cut them down. From the wild spray of bolts, Dav suspected that Vin was doing most of the shooting.

It took less than five minutes to finish the rest of the guns off. Some of the crews escaped, running away into the smoke and rain. The leejes let them go.

Stump circled his hand above his head, and the legionnaires assembled back at the cleft they'd climbed to get up on top of the hill. Dav had shouldered Hesand's body, unwilling to leave it unattended and unburied if he could help it.

The kid might have been an idiot, might have been a basic, but he'd still been one of his, and if Yuso got treated that way, there was no way in hell that Dav was going to leave Hesand to the scavengers and the elements.

He wasn't the only one, either. Three of Stump's legionnaires lifted their brothers' bodies and followed as the point fire team led the way back toward the rally point and the LZ beyond it.

Behind them, the MCR forces' artillery support burned fiercely. Another explosion rocked the hills as more ammunition blew up.

25

Vin gave Dav a look as he appeared out of the gloom with Hesand's body over his shoulders, but if he had anything to say, it was silenced by the fact that three of the legionnaires were carrying their own dead. With the men hauling the casualties in the middle, the surviving legionnaires and contractors formed a diamond formation and stepped it out for the LZ.

Stump was already on comms to call in their extract vehicle. To Dav's surprise, the pilot announced that she was still in position at the LZ, waiting for them.

With a quick hand signal, Stump got them stepping it out faster toward the landing zone. The MCR had just taken a hit, but they were hardly out of the fight.

And if Cel Tradat really wanted Triste out of the way, there was no way he was going to let the loss of a handful of ancient artillery pieces slow him down.

The thrum of the speeder's repulsors became audible as they moved down the hill and back through the trees, and soon, through sheets of pouring rain, they spied the dark bulk of the vehicle crouched in the clearing, waiting.

It took seconds to get everyone back aboard, the dead piled on the deck at their feet, and then the pilot was adding power, lifting them over the trees and pivoting the speeder back toward the hills and Triste's compound beyond.

Dav sat in his jump seat and looked down at Hesand's body, and felt nothing.

Dav more than half expected to return to a street-to-street, house-to-house fight for Barsota, but instead, aside from some desultory, harassing blaster fire from long rifles and the occasional heavy blaster at the south side of the town, the valley was surprisingly quiet when they came in to land. Smoke still rose from some of the structures that had been pulverized by the artillery barrages, but the enemy didn't seem to have moved much at all.

Contractors and legionnaires helped unload the dead, hauling the bodies down to the basement to join Yuso. Vin was silent, though he helped with Hesand's corpse. Dav kept an eye on the man, but if he was being honest, Vin suddenly appeared old and tired. He wasn't so much mourning Hesand as he was just... broken.

Dav still considered the man a problem, but he now had the sense that he didn't need to worry so much about being shot in the back. No, now the worry was that Vin would do something stupid to make things up to a kid who was past caring about what happened among the living.

The former sergeant major had likely seen Hesand get shot from the support by fire position. The kid's armor was designed for security work rather than infantry combat, and he'd been plenty visible. That was probably a big part of why he was dead.

"They weren't expecting that." Droma had come up to join them and was overseeing the disposition of his dead legionnaires. With his bucket off, he looked as weary as Dav felt. Dav knew the feeling of seeing the kids who'd followed his orders and died for it. It wasn't easy. But you learned to compartmentalize it, stow it away for the times where you had the liberty to mourn the dead and question your own decisions. "There's been no real movement from their lines since the arty went silent."

Dav pulled his helmet off, the chill settling into his sweat-slicked hair. Krall armor might be some of the best on the civilian market, but it didn't have the climate controls of Legion armor. "So, what's the plan?" He looked around. His mech was parked where he'd left it, while the others were stationed on the high ground around the compound, weapons ready to engage any and all comers. Additional equipment was coming up out of the vault to be passed out to the locals in Barsota, as well as Triste's household, but they were awfully limited. Hardly the kind of supplies Triste had let his enemies believed he possessed.

Then again... they had mechs now. That could make a galaxy of difference.

Droma ran a hand over his face. "Dig in. Those mechs will help even the odds, but we're still outnumbered. No surviving a direct engagement. Legion or not." That had to sting to say, but the Legion didn't breed bravado. It bred warriors, and that required a certain pragmatism. Surviving and winning takes the judgement to be able to know when to attack and when to defend.

"We won't sit and wait for the fight, though." Droma paused to think. "Hop in your mech. Sones is already mounted up. I'm sending you all down for some urban warfare."

Dav had been through more than a few towns under threat before. At least a dozen during his last rotation aboard the *Reliance*. Barsota in its current state looked similar.

Most of the town was still untouched, though smoke drifted through the avenues despite the rain contending with the fires started by the artillery bombardment. The streets were empty, aside from the occasional vehicle abandoned on the sidewalks or the mad dash of someone who decided to be anywhere but there—and quickly. The remaining locals were hunkered down, which might be a viable strategy since most of the low, solid duracrete buildings could almost as double bunkers.

Dav's mech's footfalls thumped down the lane, the clawed footpads digging holes in the packed earth vitrified into pavement. These roads hadn't been built for a KSR-74 mech, but they would hardly be the only thing in Barsota in need of repair by the time this was over.

He followed one of the Legion combat sleds, with another coming behind him, Sones bringing up the rear to monitor the more inexperienced pilots. They weren't all going the same place, but this route through the town seemed less likely to be spotted by enemy peepers.

Legion snipers were doing their best to keep the observation bots from seeing too much. A blaster bolt snapped through the smoke up ahead, punctuated by a bang and a flash as another MCR bot died.

The lead sled took the next turn and howled off toward the eastern edge of town. Dav kept going, weaving between barricades built from duracrete and scrap metal. They wouldn't stop one of those Atavist tanks for long, especially since most were just piles of rubble, but they might slow them down enough for the legionnaires to get a charge on one.

Dav slowed as he got closer to the southern edge of town. More blaster fire could be heard up ahead, and his mech's displays highlighted directions and distances. The fighting was almost a klick away. The local militia's outer scouts were trading blaster bolts with the enemy's lead elements, though neither side had made much of a move yet.

Dav was glad of that. It gave them more time to get into position to thoroughly wreck Cel Tradat's day.

He eased his mech around another barrier, and a man in rough work clothes, carrying an old PK-9, stepped out of a partially ruined building and raised a hand. Dav took one more step and brought the mech to a halt.

Popping the tiny view canopy, he strained to peer out.

The man stepped closer. "Where did you find that thing?" The local's eyes were wide as he took in the battered old war machine.

And here Dav thought the militiaman had some important intel to provide. So much for that.

"Long story," Dav said. "We're moving up to the forward positions. You got any intel we need?"

Still studying in the mech, the man said, "They're taking shots at us, but they've pulled all but the tanks back into cover. We don't know what's coming next."

That wasn't much but Dav gave his thanks and buttoned up again, starting the mech lurching down the road once more.

It didn't take long to get to the outer defenses from there. The artillery damage along the way was much worse here at the edge of town. Massive holes were blown in their walls and ceilings, some buildings were hit so hard that they weren't much more than piles of rubble with short, battered chunks of wall still sticking up through the debris.

The militia was dispersed among the wreckage, and the KSR-74's sensors was picking up a few of them, highlighting them in the mech's HUD. Dav spied a number of troopers the sensors missed, and the old mech's rudimentary targeting system had no way to identify who was an enemy and who was friendly. Transponders were required for that, and while there may have been some amid the supplies in the mountain vault, those hadn't been distributed to the local farmers, ranchers, mechanics, and shopkeepers who had taken up arms to defend their town. Most were lucky just to have the basic flak armor that had come out of Triste's vault.

Dav paused to scan the wreckage and the slope leading down to the main road and the enemy positions. He grimaced. There weren't a lot of places where he could take cover with the KSR-74. Mechs weren't exactly built with cover and concealment in mind, unlike tanks, or even combat sleds, which could slide back into defilade easily enough.

He thought about pinging Sones on the comms for some advice when a combat sled rumbled past him, moving toward a nearly flattened building that had already been cleared away, leaving a glorified revetment for the vehicle to slide into. The twins were about the only part of it that stood above the rubble once the leej who was driving powered down the repulsors and lowered the skirts to the ground.

Deciding that he probably wasn't going to find a better spot, Dav eased the mech in close to a boxy, two-story building with shattered windows and a smashed, illegible red-and-white sign. It wasn't perfect cover, but he could get the bulk of the mech out of sight from the road.

And not a moment too soon.

A hail of mortar rounds came whistling down out of the sky, hammering the wrecked buildings along the main road. Even as they threw fountains of dirt, mud, and even blood skyward, the Atavist tanks, howling like banshees, throttled up and started down the slope, their repeating blasters shifting, searching for targets.

Behind them came the technicals and the crude combat sleds, maneuvering through the wreckage of the kill zone where the Legion had stopped their column cold earlier in the day. It felt like far longer, but then, that tends to happen when sleep is a luxury.

In a full Legion operation, there might have been a detailed fire plan, but Dav hadn't gotten a range card for this position, and he sure hadn't had time to work one up except in his head. Once the first local militiamen opened fire randomly with blasters, he had no choice but to join them in support.

One of the technicals returned fire immediately, a heavy blaster bolt taking the head off the man right in front of him. Then the lead Atavist rotated its turret and unleashed a torrent of blaster fire on the nearest wrecked building, bolts punching glowing holes through duracrete and turning the men covering behind the crumbling walls into smoking meat.

It was time for Dav to act.

As devastating as the KSR-74's heavy blaster cannon could be, Dav didn't think it was going to do much more than scratch those light tanks. It would require one of the rockets in its boxy launcher over his left shoulder or nothing.

And that meant he would have to expose himself to those heavy repeating blasters.

The KSR-74 wasn't designed to sidestep, so Dav had to get inventive with his next maneuver. He backed up and then started to turn, pivoting the mech's weapons toward the corner as he stepped out into the street.

One of the Atavist's main cannon bolts could probably punch straight through his armor, something Dav was entirely too aware of as he stepped out into the open street, laid his rocket launcher's aiming reticle on the nearest tank, and cut loose.

The launcher had been set for a ripple fire, which he hadn't intended. Three rockets streaked across the opening on tongues of flame, crossing the not-quite-hundred-meter gap in an eyeblink. One didn't clear the ruin directly before him, smashing into a duracrete wall in a thunderous explosion that spewed fragments and dust toward the tank.

The second rocket missed, careening over the Atavist's turret to blow a crater in the muddy, rocky ground beyond it.

The third hit the tank dead center.

Those rockets were equipped with warheads designed to punch through the armor of MBTs, albeit MBTs from a century before. The Atavist, while not quite that old, was lightly armored enough not to stand a chance.

The warhead drove right through the relatively thin side armor, punched deep into the hull, and detonated, sending a jet of white-hot flame roaring up through the turret, blowing the hatches off and sending them flying.

What little of anyone still left inside that vehicle was thoroughly cooked and dead.

However, Dav had made himself a target, and now he backstepped quickly, even as the Legion combat sled opened fire with the twins, stitching heavy blaster bolts across three of the technicals that had been moving up behind the Atavist. The combat sled's driver was already starting up the repulsors and beginning to fall back, even as another volley of mortar rounds whistled down out of the sky.

The militia was falling back too. They weren't exactly breaking contact in good order, though. Most were just scrambling out of their hasty cover and turning to run. Many of them paid for that haste, despite the legionnaires doing their best to lay down covering fire.

Another Atavist roared up onto the hill directly south and hosed down the ruins with blaster fire before spotting Dav's mech, his rocket launcher already rotating toward it, and retreating back into defilade to the south.

Dav let out a breath he hadn't realized he'd been holding as he continued to backstep toward the corner behind him. He hoped that the fleeing militiamen—those few who had survived being mowed down by that long burst of blaster fire to get behind the wreckage acting as barricades—were aware enough to stay out from underfoot.

The Legion sled paced his mech while mortar rounds and heavy blaster fire raked the outskirts of town. Dav kept his blaster cannon hot while the legionnaire on the twins put even more fire down. They weren't the only ones, either. Something exploded somewhere off to Dav's left, sending a massive fireball skyward, and more and more blaster fire crackled and roared in that direction, where he'd last seen the lead sled headed.

"Toron, Droma." He could barely hear the comm

over the cacophony outside. He swept his blaster cannon across the street, this time catching a squad of MCR infantry attempting to advance. His bolts blew at least two of them apart in the first hits. "Fall back to Horegosk Street. We're going to pull them the rest of the way in, then slam the door. Sones's mech will cover."

Dav sent another burst of blaster fire raging down the street. Then, as the sled pulled in behind him, the twins oriented to the rear and still laying the hate, he pivoted and went stumping back through the barricades toward the next line of defense.

26

Without an L-comm, there was a limit to how much battle data Dav could get; the mech helped with that. It wasn't particularly sophisticated, being bare-bones and simple even for its time, but it had a data link that allowed Droma to push a packet to him.

The Legion NCO's message was encouraging. They'd bloodied the MCR forces, all right. Two Atavist tanks burned, and half a dozen technicals lay destroyed, shot full of holes and either smoking or outright on fire. Bodies were strewn across the main road, swathed in smoke.

The Mids were getting cautious again, but they hadn't pulled back. The two remaining Atavists advanced up the main road, this time with full infantry support. Men with blasters and flak armor paced up the street on either side, just ahead of the tanks, looking to ferret out any ambushes.

Either they were learning, or the Active Stupid Mids were already dead. Dav had fought the Mid-Core Rebellion enough to know that they weren't always on the same page, and a lot of their commanders were rank amateurs who really didn't know much about warfare.

The rebels pushed toward the stubby tower at the center of the town, the hub from which the spokes of the "wheel" that was the town's layout radiated. Triste was another matter—if it really was him that they were after. After taking the town center, they'd need to besiege the man's compound on the hill above Barsota. Then again, Dav told himself, possibly they had no intention of taking the town at all, but were just trying to push through the city instead of tackling the rougher terrain to the east that might put them on Triste's flank.

The contractors and legionnaires had fallen back with the Barsota constabulary to a line about three blocks from the city's central tower. They hadn't quite formed a perimeter, but were arrayed in something more like an arc, running from the small industrial district to a series of residential blocks along the eastern edge of the town.

Dav had his KSR-74 hunkered down in a walled compound near the inside edge of that residential area, next to Sones's mech, while Sayavong, Aguilar, and Vin were set into the surrounding structures. Meathook's squad was set in on their right, in a series of small commercial buildings, using the thick duracrete walls for cover from blaster fire and explosives.

Beauty was several blocks ahead of them, closer to the destroyed southern district that they'd just fallen back from. Dav wasn't entirely sure where Tiny and Droma were at the moment.

This part of town had been spared all but one or two of the artillery shells. It still looked rough. Like most edge-world cities, Barsota was not wealthy; the weather had worn the place down well before the enemy ever arrived and the locals had few resources to spend on maintenance. Dav saw the wisdom of those first colonists who'd printed their duracrete buildings so solidly—it was necessary just to keep them standing. The first leg in a race against time where those pioneers hoped that prosperity would come to future generations before what they'd left them was finally eaten away by the planet itself.

Sporadic blaster fire echoed across the city, and the MCR mortars continued to pound its southern edge, which was now a smashed and desolate no-man's-land set between the rebels and the legionnaires and the local militia who had fallen back. As long as those rippling chains of explosions continued, Dav figured the enemy's advance would wait.

Of course, as soon as he thought that, the mortar fire stopped.

"Here we go." Sones was getting downright chatty now that he was behind the controls of a KSR-74. Maybe old memories were loosening him up a little.

For a few minutes, all was still. Dav wished that his mech had its own observation bot, like the combat sleds, but a moment later a data window opened up with the feed from Droma's battle board.

"Obs-bot has visuals on advancing MCR," Droma reported.

Several technicals were working their way into the side streets, supporting infantry that carefully picked their way through the rubble. From the observation bot's feed, it looked like there were two such elements working their way up along the flanks of the two tanks, each one with its own additional dedicated infantry support.

It was almost textbook. Except that they should have kept up their artillery support, but Dav and the Legion had denied them that ability.

Tiny's legionnaires lay in wait for the flankers. Dav couldn't see them from his position inside the small compound, but the battle board feed fixed them on a map of the city. Droma was keeping contractors as informed of the situation through comms as the legionnaires were through their buckets. Dav appreciated it.

The Mids were bordering on being too cautious. The flankers were falling behind the tanks. The MCR battlefield commander should be fixing that, but as time went on, the flankers only continued to flag behind. That told Dav that the rebels were rather lacking in the coordination department, too. So much the better.

Tiny and another of his legionnaires stepped out from behind a low duracrete garage with AP launchers already shouldered. The missiles slammed down the street, one almost skipping off the top of a barricade of duracrete blocks and what looked like an ancient, broken-down tractor. A wheeled one, even.

The first technical got hit right in front of its cab. White-hot plasma blew right through it and out the other side, immolating the gunner on the old GKV-14 medium blaster mounted in the bed. The crude, bolted-on armor didn't so much as slow the warhead down.

The second took more of a glancing hit, but it was enough. The blast knocked the sled halfway around, its skirts plowing into the rubble as its repulsors lost power. The warhead's detonation sheared half the front away, and if it hadn't hit quite the way it had, the vehicle might have flipped over.

Then the power cell exploded, ripping the sled apart and taking the dazed gunner and his weapon with it.

Tiny's squad was moving ahead of the two Legion heavies, who, with the damage done, dropped their AP missile launchers and slung their N-4s to follow.

A Legion SAB gunner swept the street from his position in a second-story window, while the legionnaire on the N-18 smoked what looked like a patrol leader just beyond the wreckage of the second sled. The rest of the squad burst from the buildings on either side of the street and began to bound forward, first on one side of the street, then on the other, each element laying down more blaster fire to cover the movement of the other as they leapfrogged from building to building.

Blaster fire ripped through shocked and dazed Mids, sending them sprawling across the smoking rubble. A few shot back wildly, but they were caught in the open and knew it and soon threw themselves behind whatever protection they could find. The legionnaires moved from cover to cover, never without high-intensity blaster fire to keep enemy heads down. Every time a covering MCR element started to get reasonably effective fire on the advancing legionnaires, they received serious attention from the guys on the SAB and the N-18.

Being legionnaires, neither man missed much.

The MCR might have stood a chance if they'd fallen back immediately and in good order. The legionnaires were outnumbered, even after destroying the two sleds in the initial salvo. It was the sheer violence of the leejes' advance that had the MCR lose any hope of a rallying to counterattack as they either ran for their lives—most of these were cut down by devastatingly accurate blaster fire —or desperately fighting in small, isolated knots that were quickly cut off and surrounded by the advancing legionnaires and their fire support.

"Prodigal, Meathook. That's our cue." Dav blinked dumbly for a moment before realizing that Meathook was addressing him. He hadn't heard who'd come up with the nickname "Prodigal" for him, but he had to admit that it kind of fit.

"Moving," Dav replied. He'd been keeping the mech's systems on standby except for the comms and the most basic detection systems. Now he brought the rest of it up, starting the drive engines working and stomping out of the gate and into the street.

More blaster fire flickered from down the street, beyond where the legionnaires were cleaning up. It struck just past his mech's shoulder, blowing a glowing pit in the duracrete wall behind him. A large fragment blew back and struck the back of the mech's armor. The hit rang his bell and the bang echoed through the mech painfully. Several warning signals lit up his HUD as he adjusted his aim, and the HUD flickered out. He cursed, ready to fire anyway, aiming reticle or no, but thankfully it flickered back on again.

The legionnaires hadn't quite gotten everyone. About a block back from where Tiny and his boys had dusted the two technicals and its escort, a heavy blaster team had dug into the rubble set back behind the wreckage that had once been a house. They were concealed well enough that he took a glancing hit to the top glacis before he spotted them.

Dav pivoted, bringing his blaster cannon to bear as he zoomed in with the mech's targeting computer. He fired just as the reticle came back, blasting a high-powered cannon bolt down the street and through the narrow gap that the Mids had been using as their firing window. More rubble collapsed in the aftermath of the flash, and the heavy blaster fire ceased.

"Come on, baby, stay with me." Checking his systems as he continued out into the street to follow the legionnaires, whose fire had slackened for lack of targets, Dav saw that the mech was still operational.

Sones checked in. "Dav, systems still live?"

"Yeah," Dav said, "I think I'm good." He spoke with a confidence he didn't fully possess. That hit had been worrying. As powerful as the machine might be, it was still old.

Just got to keep it running through this fight. Kick the Mids out of Barsota, and then we can figure it out from there.

He kept moving, the mech's claws stamping into the road. There was a faint sluggishness in the controls, but as far as Dav could tell, he wasn't moving any slower than before. With Aguilar following in trace, he moved toward the kill zone, pivoting his mech's torso toward the main road while keeping his eyes on the scanners.

Dav found himself wishing that he was engaging

on foot.

Should have passed this off to someone else. I'm too high up and too slow. It didn't matter that much that the mech could move faster than a human. It didn't feel that way, and he'd be a lot more comfortable on his feet, in his armor, with a blaster in his hands. He was a legionnaire, and very rarely did they ever do much more with vehicles other than ride them to the battlefield. He was sure that anyone—maybe excluding Vin—could have figured the control systems as well as he had.

Maybe he was selling Vin short, though. Maybe the other man would have done better in a mech, with the vehicle's systems to do more of the work for him.

Maybe Dav was getting more charitable in his old age.

It was too late to do anything about that now. He'd hopped in the KSR-74, so he was going to have to ride it out.

The feed from Droma's battle board showed that the tanks and their infantry support were getting closer and closer to the center of town. He and Sones were going to have to move fast. He brought his rig as close to a run down the street as possible, careful to avoid stepping on any of Tiny's legionnaires as they swept through the kill zone where the MCR technicals were still burning.

"Keep it smooth, Dav," Sones instructed. "Don't run out faster than you can react. You're not a legionnaire on the ground with an N-4. This rig doesn't have the same reflexes."

"Roger," Dav said.

Two blocks down and he was almost to the structure where the Mids had set up that heavy blaster that had winged him. Then he turned to the left, taking one side of the street while Sones took the other. The street was almost wide enough that the two mechs could go side by side, even with the handful of parked vehicles on either side. It curved as they advanced, forming a single ring around the central hub of the tower at the middle of town. Visibility was slowly opened up as the two mechs advanced toward the main road.

Dav stepped out along the street just in time to see the snout of the lead Atavist push past the corner. The tank's infantry support lagged behind, and the vehicle was halfway into the intersection before the first blaster-wielding Mids in gray appeared, cautiously easing around the corner of the building.

"Dust 'em!" Sones called.

Dav's fingers were already on the fire controls.

27

Dav put his targeting reticle on the tank's side armor as the turret with that heavy repeating blaster started to swing toward him. He fired one of his remaining missiles.

A tongue of flame belched from the boxy launcher, propelling the weapon across the gap between vehicles almost too fast to see. The missile hit the side skirts, punching through armor and rocking the tank as the explosion ripped through the hull and blew out the other side. At that range, Dav could hardly have missed and against that target, the effect was spectacular. There was a reason the Atavist had long ago been relegated to scouting and infantry support duties in planetary militaries beyond the core worlds.

Dav kept advancing, mainly because he needed to give Aguilar room to bring his own mech's weapons to bear. So far, the mechs could handle the tighter spaces of the urban environment better than most tanks could, but mechanized warfare in a town was still a nightmare. The only advantage the combined force of local militia, constabulary, legionnaires, and contractors really had was playing defense—the MCR hadn't had a chance to burrow into the buildings and the rubble, and they were that much easier to kill because of it.

The tank's hulk was smoking, though the fire hadn't really set in yet. It wasn't moving, though, and the turret had frozen while the heavy blaster was still pointed at the corner just ahead of it. No one had gotten out.

Dav pounded to the corner, still checking beyond the wreck of the tank and around the rest of the intersection, just in case the Mids had pushed a foot-mobile team ahead, armed with something heavier than blasters.

Nothing else moved, though the blaster fire across the southern edge of town continued to intensify as the militia and the legionnaires closed the jaws of the trap on the MCR's advance. With one entire flanking element destroyed, Tiny's legionnaires were now leading close to two companies of militia against the enemy column's western flank.

Droma hadn't deployed Dav and Sones to be the main effort here. Their job was to stop the column, or at least slow it down enough for Tiny and his boys to tear its guts out.

Sones sped up as Dav reached the corner and stepped out into the street, though not before launching a disruptor smoke grenade out into the lane. The grenade popped about half a block down, right in front of a second Atavist, suddenly filling the roadway with a conductive white obscurant that turned every electronic sensor within a hundred meters into hash. It wouldn't last long, since the stuff was also hot enough to blind most thermals, but it would buy him some time.

He'd marked the location of that light tank as soon

as he'd launched, and now blind-fired another missile into the smoke.

That one didn't hit as squarely as the first. It glanced off either the turret or the front glacis, slamming into the two-story block of a building behind the tank with a flash and a shower of pulverized duracrete, followed by a catastrophic crash. The corner of the building slumped into the street, cascading broken duracrete and steel on the tank while it hammered half a dozen heavy blaster bolts back toward him. But the tanker was firing as blindly as Dav had been; the cannon shots punched massive holes in the building and the sidewalk right in front of him but missed his mech altogether.

He backstepped, responding with his own blaster cannon. He had two missiles left out of the six he'd left the vault with, and he had to make them count.

Sones, apparently aware of this fact, gave a curt reminder. "Save those for sure things, Dav."

Way ahead of you. He held his peace, though. His fellow contractor wasn't wrong, and had a lot more experience with these monsters than he did.

More blaster fire flickered down the street as the tanks' infantry support and a couple of the technicals farther back in the column opened fire. Several of them were far too exposed to have tried it, and they died quickly in another storm of blaster fire from off on their flank. Tiny's legionnaires were putting in work.

The remaining Atavist's crew surely saw what the mechs were capable of, but they weren't going down without a fight. That heavy repeater kept spewing bolts at

Dav's corner, forcing him to backstep still more. Sones was across the street, having sprinted through the intersection while the obscurant covered his movement. He had the bulk of the dead tank between him and the surviving Atavist and was maneuvering around it when something drew away his attention—and fire—off to his flank.

"Got some Mids over here I need to take out," Sones reported over the comm.

"On it." Aguilar and Sayavong had kept pace with them, and while Dav had lost track of where Vin was, he trusted Aguilar to have at least set the man in where he might do some good.

The two contractors moved through the dissipating obscurant like ghosts, and then a burst of blaster fire erupted somewhere in the rubble off to Sones's left.

Some of the rebels must have worked their way around, or the eastern flankers hadn't been dealt with as decisively as Dav had thought.

As the fire from that direction intensified, followed by a tooth-rattling explosion, Dav started to suspect the latter. He couldn't spare too much attention, as the Atavist in front of him had freed itself from the rubble and was advancing on the intersection now, fixated on Dav's mech and continuing to blast chunks out of his meager cover with that heavy blaster.

The mech's armor *might* hold up to a direct hit from that cannon, but after the near miss he'd had earlier, Dav wasn't at all sure.

Backing up into the street, he retreated from the storm of fire coming from the tank. Fortunately, this wasn't a do-or-die line that needed holding. They'd done their part in slowing the column for Tiny and had the freedom to stay or go after that. It was time for them to go. But he couldn't leave Sones and the others with their flank exposed to that tank.

The mortar fire picked up again as some desperate MCR commander tried to suppress the flanking attack on his main drive into the city. Another burst of heavy blaster fire chewed into the building on the corner again, and it collapsed, cascading shattered duracrete into the street. Dav barely avoided having one of his mech's legs get crushed as he fell back.

He armed one of his last missiles. He'd been hoping to hold on to them for potentially greater threats, but if he got blown to smithereens before he could use them, he'd do himself and the legionnaires zero good.

Sones was thoroughly engaged on the other side of the street. "Toron, Sones." He sounded like he was talking through clenched teeth. From his vantage point, Dav could see Sones's mech spray blaster cannon fire into the increasingly blasted and glowing ruins to the south. "Things are getting hot over here. I'm diverting to support the militia on Casteria Street."

Dav acknowledged and took several long steps back, crossing the street and putting more of the rubble of the collapsed building between him and the tank. Locals, mostly carrying old blaster rifles but a few toting shoulder-fired missiles, came running up the street behind his mech, dashing from parked vehicle to parked vehicle. They might well be running to their deaths if Dav didn't do something to end the brewing fight between tank and mech before the militia was caught in the middle of it.

Content with his positioning, Dav set in and prepped the missile, keeping the aiming reticle on the corner, his finger hovering on the firing button. He'd have a split second to take the shot once the tank pushed past the hulk of its fellow.

The tank didn't come. Blaster fire continued to rage a block to the south, and more chunks of the ruined building on the corner kept getting pulverized by blaster cannon fire, but there was no sign of the Atavist.

The column had either halted or retreated. Dav had been so focused on his own targeting that he hadn't checked the observation bot feed for a minute.

They were falling back. The tank had reversed and was slowly tracking back down the main street while the Mids on foot streamed toward the south, chased by devastatingly accurate blaster fire that cut several of them down as they raced across the side streets. Tiny and his boys were still at it.

The mortar fire from beyond the outskirts was able to rain heavily now that the MCR was out of the box, and the legionnaires soon broke contact and fell back as more and more shells came howling down out of the clouds to blow holes in the streets and buildings.

"This is Droma." The platoon sergeant was on the all-force net, addressing the legionnaires, contractors, and local militia in the same call. "The enemy is retreating. All units fall back to Korivaneu Street and hold positions.”

28

Despite Droma's order to fall back, Dav waited. He had the mech and figured he could still do a lot of damage to the infantry and the technicals. And the more they could hurt the Mids out there in the outskirts, the better. Tiny was still out there and engaging. Dav decided he could do the same for a while.

There was also no way he was going to go back before Sones and the others.

He drove a block over and proceeded to move down a street roughly parallel to the main drag down which the Mids were retreating, all the while looking for an opening between buildings. He passed quite a few militia heading for the next line of defense before he came to the street where Tiny's legionnaires were still set in and fighting.

There wasn't a good field of fire down that lane. He could see the flashes from Tiny's squad's blaster fire, but that was it. He would need to move in closer. Dav started down the lane, the mech's footfalls muted in comparison to the crash of heavy blaster fire and the thump of mortar impacts.

Tiny's squad was hunkered down in a pair of buildings, hotly engaged with shooters in several buildings on both sides of the intersection. The sheer volume of blaster fire would have had anyone but legionnaires pinned down so thoroughly that they could only call for help and pray that Oba got them out. Tiny's squad, green as they might be, were fighting back admirably. Every time a legionnaire fired, one less blaster was shooting back at them.

Even so, if the MCR opted to halt their retreat and commit forces to clearing Tiny's team out, the legionnaires would be quickly overwhelmed. Dav waded in.

His mech brought its blaster cannon to bear and opened fire.

Heavy bolts smashed through the wall of the slightly taller building on the far side of the main road, obliterating several covered positions where rapid-fire blaster bolts had been pouring out across the street.

In the sudden lull in hostile fire, Tiny's legionnaires turned the full fury of their own fire on the nearest positions. In moments they were up and leapfrogging down the street behind Dav's mech as he tracked across the buildings, dragging a storm of destruction with him as he held down the blaster cannon's trigger.

"Toron, Tiny. We're clear." A glance in the small mirror mounted in the upper right quadrant showed him the Legion squad leader crouched behind a ground car half a block back. His hood had fallen back, and the wan light of day gleamed off his helmet.

Dav put the mech into reverse, continuing to rake the buildings and the street beyond with blaster fire. A few bolts smacked into the front of the mech's armor, but they were small arms, blaster rifles and pistols, and they barely managed to carve pits in the surface. He responded with full-power cannon bolts, silencing the oncoming fire with every ravening blast.

He continued to fall back until the curve of the street cut off his field of fire and that of the enemy. Then he followed Tiny and his squad back toward the second line of defense.

Behind them, a mortar barrage lashed the street they'd just left, sending still more rubble cascading onto the pavement and detonating a power cell with a thunderous *boom*.

"Thanks for the assist," Tiny said over the comm.

Dav smiled. "Couldn't let you leejes have all the fun."

Sones was checking over Dav's mech once the contractor had arrived at Droma's crude forward operating base set up in an industrial garage just behind the line of Korivaneu Street. "Power cell's still working. Armor's intact." He looked at Dav. "How's it driving?"

Dav shrugged as Droma stepped up to hear the assessment. "Felt a little slower than when we first took it out of the mountain. Computer's getting a little sketchy."

"Missiles?"

"Two left," said Dav.

Droma looked up at the machine next to him. "Better than nothing. Smead is gone, along with his mech." He let out a long, frustrated hiss. "We could have used the three missiles that chain-fired, too."

Coming from a point, that might have been cold. Points tended to be politicians—not always good ones— and often had the bottom line in mind. Coming from Droma, though, it said something about the desperation of their situation.

"We will need every munition we can get," Triste said, joining them. The old man wasn't heavily armed, but he *was* armed. That he was here, this close to the fighting, caught Dav off-guard. "We do have allies elsewhere on the planet, but it will take them time to get here, and from what little I have heard, they are facing resistance from some of the remaining TDF units in their vicinity. The governor—or someone claiming to be the governor—ordered them to 'pacify' their respective districts. Worse, I've heard from some friends in Temugol City. It sounds like two more ships have arrived, with more fighters, more vehicles, and more weapons. If they're right, even a couple of starfighters."

"Starfighters." If Droma hadn't been a legionnaire, his shoulders might have slumped. "Any sign that they're heading this way yet?"

Triste shook his head. "Not so far. I have lookouts up at the compound watching the sky, just in case."

Droma nodded, as Mayor Yalorak, a surprisingly young-looking man in flak armor and carrying a well-used PK-9, joined them. "The mortar fire has died down and most of them have retreated, except for the pocket just off Casteria Street."

Dav looked out at the street. Night was falling, made darker by the fact that no one in the city dared show lights, and the weather was closing in again. Dav had been on Temugol for about a week, and so far he'd only seen rain, snow, and fog.

"What do you think, Sarge? Use the dark and the weather to do a little raid?" Dav stifled a yawn. "After a couple hours' rest."

Droma considered it. "It's an idea. I've been looking for their headquarters when I've had a chance, using the obs bots. We might have a target, though they've pushed into the city, so it's not going to be near as easy as hitting that artillery pos earlier."

Nobody mentioned that that "easy" hit had resulted in one dead contractor and three dead legionnaires.

Sones stepped away from the mech, now interested in the discussions. "How many are you thinking?"

Droma rubbed his shorn scalp. He was showing some stubble over the last few days. "No more than a squad. I don't think we'll be able to just sneak through, either. We might be able to circle around the outside of town, but they'll be on alert."

"Diversionary strike," said Aguilar. Dav had been about to say the same thing.

Yalorak was looking at a datapad with a holographic map of the city projected above it. His eyes lit up at the possibilities as his fingers searched for potential locations for such a strike. As mayor, the man knew the city and surrounding region as well as anyone. "Perhaps here, in the old industrial district, off to the east of the pocket?"

Triste eyed the suggested location. "That is quite close to where Sergeant Droma estimates their headquarters is."

"It is." Yalorak didn't seem deterred. "That could work to the raiders' advantage, though. They will likely think that a diversionary attack would be far away, and so they will probably concentrate their forces elsewhere."

Dav frowned and glanced at Droma, who had done the same and looked to Sones. That wasn't exactly the best tactical wisdom he'd ever heard. In fact, it smacked of an amateur overcome by his own cleverness and a healthy topping of wishful thinking.

"I don't feel comfortable betting on that reaction, Mayor Yalorak," said Droma. Despite the Legion NCO's obvious fatigue, he was playing it diplomatically. "Tactically, we have to try to draw as many of their forces as far away from the target as possible."

Dav glared at the map and the dim red blotches that represented the probable enemy positions. They'd set in along an arc around the southern quarter of the town, except for that bulge of the pocket on Casteria Street. "That pocket's the most logical place to hit."

The contractor knew it wasn't his place to make such a suggestion, but he was tired, and for that moment had almost forgotten he wasn't a legionnaire anymore. But Droma only nodded, encouraging him to continue.

"It's exposed, and it's deep enough into the city that it makes the most sense that we'd try to reduce it quick, before they use it to push deeper. Hit it hard enough and they'll either reinforce it, or they'll pull it back while reinforcing their main line in case we try to exploit the retreat."

"Good," said Droma.

Yalorak looked simultaneously chastened and offended. But the man was an indig, and there was only so far the Legion would cater to the native populace they supported. To the Legion, winning the fight took precedence over being liked by the locals. The House of Reason, of course, saw it differently.

But nobody representing the House—the point or the special aide—was present. Or even still breathing. And the staff was huddled underneath Triste's house.

Droma focused on Dav and ignored the mayor's sulking. "Toron, I know you've gotten stuck in pretty good already, but we're shorthanded. I won't order you or your boys to go, but if you can send a couple, it'll help."

Dav was going. To the contractor, that was a foregone conclusion. "I'll see who else will come. Sones?"

"Given his experience with the mechs," Droma said, "I'd prefer he stay with the machines."

"Was gonna suggest the same," Sones said. "No offense."

Dav saw the wisdom in that. "Aguilar and Sayavong are always up for a fight. See you guys soon."

Droma waved a half salute at him, and went back to studying the map as he pulled his bucket down over his head to use the L-comm.

Dav looked around the apartment where Aguilar had brought the rest of the contractors. It had been a small family dwelling at some point, on the second floor of another boxy building with a clothes shop downstairs, but the family wasn't there. Hopefully they'd been evacuated to Triste's compound, or even to another town. The furniture was all in place, and Sones and Vin were sprawled out on any horizontal space they could find.

"Got a potential mission tonight," Dav announced.

Vin was snoring when Dav came in, but woke with a yelp as Sayavong dug a boot in the former basic sergeant major's ribs. "Got a mission," Sayavong told the man.

Dav continued. "I'm going, and I'd like some support, but I'm not going to tell any of you what to do." Dav had been thinking it over since Droma's words in the garage. They were contractors. There was no real chain of command in place for them. Dav was going because it needed to be done. Anyone else who came would likewise need to be a volunteer.

Aguilar laughed. It was a strange laugh, almost silent. "When do we step off?"

"Don't talk stupid, Dav." Sayavong was already reaching for his gear. "We've come this far. I may not have been a leej, but I never complained when we got to fight alongside 'em."

Dav turned to Vin, a little reluctantly. He already knew what the shorter man was going to say. And right then, he was just too damned tired for the inevitable fight. If it wasn't about the raid, it would be about Hesand, or something else. Vin wasn't going to volunteer. He should just leave it, get his gear ready, and get some sleep for the roughly two hours he'd have before they needed to leave to link up with Droma's assault force.

"I'm in." Vin didn't look at him, but he made a point of checking his gear. "Like Aguilar said. When do we go?"

Dav kept his surprise off his face as he studied Vin for a moment. The other man still wasn't looking at him, but something had definitely changed.

Maybe it was just fatigue, but Dav felt a flash of hope that maybe they'd get through this. That maybe this team was something more than a handful of only vaguely professional strangers thrown together for a paycheck.

He brushed it off. If Vin had found his impervisteel, he'd show it over the next night, or he'd be a corpse out there in the rubble.

He might end up doing both.

So might Dav.

So might all of them.

29

The rain had lifted by the time the raid force got into the two combat sleds and headed north, out of town and toward Triste's compound. The night was quiet except for sporadic blaster fire to the south, and the even more sporadic whistle and thump of mortar fire. The latter was spread out enough that it sounded more like harassment, rather than covering any sort of advance, was the goal.

Soon the sound of weapons fire was lost in the hum of the repulsors as the sleds wove their way through the web of streets and out into the fields. Dav watched the feed on the holoscreen between the troop compartment and the drivers. Droma had linked the feed from the sled's observation bot.

The valley was darker than any urban environment Dav had seen before. The locals had shrouded their windows and turned out the lights, so the only artificial illumination was coming from blaster fire. Clouds overhead blotted out the stars, leaving the legionnaires' buckets to struggle with light amplification.

Fortunately, other sensors could make up for the lack of ambient light. As the sleds turned west and headed for the ridgeline that ringed the valley of Barsota, navigation algos mapped out the rough ground beyond the fields, highlighting the herds clustered up against the ridge, away from the noise and fury of combat.

If not for those ridgelines hemming the animals in, the locals might have required months of work to get their livelihoods back together after the fight was over.

The sleds turned again, starting to parallel the ridgeline toward the south, circling toward the MCR positions. They planned to stop before reaching the rebels, however, intending to drive just to the outcropping beneath the shadow of a sheer-sided peak that stood out against the distant horizon like a black figure in the dark.

The sleds would be staged there and those inside would proceed on foot through the scattering of small dwellings and farms on the outskirts of town, slipping into the wreckage and rubble of the southern edge before the Mids knew they were there. The legionnaires had hoods up and cloths wrapped around the rest of their shiny armor as best they could, though the occasional glint was unavoidable. It would make infiltration tricky.

All too often, plans turn out to be a list of things that don't happen. So it was with them now.

"Sket!" cursed the gunner on the twins, a whip-lean legionnaire named Evan Boldt. "Our indig just went loud early."

The feed on the relay screen pivoted, and sure enough, a ferocious exchange of blaster fire was lighting up the blocks around Casteria Street. Either the Barsota militia and constabulary had indeed gone early—surely despite the advice of the legionnaires who'd stayed behind —or the Mids had decided to push out and try to drive through the locals under cover of darkness, before they could do exactly what they were preparing to do. Either way, the raid force was now out of position.

Droma called an audible. "Keep moving. We're staying with the sleds all the way in. Buckle up, boys. You leejes on the twins, keep your heads up and your thumbs on the triggers. We'll get as close as we can before we go loud, but be ready to rock when the time comes."

Dav checked his EH-7 for the umpteenth time, knowing full well it was as ready as it was going to get. There was only so much he could do, sitting in the back of a combat sled, but he felt like he had to do *something*.

He'd known legionnaires back in the day who were so icy, Parminthian cold, that they could wait in absolute stillness until things went loud. Dav had never been that way. He'd always preferred to be on the twins when he'd been in the Legion. It gave him more to do—and a chance to get stuck in first if it dropped in the pot.

They surged forward as the driver got them moving. The nearest buildings slid past quickly as the gunner up on the twins rotated left and right, trying to cover every angle he could as they raced into the south-side ruins. Artillery and the mortar fire had done some damage in this part of Barsota, but not as much as they would see as they got deeper. A few holes had been punched in roofs, windows had been shattered, and craters pocked the street. Walls were collapsed into rubble, and although many buildings remained intact, that often only made the situation riskier. A building that had already collapsed felt a whole lot safer to be around than one that might be on the brink of teetering over, and in Dav's experience, you often couldn't tell it was going to fall until the wreckage started to come down on top of you.

Droma was in the lead sled, a good block ahead as they entered the outskirts. That, plus the city's wheel configuration, made it difficult for the gunners to support each other, but the dispersion was necessary. If the Mids had just one team on flank security with a shoulder-fired missile, this could turn into a very bad night in a heartbeat.

They traveled three blocks, getting into the severely damaged parts of town without incident. Several buildings had been outright flattened, though most still had a large part of their walls and roofs standing. The street's surfaces were almost entirely covered by rubble, and several local vehicles, now burned-out wrecks, presented further obstacles that the sleds had to navigate.

A good hiding place, Dav thought as they passed one of those vehicles, *for a bomb big enough to turn a combat sled into a pile of twisted impervisteel and mangled flesh.* He waited, tensed, until they passed by. *Come on, let's stage and move up on foot.* If he couldn't be up in the turret, he'd rather be on the ground, a much smaller target.

The display on the relay screen shifted to an overhead image of the town, with the two combat sleds marked by blue triangles. A red circle pulsed about three more blocks ahead. That would be their drop-off point.

They didn't quite make it.

Blaster fire crackled from a low crumbled wall, splashing off the lead sled's front armor plating before its gunner pivoted and unleashed the full fury of twin N-50s on the Mid's hiding place. Heavy blaster bolts tore the MCR fighter apart, and sent blasted and glowing masonry to half-bury the man's body.

The lead sled kept pushing, actually speeding up instead of moving more cautiously. Dav's follow-on vehicle sped up too, closing the distance. The fact that it had been blaster fire rather than a missile or an IED was somewhat reassuring. They'd caught the enemy off guard, at least a little. They were still a good six blocks from their target, though. A lot could happen in six blocks.

Especially when Cel Tradat's MCR allies knew they were there.

Speed was essential, but the deeper they got, the more difficult movement through the ruin became. Rubble and wrecked ground cars choked the streets, forcing the sleds to slow to a crawl to get through the debris. That made them increasingly vulnerable, and gave the enemy time.

Sure enough, after about two blocks, someone opened up with a heavy blaster from a second-story window.

Searing bright bolts slashed across the street, skipping off the sled's roof and barely missing taking the gunner's head off. The kid—Dav had no idea which legionnaire was on the lead sled's twins, but they almost all looked like kids to him these days—ducked low, pivoted, and responded with a burst of N-50 fire that pulverized the front of the building and silenced the heavy blaster.

Droma had a decision to make, and he made it

swiftly. They still had four blocks to go to get to their target, but the more resistance they met, the harder reaching it via the sleds would be. "Everyone out. The sleds will conduct a fighting retreat back to the staging point. We're on foot from here."

There was no gung-ho, moto speechifying. It wasn't the time or the place. The legionnaires knew what needed to be done. So did Dav. And so, he hoped, did his contractors.

The ramp dropped, and Dav was one of the first ones out, almost desperate to exit the impervisteel coffin to the open air where he could fight.

The contractors and the legionnaires spread out on either side of the street, blasters ready and trained up and down the long axis of the avenue. They appeared to be in the clear. The only fire was coming from the lead sled, as the gunner on the twins laid the hate to cover for their dismount.

Dav saw a light source come on and then just as quickly go off from the recesses of one of the still-intact buildings nearby. Like someone had mistakenly shone an ultrabeam at their own ceiling. There were probably some civilians in those surrounding buildings, people who hadn't had a chance to get out before the Mids moved in. They'd do best to get low and wait things out.

Fortunes of war.

Droma and Beauty were near a bombed-out building at the center of the block. "This is Droma. Collapse on me. Beauty's got point."

Dav checked his surroundings. He was crouched

behind a burned-out sled that looked like it had taken a mortar round right through the roof. Vin and Aguilar were with him. Sayavong was in the lead sled with Droma. He pointed to Vin, then toward where Droma was ushering the rest of the leejes into the rubble.

Vin nodded and dashed across the street, between the sleds, both of which were pouring blaster fire into the surrounding buildings. Sones followed, with Dav and another legionnaire taking up the rear.

Droma was crouched at the hole in the wall, his N-4 in his hands, his hood pulled far out over his bucket. There was a lot of blaster fire ripping through the night, and while it was hopefully enough to dissuade anyone on that street from sticking their heads out, it was putting out a lot of light that might glint off a new Legion helmet.

Dav might have griped about how reduced his Krall helmet's capabilities were, but at least it was a flat tan that wouldn't shine at the wrong time.

Droma let the small team of raiders slip into the rubble, holding security while the sleds started to reverse out, still raking the ruins around them with blaster fire. They were putting out a lot of sound and fury, but after taking contact, they were probably hoping to draw the Mids' attention and make them think that the attack force had decided discretion was the better part of valor.

It took a few minutes, as the legionnaires and contractors wormed their way into the ruins, before the sound of repulsors and N-50s faded into the general noise of the violent night. Droma reminded his team—really it was for the benefit of Vin and the other contractors—not to fire unless ordered to. Their survival depended on moving undetected.

They made their way down to the remains of the next street, often down on their hands and knees, crawling through gaps between shattered walls and collapsed floors.

Dav was bringing up the rear by the time they crawled out onto the next street. It was every bit as cluttered with debris as the one they'd just left, but that was all to their advantage now. He hauled himself out of the rubble of a storefront that had collapsed outward and took cover next to Droma, using a fragment of the wall as a rest for his blaster rifle. Dav didn't have thermal scanners in his helmet, but he carefully searched their surroundings with every bit of night vision capability the Krall had available.

He could see the other legionnaires a little too well despite their taking full advantage of what cover they could find. No other movement met his eyes. This block had taken a pounding. Nothing of any building stood more than a meter high. Most of the vehicles that had been on the street were mangled piles of blackened junk.

Droma dug his TT-16 out, sent it aloft to circle, then retrieved it. "We're clear."

With Beauty's point man in the lead, they began to move from cover to cover through the nightmare landscape toward the MCR's command post.

30

The MCR command post was easier to find than Dav had expected, but when he thought about his experience fighting the Mid-Core Rebellion over the years, he shouldn't have been that surprised. Most of the Mids weren't professional soldiers. Some had no military experience or training at all. They could still be ferocious fighters, especially those recruited from harsh worlds closer to the edge, but they made more mistakes than the better-trained Republic troops.

From their perch in one of the few standing structures, Dav, Droma, and Beauty could see the slapdash camp that was serving as the MCR field headquarters. Two old UT-70 sleds were drawn up in what had once been a motor pool for a delivery company, both with single medium-heavy blaster cannons pointed north toward where the Barsotan militia were fighting like hell for the pocket near Casteria Street. A much more modern sled, without weapons, was parked between them, sprouting a small forest of comm antennas. Dav didn't recognize the model, but it looked military. Probably from an actual mid-core world's arsenal.

"Man, we should have brought some AP missiles." Beauty's external speakers were turned way down, his voice a raspy whisper. "Three tubes and we'd be done and out of here."

"What missiles?" Sayavong asked, in an even louder whisper. Droma had decided to husband their few remaining missiles for bigger threats, such as tanks. "Somebody been holding out on us?"

Dav continued his scan, wishing more than ever that he had thermals. He didn't see any infantry on the ground or in the structures around the three sleds. Those vehicles appeared to be it. If they'd had any security teams out, they must have pushed west in pursuit of the sleds after that heavy blaster had been destroyed. Or else they'd buttoned up in the sleds as soon as things had gotten hot.

"Nobody move yet." Droma pointed up, and Dav grimaced. He'd gotten so focused on the sleds that he'd missed the observation bot hovering above. The enemy wasn't completely blind.

The bot was going to make this a lot more difficult. The team had to get down there to the sleds and deal with them the old-fashioned way, which meant planting explosives and being ready with blaster fire to clean up any that escaped the subsequent blasts. If the observation bot spotted them on approach, they might never get close enough to execute.

"Think we can get any closer without getting burned?" Dav asked. He was trying to gauge distances and lines of sight.

"Doubt it." Droma and Beauty spoke at almost the same moment.

This part of town was pretty close to leveled, and

while there were plenty of low walls to hide behind and fine concealment from a ground-based observer, the observation bot hovering twenty meters overhead would spot them easily.

Dav was fairly confident he could hit the obs bot with a blaster bolt from where they were, which meant that the rest of the leejes definitely could, especially Spencer "Spen" Bromley with the N-18. He began to think out loud. "If we pop the bot, then Spen can dust the far gunner, while Vin, Aguilar, and Sayavong lay fire on the closer one. Then the rest of us move in, toss charges, and get out."

The contractor knew all too well just how dicey such a plan was, relying as it did on the assumption that there were no other reinforcements within a few seconds of the CP and that their accuracy would be perfect on the first shot.

He expected any legionnaire to be mostly perfect in a fight, but he had seen that Droma's men weren't *quite* as accurate as he remembered leejes being back in his day. Maybe it was just fatigue, but then again, leejes were built on fatigue. Which in Dav's mind meant it was due to slipping training standards, thanks to the points that were infiltrating the Legion. Regardless, they'd all have to keep their shots tight and fast to make up for any misses. Failing to take out even one gunner would result in the assaulters facing concentrated heavy blaster fire as they tried to cross the rubble-choked street and get in close to the vehicles.

Provided the drivers didn't just run them over

while speeding to relocate.

That was another problem. But the charges they'd brought were limpets that would arm as soon as they magnetically attached to their targets. Like everything pulled out of the pirate vault, they were old, but they appeared to be in working order. All the legionnaires had to do was throw the charges hard enough that they got close and stuck, then get out of the way.

Droma rolled back into the cover of the broken wall and pulled off his bucket. It was easier for him to talk to someone without an L-comm that way. "The other option we've got is to fall back and think up another plan."

Beauty didn't want to give up their current opportunity. "They might not be here, and they have to know that we gave it a shot already."

Dav was right there with him. They might not get another chance at this.

It wasn't a foregone conclusion that the MCR assault would collapse if their leadership was taken out, but it was likely. Again, the MCR wasn't all that professional, and without direct coordination, in Dav's experience, they tended to fall apart. The true believers would fight hard, but without that central command, they wouldn't do it well.

Dav checked his chrono, carefully sheltering it to avoid showing any light. "They don't seem to have spotted us here yet. Why don't we give it an hour, set security, watch and wait?" He looked between Droma and Beauty. "If they think we retreated with the sleds, maybe they'll start to feel secure. Might even pull the bot back."

Droma didn't seem convinced as he considered the idea, but nodded. "We've got some cover here. And we might be able to pick out any concealed security we've missed so far." He ran a gloved hand over his scalp before he pulled his bucket back on. "We've got about six hours of darkness left. Let's make use of it."

The next hour went by with agonizing slowness.

They lay in the wreck of the building and watched their target. Dav had never been on an official recon team, but Legion squads often had to fulfill just about every function of an infantry company. It was in the independent nature of how the squads were deployed. Especially on planets like Porovus, during that nightmarish six months before Keram had redefined the word. The planet and situation was different this time around, but the goal was pretty much the same.

Infiltrate, watch the objective for a pre-determined time while building a thorough map of the target area and figuring out exactly how many bad guys were there, what their pattern was, and what weapons and equipment they employed. Then, once sure that the squad could take their target without additional Legion support, they would wait until it got dark, slip down out of cover, and end them all in a ten-minute storm of blaster fire before disappearing into the dark again.

And hopefully, like on Porovus, Dav and his team squad would make it out alive and intact.

He hadn't thought about Porovus in a long time. Not everyone in Tiger Company had been as lucky as he.

As the MCR went about whatever preparations they needed prior to assaulting the city center, the legionnaires and contractors watched and waited. The hidden observers were crowded too close together, which gave them little room to switch off observers. They weren't going to be staying in place long enough for it to matter. They had four hours to observe, make their move, and get out. Dawn would come early, and while modern sensors made light and dark much less of a contrast, there were still going to be a lot of Mids out there relying on their eyes instead of fancy tech to see in the dark.

They'd been watching for about half an hour when he heard a hiss from Sayavong, who was watching the road they'd come from. Dav twisted his head around to look.

Four Mids with blaster rifles, plus another supporting a wounded man limping along, were making their way through the rubble toward the sleds. They looked shell-shocked, and they weren't keeping much of any formation. Blasters hung slack in weary hands.

They must have pursued the combat sleds, and it had ended rather predictably.

It would have been easy to end them right there, but doing so would require them to also attack the sleds immediately, or else break contact and get out. So they watched and waited.

For a moment, Dav worried that Vin would find the target too juicy and take it upon himself to drop the rebels, but all the hidden guns remained quiet. The little group staggered into the smashed-up motor pool that now housed the MCR command post. The UT-70s didn't show much reaction, except for the gunner on the nearest ZX-60, who lifted himself out of the turret to ask a question. The response he got was venomous, and he slid back behind the blaster.

The comm sled's ramp opened, spilling green light out into the lot, and a short Endurian came down, his hands on his hips. He didn't step off the ramp, just stood there, waiting impatiently for the patrol and the wounded man. The gunner on the other UT-70, on the far side, watched the tableau.

They think all the fighting is up north, and that we booked it out of here. There probably wasn't going to be a better time.

Droma thought the same. "Now."

Spen kicked things off with the N-18. Its *crack-bdew* echoed across the narrow street and off the fallen walls of ruined buildings. The bolt took off the top of the Endurian's skull.

The man crashed onto his back on the ramp, and the rest froze.

The attacking legionnaires and contractors did not.

Their blaster fire flashed across the street with a howling crackle, lighting up the night as they cut down the men on foot. Aguilar and Vin pumped bolt after bolt at the gunners. Glowing pits were blasted into the splinter shields and the turrets, which were still pointed the wrong way, and at least one gunner was hit in the head, dropping out of sight.

A bolt hit the ZX-60's gunner as he tried to bring his weapon around to return fire. The blast ate most of the gunner's head.

The wounded man and his helper had been the last ones to die, as Dav, Droma, and Beauty cut down the Mids with weapons first. They probably wouldn't have been spared anyway, but both had done the stupid thing and reached for their blasters after first freezing for a confused moment.

It was all over in seconds. The street fell silent, as the legionnaires and contractors had no more targets.

Droma, however, wasn't going to sit there and wait for something to happen. "We need to sweep that command post before someone comes to help."

Such a request had probably already been made. If they moved fast, they could get down there, kill whoever was left, blow the vehicles, and get out, hopefully before reinforcements arrived.

Beauty was already on his feet and scrambling down the low slope of smashed duracrete in front of their hiding place, his blaster rifle in his hands. Dav and Droma followed with the rest of the assault team coming after. There wasn't time to worry about order of movement. They just naturally fell into a formation, blasters up and scanning for targets.

Dav saw movement near the body on the ramp of the comm sled, and snapped his blaster to his shoulder. He fired a split second before the Mid could bring his own pistol to bear. Dav's bolt blew through the Kimbrin's throat and dropped him onto the Endurian's body.

Then they were across the street where more blaster fire snapped through the night. One of the UT-70 drivers had stuck his head out of the hatch, and Beauty proceeded to put a single bolt through his helmet. The second sled was starting to move, and Droma dashed forward, pulling his limpet charge out of the pack at his waist.

He threw the charge as the sled pulled out of its crude revetment. It struck with a clang, and then the legionnaires and their contractor allies were diving for cover.

The ten-second timers on those chargers couldn't be adjusted.

Dav's time on the ground felt much longer than the seven or eight seconds it truly was before the limpet blew with a deafening *crack*, splitting the sled's hull with a flash and a tongue of flame ten meters long. The blast threw the vehicle sideways, where it rolled over onto its back, repulsors dead and flames beginning to lick outside the hatches.

Beauty and the leej with him—Brad Chenoweth— were already up and driving on the comm sled. More blaster fire split the night, muted and quiet compared to the catastrophic death of that UT-70, as they cleared the inside compartment. Then Beauty tossed another limpet inside, and the two of them ran for the wall as Dav tossed his own charge at the nearer UT-70. The gunner of that sled was dead as was the driver, but there was no reason to leave it for the Mids.

The two vehicles exploded seconds apart while the assaulters fell back toward where Spen and Sayavong covered their movement from the hide.

That was when things went sideways.

An approaching technical with about half a dozen Mids in the back, and another wheeled technical following close behind, hadn't been heard because of the blaster fire and the explosions. It seemed to have appeared on the main street through a magical teleportation, weapons manned and ready for trouble, just as the assaulters were moving across the street, less than a hundred meters ahead.

Blaster fire snapped and howled down the street, driving two of the legionnaires, Sayavong, and Aguilar to sprint the rest of the way to get out of the line of fire. Dav, Droma, Beauty, and Vin found themselves cut off, taking cover on the near side of the street, not far from the burning hulks of the MCR vehicles.

Droma risked a peek up the street, shooting back even as Spen took the gunner's head off with a relatively close-range N-18 bolt.

The heavy blaster fire slackened abruptly, and the technical came to a lurching halt as the rest of the MCR troopers opened fire, raking the street and the vehicles with blaster bolts. The assaulters fired back just as furiously, and several Mids in the back of the technical were killed immediately, while others gave up their offensive and bailed out and sprinted for cover on either side of the street.

"Go!" Droma's external speakers blasted his raspy

command.

Dav, Beauty, and Vin got up to run, shooting as they went. Droma surged to his feet as they started their sprint, partially covered by Sayavong and the other legionnaires on the west side.

The technical coming up behind the first opened fire.

Searingly bright bolts crashed down the street, chasing the hunched and running figures across the open space. One stumbled and fell as molten duracrete blew apart right under his feet.

It was Vin.

Dav got to cover and turned, only to see the contractor down on his belly in the street. He was alive, moving, crawling to cover, but one mangled leg dragged behind him impotently.

The former legionnaire didn't think. His mind provided no snark or cruelty, no eye-rolling disdain at the man's slowness in making it across the street. He only turned back and dashed toward that torrent of blaster fire, even before Spen took the technical's gunner down, and added to the Legion sniper's personal reaping. He grabbed Vin by the drag handle and hauled him up toward cover.

They threw themselves behind the fan of debris below the wall, both men panting, Dav with exertion, Vin with pain.

Bolts smashed into duracrete and showered them with fragments. The Mids who had found cover were now shooting at them. And more were coming, judging by the howl of repulsors echoing ever louder down the street.

"We've got to go," Dav said, looking down at Vin. "Can you walk?" He really didn't want to have to carry the man, but hostile history or not, he couldn't just leave him to his fate.

Vin tried to get up, winced, and sank back down. "Leg's karked. Can't even start to put weight on it."

Dav cursed silently as he looked around. He didn't think he'd be able to get the shorter but stockier man up that fan of debris, even if it wasn't currently being pelted with blaster bolts. When he was young and in the Legion, maybe. But now... that would be difficult, and it would take him completely out of the fight. He saw an avenue around the side of the building, though. It would expose them to more fire and cut them off from the rest, but it was a manageable chance. "Okay, then. Buckle up." He reached for Vin, intending to lift him in a fireman's carry.

To his surprise, Vin shook his head and deflected Dav's hands. "You try to carry me out of here and we'll both get dusted. I'm not as fat as some of my old buddies, but I'm no lean, mean, killing machine, either." He laughed softly, a strange sound coming from such a bitter man. "Never really was, come to think of it." He shifted his position, rolling onto his front and starting to crawl up to where he could shoot over the rubble. "Leave me a few extra charge packs, will you?"

Dav just stared at him. Was this the same Vin he'd butted heads with for the entirety of the contract?

It wasn't the time or the place for any further conversation. Vin was right, as much as it might pain Dav's Legion-inflated pride to admit it. He *wasn't* going to be able to carry the man for long, not the way they would have to move to get clear. The blaster fire from the surrounding ruins was not only intensifying but coming from more and more angles. They were being surrounded, as Mids flooded in to the aid of their already dead commander.

Dav pulled two of his precious charge packs out of his gear, set them on the rubble next to Vin, and got a nod of thanks. There was nothing else to say.

"Come back for me when it's all over," Vin said. "If you can."

"I will," Dav said. He didn't want to be buried on this icy rock either.

The contractor ducked and surged up the slope as Vin opened fire on the street, pouring blaster bolts into every opening he could spot, running his PK-9M as fast and as hot as he could.

That was the last Dav saw of Vin. The man who'd been a thorn in his side from the beginning was last seen down in the prone, drawing every Mid's blaster fire on himself as he poured covering fire into the night, giving the other contractors and the legionnaires a chance to escape.

The assault team slipped away. Blaster fire behind them rose to a crescendo, then stuttered to a stop.

None of the legionnaires said anything when Dav rejoined them without Vin. Even when the blaster fire started up behind them, they understood. They'd seen the hit the smaller man had taken, and no leej was going to take a man's last stand away from him.

They kept going, but Dav couldn't help but look back as the blaster fire died down. He couldn't see anything. His guts twisted, then twisted still more when several more bolts snapped in the night, answered by a storm of fire that sounded like the galaxy's biggest sheet being ripped in half.

The blaster fire died down after that.

31

It was just after dawn by the time they got back to the command post behind the front line, which had pushed south during the night's fighting. The movement on foot through the ruins to where they could link back up with the sleds, which had needed to go pretty far to avoid the MCR forces that had pursued them, had taken hours, in no small part because of the number of times they'd had to go to ground. The front line had turned into a fluctuating no-man's-land for several hours during the night, and it had taken entirely too long to get clear of it.

The garage was about the same as it had been, except the mechs parked inside looked a little worse for wear. Sones had clearly been using them to keep things from going sideways in the night.

The town had gone quiet with the coming of the light. Everything was hushed, as if the Mids and the locals alike were wondering what was going to happen next.

Dav was almost too tired to wonder. Tired, worn out, and increasingly bothered by what had happened back there.

He'd gotten used to holding Vin in contempt. Now that the man was dead, and given the manner of his death, he had to think of him differently. That was going to take some getting used to.

Droma met with Triste and Yalorak, while Beauty, the rest of the legionnaires from the night's foray, and Dav and his fellow contractors, crashed for a few hours.

Dav found he couldn't sleep much.

He was checking over the mech that he'd somewhat inadvertently become a pilot of when Droma, looking drawn and haggard as if he hadn't even tried to lie down, found him.

"Leadership in the TOC, five minutes." The platoon sergeant's voice was as hoarse and raspy as his appearance was grim.

Dav left the mech alone. He was just trying to kill time. He had no tools to fix anything, even if he knew how. And anyway, Sones likely had the thing humming as well as it could. Dav was a lot more comfortable on foot during the raid, and hoped that perhaps someone else had been found to pilot 'his' rig.

Droma led Dav inside the command room. Dav's eyes were drawn to the holomap which had been updated with red lines traced around suspected MCR concentrations. His eyebrows went up. Most of those lines were considerably farther back and smaller than they had been the last time he'd seen the map.

"The Mids are falling apart." There was an alarming lack of satisfaction in Droma's voice that put Dav on edge. "It looks like our little end run, combined with Sones's use of the mechs last night, worked. They're still dangerous, but they're fading and drawing back. The harder the locals push, the faster they pull back, though they're still laying down a lot of fire to cover their movement, so it's not a rout."

Dav looked for Sones and saw him sitting in a corner, eyes bloodshot and looking every bit as tired as Dav felt. The Legion squad leaders present didn't look much better.

"What's our next move, then?" Dav asked. The question came from a part of him that desperately hoped that they could rest, at least for a while. "We're not exactly equipped to go hunting."

"No, we're not." The fatigue and deadness in Droma's voice, and the fact that he was still staring at the holomap, told Dav that a rest wasn't in the offing.

"I heard from my friends in Temugol City," Triste said heavily. "It seems that Governor Nisa survived the attack on the Republic compound after all."

The de facto ruler of the valley looked to Droma, who simply waved at him to continue.

"Governor Nisa has officially abdicated all Republic control over Temugol to Cel Tradat and has accepted a position in the man's new cabinet. As such, he has also turned over the full command of the Temugol Defense Force under General Huno to Cel Tradat. Cel Tradat, for his part, has placed them 'temporarily' under command of General Kade Orvannos of the Mid-Core Rebellion." Triste sounded like a defeated man; his shoulders slumped as he spoke. "My source does not have a great deal of access, but he tells me that TDF units are arriving from other cities to the east, massing for a move west. They are coming here."

"Can't have the only rival for the governorship holding his own city." Dav kept his tone as light as he could, even as he came to understand just why Droma looked so exhausted. They'd taken losses and wrecked nearly a third of Barsota, trying to keep just a battalion of Mids out. If the entire TDF, with MCR reinforcements from the ships that had been reported as arriving, came next, there was no way they could hold. Even with the resources of Triste's vault, they simply didn't have the trained manpower.

"Are there any other places back in the hills where you could hide?" Dav said, recalling some of his experiences on the edge, especially on worlds like Porovus. The local warlords there, with support from the MCR, had faded into the punishing wilderness as soon as they'd gotten hit, leading the Legion on wild chases through mountains, deserts, and jungles. Temugol was far harsher, in its way, than Porovus had been, but there had to be *some* places they could wage guerrilla warfare from.

"Nowhere I could get enough of our people in time." Triste looked downright defeated. "There is no way off the planet, either. Not from here."

Dav got the sense that he was the last one to know the score, seeing as how only he seemed to have any questions. He looked at Droma and then Sones. Neither man looked like they had anything to say. Maybe they were out of ideas. The situation was dire.

"There might be a way." Dav knew that what he was about to suggest was a desperate throw of the dice, but that might be what it took. He looked at Droma as the legionnaire turned to him with a faint frown on his face. "Sergeant, which destroyer are you based off of?"

"The *Indomitable*." Droma started to think about it and quickly grasped Dav's plan. "Do you have any idea what a long shot that is?"

"Kindly fill me in," Triste said. "That *what* is?"

Dav ignored the rancher and answered Droma directly. "Unless she's due in the next few days, I don't see that we've got any choice."

Triste looked from one to the other of them, while Meathook, Beauty, Stump, and Tiny listened impassively. From the faint flicker of expression in Sones's eyes, he knew exactly what Dav was talking about, and was all too aware of how it would probably end up.

Sones had probably been in this position before.

Droma turned back to the holomap. "Timing would be critical. We don't want to go in there with the majority of their forces massed in the city. We wouldn't get half a klick. At the same time, we can't wait until they're right on Barsota's doorstep, either, because if Triste's killed or taken, then we've got a full-planet pacification on our hands, provided we can get through and call the *Indomitable* in the first place. If we can't, then it just gets worse."

"We won't be here to worry about it in that case, anyway," Stump muttered.

"True enough." Droma had his battle board out. "We've got some planning to do."

Dav was tired. The night's fatigue—and the aftermath of hardly being able to sleep, despite his exhaustion—weighed on him like double gravity.

They'd moved to the central tower and assumed the top-level constabulary's offices as planning center—Dav wasn't sure why they hadn't used it as the command center to begin with, perhaps local politics—but they were moved in now.

The MCR, content to wait for reinforcements, hadn't done much beyond harass anyone too close to their positions with sniper fire. That left plenty of time for an all-hands, all-night planning session. The remaining legionnaires and contractors had been included while the militia kept an uneventful watch. A break had been called and Dav and his fellow contractors decided to head out onto the roof to catch some fresh air.

None of them had put it into words, but Dav understood them all to be on board to the end. None of this was about Yuso anymore. If it ever had been. They saw a fight worth fighting, and had signed on. And not without risk. Contractors working for a House of Reason special aide would be treated as enemy combatants by the Mids and summarily lined up against a wall and shot. For his part, Dav had seen enough of the MCR over the years to know that he'd happily put more of them in the ground.

He yawned, mixing his stale breath with the faint night mist as he rubbed his gritty eyes. He was still in his armor, minus his helmet. He kept his EH-7 slung in front of him and would keep it that way until he got off this rock.

Sones and Sayavong stretched their legs and looked out at the city, but soon decided that some rack time would be of better use than taking in the view. That left Dav and Aguilar, who lit up a stimstick. Dav hadn't even known the man indulged, but after what they'd been through, it wouldn't surprise him if an old habit reasserted itself.

Neither man spoke. There was no need for it. Aguilar leaned on the parapet that surrounded the roof, while Dav stood tall and stretched, feeling his back pop.

After a few minutes, Aguilar looked up at the sky and let out a stream of smoke. He laughed, tiredly. "And to think. I could have stayed on ship."

Dav looked over at him. "I always kind of figured you were a hullbuster."

"I was." Another drag on the stimstick. "Long time ago."

Aguilar took another long drag while Dav considered his teammate. Seemed he had a story to tell. He was never one to pry, but… maybe this was something the man needed to let out. So he asked.

"What happened?"

Aguilar gave him a look. "You really want to know?"

Dav shrugged. "If you want to tell it. We've got time."

"True. Well. It was about the time that the Marine Corps decided to concentrate more on the ship-to-ship boarding aspect. They didn't like what the old guys had gotten into on Psydon. I think it was a combination of the casualties and the officers, who'd done everything they could to avoid that hellhole of a planet, wanting to make sure they didn't get sucked into another one." He shook his head. "So, naturally, I had to go looking for dirtside action after I got out."

Dav leaned on the parapet next to him. "Something tells me you're not talking about this gig."

Another dry laugh, laden with years of regrets. "No." He hesitated, as if wondering whether or not to say anything more. "I joined up with the Corwon Company."

Dav felt his eyes widen as the name clicked. "I thought they were all wiped out on Verseim."

Aguilar was staring, unblinking, at the clouds above. No, not at the clouds. At somewhere far, far away. "Most of us were. Those who survived and got off that rock had a vested interest in not letting the rest of the galaxy know that we had." He almost seemed to shudder a little, finally dragging his gaze back to the present. "Talk about backing the wrong side."

"It's a risk every merc outfit takes." The action on Verseim, though, had been a singular, prolonged bloodbath. "From what I've been told, Verseim made Keram look like a cakewalk."

Aguilar shrugged. "Maybe. I don't know. I wasn't there for Keram." He laughed again, and there seemed to be some actual humor in the sound. "Besides, it ain't a contest."

"Tell Sayavong that." That elicited more of a genuine chuckle. Both of them had been through their big comrade's grilling about their background and combat experience, back when they'd first boarded the *Inspiration* with Yuso.

They both got quiet again. Aguilar seemed to have gotten something off his chest, and Dav had put a few more pieces together about his friend. Verseim had been a hell of a fight, and if he and his fellow mercs had needed to escape and evade to get off the planet, it explained some of Aguilar's skill sets that wouldn't have been taught to a hullbuster.

His companion wasn't quite done yet, though. After a moment, Aguilar turned to look at him, taking another drag off the stimstick. "I got to admit, brother. This feels like déjà vu." He blew smoke skyward. "Except I'm not sure I didn't use all my luck on Verseim."

Dav wasn't sure what to say. He wasn't given to inspiring speeches. And he couldn't say that he necessarily disagreed with Aguilar about their chances, either.

Something made him look up. He couldn't identify the sound at first, but after a second's scanning, he saw the small black dots coming through the gray, the clouds having lifted just enough that he could spot them while still just far enough out.

"Preyhunters." Aguilar identified them first. "Sket."

Dav keyed his comm. "Droma, Toron. Get everyone to cover. We've got inbound Preyhunters."

He and Aguilar were already hurrying for the steps as he spoke. The howl of the starfighters' engines rose as they moved.

Heavy blaster cannon fire streaked from the sleek,

snub-nosed starfighters, smashing into buildings and vehicles as they stitched their way along the north edge of town. Explosions bloomed on the streets, and a few buildings, already shaky from the bombardments of the previous day and night, collapsed. The starfighters howled as they climbed back into the sky and banked for another pass.

Dav raced down the steps to the command post. Droma already had a feed playing on the big relay screen on the wall. "I've got the sleds moving north. The twins will make short work of those old crates, if my boys can get a shot."

"Not sure we're the main event." Dav nodded toward the screen, which showed the two Preyhunters lining up Triste's compound. The starfighters sent more blaster fire streaking through the gray of the morning to blow holes through the ranch's outer walls and the main house before they nosed up again, climbing over the ridge and momentarily disappearing into the clouds.

"Guess that means they don't have bombs or they'd have used them on the first pass," Aguilar commented. A moment later, his suspicions were confirmed as the two Preyhunters dove out of the clouds once more, again strafing Triste's compound. Blaster cannons only. No bombs.

"They're trying to do the same thing we did last night. Take out the leader so that there's nobody for Cel Tradat's enemies to rally around." Droma ran a hand over his face, then turned to where Triste was drinking kaff at the chief constable's desk. "Good thing for us he had the balls to come down here instead of hiding up there."

Dav wasn't as impressed with the MCR's strategy. "If he'd stayed there and gone underground, those Preyhunters might as well have been throwing spitballs. This is harassment, with the outside chance that they might get in a lucky shot. The MCR wants a victory *without* the TDF involved if they can get one. We just stomped their skulls in, and they don't want that being the last contribution to Cel Tradat's regime they make."

The Preyhunters continued to make passes, damaging the compound as best they could. Dav was impressed with how tough Triste's home was. It had taken a beating, but fared far better than most of the buildings in the city, withstanding multiple direct hits and shrugging them off. With the Legion combat sleds waiting with their twin cannons should the starfighters make another go at the city, the two Preyhunters finally broke off their engagement and disappeared into the clouds, not to return.

Yet.

"Whether that allowed them to save face or not, I don't know," Droma said as he turned back to the holomap. "But if Cel Tradat's forces, the MCR, and the TDF are really allied rivals like you think, Dav, then let's try to find some possible ways to exploit it. We can use all the help we can get."

32

The speeder pilot was visibly more nervous than the last time. She had been willing to risk it all to get that artillery, but as Dav watched the woman fidget, he was increasingly convinced that that had been before she'd seen what real war was like. But to her credit, she'd agreed to fly the mission when Triste asked it of her. Dav had to admit, as he climbed into the speeder with Droma, most of Tiny's squad, and his three remaining contractor teammates, that flying into Temugol City, the heart of the enemy's new territory, was going to be a lot hairier than going one ridge over to pull an end run on the MCR's firebase.

Brian "Tomahawk" Callahan, another SAB gunner, was as close to the door as he could get and would act as door gunner in the civilian model speeder. Dav hoped that the pilot had the presence of mind to put them down with that door facing the enemy when it came to it.

Stump, Beauty, and Meathook had left in the combat sleds and remaining mechs a couple of hours before and had an easy time navigating through the wilderness to get around the battered remains of the original MCR force without being detected. The sleds should just about be closing in on Curwasta. They could probably slip around the town and the mines, but the terrain up there also provided a good chokepoint to ambush the TDF column that they were sure was already on its way. It was for that purpose that the legionnaires hadn't gone alone. About a hundred of the Barsota constabulary, with almost as many local militia, had gone along behind the sleds, in farm trucks, utility sleds, and commandeered technicals that the Mids had left behind inside the city.

Dav had his helmet on and watched the Triste's ranch below as the speeder rose into the air on its repulsors and pivoted toward the east. The plan was sound. A long shot, but sound.

That didn't mean he expected to live through it.

The speeder surged into forward flight, staying low to keep off the TDF's scanners. The other contractors and leejes were likewise ready for action. Other than the pilot, the craft was free of nervous emotion. That was a thing of the past. It was game time.

Dav watched the rocky ground race below him as they hurried toward Temugol City and whatever destiny awaited there.

The TDF reached the mining town of Curwasta before the legionnaires.

The flicker of blaster fire was visible from the air long before Dav's speeder got close, even though the pilot was keeping low, near the peaks of the coastal mountains.

There was a hell of a fight going on near the coastal road.

At least, that was what it looked like initially. Dav was sitting on the right side of the speeder to watch as they got closer, and the first thing that struck him was that neither side seemed to be moving much.

Maybe it was an illusion. Maybe they really were, but the speeder's height and velocity made it seem like it was a static exchange of fire down there.

The pilot could see better, though. "Either I'm losing my mind, or that whole column of TDF vehicles is stalled out on the coastal road and just spraying blaster fire at the hills."

Twisting to look, Droma scanned the ground below. "You're right."

Dav's perspective improved as they traveled. Sure enough, the column was halted, with some of the lead UT-70s off the road throwing blaster fire wildly at the hills above Curwasta. Some fire was coming down from those hills, but only when a target presented itself. Whenever it did, the outgoing fire slackened for a moment.

"Doesn't look like they really want to fight," Dav said.

"Can you blame 'em?" asked Droma. "Doesn't take a Melenic scholar to figure out that it was the Mids who dusted the TDF base outside Temugol City. Whatever kind of sket story Cel Tradat and Nisa put out, the indigs have got to have doubts about this whole war, especially since they've been fighting Cel Tradat for the last ten years."

"And now all of a sudden he's governor," Sones said.

Droma nodded. "And all of a sudden he's the governor, yet it's the TDF being told to go into a meat grinder that the Mids out this way just ran away from."

The pilot accelerated, and Dav braced himself against the surge as they roared past the flickering exchange of blaster fire and disappeared into the clouds again.

Temugol City—and the spaceport—awaited.

33

The weather grew nicer as they got closer to their destination; some of the seemingly perpetual cloud cover broke up and showed blue sky and actual sunlight. It might have been heartening under different circumstances, but to Dav, it was all dread and bad luck. He wanted every bit of fog, rain, sleet, and hail imaginable to hide in. Clear skies would not help.

"I'm getting painted by targeting scanners." The pilot dipped the speeder's nose, getting lower still and veering off toward the north and the coastal mountains again. "I don't know how close I'm going to be able to get you."

"As close as you can," Droma said, watching the dark skyline of the triple-lobed city below them and to the southeast. "If you've got to go over the peaks and come back from the east, do it."

"Oh. Yeah. Hadn't thought of that." The pilot sounded scared stiff. Dav couldn't really blame her, but they were committed, and he hoped the gal didn't finally lose what was left of her nerve and decide to scrap the whole plan. He was pretty sure that Sones, who was sitting right next to the cockpit, would put his Garmian to the woman's head and *make* her finish the insert. Then again,

Sones might just know how to fly the rig himself, like he did with the mechs. Neither option was ideal, though.

The pilot kept a steady hand on the controls as she dipped closer to the rocky terrain below and sped toward the snowy outlines of the coastal mountains again. Dav gritted his teeth and hung on. He wasn't that confident in the pilot's nap-of-the-earth skill, and hated riding along at any altitude when there were potentially heavy blasters and AP missiles pointed at his vehicle.

Just get me on the ground with a blaster in my hands. Let me be at least that much the master of my own fate. Then I'll be fine.

G-forces pulled at Dav as the pilot banked along the slopes of the hills, staying below the tops of the peaks. She was trying to be as tactical as possible, though Dav thought that maybe she shouldn't try quite so hard. This close to the city, they'd actually stand out *more* to any MCR and TDF observers. Act like just one more everyday speeder, and they probably had a better chance.

He was about to point that out when Droma did it for him. "Ease up, ma'am. Let's not attract more attention than we need to."

The pilot was breathing hard, and Dav could hear it over the speeder's simple intercom. She steadied and turned hard north, climbing toward the top of the ridge of the coastal mountains. The buffeting continued, but it felt better, as if some of it had been because of the pilot's nerves more than the atmospheric turbulence that close to the mountains.

The speeder bucked and rocked on the updraft as

the pilot hurtled over the ridge, dropping down below the crest and banking toward the east. She accelerated again, speeding away from Temugol City.

"Going to head toward Yovasteu, then circle back. We might be able to disappear in some commercial traffic." She was calmer now, but still sounded nervous. "If there is any commercial traffic."

Dav doubted it, didn't comment. The pilot needed to keep her mind on flying.

They climbed as they got farther away, rising into the clouds and then above them, where the sunlight shone in a blinding brilliance that seemed to belong to another world and not the gray, cold rock they'd all grown accustomed to. They leveled out at what was still a relatively low altitude for commercial speeders, and headed east.

After about half an hour, they turned back toward Temugol City, dipping into the clouds once more. Dav waited through the blindness as they went through the cottony gray veil, then peered out at the city below and ahead as they dropped out of the cloud ceiling.

"Sket." The pilot's voice was strangely calm. "The spaceport's asking for identification and a flight plan number. We don't have one."

"Make one up," said Droma.

The pilot shot an incredulous look at the legionnaire. Droma had to understand just how delicate their current situation was, but he was right—they had to improvise. There was no turning around.

Aguilar chimed in. "Keep on course and buy as

much time as you can. Every second gets you closer. Set down if they tell you to, even if it's outside the city."

"Right. Right." The pilot seemed to be trying to convince herself as she continued on her flight path toward the spaceport.

Dav could only hear one side of the conversation between the pilot and the spaceports local traffic control tower. So far, the approach sounded normal, but Dav started to tense up.

"Patch that through the interior comm," Droma told the pilot.

Dav leaned forward in his seat, scanning the buildings below more closely as he listened to the conversation between pilot and tower.

Temugol City was somewhat jarring in just how *normal* it looked compared to the besieged ruin they'd left. It had only been a few days, but he'd almost gotten used to the destruction wreaked on Barsota. To see a place not that far away, still intact and apparently normal—except for the crater that was about all that was left of the main TDF base on the other side of the city—felt strange.

The tension Dav felt mounted as he listened. There were strange pauses and hesitations between the controller's responses to very simple and mundane questions and requests for clarifications—all stalling tactics—from the pilot. They were clearly communicating with a person and not a bot, which was also somewhat unusual. The voice of the tower controller was stiff and odd. Dav didn't know if Droma was picking up on it, but his time in security contracting had taught him to be a lot more cognizant of verbal and physical cues pointing to threats than he'd needed in the Legion. As a close protection specialist, he needed to spot trouble before things dropped in the pot, so he'd had to learn more about various human and alien mannerisms in order to pick up on the more subtle threat indicators before they became full-blown problems.

"That controller is taking answers from someone else in the background," Dav told the others. He tapped the pilot's shoulder. "Break off, get low, and get us out of here."

They'd have to find another infiltration route. It might cost them more time, but that was sure as the Nine Hells better than being turned into a fiery scar on the landscape by flying into an ambush.

For a second, he thought that the pilot or one of the legionnaires was going to argue with him. Neither did. She banked hard, dipping toward the ground as she pulled away from the spaceport. Alarms lit up in the cockpit.

The clouds around them strobed with bright light. A TDF combat sled came roaring out of the industrial area just outside of the spaceport gates as the spaceport's air and space defenses opened up, springing the trap prematurely and filling the air around them with blaster fire.

"Hang on!" The pilot twisted and banked, trying her best to avoid the torrent of bolts, but she wasn't a combat flyer, and the speeder wasn't a military model built with that kind of performance in mind.

Two bolts hit the wing, blasting glowing holes through the metal, and a third struck the repulsors as the speeder dipped and threatened to spin out of control. The entire vehicle rocked as a small explosion blew out half the repulsors. Then they really were out of control, the speeder went into a flat spin toward the warehouses on the outskirts of the city.

"Brace for impact!" Droma was already suiting actions to words, tucking his knees and his head, his blaster cradled in his arms. The others did the same.

They hit with a catastrophic roar, and everything went black.

34

Dav knew he was alive because everything hurt too much for him to be dead. His entire body, armored or not, felt like an enormous bruise as he awoke. He tasted blood.

He opened his eyes and found that he was in almost as much darkness as when they were closed. He heard someone groan in pain as he clawed his way out of a deep mind-fog and back to full awareness. Then he heard other sounds, much worse than the groan.

One was the crackle of flames. The other was the thrum of repulsors.

He looked around, his head splitting as he surveyed the inside of the speeder, his eyes adjusting to the dark.

Droma wasn't moving. Given the way he—like the pilot—had been crushed between his seat and the forward bulkhead, he probably wouldn't move ever again. The old Legion armor *might* have saved him, but the shinies... not so much.

A simple crash-foam safety feature might have saved them, too. But out on the edge, you often didn't find such core and mid-core regulations being followed.

He couldn't see Aguilar, but judging by the mangled nest of smashed synthetic and twisted durasteel where his seat had been, he knew the man was gone.

Sones was moving, extricating himself from his folded-over seat. So was Sayavong, though the big hullbuster was obviously in pain.

Tiny wasn't moving. From the amount of blood that had flowed out from under his bucket, painting his shiny breastplate red, Dav didn't expect him to.

Only four legionnaires looked alive. Two had limbs that were bent the wrong way, and one had a fragment of the fuselage right through the synthprene at the back of his knee. Neither would be able to fight. The others, a leej named Sean Clifton and Tomahawk, looked as bad as Dav felt—meaning they were beat up, but capable.

Taking stock, Dav was surprised to find that, despite the ache that throbbed through his every tissue, he didn't seem to have anything broken. More importantly, his EH-7 was intact. A good thing, because those repulsors were getting closer.

"Sones, Clifton, can you get out?" His voice was a sandpaper rasp in his ears.

"Yeah." Sones was pulling himself free, checking his R-6 to make sure it functioned.

Clifton was in pain, but he was game. "I'm up."

"Good. You're with me." He pointed to the big leej with the SAB, who was still prying himself loose. "Callahan, get everyone else free and ready to go. Triage the wounded as you can, but we're going to have to move." He looked at his little fire team. "Let's go."

It took some more doing than he'd hoped to get the crushed and warped side door open, but its seals had been popped in the crash, so, with Sayavong's help, he finally pried it far enough from the fuselage, putting his armored shoulder to it and pushing with his legs, to drive a gap wide enough to crawl through.

Not a moment too soon.

He was still groggy and his head felt like it was in a vise, but he didn't seem to have been out for that long. Otherwise, they'd be surrounded already, but the fenced lot around the warehouse they'd hit was empty, and the thrum of repulsors was still coming from the far side of the line of industrial buildings beyond the fence.

With Sones and Clifton, Dav ran for the smashed gap in the fence. He wasn't moving quite as fast as he would have liked, but he reached the fence in seconds, Sones limped as he joined him, blaster up and covering his back. Clifton moved faster than them both. Younger and in better shape, the kid was bouncing back quick. Good. He'd need to.

Dav pointed to the next building, a one-story, windowless duracrete block about two hundred meters long. It would give them some cover, provided he was judging the direction of the repulsor hum right. It was echoing from the cross street at the far end of that building, and that was the closest avenue to the spaceport.

He held security on that corner while Sones and Clifton sprinted across the street and dropped to a knee at the corner of the building. Then, while they covered him, Dav ran to join them.

Just as he skidded to a halt near Clifton's shoulder, the old UT-70 sled came purring around the far corner, right where he'd expected it to emerge. It was followed by two more.

His EH-7 wasn't going to scratch that thing, especially since the gunner was hunkered down low behind his medium blaster. But the UT-70s weren't the most thoroughly buttoned-up vehicles, either. He just needed to get closer.

A part of him rebelled at the idea. He was hurt, and it was a long sprint to reach it. The mission was all but over. He'd never get to it.

But the part of him that still held onto that Legion crest, even though it had long ago been put away in a locker, knew he couldn't just sit there and let the rest get slaughtered. He had no doubt that Cel Tradat and Nisa would have them all killed and quietly disappeared. Let word about what had happened out here get to the galaxy at large, and they'd be in trouble.

He got up and moved.

Rolling away from the corner, he hissed, "On me," and headed for the front of the building.

A low line of shrubs had been planted along that main street. Dav had seen them on first arriving, but now suspected they were off-world transplants. They didn't look like any of the sparse and generally low-lying vegetation he'd seen on Temugol.

But these would help conceal the three of them as they moved in on the TDF's flank.

And those vehicles *were* TDF. They were the same gray, with the same markings, as the sleds that had been out front of the governor's compound when they'd first arrived, what felt like a lifetime ago. That might work to their advantage, if the TDF was as shaky about the new power structure as they'd appeared to be when the speeder had flown over Curwasta.

Staying half crouched, he rushed along the front of the building, keeping his helmeted head below the tops of the bushes, his blaster in his hands. Clifton was right behind him, with Sones bringing up the rear. The contractor was lagging a bit, his leg clearly bothering him, but they could worry about that once they'd secured the crash site.

There were three sleds. The gunner on the lead vehicle was hunkered down in his turret, but the second was all the way upright, the triggers for his medium blaster right about at the center of his chest. The rear sled's gunner wasn't even paying much attention. He wasn't turned toward the rear, but had his ZX-60 pointed up at the sky, one hand resting on the receiver. They probably didn't expect anyone to have survived that impact.

Dav crouched down behind the shrubs near the entrance as the third sled hummed past the corner, leaving the street empty. There might have been some locals peering out of buildings, but if they were smart, they were down on their floors, keeping away from windows and doors.

The one thing Dav figured they had going for them was that the locals probably didn't have a direct comms line to the TDF, if they felt like reporting the armored men with blasters hiding in the bushes. By the time they could get word to the troopers in the sleds, it would all be over.

One way or another.

He paused just short of the corner, took a breath, and made sure that Clifton and Sones were with him. This was going to take swift, violent action by all three of them. Rear security was going to have to go by the wayside for a few seconds.

He eased around the corner, blaster muzzle first, verifying what they were up against. If that rear gunner had remembered which way he was supposed to have his blaster pointed, this could be over before it started.

The TDF trooper had lowered his ZX-60's muzzle, but it was pointed at the crash, the same as the other two. The three sleds had fanned out and now formed a slightly arced line facing the crash site. The fence was still between them and the wreckage, but there wasn't any visible movement at the wreck, so they weren't in a hurry.

If everyone had been killed, all they needed to do was mop up.

Ducking around the corner, Dav started to close on the nearest sled, moving fast and staying low. There were no eyes on him; he needed it to stay that way for the next twenty meters.

He covered it in seconds. The UT-70s had handles on their hulls on either side of the back ramp to allow a gunner to climb up and drop into the turret from above. Dav took hold of them and hauled himself up one-handed, his EH-7 clutched in the other hand.

The gunner must have felt something—likely Dav's weight making the sled sway a little—but by the time the trooper turned, Dav had his blaster leveled.

Two bolts, fired as fast as he could rock the trigger, blew through the gunner's helmet and skull, dropping him into the sled below. There might have been a yell from one of the other gunners, but Dav was already climbing up the rest of the way and couldn't be sure. He heaved himself up onto the roof and shot the gunner a sled over before the limping Sones could mount the back of that sled. More blaster fire snapped as Clifton went to work on the third sled.

Dav dropped down inside the turret, making the entire sled rock with the movement—a testimony to the vehicle's weak repulsors. He landed awkwardly on the gunner's corpse. His finger was tightening on the trigger as he sighted two stunned TDF soldiers, still in shock at the sudden arrival of the dead gunner at their feet.

There would be no prisoners here. Dav shot both Temus, not bothering to aim at that distance. His EH-7 sprayed bolts in the confined space, cutting them down in as long as it took to get one boot planted on the deck.

He pivoted, lashing out with a boot to kick the driver in the head as the man tried to bring his sidearm to bear. The driver sent an errant blast into the empty co-pilot seat.

Meanwhile, Dav struggled to get his rifle maneuvered around fast enough in the narrow space. He let go of the weapon, snatched his curved fighting knife out of his belt, and stabbed the driver in the neck.

Blood sprayed across the control console, and the man dropped his blaster as his hands went to his throat to make a desperate and futile attempt to stem the flow. Dav left him to die, ducking under the overhead and standing up on the dead gunner to make use of the sled's blaster cannon.

Once topside, he found that there was nothing to shoot at. Clifton stood on top of the third sled, his N-4 pointed down into the turret. The driver had been riding with his hatch open, and his helmeted head now slumped against the coaming, a blackened hole punched through the helmet. Smoke rose from inside the sled. Clifton must have tossed in a fragger.

Sones stood atop his sled, calmly changing charge packs. Smoke billowed out of the open hatches and gunner's cupola. Dav didn't know what his teammate had done, but it was over now and clearly had worked.

"Bring it in. We'll drive back to the wreck and set security." Dav dropped back down inside the sled and pivoted the vehicle to out away from the wreck, ready to move into the city.

Sayavong was hurting, but had still managed to post up behind the wreck with his blaster held ready. Tomahawk had pulled three more legionnaires out of the wreckage, and though they were all looking the worse for wear, they were mostly alert and keeping their weapons ready. That was better than Dav had expected in the immediate aftermath of the crash. For a moment, he felt a pang of hope that maybe Droma had survived, but the Legion NCO's body was still inside the speeder, unmoved.

Also unfortunate was the condition of those leejes with broken arms and legs. They wouldn't be able to move under their own power. The sled Dav had cleared, at least, still functioned, but it was much smaller than a Legion combat sled; not everyone could fit inside. Some of the survivors would have to remain on foot.

Tomahawk gave Dav a status report on his return. "We got some charge packs off the others." The legionnaire was holding it together admirably, considering that his platoon sergeant and squad leader had just both been killed. Once, Dav wouldn't have expected anything less. He was glad to see it now. "LS-340 and LS-523 can hole up until we can come back for them."

Dav realized that the legionnaire was speaking of the two troopers with broken arms and legs. It seemed that a decision had already been made that they would stay behind. The cold truth was, they had a mission, one that would be impossible to complete if they stuck around to protect the wounded. But they all had to know that leaving them there meant consigning them to death. No friendlies were coming, but further hostile forces were sure to. Dav didn't think that was the only way, but he needed to get a clearer idea of how they could complete their mission before worrying about it any further.

They still needed to get to the spaceport control tower and the planetary hypercomm. Getting there would be hard enough. After that... things could easily grow complicated without Droma.

Dav wasn't an active legionnaire and lacked any compelling reason for the *Indomitable* to actually listen to him, even if he could reach them. Let some random chungo come over the hypercomm without verification, and he'd be cut off so fast that he might as well suck-start his blaster right then and there. "Any of you have the codes that will get the *Indomitable* to listen to us?"

Back in Dav's day, every legionnaire had that kind of authorization because every leej knew the intent of the mission and was expected to finish it no matter what. Now, with so many points, he wasn't sure.

"We all do." Tomahawk's voice sounded slightly stiffer than his bucket's exterior speakers could account for. "Sergeant Droma made sure of that before we lifted."

Dav nodded. "All right. We're going to mount up on this sled." He looked at the injured leejes. "*Everybody.* Except the dead." He jerked a thumb over his shoulder to the remaining functional TDF sled. "Let's get the bodies out of that sled. Leave the others unless it's to find an intact helmet for our gunner to wear. That'll keep us from too many second looks."

"I could use a bucket, so I'll do it," Sayavong said. "My old one saved my skull, but it's cracked. Useless."

Dav nodded. "We need to be gone from here in two minutes, tops."

With the legionnaires helping their wounded brothers, they got the ragged, battered remains of the assault force into the sled. Dav waited by the ramp, watching their surroundings over his EH-7, sweating under his armor despite the chill in the air. The clouds had covered the sun again and the gloom he'd hoped would cover them returned *after* their crash. Typical.

He could already hear repulsors approaching, and the comms aboard the sled were blinking unanswered. Someone was demanding an update.

Sayavong set up on the sled's cannon. His new helmet was slightly too small for his head, but he made it work. "We're up. Let's speed."

Dav clambered up into the back of the sled as Ben Davis—a leej they all called "Paranoid"—raised the ramp. He held on as the sled surged into motion, battering through the crash site wreckage and heading away from the warehouses, north toward the second ring of the city. They turned a corner and just escaped from the view of the follow-on forces that emerged to cautiously approach the two dead UT-70s—and aerial speeder—they'd left behind.

35

After about three blocks, Dav was reasonably sure they'd gotten clear. The more curious of the locals were now out in the streets, but avoided the sled. Some shot dark looks at them as they passed, and Dav wondered about it. He'd seen the MCR do some pretty heinous stuff, all in the name of "freedom" from the "corrupt Republic." But unless Cel Tradat had already started hanging people in the street, it seemed premature for the locals to aim such ire at their own defense forces.

As Clifton drove, starting to circle back toward the spaceport, Dav watched through the narrow viewports in the sled. He felt the hesitation in their forward movement and heard Sayavong curse before seeing for himself what had given both the legionnaire and the former hullbuster pause.

They'd just driven past one of the larger markets centrally located on the southeastern wheel. There was no mistaking the blood-spattered wall and the scorch marks of blaster fire. Though the bodies were removed, this was clearly the site of a mass execution.

The purges had begun.

How much of that was the MCR and how much was Cel Tradat—or even if there was a difference—Dav didn't know. Nor did he care. He was living on borrowed time, same as everyone else on this sled. He would spend it killing as many of these kelhorns as he got the chance.

"New planet, same MCR," Sones mumbled.

Clifton kept the sled moving, even as Sayavong kept rotating the turret, scanning for hostiles. Dav considered telling the hullbuster to stop. That was going to attract attention, since the TDF hadn't been doing that on their way to the crash site. Under the circumstances, though, he decided that security was probably more important than a low profile, especially since they were a single sled and probably well off the TDF's regular patrol routes. Things were going to drop in the pot sooner or later.

Better to have Sayavong up and ready when it happened.

They progressed closer to the spaceport, Oba smiling on them. So far, there were no incidents. Dav had felt as though the fight would begin almost as soon as they sped away, but no... they were hardly noticed at all except by the locals. The contractor was doing what he could to watch both sides through the narrow slits of armored plastite. There was more civilian traffic on the streets around the market, but so far...

Their luck failed on the next turn. Clifton selected an avenue leading inside the spaceport, and they came face-to-face with a checkpoint. Nobody was surprised, of course. They all knew getting inside wouldn't be *that* easy.

As checkpoints went, this was about as good as they could hope for. There were no combat sleds, but only two trucks, one repulsor-powered, the other wheeled. They were ordinary vehicles, not technicals—only the guards were armed. The trucks were parked in the street to form something of a serpentine obstacle they'd have to slow to get around. Half a dozen men and women in TDF gray fatigues and carrying PK-9 blaster rifles stood, some of them smoking stimsticks, most of them lounging around and looking at their comms.

They grew more alert as the UT-70 slid around the corner and hummed toward them. Dav tensed as Sayavong shifted his weight behind the ZX-60, ready to lay waste.

But all that the TDF troopers at the checkpoint saw was a TDF sled with a TDF trooper wearing a TDF helmet at the medium blaster up in the turret. One of them waved the sled through, while another hopped in the repulsor truck and started to swing it aside, out of the way.

Dav leaned back to avoid silhouetting himself in the vehicle's window, watching the troops while the sled hummed through the checkpoint. Most looked bored, but there was something else there, too. They were nervous, uncomfortable, and jumpy. Some looked over their shoulders with too regular a frequency to not be bothered by something.

Droma had theorized that the rank-and-file TDF might not be all that gung-ho about backing the warlord they'd been fighting for the last decade or so, especially after that warlord's allies had flattened their biggest base on the planet. Is that what Dav was seeing now? He thought it might be, but wasn't ready to recruit the gray-uniformed troopers into his cause.

Still, the sight gave him a glimmer of hope. Maybe this really was doable. If the TDF believed that Legion help was on the way, and that they didn't have to just knuckle under, maybe that would be the time to trigger a mutiny, overthrow Huno and Cel Tradat, and end this.

Maybe. He'd never been in Dark Ops. Guerilla warfare wasn't quite his forte. It was also probably the sort of thing that took days, if not weeks and months, of gaining trust.

Even then... Dav had been around the galaxy too much to get too optimistic about their chances of relying on anyone who wasn't already inside the sled with him.

They left the checkpoint behind and kept going. Sayavong kept the ZX-60 pointed forward and a little high. It had to take every bit of self-control the man had not to pivot back to cover those troopers at the checkpoint as they glided away, but he managed, and it was well that he had. A few blocks later, they passed another checkpoint, then another. Dav was starting to think that maybe he'd been overly paranoid. The TDF had to know that one of their sleds was missing, but no one had given their sled a second glance.

It was just like so many other indig militaries he'd had to work with out on the edge. Dav, like most of his fellow leejes, had held the basics in contempt, but the indig defense forces were often far, far worse. Lazy, entitled, and poorly trained on top of it.

He looked across the compartment at Paranoid. The kid had his bucket down, like all the rest. The shiny exterior was scarred, dusty, and scorched from the fire that had started after the crash. On a sudden impulse he asked, "This your first Legion rotation, son?"

The legionnaire nodded. "Turned out to be a hell of a hitch, sir."

"I'm no sir. I was an NCO." Dav looked out at the last checkpoint they'd passed. "They're not all like this, though enough of 'em are. This is the edge, no matter what the House of Reason tries to say."

Sones was expressionless behind his helmet, but his fingers tapped his R-6. "The edge, some of the mid-core, and even a few neighborhoods on a few core worlds... it's all the same. People gonna have wars. Small ones or big ones."

Dav nodded toward the outside. They had slowed as a patrol went by, not even offering second glances at the sled once they'd seen the gray hull and the markings. "Is this what the TDF's been like the whole time you've been here?"

Paranoid peered out through the plastite windows. "Pretty much. They might be a little sloppier and more discontented now, just from the looks of things."

Dav filed the intel away. He realized that he was past hoping for a break. Past hoping for an advantage. They were committed, and whatever happened, they would have to move fast and KTF.

KTF. It was a Legion thing. Yet, looking at Sones and Sayavong, he was pretty sure that those two knew how to KTF, too, even if they'd never worn the Legion armor. Even if, as a hullbuster or a merc, they had believed all that Legion bravado was just marketing.

As glad as he was to have legionnaires with him again, he was just as glad to have those two along.

They passed another block, and Clifton sped up, just a little.

"Hey, Dav." Sayavong dipped his head to be heard inside the sled. "Something's weird out here."

He was right. The streets were empty.

"No patrols, no checkpoints." Sayavong was ducking his head to speak, trying not to take his eyes off their surroundings, rotating the gun left and right as they drove. "We're three blocks from the spaceport. Shouldn't there be *more* security?"

"Clifton, hold up." Dav was getting the same bad feeling that Sayavong was. The legionnaire didn't hesitate or ask questions, just pulled the sled over to the side of the street. He kept it powered up, but didn't move.

"What's the plan, Sarge?"

Dav realized that the legionnaire was speaking to him. He'd taken charge with Droma dead, and now these legionnaires, who knew that he'd been one of them, were looking to him to continue to lead. He'd told them he was an NCO and now they were treating him like one.

It gave him pause. He'd been running on inertia and adrenaline, old habits taking over in the wake of the crash. But now it sunk in. He really was the closest these guys had to an NCO. The mission was on him.

That meant he had to reassess and do some planning.

"Okay, there's got to be a reason the TDF's karked

off and left the area around the spaceport a no-man's-land. We might be short on time, but I'd rather scout around a bit and make sure we're not about to drive right into a blockade or a bunch of tanks." He really wished that he'd retrieved Droma's TT-16 observation bot, but there had been no sign of it in the wreckage.

"Sones, Paranoid, you're with me. Everyone else, hunker down and hold security. If you have to relocate, contact Paranoid on the L-comm and he'll pass it to me."

Fortunately, the old UT-70 still had a basic version of a battle board, and he could bring up the map of the surrounding area. "We'll move up this street to this three-story building here." He was still wondering just how they were going to get to the top without alerting anyone. Despite the war and the heightened TDF presence on the streets, it looked like most of Temugol City was still going about its business as usual.

That was more normal than it might seem. Most people, whether on a core world or the farthest-flung dirtball on galaxy's edge, had to work and go about their daily lives despite the violence and the disorder. They might be more furtive, they might not get to work on time or as often, but they still needed to feed their families.

Unfortunately, that fact presented some problems when trying to conduct reconnaissance, in full combat armor, while being hunted throughout a city.

Clifton traced a route on the battle board from his own miniature version in the sled's cockpit. "If we go this way, we shouldn't need to dismount. It'll take a minute, but I can get us there without getting too much closer to the spaceport."

"Do it." There might have been other considerations to mull over, but Dav was past mulling and already felt like he was operating at his peak mental abilities—which he knew were highly degraded due to so much lack of sleep. He was just as likely to fall into an open-mouthed stupor than come up with a more viable plan. He had to roll with the punches and adapt. If they were going to get onto the spaceport and take that hypercomm station, they'd need to move fast.

Clifton backed the sled up, then pivoted it and headed down an empty side street. Sayavong kept turning, rotating the medium blaster in the turret ring, watching for threats. Two more turns put them in an alley behind the three-story building Dav had pinpointed as their vantage point. "This is your stop, gents."

Dav hit the ramp's controls, and it dropped. He and Paranoid were ready, leaning back and staying in the shadows as they scanned the alley over their blasters.

The alley was empty, much like the nearby streets. It was as if the spaceport was some cursed place that no one wanted to get near.

Dav led the way out of the sled, pivoting to clear their flank before he turned back toward the building.

With Sones at his heels and Paranoid following behind, the driver buttoned up the sled's rear door and waited while Sayavong covered the scouting team's movement toward their target building.

The building's door opened easily, which brought a frown to Dav's face. He suspected that they were entering another trap, similar to the one laid for them before the crash. He eased through the door, leading with his blaster. The interior was dark and quiet.

The three of them padded toward the nearest stairwell, checking each door as they passed. The building was utterly still, except for the faint hum that told Dav the power was still on.

Everybody's cleared out. As they climbed the stairs toward the top story and the roof, that impression of abandonment grew stronger. This building, and the streets surrounding it, were empty. The question was, why?

He could guess. So far they'd seen almost entirely human troops on the street, all in the TDF uniform. No MCR at all. It was possible that the Mids had all gone with the column heading for Barsota, but he didn't think that was likely. Instead, Dav toyed with the idea that the MCR had taken over the spaceport, in no small part to try to keep anyone from doing what he and his legionnaires were about to try.

Reaching the top floor, they spread out and quickly cleared the half-dozen offices arranged around a central meeting room. Then Dav moved back toward the office that overlooked the main entrance to the spaceport.

"Well, well, well." Sure enough, there was a technical parked just inside the gate, with a pair of rusty light repeating blasters mounted on top. Looked like a Hool behind the guns, too. In most instances, any Hools involved with the MCR were there as hired guns rather than enlisted believers. A fellow contractor, then.

Even when under employ, Hools weren't known for their law-abiding natures or calm demeanors. There were exceptions—Hools could occasionally be found in the Repub military, though not the Legion—but they were generally violent and unpredictable when provoked, and it didn't take much to provoke one of their species. All the worse thanks to the quills running from the back of their heads and down their spines, each which carried enough neurotoxin to kill a herd of bullitars. Dav had first encountered the aliens when the Legion was tasked with taking down an organized crime ring that had crossed the wrong member of the House of Reason, most likely.

It seemed fitting to see Hools now with the MCR.

With time pressing, Dav considered pushing on and attempting to reach the tower's hypercomm, but he wanted every bit of intel he could get. The contractor settled in to watch.

He was rewarded with a changing of the guards. The Hool got down from behind the guns and a Kimbrin took over. Even from far away, Dav could see unease down there. The Kimbrin didn't like being that close to a Hool, or at least this particular Hool, and the Hool could not only sense it, he was downright reveling in it.

That was when Dav noticed that the Hool wasn't wearing the same tan fatigues that most of the Mids had been wearing. He wore black, his jacket made of some exotic animal's hide, punctured through with holes for his quills.

"More of 'em." Sones pointed to more of the aliens, all wearing the same black jackets and armed to the teeth.

The Hools sauntered along the fence toward the technical, where the first Hool waited.

Dav turned his attention back to the Kimbrin behind the guns. The Mid was watching the Hools, not his sector, and from the looks of things, he was more than ready to pivot those blasters toward the poisonous reptilian aliens and open fire.

Interesting.

He expanded his scan. Unfortunately, the section of spaceport encircling the tower didn't have a ray-shielded fence, but was walled in by solid duracrete. It was impossible to get over or through that with a sled. Given the sensitivity of what was inside that perimeter, he was equally sure that there would be some kind of security measure installed to keep anyone from climbing over it, too. It looked like the gate was the only way in or out.

The spaceport was laid out in a big circle, with three rings of landing pads surrounding the central control tower. It would have been nice if there were another hypercomm on the planet, and Dav had hoped that Triste would have had one. But the devices were expensive, and though Triste was wealthy for Temugol, he wasn't so rich as to afford, or apparently need, such a luxury out here on the edge. To the best of Dav's knowledge, the spaceport was it.

"There's a bright side, though," Sones said, still watching the Hools.

"What's that?" asked the legionnaire with them.

"No tanks."

That was true, and as soon as Sones had

mentioned it, Dav nodded. "See that ship over by the outer landing pads?"

The others grunted that they had; it would have impossible for them to have missed the craft. It was the biggest ship in the spaceport by a considerable margin. "Last time I saw a ship like that was on a raid out in the Rutara Verge. Pirates. I'll bet whatever charge packs we've got left that this one came from the same illegal shipyard. Which tells me those Hools are probably pirates, not Mids."

That fit what they'd all observed about the MCR after its initial idealistic founding. The rebels talked a big game about freedom and liberty, then resorted to the scum of the galaxy to brutalize their "liberated" populations into handing over their stuff.

A plan formed in Dav's mind as he watched the pirates and the Mids interact. A lot of the rebels clearly didn't want to have much to do with their murderous compatriots. That would probably change as soon as the blaster bolts started flying, but the distrust could be used to tilt the scales if they were smart about things.

Turning away from the window, Dav addressed Sones and Paranoid. "I have an idea. But it means we probably won't get out of that spaceport once we're inside."

Paranoid still had his bucket on, so he didn't visibly react at all. Sones just laughed, a low, dry sound. "It's cute you thought we might have before. Look. I've been living on borrowed time for years and parsecs, son. Lay it on me."

He did. They listened, Paranoid relaying it to the

rest over the L-comm.

None of them had a better idea. No one complained about being stuck. They just started getting things ready while Dav, Sones, and Paranoid headed down the steps to the alley.

36

The Kimbrin who had taken over the light repeater hadn't let the Hools slip from his mind, even though the aliens had long since slipped out of sight. The yellow-skinned alien with a dermal ridge of short, nubby spikes running along its jawline kept looking over his shoulder, probably expecting the Hools to come back at any moment. That worry kept drawing his eyes away from his sector and the gate, which was the whole reason for his presence there in the first place.

The technical he stood in was powered down, with no driver in sight.

Which meant that there was no one else to pick up his lapse in duty as the Kimbrin's eyes again shifted off the one spot he needed to be watching, at precisely the wrong time.

The confiscated UT-70 combat sled came tearing down the avenue toward the spaceport gate, passing the same place where Dav and Aguilar had engaged Cel Tradat's raiders as they'd unloaded their wheeled utility truck, about a week, plus or minus a lifetime, ago. It didn't slow down as it bore down on the gate, and the MCR gunner's eyes widened as he turned toward the sound of approaching repulsors.

He should have bailed. There was no time for anything else as the sled came straight for the security vehicle set up in front of the ray-shielded gate. Instead he froze, and when the UT-70 slammed into the technical at sixty kilometers per hour, he was thrown clear and broke his neck as he hit the ground. The impact tossed the technical into the ray shielding, causing it to skip and falter as Dav's sled roared its way inside the gate. The powerful anti-materiel shielding caused both vehicles to cook and then erupt as their power cores were compromised. The subsequent dual blast in those tight confines brought the shield down altogether.

In a more sophisticated star port, such a thing would have set off alarms and caused a blast door or other physical obstacle to close off the breached entrance. But this was an edge world, and the way inside the perimeter was now wide open.

The *crack* of the explosions rattled windows and shook duracrete. As smoke billowed out in an expansive, choking cloud, Dav, Sones, Sayavong, and the legionnaires sprinted for the gate while those too wounded to move were holed up inside an empty building several blocks back.

It had taken more work than Dav had hoped to get the controls rigged not only so that the sled would stay on its collision course with the technical as Clifton bailed, hitting the pavement with a roll that further scratched up his armor, but also to fix up the power cell to explode and create enough obscurant and chaos that they could get through. That second bit hadn't been necessary—the ray shielding had done it for them—but industrial chemicals pulled out from the building they'd used as an observation post, planted around the hot-wired power cell, caused an even fiercer burn once it went up.

Black and gray smoke poured out of the wreckage, rising into the sky and blanketing the entire gateway and almost half the spaceport. The assault team survivors sprinted right into it.

Sones and Sayavong split off as soon as they got inside the wall. Dav hated to split up their tiny force and lose whatever maximum firepower they could bring to bear, but they were outnumbered and outgunned no matter how he looked at it. Spreading the chaos as much as possible was their best hope for keeping the enemy guessing and jumping at shadows, hopefully long enough for Dav and the legionnaires to get to the hypercomm and get the message out.

The smoke was thick and disorienting, and some of it was getting through his Krall helmet's filters. The legionnaires didn't seem bothered, which was a good thing. Hopefully, the cheap buckets still had the old environmental control systems, or at least something close. Sayavong was a different story, and though he did his best not to breathe in the foul toxins, Dav could hear him coughing violently once they were through it.

He carried on, though, and went one way with Sones, while Dav and the legionnaires went the other, ducking into the shadow of a landing pit. Paranoid quickly breached the door. It wasn't an armored door, and a small charge quickly sheered through the lock. Absolutely inexcusable for a spaceport's inner security. Dav wondered if this might not have been part of the little game the planetary government and Cel Tradat had been playing before everything came to a head. Then they were into the maintenance corridor, out of sight.

"Do you have comms with Sones and Sayavong from in here?" Jared Plathe sounded a little nervous. He was a leej, but he was young, and this was probably his first time quite *this* out of the box.

"No." Dav took point, no longer worried about chain of command or anything else but the mission. With the legionnaires forming up behind him, he paced quickly down the corridor, his blaster up and ready. "They know what to do. If they can, they'll meet us at the control tower. If they can't... well, neither one of those guys is going to go down easily."

Sones was hard as a Kungalorian cyclax's hide, and Sayavong was the same, only built like a bullitar. They'd hold their own.

Dav's team worked their way around the landing pit. The corridor was dark and quiet, in marked contrast to the pandemonium outside just before they'd entered. Dav moved fast, the legionnaires keeping up easily. The contractor was looking for a door, one leading in and down, rather than back out into the open avenues around the landing pits.

There wasn't one. The spaceport's maintenance

facilities were less advanced than he'd hoped. Maybe *that's* why they felt comfortable skimping on the locks.

"Plan B," he told the legionnaires and then stacked up on a door leading outside, glad that at least his helmet had enough of a HUD to give him a compass readout. It would have been easy to have gotten turned around looking for the type of underground passages that were common in spaceports throughout the mid-core and the core. He held on the door and said, "We've got two more landing pits to get around before we can reach the control tower. Move fast and do what you can to avoid contact. There's a sizeable open area around the tower itself, so once we reach it, and depending on the amount of smoke that might conceal us, Plathe and Ralston will hold security while the rest of us get across and breach. Once we've got our foothold, then you'll join us."

He got nods from faceless, chromed buckets. They were ready. He triggered the door open and went out fast, blaster up.

They were let out into a narrow alley between landing pits, just off the main ring road, sheltered from the entrances to the two landing pits. He cleared the outer space as Clifton covered his back, checking the alley leading toward the inner road. Smoke drifted through the spaceport. From the sounds of things behind them, close to the gate, the Mids had figured out how to get the fire suppression sleds into action.

There was no blaster fire yet, which meant that the other contractors remained undetected. Still, they didn't have much time. The smoke would only cover their movement for so long and once the fires were out... that would be it.

Clifton took point. They had to slow as they neared the inner ring road, checking that they weren't about to rush out in front of a pirate or Mid technical. Dav moved to one side while Clifton shied to the other, both shifting their aim to check as much of the ring road as they could.

Dav dipped his blaster's muzzle, Clifton did the same, and they pivoted out into the road, covering down their respective directions while Paranoid led the rest of the legionnaires in a dash to the next landing pit.

As soon as they were across, Dav and Clifton hurried to join them.

They were at another landing pad maintenance door while the designated legionnaires held security on the pit and the ring road outside it. The maintenance tunnel's lock soon gave way.

Dav didn't wait for one of the legionnaires to take the door, but pushed in himself, Plathe on his heels. They moved through the maintenance tunnel quickly, Dav hardly able to believe just how deep they'd already gotten without being detected.

As soon as he opened up the next door, though, he could hear blaster fire. Sayavong and Sones had started to raise hell.

That familiar sound, punctuated by a fragger's bang, made him throw stealth and caution to the wind. He burst out of the door into the alley, quickly pivoting to check his six while Plathe took the other direction.

There was nothing to see but smoke and maybe a

dim figure running past. The movement was so quick in the murk that Dav couldn't be sure he'd really seen it. He turned back, joining Plathe as the legionnaire pushed to the edge of the open ground outside the control tower. The rest of the legionnaires poured out of the door. Dav sped up as he got closer, his adrenaline spiking as he kept hearing Sones and Sayavong under fire.

Shouldn't have let them go alone. The brotherhood between contractors had been cemented as the fighting had broken out on Temugol, and if he'd had the time to think about it, he would have been forced to acknowledge that even Vin had finally joined that brotherhood, there at the end. Sones and Sayavong hadn't been legionnaires, but in the crucible of combat, that didn't matter so much anymore.

The clinical part of his mind acknowledged that there hadn't been any way for him to stick with one or the other team. They'd needed the diversion, and Sones and Sayavong had rogered up. Dav figured every last one of them would be dead in the next few minutes, anyway. He just hoped he could get that message off first.

It hardly seemed like the heroic last stand that every legionnaire secretly thinks about. Trying to call for help on some desolate, frozen, backwater world, because the locals couldn't govern themselves without violence and the Mids wanted a base close to a strategic Republic installation. But a man doesn't get to choose his time or place of dying.

Just how he faces it.

The tower was a squat, five-sided column of

duracrete, with a flared-out command center at the top that formed a cut-stone-looking crown. There were some decorative planters on the plaza around it, which might provide some cover, especially since the planters—like everything else on this rock—appeared to be solid duracrete.

Not that they were going to do much bounding from cover to cover. Not across fifty meters.

"On me." Dav took just long enough to check the innermost ring road to make sure they weren't about to rush out in front of a technical and more light-repeaters, then launched himself toward the tower door.

Fortunately, he hadn't completely gone into a sprint, but was gliding fast toward the door, his EH-7 at the low ready. That meant when the door slammed open and the man in tan fatigues opened fire through the opening and down the alleyway, he was able to return fire as he dove for one of the duracrete planters.

Joe Ralston wasn't so lucky. The legionnaire went down with a crash, even as the rest of the legionnaires bombshelled out of the alley, pouring more blaster fire into the open doorway. The Mid who'd killed Ralston suddenly didn't have a head anymore, and his body collapsed.

Dav was up and moving, determined to get to that door and take it before any more Mids or pirates could pick up the fire. Clifton was right next to him, starting to outpace him on the way, as the rest of the legionnaires continued to pour blaster fire into the open door to dissuade anyone else from sticking their head out.

Clifton was about two steps ahead of him when

they got to the door. The legionnaire slammed into the wall shoulder first, paused just long enough for Dav to give him a bump, then went through the door, his N-4 already in his shoulder, as the covering fire ceased.

Dav was right behind him, hooking through the door and into the bottom floor of the tower, Clifton's blaster spitting bolts and transfixing the Kimbrin hunkered down away from the door. Dav drove through the opening and pivoted to cover Clifton's back as he cleared the room, finding himself facing the stairs leading up toward the second floor and the control center above it.

The other legionnaires sprinted to join them, getting out of the smoke-wreathed, but still far too open, courtyard as fast as they could. Not quite fast enough.

One of the MCR technicals, a heavily modified sporting sled painted in a jagged camouflage pattern and mounting two light repeating blasters, roared out of the smoke and onto the innermost ring road. A Hool pirate behind the guns sprayed bolts blindly through the smoke, and then walked his energized fire to where the legionnaires were pushing inside the tower. Paul Roder went down hard, smashed off his feet by the high-energy bolts that also blew apart duracrete planters with titanic flashes and sprays of pulverized fragments.

"Sket!" Plathe barely got inside the tower and was driven back from the door and his fallen squad mate as more high-powered bolts slammed through the opening. He paused at the threshold, and for a moment it looked like he was waiting for a lull in the fire to run for the other legionnaire's body.

"He's gone," Dav said, grabbing the younger man's armored arm. Under different circumstances, he'd never leave a man behind until he was damned good and sure that he was dead, which meant getting to the body and checking. He'd seen the heavy blaster bolt hit Roder in the neck, though, almost blowing his head clean off. "Getting yourself killed won't bring him back. Come on, we need to finish this. They can't drive that thing in here anyway."

He started toward the steps, his EH-7 rising to cover the stairs as he went.

The rest of the legionnaires collapsed on the stairs, two of them having to circle around to avoid the blaster fire punching deep, smoking pits in the duracrete floor, and then they were moving up, Clifton and Plathe taking turns covering their six as they went.

37

Dav took the steps as fast as he could while still keeping his blaster rifle leveled. The pirate on the technical continued to dump bolts through the open entrance a floor below despite the lack of targets. If nothing else, the Hool gunner was making sure Dav and the legionnaires couldn't come back out the way they'd come in. The contractor blew past the second floor and onto the third, pivoting to cover the opening as he went, then relinquishing it to Paranoid.

"Contact!" Paranoid shouted, his voice barely audible above the sounds of his blaster rifle. Dav looked back toward the stairs and saw the legionnaire dropping an MCR trooper.

Dav's heart pounded and his breath rasped in his lungs. He kept turning as he moved up. There were rebels in the building, a few on each floor, it seemed, but no concentration of hostiles that forced him to slow his climb to the top. Soon, he was at the entrance to the control center.

Whether the control center had automated security, MCR soldiers, or something else on the other side of that portal, he didn't know, but he would take no chances. Rifle up and ready, he moved cautiously toward the door.

There were four of them left inside the control tower now. Sones and Sayavong might still be raising hell outside, but Dav couldn't hear anything beyond the tower's confines except the crackling thunder of the technical's light repeating blaster fire. It was probably too much to hope that they were still alive, though the pirates and the Mids had to be shifting their focus to the control tower now that the real target had become apparent.

Don't doom the world yet, Toron. You're still alive.

The control center's door was probably locked. That hadn't been a problem so far, but as Dav went to its coded access panel, he figured that *this* would be the place where the planetary government finally spent some credits on security.

He really wished he had Aguilar with him again. The door was more solid-looking than the earlier ones that they'd breached with charges, and so it looked like they were going to have to hot-wire the lock. He *could* do it, thanks to the Legion's breacher course, though that had been a lot of years ago, and it would be a brute-force approach, that might still backfire.

There wasn't any other option. He ripped the panel off and went to work slicing the door.

Dav was still working by the time Paranoid stacked on the door. Clifton and Plathe were a few steps down, covering behind them. A single blaster bolt raced down the stairwell as Dav got set.

"How's it looking?" Paranoid asked. "We're about to get company."

That was when he realized that the heavy blaster fire had ceased. The Mids—or the pirates—were trying to come up the stairs after them.

"I think I've got it," Dav said. "Just wanted to be sure I didn't lock us out permanently."

Nearly out of time, Dav got ready to bridge the last connection. "Okay. We're good." He looked up at Paranoid and got the nod. Returning it, he opened the door.

The portal snapped open, and Paranoid was already shooting. Blaster bolts screamed through the opening and knocked a tech with a Python blaster sprawling, the sidearm triggering a single bolt into the wall above the door as he fell. Dav followed the legionnaire inside, moving fast, blaster leveled.

A second tech huddled behind a chair, his hands in the air. He wasn't wearing Mid fatigues or the pirates' black. Probably a spaceport official. "Don't shoot! Please don't shoot!" he screamed at the top of his lungs as the two armored figures closed in on him at a ninety-degree angle from each other.

The room was clear except for the man pleading for his life. Dav wasn't feeling particularly merciful, but fortunately, his emotions were only a distant echo at that point. The man didn't appear to present a threat, so he was no longer a target. What to do with him, though, was a question.

The guy peered up at the helmeted intruders and pressed his case. He wasn't dead yet and now he was trying to keep it that way. "I just work here! They said I'd go to the work camps if I didn't stay at my post! Please! I have a wife and children!"

"Down the stairs." Dav jerked his head toward the door, where Clifton and Plathe had made entry and were now guarding the opening. "You can't stay up here."

The man gulped as he looked at the door. Going down those stairs would probably get him shot to pieces by the MCR making their way up... but he didn't have a whole lot of choice.

"Now."

With a look that was awfully close to panic, the tech scrambled for the door, screaming, "It's me! Don't shoot! Don't shoot!"

If the Mids down the steps knew who he was, they didn't care. Three bolts hit him in the chest and throat. He fell without a sound, tumbling down the stairs and out of sight.

Clifton and Plathe returned fire, driving the advancing Mids back down the steps. At least, Dav assumed they were Mids. He was too busy searching for the hypercomm to confirm anything.

The console he wanted was set aside from the traffic control consoles, centrally located with the transmission tower rising through the roof. Dav looked it over. The frequency was open and didn't look to require any special authorizations to use. After all, unauthorized personnel weren't ever supposed to be in the tower to begin with. So much for that.

Dav stepped aside. "All yours, Paranoid."

The legionnaire kept his bucket on as he punched in the codes to send a hypercomm hail to the *Indomitable,* while Dav turned to join the other two legionnaires at the door.

"This is LS-352-BC-173, on Temugol. Our CO and the platoon sergeant are dead, along with my squad leader. The Mid-Core Rebellion has sponsored a takeover of the planet and suborned the Temugol Defense Force to support the separatist regime. We are outnumbered and need immediate support."

Dav was listening with half an ear as he stepped up behind Clifton. The stairwell was empty, except for the body of the tech lying crumpled on the landing. They could probably hold this position for a while.

At least until they ran out of charge packs.

"Are you in command, Leej?" The voice on the other end of the hypercomm was hard and no-nonsense.

"No, sir." Paranoid sounded hesitant. "We are working with Republic contractors assigned to a House of Reason special aide, who is also KIA."

"Let me talk to whoever that is, then." The voice was firm, though there was the hint of a question as to why the junior legionnaire was on the hypercomm instead of the acting commander.

Paranoid turned toward Dav. "Uh, Toron?"

Dav hesitated. He wasn't a legionnaire anymore. But he had led the way in here, so he guessed he really was in command. He stepped away from the door, pulling his helmet off as he did so.

The face on the comm screen was square and chiseled, showing no more than stubble on his scalp. The legionnaire officer had been around. His skin was burned a dark mahogany, and the squint lines around his hard gray eyes were deep. That stubble on his head showed quite a bit of gray, too.

Those steely eyes narrowed a little at the sight of Dav's out-of-regulation haircut and the non-standard armor that was visible on his chest and shoulders.

"Major, I'm Dav Toron, a contractor here on a protective detail for House of Reason Special Aide Yuso, who was assassinated at the behest of the planetary governor when the Mids showed up." He glanced over his shoulder at the legionnaires holding security on the door. "We've been sticking with the platoon ever since."

"Sounds like you've been doing more than just sticking with the platoon if I'm talking to you instead of a leej."

"All due respect, sir, I'm former Legion." Dav gave his identifiers, something that rarely left the mind of a legionnaire. "I guess I just sort of fell back on old habits when Sergeant Droma was killed."

The major looked off-screen, probably reading what he could of Dav's record now that he had an identifier on the man. "Your file's fairly impressive, Sergeant Toron. Up until you got in a fight with an officer." He was still reading. "From the looks of things, the officer was a point, so I'll let that slide."

Dav might have appreciated the remark at another time, but right now, their lives were all on the line and he wanted the major to have authorized a Legion QRF yesterday. But there was always going to be an authentication period. So, Dav only nodded and said, "Yes, sir."

"Give me the rundown of anything LS-352 didn't cover."

Dav proceeded to give the major as much of a blow-by-blow of the last two weeks as he could in a short period of time. The initial raid, the breakout from the governor's mansion, the pursuit, and then the fight to hold Barsota against the Mids. "They're holding the spaceport with the assistance of what appears to be a hired pirate crew. We don't know what they've got in space, but have lost contact with our escort vessel and have seen at least two K-13 Preyhunters."

"You're going to have to hold your position, Sergeant Toron. We'll be on our way presently, but it won't be immediate, and we might need you to call out targets when we get close."

Plathe opened fire behind him. Dav ducked his head instinctively and said, "We'll hold as long as we can, Major. We're only four men, though, not counting my buddies who are down there raising hell, and the Mids aren't happy that we're up here talking to you."

"Understood, Sergeant, but I can't change the laws of time and space. Hold as long as you can. If you can break out, and you think you need to, do it. Our boys with you have L-comm. We'll figure out linkup later. KTF."

"KTF, sir."

The link went dead, and Dav pulled his helmet back on.

"Dav, it's Thomas." Sayavong sounded bored. "I'm guessing you got to the control room, because these kelhorns just got a lot less interested in us."

"We did. They've got us buttoned up pretty tight in here." Dav moved toward the windows, searching the smoke below for any sign of his compatriots. The relief he felt at knowing that Sayavong and Sones were still alive surprised him. Every other emotion had been essentially shut down since the crash.

"Well, we might be able to do a little something about that." While Dav couldn't see Sayavong's face, he could imagine the sly grin creeping across the big man's features. "We're three pits over from the pirate ship. If we can break out of here and make a push for it, we might be able to draw some of 'em off you."

Something rattled on the steps, only to get kicked back down to the landing where it detonated with a bang that was almost painful even with his helmet on. "Only if you can get clear. We need to stay in place until the *Indomitable* gets here, if we can."

There was a pause. "Well, that could be touch and go. There are a lot more pirates here than we thought. And they're damned well-armed."

"Never said it was going to be easy." Dav eased closer to the window as Plathe sent another blaster bolt down the stairwell. Sooner or later, the Mids and the pirates would get inventive and then things would get bad.

All it would take would be one RPG fired into the control center and they were karked. He should probably be thankful that they hadn't thought of that yet.

As he continued his scan, he saw another technical come out of the smoke from where the pirate starship hulked in the murk. Its heavy blaster cannon rotated up toward the control center.

"Down! On the deck!" Dav threw himself flat just before the gunner opened fire, hammering massive bolts of destruction through the plastite windows and up into the duracrete roof. Glowing fragments rained down on them as the legionnaires ducked to avoid the devastating storm of fire.

Dav could barely hear the comm say, "On it, brother." He thought it was Sayavong's voice, but he couldn't be sure.

The fire continued, scattering fragments of molten plastite and more bits of duracrete across the inside of the control center. Dav crawled for one of the corners, hoping he could get up far enough outside the cone of fire to get a shot at the gunner. It was a long shot, but it might be the only one they had before those heavy blasters obliterated the entire control center, the comms gear, and the legionnaires inside.

Something drew his eye as he started to get his feet under him. "Door!"

His warning wasn't needed. Clifton was already bringing his N-4 up as the Hool filled the doorway, heedless of the heavy blaster bolts chewing through the other side of the control center. The legionnaire had dropped flat, but now he rolled to one side and brought his blaster to bear at bad-breath distance. He stitched the Hool up with half a dozen bolts, as fast as he could rock the trigger.

At less than three meters, the blaster bolts

punched through scale and hide, the last bolt coming up under the Hool's chin and blowing spines, skull, and neurotoxin all over the ceiling. The venomous alien crashed over backward, slamming into a second Hool right behind him and sending both of them tumbling back down the steps.

A third Hool on the landing was shooting up past them, blowing more bits of duracrete off the doorframe. Plathe pulled his last fragger, primed it, and sent it caroming down the stairs.

The dual detonation sent smoke and frag billowing and snarling up through the open door. One Hool howled with rage, and Dav was pretty sure at least one other had eaten enough shrapnel to be dead or incapacitated.

Incoming blaster fire from the technical stopped. Dav heaved himself to his feet and looked for the vehicle. Smoke partially obscured it, but he spotted the massive figure of Sayavong in the back, one huge arm wrapped around the gunner's neck as he plunged his fighting knife deep into the Mid's body. Flashes of light in front of him suggested that either the driver was shooting the big hullbuster, or Sones had jumped in with him and was dispatching the driver.

Dav hoped it was the latter.

A moment later, Sayavong threw the limp body of the pirate gunner off the back and got on the heavy blaster canon. The sled started to move again. Dav felt a wave of relief. That explained where Sones was.

As the sled moved out to circle around the tower, Dav turned back to the door. The Hools had backed off, leaving the mangled bodies motionless on the landing.

Maybe they had a chance to get through this after all.

Don't throw a victory parade before the destroyer even gets here.

As if in response to his thought, repulsors thrummed through the smoke, and two TK-552 armored speeders glided out of the vast landing pit where the pirate starship was docked.

38

"Thomas, get clear. You've got two TK-552s coming up behind you." Dav had seen those on his first deployment with the Legion. A would-be warlord on a dusty speck of a planet called Corridan had gathered a motor pool of vehicles and weapons dating back, in some cases, to the Savage Wars. Much of it had been ancient and half broken-down, but while the Legion had dusted the warlord in a couple of weeks, those TK-552s had been a challenge. They were far more heavily armored than a vehicle their size had any business being, and redundant systems made them extremely hard to knock with anything short of an AP missile.

The ones Dav had faced also packed at least twelve vicious little anti-armor missiles of their own plus a turreted G-345 repeating blaster. Hopefully the pirates didn't have the same, but either way, Dav was worried for his fellow contractors.

"Got to get some of these pests off you first," Sayavong said. Heavy blaster fire was lighting up the front of the tower now. Something went off with a *crack* as Sayavong raked the two technicals, one obviously a pirate vehicle, the other a rougher-looking local sled commandeered by the Mids. The local sled was the one that had just gotten shot to pieces. Its repulsors failed, dropping it heavily to slam onto the ground.

Those armored speeders were moving in fast, though. They opened fire with their repeating blasters as soon as they cleared the side of the tower. The TK-552s' must have been operating under orders to eliminate the contractors at all costs; their shots raced toward the stolen technical and friendly pirates and MCR caught in the open, heedless of the possibility of friendly fire. Searing bolts spit across the short distance and smashed duracrete and the front of Sayavong and Sones's vehicle.

Their technical slewed halfway around and hit one of the duracrete planters. Sayavong pivoted around behind the cannon, shooting back as fast and as hard as he could.

He hit one of the speeders' turrets. The weapon was mangled and blew out the side with a flash a moment later.

Sones was driving fast and erratically, which spoke to Sayavong's gunnery. The armored speeders turned for another pass at the commandeered technical and more blaster fire skipped off the deck behind them before crashing into the tower. Sones drove to keep as much of the tower between his sled and those TK-552s as he could. As he came around the front, the remaining technical and the near dozen pirates and Mids were waiting.

Sayavong was on it. He opened up on the Mids as they roared through the hostiles, the speeders following and adding to the carnage as their shots ate up more of their own men while missing the sled entirely.

This couldn't last forever, and both contractors

knew it. Dav was looking for any way he could possibly open up a lane for Sones and Sayavong to join them in the control tower, when Sones veered away, Sayavong coming back over the comms.

"Dav, be advised, you've got a pack of Hools coming in the main entrance. You're about to get hit, hard."

Despite every instinct telling Dav he had to do something to help his friends, he forced himself to stay detached. This wasn't about him, or Sones, or Sayavong. He was responsible for those young legionnaires up in the tower with him, and ultimately, for the mission.

"Good copy. Get clear if you can." The two contractors had done more than he could have hoped to open the way for him and the legionnaires to get to the control tower. There was no way they'd accomplish anything more by getting killed out there, and they couldn't get to the control center as it was.

"Kark that. We'll be around." Sayavong wasn't going to be left out of the fight. Dav could almost hear Sones's dry chuckle in the background. Then the big former hullbuster's voice changed. "Be advised, we saw what might have been some heavy weapons going in before we moved off. You boys are about to get some love."

Dav looked down the stairwell, but the landing below blocked his view of the entryway, though he thought his helmet's auditory enhancements might have picked up some noise.

Dav knew he was going to die. There was no telling

exactly how long it would take the *Indomitable* to get to Temugol, but even if the destroyer was relatively close, hyperspace travel wasn't instantaneous. They were probably going to run out of charge packs and get overrun long before the Legion could come and show Cel Tradat and Nisa just how badly they'd screwed up.

There was a certain peace that came with that realization, though. There was nothing left to lose. A calm deeper than his usual combat mindset settled over him.

It can be immensely liberating, understanding that you're already dead.

Apparently, Clifton felt the same way. From where he and Dav stood behind Paranoid and Plathe, he looked across the doorway. "What do you think, Sarge? Push down and KTF, before they can bring that hardware up?"

It wasn't lost on Dav that the kid had called him "Sarge." Maybe it was just because the officer aboard the *Indomitable* had referred to him as "Sergeant Toron." Maybe it was because they'd accepted his takeover in Droma's absence.

He still had to think it over for a moment. "Anybody got an extra fragger?"

"I've still got two." Paranoid started to get to his feet, but Dav put a hand on his shoulder to stop him.

"Not everybody's going. *Somebody* has to hold this room, and provide cover if we have to come back up those stairs fast. Give me the grenade."

Reluctantly, the legionnaire handed over a fragger, and Dav stuffed it into a pouch on his gear before turning to Clifton. "Ready?"

"KTF, Sarge." The kid's voice was rendered robotic by his bucket's external speakers, but Dav could read some of the feeling behind his words, anyway. There was a strange mix of aggression, resignation, and a sort of fear in the young leej's voice. Not fear of dying. A part of Clifton didn't think he'd ever die. He was a legionnaire. He was blaster-proof. Never mind the others who had already died on the way in. They were different. It was a sort of illusion that most young gunfighters clung to, even as all hell broke loose around them.

No, the greater fear in Clifton's mind was that he would fail.

The two of them rolled into the stairwell, leading with their blasters. The new assault force was still out of sight, somewhere on the bottom floor, so they held their fire as they moved down, pacing each other, covering each angle as it opened up.

The second floor was still quiet, though the door on the landing was still open. Dav covered it as Clifton leaned out over the final flights of stairs, taking a knee to get a better view. When he came back, his words came over the comm. "At least six down there, with a big heavy blaster. I don't recognize the make, but it looks like it'll go through a door like a vibro-blade through paper." He was already prepping a fragger as he spoke.

Taking a split second to determine that they probably weren't going to get jumped from the second floor, Dav prepped his own fragger. "On three."

They counted down together, then lobbed the grenades down the steps, hooking both of them through the narrow opening between flights of stairs. Dav's hit the landing and bounced down the last few steps. Clifton's went deeper. They both went off with a double thunderclap that shook the entire structure.

Dav and Clifton came down the steps and around the landing fast, pumping bolts into the two Hools that were still on their feet, bleeding profusely and staggering from the shockwave. The first one didn't even have time to register that the outnumbered, outgunned prey was actually attacking. Dav transfixed his spined, reptilian skull with a single shot, the bolt slamming through one eye and blowing out the back of the Hool's skull. The other brought its blaster up and was tracking it toward Dav when Clifton slammed four bolts through its torso, throat, and mouth.

The smoking wreckage of the heavy blaster lay on its side on the floor, next to the twitching remains of three more Hools. Those five hadn't been alone, though. Dav had to throw himself flat as the three aliens who had avoided most of the blast and fragmentation filled the stairwell with blaster fire. He hardly dared to aim as he returned fire, spraying bolts as he dragged his muzzle from wall to wall. He dumped half the charge pack before the blaster fire fell silent.

Clifton was slumped on the landing and shuddering as he looked down at the scorched hole in his armor, just above his beltline.

Dav couldn't go to him immediately. He swapped charge packs as he fought his way to his feet, scanning the wreckage of the support room. Five Hools lay in pools of their own poisonous blood, one still moving despite the blackened pits blown in its chest, glaring hate at Dav as it fought to bring a blaster up with one clawed hand.

Dav put one more bolt through its skull, then backed up to treat Clifton while still holding the stairs. Comms chatter squawked from a helmet somewhere. They were far removed from being able to help Sones and Sayavong, and Dav was starting to think that all he'd accomplished was getting a leej killed.

After dragging Clifton a little higher up the steps to get him out of the line of fire, he examined the wound. "How much can your armor take care of this?" He'd gotten out just before the shinies had become general issue, and didn't know their full capabilities.

"Got some painkillers in me." Despite that assertion, Clifton sounded like he was in agony. "It's supposed to seal the wound off."

From the looks of it, it wasn't doing a great job. A puckered, blackened hole in the man's flesh showed through the gash in the armor. "I'm going to have to get a skinpack on it. This is gonna hurt."

Paranoid came down the steps. "I've got him, Sarge."

Dav just nodded, slapping his hands back on his EH-7 as he thought he saw more movement outside. He reached up as Paranoid started to pull the wounded legionnaire up the steps, and grabbed the last fragger off the stricken leej's belt. Then he twisted the smart detonator and lobbed it through the opening.

It hit with a faint metallic knock, then blew, a heavy *thud* shaking the tower while a cloud of smoke, shrapnel, and debris billowed up out of the lower level. The second fragmentation explosive followed quickly after the first as the fragger performed its shrapnel-hurling double-boom. He might have heard a scream before he turned back up the steps to follow the legionnaires, though he only dashed to the first landing before turning to cover back the way he'd come once more. All he saw was dead bodies and smoke.

No one attempted to come in after that. He held his position, watching the door as Paranoid got Clifton up into the control room. He saw what might have been a huddled shape in an attitude of violent death just outside the door as the smoke began to drift away, and a ragged howl of pain came up the steps in the quiet that followed. He couldn't hear the heavy blaster fire outside anymore.

Just as he had begun to resign himself to the fact that he and the three leejes up top were all that were left, his comm chirped. "Dav, it's Thomas. We had to break contact, ditch the sled, and are working our way back to you through the maintenance passages. Be advised, they know we're down here." Blaster fire could be heard in the background. "Could be a minute."

Dav acknowledged. He had to force his mind to reassess their position. Through sheer violence of action, they'd retaken almost half the tower, even if Clifton was in a bad way. The assault to retake it had been decisively broken, if only for the moment. If Sayavong and Sones could somehow get back to join them...

Only how many pirates and MCR still stood between them?

Judging by the size of that ship, and the fact that they're running a pair of TK-552s, a lot.

He heard repulsors a moment later. Dav couldn't see out from the second floor, but Plathe confirmed his suspicions. "Got those two TK-552s out front again."

So, they were going to try to bottle up the control tower while they figured out what to do next. They couldn't afford to leave a hostile force in command of the center of the spaceport, but at the same time, there wasn't much they could do to stop the coming of the *Indomitable*. They had to know that the legionnaires had gotten a message out. Why else take the comm tower?

What happened next was largely going to depend on what that pirate commander or whatever MCR ran the show out there decided to do.

Probably the pirates. Dav didn't think the Mids were really in charge of the spaceport. They might *think* they were, but as soon as they'd brought the pirates in, that had changed. The fact that the Hools had led the charge, coupled with the way the Mids on the gate had been obviously afraid of the venomous aliens, told Dav that much.

"Thomas, Dav. Those two TKs are out front. You're going to have a hell of a time getting across the open ground to join us." As much as he wanted the big hullbuster and Sones at his side, Dav didn't see how they could get through without getting dusted.

"Leave that to me." He could hear the grin in Sayavong's voice. "You leejes don't have *all* the tricks up your sleeves."

Dav briefly debated between trying to go down to the main entrance and going back up to the control center, where he might have a better view. Going up wouldn't let him really cover the other two contractors on their way in. He headed down.

The bodies from their initial breach were still on the floor, but he saw no movement, no other figures. He kept going, angling to keep his back to the outer wall, careful to avoid silhouetting himself or get too close to the main entrance where the man he'd shot on entry still lay flat on his back, staring blankly at the ceiling.

There was no more movement from outside. The carnage he and Clifton had wrought must have prompted the pirates and MCR to pull back after all.

That didn't mean they were out of hyperspace, but they had full control of the tower. For now.

Pivoting to the front door, he started to pie it off, looking for targets—and for Sones and Sayavong. He lacked sufficient firepower to even scratch those armored speeders, but he would lay down what fire he could. He had to.

The two technicals, one of which had been disabled by Sayavong, loomed outside the door. Dav figured that if any hostiles were hiding nearby, it would be behind or between those two vehicles.

Then the armored speeders were overhead. The one with its turret blasted away left a faint trail of white smoke. It was also the one that blew up first.

Dav flinched as the *crack* of the explosion shook the entire tower. A heartbeat later, flames leapt up from the mangled turret and the speeder began to plummet toward the ground beyond the tower. This was as good a diversion as Sones and Sayavong were likely to get, and the hullbusters seemed to know it.

"Coming to you!" Sones called over the comm.

Dav peered through the dust and smoke. As the black plume from the crash grew thicker, blaster fire erupted from somewhere beyond the dead TK-552. Sayavong sprinted out of the smoke, his blaster in his hands and a launcher tube over his shoulder. He looked up, saw Dav in the doorway with his own blaster, put his head down, and put on a burst of speed.

Sones came out of the murk behind him, just after another vicious burst of blaster fire. He had a launcher tube with him, too.

Sayavong reached the door and burst in past Dav, at about the same time Sones got halfway across the courtyard, weaving between the low duracrete planters.

There was no one for Dav to suppress—no one he could see through the billowing black smoke screen, at least. He could hardly believe that Sones and Sayavong had made that shot—with grenade launchers of all things— to take down an armored speeder on the fly. That kind of shooting was impressive for Legion, and Dav doubted he could make the shot one times out of a hundred if given the task.

Unfortunately the speeder they'd taken down wasn't the TK-552 with the functioning blaster cannon.

Massive, searing bolts slammed through the air, punching whorled tunnels through the smoke and blowing apart two of the duracrete planters near the tower in seconds.

Another of those bolts hit Sones in the foot.

The man tumbled to the ground, hitting hard, his armored boot just *gone*. For a moment, he lay still behind a half-ruined planter, its dirt and thick, purple succulents spilling over the walkway as more heavy blaster bolts raced by overhead with a sound like a close-range thunderstorm. Dav wondered if that hit had been too much for the man. Not to mention the fall.

He should have known better. It was Sones.

The older contractor rolled painfully to his side, his leg limp and dead. Dav started to go after him, but Sones saw the movement and he waved at the other two contractors to stay where they were.

Then, despite the agony he had to be in, Sones armed the launcher tube, hauled himself upright behind the planter, leveled the tube at the remaining TK-522, and fired.

Just as the grenade left the tube, crossing the bare thirty meters to the armored vehicle in less than an eyeblink, hitting just at the turret ring and killing the TK with another deafening *crack*, a flurry of blaster bolts came out of the smoke and cut Sones down in the open. He dropped limply, his helmet smoking where a bolt had punched through it, right at the level of his temple.

Dav and Sayavong returned fire, even though it was far too late for Sones. Dav picked out a faint silhouette through the smoke and blew some pirate's head off before Sayavong fell back inside, drawing Dav with him.

Dav gritted his teeth, fired one more shot that dropped yet another of the shadowy figures in the smoke, then he hit the control to the doors. He put a blaster bolt into the control box a moment after they finally slid shut, cutting off his view of Sones's dead body.

Killing the controls wouldn't keep the bad guys out for long, but it would slow them down.

He turned to Sayavong. "You hit?"

"I don't think so." The big hullbuster looked down at his armor, which was carrying a few more scars in its gray coating than it had before. "You?"

Dav shook his head. "Come on. I doubt they're done, and I don't want to be on this floor when they figure out how to get through that door."

They started up the steps. Sayavong looked over his shoulder one more time. "I'm gonna miss that crusty old kelhorn."

"You and me both, brother. You and me both."

39

The expected assault on the doors wasn't immediately forthcoming, and Dav and Sayavong continued up to the control center in relative peace.

"Any word from the *Indomitable*?" Dav asked as they reached the legionnaires. He knew that it was probably too much to hope for, but they were running out of time. Even with those TKs knocked out—Oba knew where those launchers had come from, though when he thought about it, they'd probably been in the technical that Sones and Sayavong had taken over—they still weren't in a good place. Two leejes in fighting shape, one severely wounded, and a pair of contractors... from the looks of things, he wasn't long for this galaxy if a miracle didn't happen soon. Not against whatever else the pirates, Mids, and Cel Tradat could get together to throw at them.

"Not yet. Holy strokes, that was a kelhorned sket-show out there." Plathe's voice was tinged with grudging awe.

"Hullbusters gotta learn to make do with grenade launchers," Sayavong said. "We don't get all those fancy Legion toys like APs."

Dav nodded and headed for the windows. He couldn't help but smile. Hullbuster vs. Legion. Even here, with all of them likely at the end of their lives and fighting together for survival, the rivalry lived on. Even though it was little more than banter, at this point. Every man in that tower would fight like a pissed-off Taurax for any of the others, after all they'd been through.

Outside, smoke drifted in from burning vehicles, but Dav still had a commanding view of the spaceport. He stayed back, avoiding silhouetting himself and becoming a target for some pirate or Mid sharpshooter. That meant he couldn't see the ground immediately below the tower, but for the moment, everything had gone quiet.

Looking up, he could see more speeders approaching, dipping below the level of the buildings to land just outside the spaceport. These weren't armored craft like the ones before, so unless he'd missed something, they appeared to have come from the governor's compound.

"Let's get set. They're not done. How many charge packs have we got left?"

The answer wasn't encouraging. Each man was down to three or four. Enough to do some serious damage, but not enough to win the fight outright.

Not that that had ever been much of a possibility, not since their speeder had been shot down and they'd lost so much of their assault force.

"We need to obstruct those stairs," Dav said. "Unless they decide to just obliterate the tower—and if they were going to do that, they'd probably lift off with that pirate starship and use its guns on us. Until then, best bet is that they'll try to retake this place whole."

Sayavong flexed his shoulders. "Saw some big equipment cases in the room downstairs. Probably support gear for the comms and the tracking gear. We can use those, but it might mean disabling the hypercomm itself."

"We could scrounge some packs off the dead while we're there," added Plathe.

Dav wanted to keep the hypercomm working, but as long as the leejes were alive and had L-comm, once the *Indomitable* did get there, they could call targets without it. At any rate, they wouldn't be making *any* comms to the destroyer if they were all dead, their bodies staked out as a warning to Cel Tradat's enemies.

"Sounds good," Dav said. "Let's set up a barrier plan."

Dav and Sayavong tore connectors loose and piled the electronics cases on the landing and the stairs. Dav didn't know what it took to make a working hypercomm, but the big, bulky cases—really modular housings packed with Oba-knew-what—seemed primitive as hell. Given that they were on a backwater Temugol, it was unsurprising. They were heavy, though, and while Dav strained and sweated to manhandle them into position, he enjoyed the satisfaction that they'd be even harder for anyone trying to climb those stairs under fire to move.

Even Sayavong seemed exhausted by the time

they finished and took up defensive positions behind the pile of wreckage on the landing overlooking the bottom floor and the main doors. Still, no attack had come. From the tower, Clifton had reported he could hear some movement outside, like forces massing. Repulsors, too. That was as much as the wounded legionnaire could help.

They waited. Plathe and Paranoid's thoughts went to their comrades fighting back at the mining town.

"Wonder how it's going for those guys back at Curwasta?" Paranoid asked.

"Couldn't be any worse than for us," said Plathe.

"No Hools, though."

"Probably not."

"Lucky."

"Yep."

Dav listened to the young troopers talk about nothing to ease the tension. He had never been one to join in on that particular way of dealing with the buildup. Sayavong checked his weapon, making sure that each pirate charge pack he'd taken for himself fit properly in his blaster rifle's magazine well.

"Attention, Legionnaires!"

The amplified voice reverberated through the center of the spaceport. Dav and Sayavong looked at each other, then Dav looked to the pair of legionnaires. "Better head back up to the top. Looks like the storm's coming. We'll defend here long as we can and fall back to you." He didn't say *if we can*, but the unsaid words were heard, anyway.

The young soldiers didn't argue, but headed back

up to the control room.

"If they're talking, they're not likely to be ready to breach yet," Sayavong said, after listening for a follow-up to the announcement from outside.

"Attention, Legionnaires!" the voice repeated.

"Unless that's exactly why they're talking," Dav muttered. He wasn't as trusting as the big hullbuster. "Keep us distracted while they get into position."

"They're going to have a very unpleasant welcome if they try." Sayavong patted his VS-3. "Wish I'd thought to wire that last launcher to trigger right through the doors when they open, but it's a little late now."

Dav clapped the hullbuster on the shoulder settled a little lower behind his own blaster as the voice repeated its hail a third time. Then, satisfied that they *did* have the legionnaires' attention, the man on the amplifier gave his address.

"Attention, Legionnaires. You are outnumbered and surrounded. The only ship in the system that could have supported you has been destroyed. Triste's holdouts will not last long. The Republic's hold on this world has been broken. It's over. If you surrender now and hand over your weapons and armor, you will be unmolested and allowed to leave on the next passenger liner off the planet."

In the silence that followed, Dav pinged the legionnaires over the general comm. "You guys got something you want me to tell 'em?"

A flood of expletives and curses, each as unique as the world they came from, returned.

Dav smiled. The years roll on by, but legionnaires stayed the same. "I'll tell 'em as soon as they breach the tower."

For now, silence would be their only reply.

"What do they see up there?" Sayavong asked.

Dav made the request. The legionnaires called out some movement in the smoke on the other side of the burning TK-552s, but it didn't look like there was any concerted assault in the works. The courtyard immediately below remained empty except for the dead.

"They must really be hard up," Sayavong commented.

"Maybe." Dav didn't want to get too optimistic, but they'd already brought out two TK-552s, and those were both dead, burning hulks. It was possible that they'd hurt the rebels and the pirates badly enough that they were regrouping and licking their wounds. In which case this little request for surrender might have just been one of those "might-as-well-try" attempts to end things early.

What would be their equivalent? Dav had heard the story of how General Devers, when surrounded by the MCR and their Kublaren allies, had demanded their surrender. Not that he believed much of that point's war memoir or the incessant holo-broadcasts celebrating the man's heroics. Those were probably the words of another leej who got dusted protecting the point's life.

Dav wouldn't ask the forces outside to surrender, but he started to consider that there might actually be a "might-as-well-try-it" scenario of his own. He pinged the legionnaire again. "Is there a broadband transmitter up there?"

There was a pause while this was checked on. "Looks like it. Why?"

"I'll be right inside." Dav left Sayavong at the barricade on top of the stairs and entered the control room proper. As he moved, the speaker outside repeated his message.

"Where's the transmitter?" Dav asked the moment he stepped inside the room.

Paranoid pointed. "There, but..." It took a second for Dav's idea to filter through the haze of the legionnaire's fatigue, but as soon as it clicked, he got enthusiastic. He headed for the main comm station, separate from the hypercomm, ahead of Dav.

"Hopefully it still works." Clifton was in a lot of pain, but he wasn't out of it yet.

Dav's stomach dropped. He hadn't thought about whether their stripping the lower levels for barricades might have harmed more than just the hypercomm.

"No, it looks like it's working," Paranoid said. "You want the security camera footage pushed out? Seems like it would be the most useful."

"Do it, if you can." Dav turned back out to rejoin Sayavong. The amplified voice hadn't spoken again. That meant the next blow had to come soon. "Keep your heads down."

Plathe got up to follow. "We only need one working L-comm kept alive and we've got two in here."

Dav nodded. "You're with us, then. I have a feeling we'll need every blaster we can get down on the door here in a few minutes."

"Sounds like every other day this week," the legionnaire said and then hurried out the door ahead of Dav.

The pair headed for the stairs just as a withering storm of blaster fire raked the control center. Paranoid dropped like a rock, and for a second Dav thought that he'd been hit, but the trooper rolled over and grabbed the control pad from off the comms station. He was still in the fight and still working on the plan. "Go! I'll join you in a minute! Got to get this broadcast out."

Dav threw him a thumbs-up, and then he and Plathe were pelting down the stairs, reaching Sayavong's barricaded position the moment a pair of old single-det fraggers sailed in the door and blew.

Sayavong ducked as the entryway practically disintegrated with a flash. The double *crack* of the explosions was numbing, helmet or no, and Dav staggered as the entire tower shook. He recovered quickly, though not as quickly as Plathe, and threw himself behind the barricade. Sayavong was shaking his head. Even in their armor, all three had gotten rocked. Dav barely regained his equilibrium and got up behind his EH-7 before the first blaster-wielding figures appeared through the wreckage and smoke.

40

They came fast and they came shooting. A blizzard of eye-searing bolts preceded them through the door as they sprayed down the entire room. It was about what Dav would have expected from some yokel rebels in close-quarters combat.

Unfortunately, between the shock of the explosives blowing the doors apart and the sheer volume of fire those men in blue were throwing around, the two contractors and one legionnaire couldn't immediately take advantage of the sloppiness. Still rattled by the blast, Dav had to duck as blaster fire chewed into the walls and the metal cases in front of him.

Sayavong was blind-firing back with his VS-3, but the assaulters only redoubled their fire, shifting from hosing the whole room down to focusing on the stairwell.

Their cover on the lower steps was coming apart. Plathe felt around his belt, pulled a grenade, and tossed it over the barricade.

It was an ear-popper, not a fragger, but its titanic *boom* and blinding flash at least slowed down the incoming fire. Dav and Sayavong took full advantage of the lull to rise up over the barrier and send a torrent of blaster bolts into the group on the ground floor.

Dav knew that he'd hit at least two. He was still on a low knee, the armor getting uncomfortable as edges dug into sensitive parts of his anatomy. The Krall suit wasn't designed to be quite *this* mobile. His helmet was just far enough above the mangled, smoking edge of the metal cabinet in front of him that he could shoot over it.

He dumped two more, but there were more coming in as the lead shooters died. Without another ear-popper, or better yet, a fragger, they were being forced low again as the volume of incoming fire increased. These rebels weren't karking around.

If they'd placed their barrier any closer to the doors, they'd have been dead. As it was, they were running out of time and cover fast.

Sayavong saw it too. "Hold on a second." Even with his helmet's external speakers working, he could barely be heard over the crackle and snarl of blaster fire. He dropped to the floor as more blaster bolts blew glowing chips off the duracrete above and behind them, and low-crawled toward the next flight of stairs.

Dav saw what he was doing, and popped up just enough to resume his own fire into the ground floor again, seeing in the split second that he got above the cabinet that the assaulters were spreading out around the room, closing in on the stairs from multiple angles.

One of them was closer than the others, and on instinct, Dav risked his head, rose a little higher, and twisted to bring his blaster to bear, shooting the man in the face. The fragger the man was carrying fell to the floor at his feet as his fingers went nerveless. Fortunately for the others around him, he fell on top of it. It blew the dead rebel in half but spared the rest, except for the two closest to him who staggered back, blood seeping from shrapnel wounds in the cloud of dust, smoke, and less wholesome debris.

The incoming blaster fire died down to almost nothing as smoke and frag billowed out from the explosion as the shock wave slapped the walls and rocked the assaulting force. In the next second, as smoke filled the room, Sayavong set up on the next flight of steps, leaned into his VS-3, and opened up with a savage rate of fire that only a SAB could rival.

A stream of bolts chewed into armor, flesh, and anything else they hit. Sayavong cut down two more of the rebels before the rest fell back deeper into the room, cutting off his field of fire. He slackened his finger on the trigger while Dav and Plathe duck-walked around behind him, then picked up the fire again as one of the rebels started to ease out to bring his blaster to bear on the steps again. "Oh yeah, I see you, kelhorn."

Dav and Plathe straightened as they got out of the funnel of the first flight of steps and raced up the second. Plathe vaulted over the equipment cabinets they'd piled in front of the door to the second level. Dav halted just short, crouching down and training his EH-7 down through the gap between flights of stairs. "Thomas! Move!"

Sayavong lifted the VS-3's muzzle as he swung away from the stairs. A few sporadic blaster bolts chased him around the corner, but he had just enough cover that he got away unscathed, his legs pumping as he dashed up the steps toward the second barricade.

Dav stayed where he was. The rebels would have to go over that shredded, twisted mass of metal sooner or later, and he intended to reap a few more of them before he fell back.

They didn't have a lot of space to work with in that tower, but he intended to use every centimeter of it.

He held his position there for what felt like hours, though it wasn't much more than a couple of minutes. The blaster fire died down to nothing, and it got quiet.

Mostly quiet. He could hear distant sounds that might have been blaster fire, somewhere else in the city, but he couldn't be sure and couldn't spare the attention.

A shadow moved through the drifting smoke. Dav held his fire. He wanted an actual target. This was time for killing, not for scaring the enemy.

Muted voices murmured below. He couldn't pick out most of what they were saying, but they were using the local dialect instead of Standard. That meant that they were probably Cel Tradat's people. The power dynamic on the spaceport had shifted. They were considering whether the speedlift was *totally* destroyed, or might be an option if they accessed it from a higher level.

The legionnaires had taken care of the speedlift altogether, though. There would be no reaching the top of the tower unless it was by the stairs. Dav looked forward to killing as many of these kelhorns as he needed to, right up until the *Indomitable* got there or the insurgent got to him first.

He didn't want any more of his boys to die.

And at that point, they *were* his boys. Those three legionnaires up there, and even Sayavong, who was about the same age, had followed him into this hell, and that made them his responsibility.

Two rebels approached the wrecked barricade slowly, their blasters, old PK-9s, held up and pointed at the top. They were looking through their sights, which meant they didn't see Dav until it was far too late.

In that moment, Dav would have preferred a fragger, just so he could get a few more, but since he didn't have any...

He shot the farthest through the skull, then dropped his muzzle toward the second man as he flinched and drilled him with another bolt that went slightly low, punching through the juncture of shoulder and neck and blowing out his spine.

Then he pivoted away from the landing to avoid the burst of blaster fire that chewed up the first barricade even more. A grenade hit the landing beside him with a *clunk*. Dav jumped up and over the second barricade and had his sinuses cleared as the grenade blew up with tooth-rattling force and scoured the walls with shrapnel while he was on his way down on the other side of the obstruction. He felt a few fragments hit him as he went over the second barricade, almost landing on top of Plathe, but the armor held.

Rolling back to his feet, Dav got into a kneeling position behind the barricade. He rose a little bit higher than he was necessarily comfortable with, but it gave him a better angle on the lower barricade.

Just in time. Despite the way he'd dusted those first two who'd tried to climb the barricade, the rebels kept pushing. They had to. It was either push the fight or give up. From the public execution sites he'd seen on the way here, Dav expected that the latter option was going to get them lined up against a wall and shot.

Better to take their chances in a straight-up fight.

His first shot took one of the Cel Tradat's blue-clad rebels in the shoulder, knocking the man into the mangled wreckage. The second punched into another's neck. Screams echoed through the stairwell.

An arm appeared with a small cylinder clenched in its fist. Dav pumped about a dozen bolts at it, knowing he was probably not going to hit the arm itself, even at that range, but hoping he could at least get the rebel to drop the grenade.

He hit the fragger with his last bolt, and it detonated in the rebel's hand. The arm disappeared in a black cloud as the stairwell shook again, and more screams sounded from below.

They had another pause after that. Likely the rebels were trying to formulate a new attack plan. They needed to. But for now, Dav, Sayavong, and the legionnaires—Paranoid had joined them—had the stairs locked down.

The longer that pause went on, though, the less comfortable Dav got. They were cooking something up, and it wasn't going to be good.

Sooner or later, the rebels and the Mids would probably decide to just demolish the whole tower. It would take time, but with the contractors and legionnaires bottled up, they could do it. The only question was whether they were willing to destroy the hypercomm and the functionality of the spaceport to do it.

"If they really wanted to finish this, they'd either bomb us or land on the roof and rappel in." Sayavong laughed hoarsely. "If they can figure out how to rappel."

Dav looked up. Sayavong had a point. He was no more confident in the locals' ability to pull off that kind of a coordinated assault than his hullbuster compatriot, but they might try. And here he was, a story below where he could see what was going on around them.

Gritting his teeth, knowing he was giving up some of the fight, he turned and started up toward the control center. "Paranoid, get on that corner and make sure none of those kelhorns gets a single boot over that barricade. Plathe, you're with me."

He'd gotten halfway to the top floor when he heard the repulsors.

Whatever was coming, it was big and heavy, and it was coming in from above. Sayavong's tongue-in-cheek observation hadn't been so tongue-in-cheek after all.

He slowed and stopped on the last flight. He had a feeling he was going to need the cover soon. Without an AP missile, he wasn't going to shoot down whatever was flying in to hover over the tower, so he was going to have to settle for engaging any assaulters with his blaster. Plathe crouched down on the steps next to him.

The repulsors vibrated the entire tower as the craft came closer. Craning his neck, Dav could see just enough of the reddish durasteel to realize that it was probably a shuttle off the pirate starship squatting in the landing pit on the south side of the spaceport.

So, the pirate scumsacks still wanted some. Dav was willing to oblige.

Cables dropped from the sides of the shuttle as it came to a hover above the control center, and what sounded like a repeating blaster opened up below them. The rate of fire was too high to be Sayavong's VS-3, and it was more coordinated than Dav had thought the rebels capable of. He rose from his crouch just enough to level his EH-7 over the top of the steps. Plathe was right next to him.

The pirates were still wearing black, but this bunch had traded in the outlaw gear that the Hools had been wearing for combat armor that wouldn't have been out of place on a mid-core world's police force. They were also more practiced at the rappel than Dav would have expected, all but one expertly swinging in through windows already shattered by blaster fire.

Dav and Plathe both opened fire at the same time, shooting just above the floor. Dav cut the legs out from one pirate before the man even hit the floor, his bolts smashing leg armor and bones to make the pirate collapse screaming as his boots made contact with the ground. Dav silenced him with two more bolts and dragged his blaster toward the next man along the wall, sending him spinning out of sight behind a console.

Plathe had been getting after it, too, and now the remaining three pirates scrambled to take cover behind the hypercomm station.

Dav gathered himself to move. They had to clear them out before one of them realized that there was a wounded legionnaire in the room with them. The fire from down below grew in intensity, and with a scrape of armor on duracrete, Paranoid appeared on the landing below, dragging a badly wounded Sayavong. More blaster bolts chased them up the stairs. Whatever rebel was working the automatic blaster beneath them was just holding down the trigger and hosing the steps as the rebels climbed.

They were out of room and out of time. If one of those pirates had had time to prep a fragger, it was about to level everyone in the stairwell. He pushed up and inside the control room, angling around the hypercomm station, his EH-7 in his shoulder, ready to kick the expected grenade back in their teeth while he absorbed however much blaster fire he had to so he could kill them all.

Clifton, lying against the wall with that blackened hole in his armor, hadn't moved. Dav thought he was dead on sight, and apparently the pirates had, too. They were stacked on the hypercomm console, their backs to the wounded legionnaire, as he heaved himself up, lifting his N-4, and dumped the last of the charge pack into them.

One of them screamed out as he fell, got quickly silenced, and then the fragger fell to the floor with a *thunk*.

Clifton, despite his pain, lunged to get there before Dav, grabbing the fragger and wrapping himself around it.

That shiny armor wouldn't have been sufficient to save him even if it hadn't already been compromised, but as the explosion lifted him off the floor, tearing into his midsection as it did so, it was still contained underneath him.

There was no time to mourn him. Dav pivoted to make sure that no more pirates were coming down from the shuttle hovering above. Plathe was crouched next to the hypercomm station, watching the other side, unmoving. From the sounds of blaster fire, Paranoid was still fighting back at the stairs. Wounded as he was, so was Sayavong.

Up or down? Dav asked himself. It almost didn't matter. This was the last stand. There was nowhere to go, and charge packs were getting low.

Plathe grabbed him. "Get down, Sarge!"

The legionnaire pulled him to the deck just before the pirate starship exploded.

The *boom* shook the tower harder than anything else so far, shattering the remaining windows in the control center as a fireball roiled up from the center of the hull of the hovering shuttle. The roar of sublight drives rattled the remains of the tower as heavy blaster fire stabbed down out of the sky, raking the courtyard outside the tower and a few of the landing pits along the way. Dav looked up through the smoke and the shattered windows to see Republic Lancer interceptors climbing away with a roar.

The blaster fire from below had all but ceased. The wounded shuttle managed to maintain altitude and made a run for it, only for another burst of blaster cannon fire from above to hit it square. The shuttle broke in half as an explosion ripped it apart. Flaming debris rained down on the city, not that far from the wreck of the passenger liner that had been shot down the first day Dav and the others had arrived.

A dozen drop shuttles were coming down through the clouds, the prows of the pods glowing hot while loudhailers boomed out over the spaceport, announcing that anyone bearing arms against the Republic would be shot on sight. It was slightly more diplomatically worded, but that was the gist.

"Sorry, Sarge." Plathe picked himself up. "The major called over the L-comm, and there wasn't time to pass the word."

Dav heaved himself to his feet and started down the steps to check on Sayavong. "Ooah, Leej. It's no worries at all."

He snorted out a chuckle through his nose. He'd made it.

EPILOGUE

Dav came out of the gym and nodded to a couple of the legionnaires on their way in. The *Indomitable* was in orbit over Temugol while two companies of the 173rd Legion hunted Cel Tradat through the mist-shrouded hills near the edge of the northern ice cap. The fighting in the city had been remarkably short-lived after the *Indomitable*'s arrival, in no small part because a good chunk of the TDF had immediately turned on the Mids and Cel Tradat's rebels. Some of that had been because of the *Indomitable*'s menacing presence overhead. Some had been because of the transmission Paranoid had sent out, showing them just how deeply they'd been betrayed.

Dav wanted to be with those leejes hunting the warlord, but Major Krestin hadn't given him an assignment yet.

It felt simultaneously strange and comfortable to be back in Legion uniform. The major hadn't hesitated to reinstate him when he'd asked, several days after the destroyer had arrived and the legionnaires had secured the spaceport.

Unfortunately, while he had been reinstated, he still wasn't on active duty. Which left him little to do but go to the gym and check on Sayavong in the medical bay.

He made his way back to his temporary quarters, passing more legionnaires in the corridor. The legionnaires were solely concerned with Cel Tradat and the Mids. The Repub Army had sent in a couple of battalions to handle the rest of local security, increasingly with the remnant of the TDF alongside them. As Dav and Droma had suspected, a lot of the Temus had *not* been happy about being ordered to side with the people they'd been fighting off and on for years, not to mention those responsible for the deaths of hundreds of their comrades outside Temugol City just before the coup.

He had just gotten to his quarters when a voice called out, "Sergeant Toron?"

He turned to see a powerfully built legionnaire with a major's insignia on his collar. The man had a bushy red beard and was wearing sunglasses.

"That's me, sir."

The bearded officer looked him over briefly, then jerked his head to indicate he should follow. "Let's have a talk."

He certainly didn't have much of anything else to do, and this major didn't carry himself like a point. Dav wasn't sure what he was, but he wasn't a point.

The major led the way to one of the smaller briefing rooms. "Have a seat, Sergeant." The big man availed himself of another chair, sprawling in it and wrapping one massive arm around the back. He was almost as big as Sayavong, and possibly even more ripped. "Major Krestin tells me you're awaiting assignment."

"That's right, sir. I was hoping to join one of the units currently down on the ground hunting Cel Tradat, but they're at full strength. Sergeant Droma's platoon is essentially no more, and Paranoid and Plathe are going to be reassigned too, I understand."

The major didn't take his sunglasses off. It made him hard to read as he nodded, his mouth pressed into a thoughtful line that vanished into his beard. "Well, I've got some bad news for you, Sergeant. Major Krestin has put you in for the Order of the Centurion for your actions down on Temugol. While that will insulate you from Delegate Mahat's wrath—I'm sure he was already gearing up to pin Yuso's death on you, just to have someone to blame, you or that hullbuster in the med bay—unfortunately it will also raise your profile to the point that you'll probably be on a permanent PR tour of the Core for the rest of your Legion career. After all, you are essentially responsible for keeping an entire world out of the MCR's hands, and that counts for a lot with the House and Senate. Even if they don't want to admit it publicly, because everything in the galaxy is copacetic, don't you know."

"Give Sayavong the order then," Dav said, almost without thinking. "I don't want it, sir. I just want to go back to work. And not as a poster boy."

There was a deeper truth to that statement. Just the thought of it, while those memories of blood and fire were still fresh, turned his stomach. To glad-hand and stand around for holo-ops with politicos and celebrities, all while reliving the smoke and the blaster fire and the carnage every night...

The major smiled and tilted his head, as if studying Dav from behind those shades. "There *might* be an alternative, if a cushy assignment getting feted by every pol from Utopion to the mid-core doesn't appeal to you. You'd still receive the Order of the Centurion. Major Krestin's on the warpath about that. The Order still gets noticed. Gives the galaxy at least a glimpse of what the mess the House of Reason is making of things. But there'd be no ceremony, no publicity. It would go in your file, and no one would ever speak about it until you're dead or retired, whichever comes first. We'll see what we can do to protect your hullbuster friend as well."

"What alternative do you mean, sir?" Dav was about ready to take a job as an armory tech over that.

He rubbed his beard with one huge hand. "You come work for me."

Dav was starting to get some suspicion as to just where this major was from, and despite the conflicting thoughts and emotions bouncing around in his head, he knew he was going to say yes. "And who do you work for, Major?"

"I think you already know."

Dav nodded. "I'm in."

The major's mouth quirked upward in a half smile, and he reached out one massive paw. Dav shook it. "Welcome to Dark Ops, Sergeant Toron."

JOIN THE LEGION

Subscribe to the exclusive Galaxy's Edge Newsletter to find out about the future of Galaxy's Edge

FOR MORE PETER NEALEN

Follow Peter for action packed titles at

https://wargate.info/join-nealen

And his website at

https://www.americanpraetorians.com/

THE BEST
IN
SCIENCE FICTION

For more Galaxy's Edge plus the best in new science fiction from
Wargate Books' scifi imprint, NOVA, sign into
https://wargate.info/join-wgnova

HONOR ROLL

Jason and Nick would like to thank those whose Galaxy's Edge Insider Subscriptions saw to the continued heroism and sacrifice of the legion.

Cody Aalberg
A. Isaiah Abney
Sam Abraham
Guido Abreu
Alex Acree
Chancellor Adams
Daniel Adams
Myron Adams
Chris Adkins
Garion Adkins
Ryan Adwers
Kyle Aguiar
Elias Aguilar
Dennis Aheard Jr.
Neal Albritton
Aleksey Aleshintsev
Jonathan Allain
Bill Allen
Byron Allen
Justin Allred
Paul Almond
Larry Alotta
Chris Alston
Tony Alvarez
Christian Amburgey
Joachim Andersen
Galen Anderson
Jarad Anderson
Levi Anderson

Taylor Anderson
Jennifer Andrews
Pat Andrews
Caleb Angell
Robert Anspach
Melanie Apollo
Joseph Aranda
Benjamin Arguello
Thomas Armona
Daniel Armour
Linda Artman
Jeff Asher
Nicholas Ashley
Jonathan Auerbach
Sean Averill
Nicholas Avila
Albert Avilla
David Azur
Sam Baccoli
Benjamin Backus
Zachary Badger
Christian Bailey
Marvin Bailey
Shane Bailey
Daniel Baker
David Baker
Sallie Baliunas
Nathan Ball
Kevin Bangert

Christopher Barbagallo
Caleb Barber
John Barber
Brian Bardwell
Beau Barker
Logan Barker
Felipe Barrios
Brian Barrows-Striker
Richard Bartle
Austin Bartlett
Sean Battista
Robert Battles
Eric Batzdorfer
John Baudoin
Adam Bear
Nahum Beard
Mason Beaudry
Michelle Beaver
Mike Beeker
Randall Beem
Matt Beers
John Bell
Royce Benford
Mark Bennett
Ryan Bennett
Edward Benson
Mark Berardi
Hjalmar Berggren
Carl Berglund

Brian Berkley
Corey Berman
David Bernatski
Gardner Berry
John Bertram
Tim Berube
Michael Betz
Kevin Biasci
Shannon Biggs
Gregory Bingham
John Bingham
Brien Birge
Brien Birge
Nathan Birt
Francisco Blankemeyer
Trevor Blasius
Brian Blass
David Blount
Liz Bogard
James Bohling
Rodney Bonner
Brandon Boone
Douglas Booth
Thomas Seth Bouchard
William Boucher
Aaron Bowen
Brandon Bowles
Alex Bowling
Gregory Bowman
Keiger Bowman
Michael Boyle
Derrick Boyter
Clifton Bradley
Chester Brads
Scott Brady
Richard Brake
Ryan Bramblett
Andrew Branca
Logan Brandon
Ernest Brant
Chet Braud
Josh Braun
Dennis Bray
Robert Bredin

Christopher Brewster
Jacob Brinkman
Geoff Brisco
Wayne Brite
Joysell Brito
Spencer Bromley
Paul Brookins
Raymond Brooks
Joseph Bross
Dodson Brown
Matthew Brown
RFC Brumley
Jeff Brussee
Benjamin Bryan
Marion Buehring
Wendy Bugos
Wendy Bugos
Nicholas Burck
Austin Burgans
John Burleigh
Jay Burritt
David Butler
Karl Butsch
John Byrd
Noel Caddell
Daniel Cadwell
Brian Callahan
Joseph Calvey
Decker Cammack
Van Cammack
Chris Campbell
Mark Campbell
Danny Cannon
Zachary Cantwell
John Cappleman
Spencer Card
Brett Carden
Tyler Carlson
Daniel Carpenter
Daldos Carr
Rafael Carrol
Brad Carter
Robert Cathey
Brian Cave

Shawn Cavitt
Blaine Chapa
Brian Cheney
Brad Chenoweth
Caleb Cheshire
David Chor
James Christensen
Cooper Clark
Kelly Clark
Rebecca Clark
Casey Clarkson
Andrew Clary
Ethan Clayton
Jonathan Clews
Beau Clifton
Sean Clifton
Adam Cobb
Morgan Cobb
Curtis Colgate
Christian Collins
Robert Collins Sr.
Alex Collins-Gauweiler
Jason Colson
Marcus Colwell
Jerry Conard
Robert Conaway
Gayler Conlin
Michael Conn
James Connolly
Ryan Connolly
James Conyers
Brian Cook
Devyn Cook
Dustin Coons
Joshua Coop
Kevin Cooper
Terry Cooper
Jacob Coppess
Michael Corbin
Alex Corcoran
Robert Cosler
Anthony Cotillo
Ryan Coulston
Seth Coussens

Adam Craig
Andrew Craig
Zachary Craig
Ben Crose
Justin Crowdy
Ben Crowley
Christopher Crowley
Jack Culbertson
Phil Culpepper
Scott Cummins
Ben Curcio
Thomas Cutler
Jason D. Martin
Christopher Da Pra
Robert Daly
John Dames
Anthony Damico
David Danz
Matthew Dare
Hayden Darr
Chad David
Alister Davidson
Peter Davies
Ashton Davis
Ben Davis
Brian Davis
David Davis
Ivy Davis
LeRoy Davis
Nathan Davis
Joseph Dawson
Andrew Day
Gabriel De Jesus
Ron Deage
Nathan Deal
Jason Del Ponte
Anthony Del Villar
Tod Delaricheliere
Wayne Dennis
Anerio (Wyatt) Deorma (Dent)
Douglas Deuel
Isaac Diamond
Michael Dickerson

Alexander Dickson
Nicholas Dieter
Christopher DiNote
Matthew Dippel
Gregory Divis
Jeffrey Dobbs
Brian Dobson
Samuel Dodes
Graham Doering
Shawn Doherty
Gerald Donovan
Ward Dorrity
Noah Doyle
Michael Drescher
Adam Drucker
John Dryden
Garrett Dubois
Josh DuBois
Ray Duck
Marc-André Dufor
Cory Dufour
Thomas DuLaney II
Brendan Dullaghan
Ryan Duncan
Trent Duncan
Christopher Durrant
Evan Durrant
Samuel Dutterer
Samuel Dutterer
Chris Dwyer
Virgil Dwyer
Brian Dye
Nick Edwards
Justin Eilenberger
Brian Eisel
Jonathan R. Ellis
William Ely
Michael Emes
Paul Eng
Brian England
Andrew English
Dakota Erisman
Ethan Estep
Dakota Estepp

Colton Eubanks
Benjamin Eugster
Richard Everett
Jaeger Falco
Stephen Farnett
Nicholas Fasanella
Christian Faulds
Carlos Faustino
Michael Feher
Steven Feily
Julie Fenimore
Meagan Ference
Brad Ferguson
Hunter Ferguson
Adolfo Fernandez
Rich Ferrante
Brandon Field
Jonathan Fields
Austin Findley
Albert Fink
Brooke Firth
Alex Fisher
Lamar Fitzgerald
Rhys Fitzpatrick
Matthew Fiveson
Daniel Flanders
Waren Fleming
Kath Flohrs
Daniel Flores
Matias Flores
Geoffrey Flowers
William Foley
Charles Ford
Steve Forrester
Skyla Forster
Joshua Foster
Kenneth Foster
Jacob Fowler
Bryant Fox
Chad Fox
Paul Fox
Doug Foxford
Martin Foxley
Mark Franceschini

Dennis Frank
Greg Franz
Luke Frazer
Evan Freel
Erik Freeman
Kyle Freitus
Griffin Frendsdorff
Josh Frenzen
Matthew Fritz
Timothy Fujimoto
Bob Fulsang
Jonathan Furnery
Elizabeth Gafford
David Gaither
Seth Galarneau
Sebastian Galdames
Matthew Gale
Zachary Galicki
Kyle Gannon
Dave Garbowski
Marcos Garcia
Robert Garcia
Robert Garcia
Joshua Gardner
Michael Gardner
Alphonso Garner
Mackenzey Garrison
Cordell Gary
Nathan Garza
John Gasperino
Jordan Gass
Marina Gaston
Robert Gates
Brad Gatter
Tyler Gault
Angelo Gentile
Cody George
Stephen George
Nick Gerlach
Gregory Gero
Eli Geroux
Christopher Gesell
Xander Gibson
Dylan Giles

Joe Gillis
Oscar Gillott-Cain
Nathan Gioconda
John Giorgis
Jodey Glaser
Johnny Glazebrooks
Bob Gleason
Martin GleatonJames
Glendenning
Seth Glenn
Jared Glissman
William Frank Godbold IV
Justin Godfrey
Rick Gomes
John Gooch
Bryan Goodman
Tyler Goodman
Justin Gottwaltz
George Gowland
Gordon Grant
Mitch Greathouse
Gordon Green
Matt Green
Joe Greene
Shawn Greene
Stephen Greene
John Greenfield Jr.
Anthony Gribbons
Dan Griffin
Eric Griffin
Ronald Grisham
Paul Griz
Auguste Gumbs
Robert P. Gunter
Jeff Haagensen
Levi Haas
Joshua Haataja
Owen Haataja
Michael Hagen
Kelton Hague
Levi Haines
Joseph Haire
Michael Hale
Marlon Hall II

Leo Hallak
Norman Hamilton
Chris Hammond
Brandon Handy
Chris Hanley
Erik Hansen
Greg Hanson
Jeffrey Hardy
Tyler Hardy
Ian Harper
Jordan Harris
Revan Harris
Shane Harris
Brandon Hart
Matthew Hartmann
Adam Hartswick
Reese Harvey
Mohamed Hashem
Matthew Hathorn
Ronald Haulman
Joshua Hayes
Ryan Hays
Adam Hazen
Richard Heard
Colin Heavens
Jon Hedrick
Jonathan Heiden
Jesse Heidenreich
Brenton Held
Kyler Helker
Jason Henderson
Jason Henderson
Anders Hendrickson
Fynn Hendrikse
John Henkel
Aronton Herbert
Philip Heritage
Daniel Heron
Bradley Herren
Felipe Herrera
Paul Herron
Sven Hestrand
Kyle Hetzer
Korrey Heyder

Matthew Hicks
Robert Hill
Lance Hirayama
William Hitt
Ty Hodges
Jonathan Hoehn
Arthur Hoffman
Charles Hoisington
Ryan Holbrook
Aaron Holden
Bryan Holden
Brad Hollingsworth
Joe Holman
William Holman
Clint Holmes
Jason Honeyfield
Charles Hood
David Hoover
Garrett Hopkins
Tyson Hopkins
William Hopsicker
Nicholas Hornung
Justin Horton
Jefferson Hotchkiss
Caleb House
Ian House
Jack House
Ken Houseal
Nathan Housley
Jeff Howard
Joseph Howle
Nicholas Howser
Mark Hoy
Kane Hubbard
Kirstie Hudson
James Huff
Adrian Hughes
Dante Hulin
Aaron Huling
Mike Hull
Donald Humpal
Forest Hunter
Bradley Huntoon
James Hurtado

Wayne Hutton
Gaetano Inglima
Antonio Iozzo
Randy Islas Jr.
Wendy Jacobson
Paul Jarman
Bobby Jeffers
James Jeffers
Michael Jenkins
Jacob Jensen
Robert Jensen
Tedman Jess
Eric Jett
Anthony Johnson
Caleb Johnson
Cobra Johnson
Eric Johnson
Gary Johnson
James Johnson
Josh Johnson
Nick Johnson
Randolph Johnson
Timothy Johnson
Bryan Jones
Jason Jones
Micah Jones
Michael Jones
Paul Jones
Tyler Jones
David Jorgenson
Ryan Kalle
Robert Kammerzell
Chris Karabats
Ron Karroll
Timothy Keane
Cody Keaton
Tyler Keaton-El
Brian Keeter
George Kelly
Jacob Kelly
Noah Kelly
Ryan Kelstrom
Caleb Kenner
Zack Kenny

Daniel Kimm
Kennith King
Zachary Kinsman
Caleb Kirkwood
Tucker Kitchengs
Joshua Kivett
Jesse Klein
Kyle Klincko
Brendan Klingner
Albert Klukowski
Marc Knapp
William Knapp
Robert Knox
Steven Konecni
Christian Koonce
Ethan Koska
Evan Kowalski
Byl Kravetz
Bodhi Kruft
Jacob Krute
Neil Kubitz
Mitchell Kusterer
Nathan Laidlwe
Ian Lamb
Clay Lambert
Shea Lambert
Mark Landez
Megan O'Keefe Landon
Travis Larsen
Dave Lawrence
Alexander Le
Jacob Leake
David Leal
Andy Ledford
Furman Lee
Nicholas Lee
Joseph Legacy
Benjamin Lemmen
David Levin
Luke Lindsay
Ruel Lindsay
Eric Lindsey
Eron Lindsey
Paul Lizer

John Lloyd
Andre Locker
Dominick Loele
Michael Lofland
Maxwell Lombardi
Drew Long
Richard Long
Oliver Longchamps
Litani Looby
Joseph Lopez
Matthew Lopez
Lucas Lorentz
Joey Lorenzi
Kyle Lorenzi
David Losey
Erin Lounsbury
MDavid Low
Doug Lower
Steven Ludtke
Johan Lundberg
Caleb Lunsford
Andrew Luong
Jesse Lyon
Taylo Lywood
Collin Macall
David MacAlpine
John Machasek
Brian Machimbira
Sawyer Mack
Patrick Maclary
Daniel Magano
Derek Magyar
William Mahoney
Richard Maier
Ryan Mallet
Kevin Malley
Chris Malone
Jake Malone
Adam Manlove
Andrew Mann
Aaron Manning
John Mannion
Brian Mansur
Brent Manzel

Robert Marchi
Jacob Margheim
Deven Marincovich
John Marinos
Cory Marko
Jacob Marquis
Alexande Martin
Bertram Martin
Bill Martin
Christopher Martin
Edward Martin
Jason Martin
Jeffrey Martin
Logan Martin
Lucas Martin
Pawel Martin
Trevor Martin
Tim Martindale
Joseph Martinez
Phillip Martinez
Cory Masierowski
Nicholas Mason
Tao Mason
Hunter Massey
Wills Masterson
Mark Mathewman
Michael Matsko
Justin Matsuoko
James Matthews
Ezekiel Matze
Mark Maurice
Simon Mayeski
Joseph Mazzara
Will McAleer
Timothy McAleese
Sean McCafferty
Logan McCallister
Kyle McCarley
Mac McCleary
Quinn McCusker
Matthew McDaniel
William Mcdaniel
Shane McDevitt
Alan McDonald

Caleb McDonald
Connor McDonald
Jeremy McElroy
Dennis McGriff
James McGuire
Hans McIlveen
Rachel McIntosh
Richard McKercher
Ryan McKracken
Jacob Mclemore
Jason McMarrow
Wayne McMurtrie
Colin McPherson
Daniel Mears
Kile Mendoza
Jim Mern
Dylon Merrell
Robert Mertz
Brady Meyer
John C. Meyers
Pete Micale
Corrigan Miller
Cody Millette
Patrick Millon
Darren Mills
Hunter Mills
Mark Mills
Philip Mills
Robert Milsop
Jesse Miner
Sarah Miron
David Mitchell
Reimar Moeller
Michael Molloy
Ryan Mongeau
Jacob Montagne
Ramon Montijo
Dale Moody
Eric Moore
Maxwell Moore
Sherry Moore
Mitchell Moore*
Nicholas Moran
Matteo Morelli

Todd Moriarty
Matthew Morley
Autumn Morris
Daniel Morris
William Morris
Christian Morrison
Alex Morstadt
Preston Morzelewski
Nicholas Mukanos
Alexis Muniz
Bob Murray
David Murray
Jeff Murri
Ben Myhre
Joseph Nahas
Vinesh Narayan
Colby Neal
Zane Nebe
James Needham
Ray Neel
Merle Neer
Joel Negron
Adam Nelson
Tyler Neuschwanger
Timothy Nevin
Michael Newson
Jon Newton
Ethan Nichols
Travis Nichols
Bennett Nickels
Mason Nicolay
Trevor Nielsen
Andrew Niesent
Sean Noble
Otto (Mario) Noda
Brett Noll-Emmick
Michael Norris
Ryley Nortrup
Douglas Norwood
Greg Nugent
Melissa Nugent
Christina Nymeyer
Brian O'Connor
Sean O'Hara

Patrick O'Leary
Colin O'neill
Ryan O'neill
Patrick O'Rourke
Jacob Odell
Conor Oehler
Quinn Oehler
Kevin Oess
Nolan Oglesby
Travis Olson
Gary Oneida
Max Oosten
Anthony Ornellas
James Owens
Will Page
Nic Palacios
John Park
Matthew Parker
Christopher L. Parrish
Shawn Parrish
William Parry
Eric Pastorek
Andrew Patterson
Trevor Pattillo
Yahya Payton
Thomas Pennington
Hector Perez
CD Perkins
Kevin Perkins
Zach Perry
Chase Barret Perryman
Trevor Petersen
Zac Petersen
Marcus Peterson
Nicholas Peterson
Chad Peyton
Corey Pfleiger
Charlie Phillippe
Brandon Phillips
David Phillips
Jon Phillips
Sam Phinney
Dupres Pina
Michael Pister

Jared Plathe
Pete Plum
Luke Plummer
Matthew Pommerening
Stephen Pompeo
Jason Pond
Nathan Poplawski
Michael Portanger
Chancey Porter
Rodney Posey
Brian Potts
Jonathaon Poulter
Daniel Powderly
Thomas Preston
Matthew Print
Darren Pruitt
Aleksander Purcell
Joshua Purvis
Max Quezada
Adam Quinn
Scott Raff
Shahik Rakib
Joe Ralston
Frederick Ramlow
Jason Randolph
Aindriu Ratliff
Michael Rausch
Joshua Ray
Beverly Raymond
T.J. Recio
Ron Redden, Sr.
Ash Reed-Kraus
Blake Rehrer
Ryan Reis
Cannon Renfro
John Resch
Nathaniel Reyes
Paul Richard
Cody Richards
John C. Richards
Augustus Richardson
Robert Richenburg
Eric Ritenour
Paul Rivas

Tina Rivers
David Roark
Grant Roark
John Robertson
Scott Robertson
Walt Robillard
Edward Robinson
Joshua Robinson
Daniel Robitaille
Christopher Roby
John Roche
Adam Rochon
Paul Roder
Josias Rodriguez
Zack Roeleveld
Adam Rogers
Thomas Rogneby
Thomas Roman
Aaron G Rood
Andrew Rose
Joseph Roshetko
Elias Rostad
Rob Rudkin
Arthur Ruiz
Jim Rumford
John Runyan
Nick Rusch
Chad Rushing
Tim Russ
Sterling Rutherford
Zarren Rutledge
 RW
Justin Ryan
Mark Ryan
Matthew Ryan
Greg S
Zachary Sadenwasser
Emelliano Salas
Robert Salmon
Connor Samuelson
Lawrence Sanchez
Dustin Sanders
Giovani Sandoval
David Sanford

Joshua Sayles
Levi Schaefers
Jaysn Schaener
Jason Schapp
Shayne Schettler
Jason Schilling
Daniel Schmagel
Ray Schmidt
Thomas Schmidt
Kurt Schneider
Peter Scholtes
Theodore Schott
Kevin Schroeder
Michael Schroeder
Alex Schwarz
William Schweisthal
Anthony Scimeca
Cullen Scism
Connor Scott
Ethan Scott
Preston Scott
Andrew Scroggins
Robert Sealey
Aaron Seaman
Dan Searle
Matthew Sedenius
Phillip Seek
James Segars
Kevin Serpa
Ryan Seymour
Austin Shafer
Mitch Shami
Ryan Shannahan
Timothy Sharkey
Curtis Sharp
Kevin Sharp
Christopher Shaw
Steven Shaw
Charles Sheehan
Wendell Shelton
Lawrence Shewark
Logan Shiley
Ian Short
Glenn Shotton

Emaleigh Shriver
Kaleb Sigler
Dave Simmons
Chris Sinor
Joshua Sipin
Chris Sizelove
Andrew Skaines
Chris Slater
Scott Sloan
Steven Smead
Jesse Smider
Anthony Smith
Caleb Smith
Cory Smith
Daniel Smith
Ian Smith
Lawrence Smith
Michael Smith
Robert Smith
Sharroll Smith
Timothy Smith
Tyler Smith
David Smyth
Gregory Smyth
Tom Snapp
Andrew Snow
David Snowden
Alexander Snyder
Briana Sparh
Robert Speanburgh
John Spears
Anthony Spencer
Thomas Spencer
Troy Spencer
Jeremy Spires
Peter Spitzer
Dustin Sprick
Super Squirrel
George Srutkowski
Eric Stack
Cooper Stafford
Travis Stair
Travis Standford
Graham Stanton

Paul Starck
Jolene Starr
John Stephenson
Joshua Sternfield
Tanner Stewart
Maggie Stewart-Grant
Edmond Stone
Fredy Stout
Rob Strachan
James Street
Joshua Strickland
William Strickler
Shayla Striffler
John Stuhl
Brad Stumpp
Louis Styer
Ned Sullivan
Shaun Sullivan
Kevin Summers
Joe Summerville
Ernest Sumner
Randall Surles
David Swantek
Michael Swartwout
Aaron Sweeney
Bryan Swezey
Tiffany Swindle
Lloyd Swistara
George Switzer
Carol Szpara
Travis TadeWaldt
Allison Tallon
Daniel Tanner
Blake Tate
Joshua Tate
Lawrence Tate
Kyler Tatsch
Alyssa Tausevich
Dave Tavener
Brandon Taylor
Justin Taylor
Robert Taylor
Tim Taylor
Christov Tenn

Jonathan Terry
Anthony Tessendorf
Stavros Theohary
Doug Thien
David P. Thomas
Jacob Thomas
James Thomas
Marc Thomas
Vernetta Thomas
Chris Thompson
Donald Thompson
Jonathan Thompson
Steven Thompson
William Joseph Thorpe
Beverly Tierney
Yvonne Timm
Michael Tindal
Russ Tinnell
Daniel Torres
Justin Townsend
Matthew Townsend
TJ Trakas
Jameson Trauger
Scott Tucker
Oliver Tunnicliffe
Eric Turnbull
Ryan Turner
Brandon Turton
John Tuttle
Dylan Tuxhorn
Nicholas Twidwell
Joshua Twist
O'brien Tyler
Jalen Underwood
Barrett Utz
Leo Vaccaro
Joel Vale
Paul Van Dop
David Van Dusen
Erik Van Otten
Andrew Van Winkle
Patrick Van Winkle
Paden VanBuskirk
Patrick Varrassi

Daniel Vatamaniuck
Jason Vaughn
Daniel Venema
Ronald Vera
Marshall Verkler
Abel Villesca
Cole Vineyard
Ralph Vloemans
Leo Voepel
Jeff Wadsworth
Anthony Wagnon
Wes "Gingy" Wahl
Christopher Walker
David Wall
Joshua Wallace
Justin Wang
Dylan Wannamaker
Andrew Ward
Wedge Warford
David Warren
Scot Washam
Tyler Washburn
Christopher Waters
Zachary Waters
Andrew Watson
John Watson
Bill Webb
William Webb
Bill Webb
Ben Wedow
Zachary Weig
Garry Welding
Hiram Wells
Tanner Wells
Matthew West
Jack Weston
William Westphal
Ben Wheeler
Lewis Wheeler
Paul White
Grant Wiggins
Christopher Williams
Jack Williams
Joel Williams

Michael Williams
Taylor Williams
Patrick Williford
Justin Wilson
Dominic Winter
Scott Winters
Edward Wise
Evan Wisniewski
Nicholas Withrow
Timothy Wolkowicz
Reese Wood
Ryan Wood
Tripp Wood
Robert Woodward
Sean Woodworth
Robin Woolen
John Wooten
John Work
Bonnie Wright
Jason Wright
Adam Wroblewski
Anthony Wulfkuhle
Elaine Yamon
Ethan Yerigan
Phillip Zaragoza
Brandt Zeeh
Kevin Zhang
Pamela Ziemeck
Attila Zimler
Jordan Ziroli
Nathan Zoss